W9-AZI-457

Also by Howard Frank Mosher

DISAPPEARANCES
WHERE THE RIVERS FLOW NORTH
MARIE BLYTHE

*A Stranger in the Kingdom*

# A
# *Stranger*

# *in the Kingdom*

Howard Frank Mosher

DOUBLEDAY New York London Toronto Sydney Auckland

PUBLISHED BY DOUBLEDAY

a division of Bantam Doubleday Dell Publishing Group, Inc.
666 Fifth Avenue, New York, New York 10103

DOUBLEDAY and the portrayal of an anchor with a dolphin are trademarks of Doubleday, a division of Bantam Doubleday Dell Publishing Group, Inc.

*This novel is a work of fiction. Names, characters, places, and incidents are either the product of the author's imagination or are used fictitiously. Any resemblance to actual persons, living or dead, events or locales is entirely coincidental.*

Library of Congress Cataloging-in-Publication Data

Mosher, Howard Frank.
A stranger in the kingdom / Howard Frank Mosher. — 1st ed.
p. cm.
ISBN 0-385-24400-2
I. Title.
PS3563.08844S77 1989
813'.54—dc19 89-30912
CIP

Printed in the United States of America
October 1989
FIRST EDITION
BG

*For my mother and my father*

*A Stranger in the Kingdom*

# 1

When I was a boy growing up on the Kingdom gool, my father and my older brother Charlie couldn't say two words to each other without getting into an argument. In and of itself, I don't suppose that their quarreling was so very unusual. Fathers and sons, elder sons especially, often have problems seeing eye to eye. What distinguished Kinneson family arguments from most others is that once they got up a head of steam, Dad and Charlie refused to speak to each other directly. Instead, they conducted their running verbal battles through the nearest available third person, who, more frequently than not, turned out to be me. Their disagreements constitute some of my earliest memories, and they disagreed continually, over everything from the editorial policy of our family-owned weekly newspaper to the individual and team batting averages of the 1918 World Champion Boston Red Sox.

It's a well-known fact, at least in northern New England, that the enthusiasm of Red Sox fans tends to increase in direct proportion to their distance from Fenway Park. Certainly this axiom held true for our family. We lived as far away from Boston as it's possible to live and still be in Vermont and not Canada, yet to this day I've never met more ardent baseball fans than the Kinnesons. Even my mother, who was otherwise not much interested in sports, avidly followed the ups and downs of our beloved Sox. Once a season we all made the long trip south on the Boston and Montreal Flyer (a misnomer if there ever was one) to see a game in person. And since there was no local radio station within seventy miles of Kingdom County, Dad and Charlie and I often drove up the logging road above our place into the high wild country known as the Kingdom gore to hear a game over the car radio from a downcountry station in Burlington or Montpelier. Or, depending on the weather conditions and the team Boston happened to be playing, we might pick up the Sox over enemy stations from far-flung cities that I connected more closely with their clubs' current positions in the American League pennant standings than with any particular geographical locations—cities like Detroit and Cleveland, Philadelphia, St. Louis, Washington, and Chicago.

And, of course, New York—which for a number of years in my early boyhood I assumed must be situated somewhere to the *north* of Boston because of the Yankees' perennial ranking at the top of the league.

Those long ago summer evenings usually started out as good ones. We would park in the clearing on the height of land near the tall cyclone fence enclosing the white-domed army radar station we called Russia (soon to be rendered obsolete by the DEW line far to the north). I can still see us clearly: my father sitting with the driver's door ajar and one long leg propped on the sagging running board of his old De Soto, fiddling with the radio dial while Charlie and I played catch nearby. Using the steel cyclone fence as a backstop, I'd crouch down with my hand plunged deep into the vast recesses of my brother's catcher's mitt while Charlie, who'd been a standout catcher at Dartmouth and was widely considered to be the best catcher in Vermont's Northern Border Town League, stood about sixty feet away and lobbed me an old waterlogged baseball wrapped in several layers of scruffy black electrical tape.

"Put some mustard on it, Charles," my father would call from the car. "Uncork one. Smoke her right in there."

Charlie would grin at me wickedly, double pump, heave his leg high, and pretend to uncork one. I don't suppose he ever threw anywhere close to all his might; but that rocklike black ball seemed to come hurtling out from behind his leg like one of Bob Feller's hundred-mile-an-hour express deliveries. I'd throw up the thinly padded glove in self-defense, and the ball would either dribble out of it onto the ground or, on those frequent occasions when I shied away and missed it altogether, smack into the fence behind me with a terrifying clang and bounce halfway back to my laughing brother.

By the time I was twelve, I could hang on to some of Charlie's pitches—but not without wincing and turning my head, whereupon my father would bark, "Don't quail away from the ball, James. You've got to learn to get behind it and stay behind it if you're ever going to amount to anything in back of the plate."

By then my eyes were usually watering, and only partly from my stinging red catching hand. As small and light for my age as Charlie had always been big for his, and when it came to catching, something of a natural-born quailer in the bargain, I was quite certain that I was destined never to amount to anything in back of the plate or anywhere else on a baseball diamond. If I was this scared of Charlie's half-lobs, how under the sun would I ever handle big Justin LaBounty's blazing fastballs when I got to high school? Invariably, I was relieved when my father rapped the horn once or twice to signify that he'd located the game.

Then Charlie would sit in front with Dad and I'd jump in back and from that moment on all three of us would follow every word of the play-by-play with as much interest as if we were ensconced in the best box seats in Fenway Park. Sooner or later, though, static would begin to interfere with the broadcast, and Dad would have to hunt for another station.

That was when the trouble generally started.

"Jim," my brother might say, winking back at me over his shoulder, "that Mel Parnell has one of the best curve balls in the history of the game." (Charlie and my father always referred to baseball as "the" game, as if it were the only one.)

Charlie would then launch into an elaborate and lengthy explanation of how a pitched baseball's rotation causes it to break down and away from, or toward, a batter—a phenomenon I have never really doubted and to this day have never entirely understood.

If there was still enough light left, and the light lasted half an hour longer up in the gore than down on the gool, Dad's expression as he leaned forward twisting the dial bore a remarkable resemblance to that of Ted Williams in a photograph on my bedroom wall. The picture, which I'd clipped out of the northern New England edition of a Sunday Boston *Globe*, showed Terrible Ted in profile, leaning on a monstrous bat in the on-deck circle at Fenway and staring out toward the mound at a hapless rookie pitcher just up from the St. Louis Browns' farm system and brought on in relief with the bases loaded.

"James," my father informed me sternly when Charlie finally ran out of gas, "Mel Parnell certainly does not have one of the best curve balls in the history of the game. The fact of the matter is that a baseball does not, never has, and never will truly curve. I grant you that a baseball may drop. I grant you that it spins. I even grant you that it gives the *appearance* of curving. The sun gives the appearance of orbiting the earth, for that matter. But the truth is that the sun does not orbit the earth any more than a baseball curves. In both instances that would be a total impossibility, in direct contradiction of the incontrovertible laws of Sir Isaac Newton."

Undaunted, Charlie hooked his arm over the seat and grinned back at me. "Isaac Newton never had to go up to the plate against Mel Parnell, Jimmy. If he had, he'd have been the first to agree that a baseball curves. Then no doubt he'd have demonstrated how."

"Mister," said my father, swinging around and glaring at me as though I, not Charlie, were arguing with him, "if it were demonstrable, Sir Isaac would have demonstrated it with an apple. It would be a violation of the fixed regulations of the universe for a perfect sphere hurled in a straight path to veer suddenly out of that path like a brown bat."

"That's just the point, Jimmy. A baseball has seams. It isn't a perfect sphere."

"It isn't a brown bat, either," my father told me angrily. "And that, mister man, is the beginning and the end of it."

That last remark was my father's personal trademark. For years he had concluded his strongest editorials in *The Kingdom County Monitor* with this unequivocal pronouncement, which rarely failed to delight the scant handful of subscribers who happened to agree with him on any given issue as much as it infuriated the overwhelming majority who didn't. Yet it seemed to me as a boy that Dad's arguments with Charlie had neither a beginning nor an end, but went on and on interminably, like their baseball debates in the gore. And once they started those, refuting and counterrefuting each other, calling me "mister" and "mister man" and getting angrier with each other (and with me) with each passing minute, they continued until the game ended.

Or, at some critical moment (and to all three of us every moment in every baseball game was critical), reception faded out altogether and left us with nothing but mountain static.

"Your father and brother agree to disagree, that's all," my mother told me a hundred times. "Every family has its little peculiarities, Jimmy. Arguing is just the Kinnesons' special way of visiting with each other, I suppose."

Whether Mom actually supposed such a thing, I have no idea. Maybe she really did. But despite her many reassurances to the contrary, I was certain that the differences between Dad and Charlie were very real indeed, and their marathon arguments never failed to make me uneasy—in part because I served as an involuntary conduit for so many of them, but mainly because Charles Kinneson, Sr., and Charles Kinneson, Jr., were the two men I thought the most of in all the world and I wanted to be able to agree with everything each of them said.

Which, as my father himself might have asserted, was a total impossibility.

As summer crept north toward the Kingdom, always slowly and nearly always preceded by a month or more of immobilizing mudtime in lieu of spring, my father and brother heatedly debated whether a man could catch more trout during the course of a fishing season on wet flies or dry flies. In the fall, which up in our remote mountains along the border is usually as short and lovely as spring is long and miserable, they wrangled over whether you could shoot more grouse with a bird dog or without one. When January gales came howling down through the gore out of Canada, rattling our dilapidated old farmhouse with its numerous attached sheds and barns like a vast wooden ark in a heavy sea, they edged their chairs aggressively up to the roaring kitchen stove, while I perched nearby on the lid of the woodbox, and went at it hammer and tongs over history and literature, politics and religion, current events and what they were pleased to call "the King's English," including such momentous issues as whether it was ever under any circumstances grammatically correct to split an infinitive; whether "uniqueness" could have degrees, as in "more unique" and "most unique"; and how obscure regional terms like "gore" and "gool" had evolved.

Especially gool. Ever since I could remember, my father and Charlie had haggled fiercely over the derivation of this curious old Scottish word that had come down through the Kinneson family over the generations and designated the half-mile loop of washboard dirt road roughly paralleling the north bank of the Lower Kingdom River from the one-lane red iron bridge by Charlie's hunchbacked green trailer just east of the village, past our house and the logging trace leading up the ridge by our bachelor cousins' place into the gore and Russia, and so back on into town from the west by way of the long covered bridge.

As a boy, I was at a loss to understand why Dad and Charlie made such a big fuss over a word that wasn't even in the dictionary. Only years later did I realize that this chronic point of contention between them contained the two quintessential elements of nearly all their best-loved disputes. That is to say, it had absolutely no practical bearing on any matter of real consequence to either one of them. And it seemed to be totally irresolvable.

I resolved at an early age to avoid all arguments, family and otherwise, whenever possible. As I grew older this aversion to controversy sometimes worked to my disadvantage by preventing me from stating a conviction as forcefully as I should have. At the same time, I learned a lesson from the constant disagreements between my father and brother. What they taught me, though I didn't realize it at the time, was that most disputes have at least two arguable sides—a concept I found invaluable years later when I went to work at the *Monitor* myself.

To the surprise of no one who knew him, Charlie had taken a very different professional tack from mine. Nearly thirteen years my senior and inclined from his own boyhood to be ruthlessly competitive, my big brother became a lawyer and a good one. So good, in fact, that by the spring of 1952 when I turned thirteen and Charlie was twenty-five and this story begins, it was widely reported throughout northern Vermont that if he wasn't away playing ball or fishing or hunting, young Attorney Kinneson up in Kingdom County could get you clean off the hook, and without charging you an arm and a leg, either, for anything short of premeditated murder committed at high noon on the village common in the presence of a dozen unimpeachable local witnesses.

For that, even with my brother representing you, it was generally conceded that you might have to pay a modest fine.

Which brings me back to 1952 and the tragedy that changed our lives and that is still referred to throughout Vermont today as the Kingdom County Affair. In the end, it divided our tiny village deeply, against itself and against the world on the other side of the hills, and once and for all wrenched the Kingdom—tucked off between the Green Mountains to the west and the White Mountains to the east, with its back to a vast and sparsely settled section of French Canada —out of the past and into a time when the fixed regulations of my father's universe, not to mention Sir Isaac Newton's, seemed no more incontrovertible than the northern Vermont weather forecasts.

Back in Burlington, daffodils and tulips were in bloom and the lawns were as green as they would ever get. But as my father and I lumbered north out of the city on the Grand Army of the Republic Highway, listening to the Red Sox' opening game of the season against the Washington Senators, we eased back into an earlier season of the year.

Outside Jericho, roadside brooks were still high and chalky from snow runoff in the foothills of Mt. Mansfield. By the time we reached Underhill, patches of old snow had begun to appear in sheltered gullies and on wooded north slopes. And as we chugged our way slowly higher into the mountains, I spotted half a dozen columns of woodsmoke hanging over bare gray maple orchards where a few farmers were boiling off late runs of sap, though up in Kingdom County sugaring had just gotten into full swing and my mother was getting her best runs from the maples on the ridge above our house.

We'd been to Burlington to pick up a new motor for my father's ancient Whitlock printing press, and because it was my thirteenth birthday he'd let me skip school for the day and come with him. Ordinarily I loved to go anywhere with Dad. But loaded down as the old De Soto was, to the very limit of its sagging springs, our maximum speed over the heaved concrete of the winding G.A.R. Highway was thirty miles an hour. By the time we reached Cambridge I felt good and queasy.

"What are you doing over there, getting sick?" my father said suddenly, as reception began to fade. Just as suddenly, that week's issue of the *Monitor* appeared in my lap. "What's the news this week, James?"

What's the News? was a game Dad and I had played since I was six years old and he began training me to be a newspaperman—not, I stress, a journalist: "I never knew a journalist worth the powder to blow his jargon to hell, James. If you work for me, you'll work as a *newspaperman*, and that's the beginning and the end of it"—by making me read several items from each week's *Monitor* aloud to him while he listened with a frown on his face as though someone else had composed them, badly. Even as an incipient teenager I still dreaded this ordeal. Today especially I did not think that reading eight-point type in the jouncing ten-year-old clunker Dad had bought because, one, it had a radio, and two, it was all he could afford, would much improve the condition of my stomach. Nor, as I glanced down over the contents of the front page, did I see any reason to change my long-standing private conviction that except for the gradual alteration from woods to farms and now mainly back to woods again, Kingdom County had managed to remain free of significant news, as I then thought of it, for the past one hundred and fifty years.

My father, on the other hand, staunchly maintained that news in the Kingdom was every bit as interesting as news anywhere if you but knew how to find it and go at it from a fresh angle. Besides which, when the old man said read, you read; and that too was the beginning and the end of it.

So I read. I read that yet another farm out on the county road had been auctioned off for back taxes. I read that two Canadian lumberjacks hired to blast open an ice jam in the Kingdom River just above the Lord Hollow Bridge had "unceremoniously blown up the north abutment of the bridge as well and hightailed it back to Quebec without waiting to receive their pay."

On the editorial page I read my father's scathing open letter to Senator Joseph McCarthy, whom the *Monitor* was among the first papers in New England to attack for his witch hunts and whom, partly as a result of my father's urging, Vermont's Ralph Flanders would subsequently be the first to denounce on the floor of the Senate. I read that at long last the United Protestant Church of Kingdom Common had hired a new minister, one Walter Andrews from Montreal, Canada, a former chaplain in the Royal Canadian Air Force. And finally, under the weekly court news on page three, I read that on the same day the ice jam was dynamited, Sheriff Mason White had discovered a moose head buried in my cousin Resolvèd Kinnesons's manure pile and a side of moose meat in Resolvèd's woodshed. According to my father's terse report—"Less is more, James, and don't you ever forget it"—Sheriff White had confiscated both the meat and the head, and our illustrious relative was slated to be arraigned in court that very afternoon.

"Maybe this time Judge Allen'll lock up old Resolvèd and throw away the key," I said, folding up the paper and then hastily reopening it in case I needed something to wrap up what was left of the two hamburgers and three Cokes I'd consumed an hour earlier.

My father snorted. "Maybe he will. And maybe the Sox will come through for us and win their first championship since 1918. But I doubt it. Boston will wilt with the heat of July like last week's lettuce, and Charles will get Resolvèd off scot-free as usual. The fact is that Zack Barrows probably won't bring the case to trial anyway. With elections coming up in the fall the last thing that dithering old sot wants is another courtroom embarrassment. No doubt he'll cave in and agree to some eleventh-hour plea bargaining deal concocted by your smart-aleck brother."

Now that Dad had gotten onto the subject of Charlie and Zachariah Barrows, whom he frequently referred to in the *Monitor* as Kingdom County's nonprosecuting prosecutor, he was off and running. "As you very well know, James, there's never been any real law and order in Kingdom County. Since your brother hung out his shingle, there's been less than ever. Charles seems to regard himself as the Green Mountains' answer to Clarence Darrow, but I'm here to tell you that he's becoming a very large part of the overall problem. The truth is that he goes out of his way to defend any scalawag who staggers down the road these days just for the very dubious satisfaction of winning another case. All this is killing your mother, by the way; you know how finely tuned she is."

In fact, I did not know how finely tuned my mother was, though my father often said this. For years, especially when he was upset with my brother, he invoked this mysterious infirmity of Mom's and strongly implied that her life was in imminent jeopardy because of Charlie's wild ways.

I didn't want to get into an argument but I felt obligated to put in a word for Charlie. "That's his job, isn't it, Dad? Defending outlaws like Resolvèd?"

"A job is something you get paid for, mister man," Dad said, and thrust his long arm out the window to signal a turn.

Ahead on the height of land above the Lamoille River, just in the nick of time for me and my tumultuous stomach, was the Ridge Runner Diner, our traditional halfway coffee stop between Burlington and Kingdom County.

To this day in northern New England, it's a myth that truckstop food is always first-rate. Depending on its current management, the Ridge Runner's burgers and fries might or might not taste more like stale fish, though my father claimed that the coffee, which for a reason I never fathomed he insisted on calling "java," was reliably fresh and hot. Be that as it may, the place was never crowded.

The diner itself intrigued me considerably. It was a long trailerlike affair converted over from a superannuated Central Vermont Railway dining car, whose most remarkable feature since its halcyon days as the pride of the CVR rolling stock had never been its bill of fare anyway, but a slightly concave rectangular mirror running the entire length of the wall behind the counter, in which any customer could visit with any other customer without leaning forward or sticking an elbow in his neighbor's soup. In the mirror's upper left corner was a star-shaped shatter mark about the size of a fifty-cent piece, which according to a former proprietor had been made by a G-man's bullet back during Prohibition when the dining car had allegedly done double duty as a mobile speakeasy. Probably this tale was apocryphal. My father, with his ingrained newspaperman's skepticism of the romantically improbable, always thought so. But to a daydreaming boy brought up on Robert Louis Stevenson and Mark Twain and Dad's wonderful stories of our own family's odd history, the curious shatter mark in the curved mirror seemed marvelously emblematic of an exciting bygone era.

At three o'clock on a weekday afternoon in late April, we were the

Ridge Runner's only customers. We sat halfway down the counter at the row of cracked leather stools and Dad ordered a cup of java and I ordered a glass of ginger ale to settle my stomach. Out in the kitchen the Sox game was blaring. Ted Williams had just belted a triple, Mel Parnell was pitching like Cy Young, and Boston was ahead 3 to 1; but I couldn't follow much of the play-by-play between the crackling static and the waitress. She was a mousy little woman with a narrow corrugated forehead that reminded me of the stiff grooved paper separators in the Whitman Samplers my father bought for my mother (who never ate candy) at Easter. As the waitress got our drinks she complained to us steadily in a whiny voice about the late spring.

Outside, a new green sedan with out-of-state plates pulled into the parking lot. It was towing a canvas-covered trailer. Two people got out, a man about forty and a boy two or three years older than me. Both, to my surprise, were black.

I had seen black people from a distance before, on our annual trips to Fenway Park and once or twice in Burlington. But I had never seen a Negro, as I then thought of blacks, this close to Kingdom County. I was as curious about the two newcomers, especially the boy, as I was surprised.

So was the waitress. "Say, Bruce," she whined back over her shoulder. "Take a gander out here and get a load of this."

In the entranceway of the kitchen there appeared a wiry, dissatisfied-looking man about my father's age, fifty-five or so. He was wiping his hands on the filthiest apron I'd ever seen. Beneath it he wore an equally grimy strap-over undershirt without a shirt. He had not shaved that day or, probably, the day before.

In the long mirror I saw my father—who got up before the birds and shaved twice and unless he was going fishing or hunting put on a freshly pressed white shirt and a necktie and shined his shoes for two or three minutes on an old issue of the *Monitor* spread out on the woodbox lid in the kitchen, seven days a week and fifty-two weeks a year—staring at this character with unconcealed displeasure.

"Yes sir," Bruce said, slurring the expression together for maximum ironic inflection. "Darkies. And it ain't even Decoration Day yet."

"Darkies" was a word I'd previously encountered only in Stephen Foster's "Old Folks at Home." It took me a moment to realize that the cook was referring to the two people in the parking lot. The black man, in the meantime, was checking the ropes fastening the canvas sheet over the sides of the trailer. Although he wasn't as tall as Charlie or my father, he was a big athletic-looking man with a build like a boxer's. The boy was pegging gravel at a utility pole across the road. He was nearly as tall as his father but much lankier.

"Looks to me like they'd be moving up this way," the waitress said.

Bruce shook his head. "Don't you believe it, Val. This country's way too cold for them people. You think the winters seem long to *you*. Darkies can't take the cold a-tall. Not a-tall. They'd be part of a traveling show, no doubt. Minstrel show or some such outfit. See that new automobile? That's show money. You can lay odds on it. You and I, now, we couldn't afford a road hog like that."

Shaking his head in disgust, Bruce returned to his kitchen. The black man and his son came in and sat down at the counter two stools to my left. The man was dressed, I thought, like a city person on vacation in the country. He wore a light tan spring jacket over a blue sport shirt open at the neck, corduroy slacks, and expensive new hiking shoes. Except for the fact that he was black and this was 1952, he could have just stepped off the cover of Charlie's L. L. Bean spring catalogue. The boy was dressed like any other boy his age. Like me, for that matter, in jeans, scuffed-up Keds, and a sweatshirt loose in the shoulders and short in the wrists. His features were smaller and more delicate than his father's and his complexion was lighter. Here was a revelation that interested me considerably. Until that instant, I had supposed that all Negroes were exactly the same color!

I was surprised again when the man ordered a cup of tea for himself in a voice not much different from my father's or mother's. Without ever giving the matter much thought, I'd also assumed that Negroes all talked like Amos 'n' Andy, or Rochester on *The Jack Benny Show*, which we sometimes picked up over the car radio in the gore before a Red Sox game.

"Coca-Cola, chum?" the man said. "Wedge of lemon pie?"

The boy twisted restlessly on his stool, half a turn in each direction. "No," he said softly.

"No, what?"

The boy sighed. "No, thanks," he said, and continued to pivot back and forth. After being carsick, it made me dizzy to watch him.

"Just the tea, then, if you please," the man said to the waitress, and got a Socony road map out of his windbreaker pocket and began to study it.

Abruptly, the boy spun off his stool and slouched over to a squat jukebox by the door. I sipped my ginger ale and looked at the black man in the mirror. He glanced up, caught my eye, and winked. I looked fast at the shatter mark, as though I'd been scrutinizing it the whole time. It occurred to me that my father was probably right about it not being a bullet hole; almost certainly a bullet would have gone completely through the glass. I turned to Dad and started to tell him, then changed my mind. He was staring toward the entrance of the kitchen, his coffee still sitting untouched on the counter in front of him, his long, closely shaved jaw set in a way I understood all too well.

The boy drifted back to the counter. "Nothing but cowboy stuff. Hank Williams, for cripe's sake. I counted eight by Hank Williams."

The man smiled. "When in Rome, old chap. Why don't you sit down, have a bite and something to drink?"

"I've been sitting all day, and I'm not hungry. Can I go out to the car?"

"May I go out to the car."

"All right, then, may I?"

"Go ahead. And Nathan, it's only—" It was too late; the boy was already through the door and into the parking lot.

The black man bought a package of Lucky Strikes from the waitress, lit one with a small silver lighter, and continued to study his map as he smoked. Outside, the boy was throwing at the utility pole again. He had an easy, smooth delivery, and I wanted to go out and join him but I wasn't sure what to say when I got there. My father was still staring toward the kitchen.

"You ready?" I said nervously.

"No."

The waitress brought the black man an ashtray from down the counter. "You folks been on the road long?"

"To my son it seems like a long time. Actually, only since about noon."

"I know how your boy feels," the waitress said sympathetically. "I rode clear to Washington once. Washington, D.C.? On a high school trip. We left here before it got light in the morning and didn't pull in there until way long after dark, and I just about thought my fanny was going to fall off from sitting on it the whole time. The apple blossoms, or maybe it was pears, was supposed to be on, only it was a late spring there too and they wasn't yet. Not that most of us kids would have seen them if they had been. Mister, we were hot the whole trip. Hot or hungover from getting hot the night before or getting ready to go out and get hot that night. You know, bunch of country bumpkins from Vermont—'Ver-mont! What state's that in?' folks kept asking us—never been off the farm before, most of us."

The man smoked his cigarette and chatted with the waitress about Washington. He had a relaxed manner, as though he was used to making light conversation with strangers. And though he talked in what Kingdom County natives would call an "educated" way, I began to detect a slight regional burr in his speech, which I supposed might be a mild southern accent. His voice was resonant, like my father's when he was telling a story, and pleasant to listen to like a radio sportscaster's, making me think the cook might be right; he could be some kind of singer or stage performer.

"They took us to where they make the money," the waitress was saying. "That's what I remember best about good old Washington, D.C. That and getting hot and hungover."

"Val."

Bruce had materialized in the kitchen entranceway. He wiped his hands on his dirty apron and jerked his thumb backward. "Out here. You're needed."

Val, who all of a sudden I liked better, rolled her eyes toward the ceiling and mogged back out to the kitchen. A minute later the black man stubbed out his cigarette butt, paid Bruce at the register, and left.

My father waited until the man and his son had pulled out of the parking lot. Then he stood up and took two long strides to the cash register. As Bruce rang up our slip he tilted his head back toward the kitchen, where the waitress was slamming pans around in the sink.

"Talk, talk, talk," he said. "And she don't much care who to, neither. She ought to learn when to keep her frigging mouth shut."

"You ought to shave and wash your hands and put on a clean apron and a shirt," my father said. "Expect a visit from the state health inspector."

And he walked out without his change, leaving his cup of java untouched on the counter behind him.

As you travel north in Vermont toward Kingdom County and the Canadian border, you will notice that even small streams are often designated as rivers on bridge signs and road maps. Half an hour later, when my father and I crossed the Gihon River, which you can easily throw a fly across at its widest point, he automatically assessed the water on his side as I did on mine—as we had done and would do hundreds of times crossing scores of different streams together.

"James," he said, "I wouldn't go brook trout fishing with that son-of-a-bitch back there if he and I were the last two men on the face of the earth."

Ever since I could remember, my father's acid character test was whether he would or wouldn't go brook trout fishing with a person. Not just fishing. Not even trout fishing. *Brook trout fishing.*

He applied this unique standard to neighbors, colleagues in the newspaper business, politicians, authors, and baseball players. Once in a blue moon someone actually measured up to it, though I'd noticed that most of the select few (F.D.R., Samuel Johnson, Ty Cobb) had been dead for years. And in point of fact, I'd rarely known Dad to fish with anyone but his own two sons and his one close friend, Judge Forrest Allen.

"Well," he said, "to hell with that ignorant bastard. If I were ten years younger I probably would have muckled onto him right there in his place of business and thrown him into the biggest snowbank south of Labrador. He can count himself lucky."

This was a common threat of my father when I was growing up. Once or twice a week he informed me with great earnestness that if he were ten years younger he would certainly "muckle onto" someone and throw him into the biggest snowbank south of Labrador. Quite often it was Joseph McCarthy, whom my father had a particular desire to muckle onto, though Sheriff Mason White and the nonprosecutor Zack Barrows were also high on the list of likely candidates. In fact, I have to confess that for a number of years I was somewhat unclear in my mind as to exactly what Dad meant by "muckling on." Yet I had no doubt at all that muckling was a most dire form of corporal retribution, with very grave consequences indeed for the mucklee.

"To hell with him," my father repeated. "As your grandfather used to say, James, coming home is always the best part of going away. Which, I am here to tell you, Thomas Clayton Wolfe's overquoted dictum on the subject notwithstanding, you most certainly *can* do if that's where your work happens to be."

As we came through the snowy woods on top of Lowell Mountain and looked abruptly out over the entire thousand-square-mile expanse of Kingdom County, I sensed something of what my father meant about coming home. Heading down the mountainside toward the village of Kingdom Common, we might have been entering a much earlier part of the century as well as an earlier season. Rickety old horse-drawn hay loaders, some abandoned not many years ago, sat out in hedgerows between stony pastures. Most of the farmhouses still had faded brown Christmas wreaths hanging on their doors, a tradition meant to ameliorate the grueling dreariness of our seven-month winters, though by this time of year they seemed only to call attention to the fact that it was already late April with warm weather still weeks away. The houses themselves had long ago faded to the same toneless gray as their attached barns; and the few farmers and loggers we passed looked as old and weathered as their buildings.

Three or four of the barns were decorated with faded murals of pastoral scenes: cows lining up at pasture bars at milking time; hefty work horses pulling loaded hay wagons; a yoke of oxen hauling logs out of an evergreen woods. They'd been painted in a rather primitive style by an itinerant artist known to me only as the Dog Cart Man, a deaf and mute individual of an indeterminable age, who at unpredictable intervals during my youth appeared in Kingdom County with an American Flyer child's wagon containing his paints and brushes and pulled by a motley pack of half a dozen or so mongrel dogs harnessed together with an incredible assortment of kite string, bailing twine, fish line, leather straps, and clothesline rope. Yet even these cheery murals, depicting impossibly idyllic scenes in an unimaginably distant summery season, seemed only to heighten by contrast the austerity of the time of year and the rugged terrain.

Many travelers, coming into these snowy granite hills, would have found Kingdom County a harsh and forbidding place. But despite my edgy emerging adolescent restlessness, which in another year would become a chronic driving urge to visit new places and see new sights at every opportunity, there was a deep and nameless appeal to me in the long stark hiatus between late winter and early spring in the Kingdom, which, like that similar uncompromising interval between late fall and early winter, seemed to reveal our remote corner of Vermont at its truest and best.

We entered the Common along the short south side of the rectangular central green. The clock on the courthouse tower said 5:15, and it is oddly comforting to me even now, decades later, to reflect that in a few days, when most of the rest of the country leapt automatically forward into daylight saving time, those long black iron hands that had regulated the comings and goings of Commoners for a century and more would not be moved ahead one second. Nor would most private households, including ours, adjust their clocks forward to accommodate someone else's notion of the way time ought to be kept. In Kingdom County in 1952 there was one time, year-round.

My brother's old woody station wagon was nosed diagonally in against the east side of the common just across from the courthouse. "Good," Dad said and stopped beside it.

"You want to see Charlie?"

"I want you to see him. Tell him I'll spring for steak sandwiches over at the hotel as soon as I get this motor unloaded. It'll be your birthday dinner."

"Won't Mom be waiting supper?"

"She'll probably have a cake for you when you get home. Your mother and two or three others have been killing themselves all day getting the parsonage ready for the new minister. I told her not to bother with supper."

"What if Charlie can't come?"

"He can come. It's your birthday, James. He'll come, all right, and that's—"

"—the beginning and the end of it," I said, and hopped out.

My father almost smiled. Then he and the De Soto rattled off past the Academy and the library, turned west along the Boston and Montreal tracks running down the middle of the street in front of the hotel, swung south again along the brick shopping block, and stopped in front of the *Monitor*, and I dashed up the granite steps of the courthouse to see my brother.

During the great November flood of 1927, most of the legal records of Kingdom County floated off the shelves of the storage room in the courthouse basement, out through the smashed windows into the inundated street, and north up the Lower Kingdom River to Lake Memphremagog and Canada. Days later, a few papers were retrieved from debris snagged by the tag alders growing in the swamp north of town. But except for a couple of ancient deeds written in butternut juice, which will last nearly as long as the paper it's printed on, none of these documents could be deciphered. Last wills and testaments, probate and county court proceedings, real estate transactions large and small—all were washed off into oblivion by that freak fall deluge that laid waste to so many towns and villages throughout Vermont and elsewhere.

After the flood subsided, the courthouse basement was converted to a three-cell jail. As new documents began to accrue, they were relegated to the third floor of the building, a single dim, musty, low-ceiled, coffin-shaped room tucked up under the slate eaves overlooking the common to the west and the American Heritage furniture mill and Boston and Montreal railyard to the east. At the far south end of this dreary garret, partitioned off from the post-1927 deeds and death certificates by four thin sheets of unpainted plywood, was the cubbyhole where my brother conducted his business.

For not much more than the twenty dollars Charlie shelled out to the county each month for the use of this cubicle he could have rented a spacious room on the first floor of the courthouse next to Sheriff Mason White's office. But as my brother had often told me, he preferred his lofty quarters for several reasons. First of all, he was much less apt here to be pestered by courthouse loiterers and members of the Folding Chair Club, who routinely poked their hoary heads into the more accessible first-floor offices to say good morning, then remained, unbidden, to pass the time of day for twenty minutes or longer. Here, too, by hitching a metal coat hanger to his portable radio and sticking the end of the hanger out his window, Charlie could occasionally pick up a Red Sox game. The window was also high enough to allow him to look out over the village rooftops when the leaves were off the elms on the common and watch the weather coming in off the Green Mountains, so that he always knew well in advance the best times to go hunting and fishing—avocations my brother pursued with unflagging zeal on two particular kinds of days: fair and foul. Which brings me to Charlie's principal reason for not moving downstairs, and that is that he simply didn't need a larger or more conveniently located office because in those days he spent as little time as possible there anyway.

My brother must have seen me get out of Dad's car and cross the street. As soon as I reached the third-floor landing he appeared in his doorway, hollering my name and exhorting me to hurry, he had something "new and wonderful" to show me.

Old and wonderful would have been closer to the truth. As I stepped into his office I was momentarily overpowered by the blended aromas of old sweat, old unwashed wool, old chicken manure, old fish scales and Old Duke wine. Tilted back in Charlie's swivel chair with his rubber barn boots on the desk was my old outlaw cousin, Resolvèd Kinneson.

I stopped in my tracks. "Sorry. I didn't know you had somebody with you."

"He don't," Resolvèd said. He leered at me out from under the limp greasy bill of his feed store cap. "I'm here on family business. Nothing else."

Charlie was leaning against the wall with his elbow on the windowsill. He winked at me and motioned with a clipboard at the single straight-back chair in front of his desk. "Have a seat, Jimmy. You're in for a real treat this afternoon."

Charlie's office was just large enough to sit down in without stretching your legs. Even so, it was ordinarily as pleasant a spot to drink a soda and shoot the breeze as any I knew in Kingdom Common. On the walls hung old-fashioned prints of men with dogs and guns, photographs of Red Sox players, and topographical maps of the Kingdom quadrangle and the Canadian bush country across the border to the north, all heavily crosshatched with red, blue, and green X's and O's designating the probable lairs of big trout and big bucks. The desktop was strewn with trout flies and fly-tying paraphernalia, boxes of shotgun and rifle shells, the second-place trophy from last year's Smash-up Crash-up Derby, and more outdoor periodicals than the magazine rack in Farlow Blake's barbershop in the back of the hotel, all presided over by an eight-by-ten framed color photograph of Charlie's longtime fiancée, Judge Forrest Allen's daughter Athena, smiling archly out over my brother's cluttered bailiwick.

There were no bookshelves in my brother's office. The flimsy plywood walls wouldn't have supported them. Piled everywhere, though, in the corners and against the desk and on the windowsill, were books on every conceivable subject that interested Charlie, from turtles to Turgenev—with one notable exception. In my brother's office there reposed not a single volume of the law of the land. Those he kept in the county's legal library adjacent to the second-floor courtroom and consulted, as nearly as I could determine, only during the ten or fifteen minutes immediately preceding an upcoming trial.

Ordinarily at this time of the day and year, I would have settled happily into these comfortable surroundings, cracked open a Coke from Charlie's beer cooler, and discussed with my brother the Sox' prospects for a good start or the approaching trout season or some other suitably vernal subject. Not today. Today I had no intention of spending ten seconds longer in the presence of my smirking outlaw cousin, who was one of the few individuals in Kingdom County I unequivocally detested and, to an extent, actually feared.

I was about to tell Charlie to meet Dad and me at the hotel when he said, "Jim, buddy, you probably aren't going to believe this, but Cousin Resolvèd has finally decided to avail himself of my wise counsel and find himself and Brother Welcome a pretty little housekeeper."

Resolvèd shifted his boots on a back issue of *Field & Stream* and gave me a malevolent look.

"If you don't mind, Cousin," Charlie continued, "I'd like to show Jimmy what a splendid letter you dictate."

"I don't give a Frenchman's fart what you show him," Resolvèd said. "It'll be in print for all to read soon enough anyway, and I don't mean no two-bit once-a-week gossip sheet I wouldn't use to wipe my ass with, neither."

Charlie laughed uproariously at this compliment to our family's one-hundred-and-fifty-year-old newspaper and handed me the clipboard he'd been holding. Attached, in my brother's flourishing handwriting, was a letter to the lonely hearts column of a Montreal tabloid called *Young Love, True Love*. It said:

> Dear Lonely Hearts:
>
> My name is Resolvèd Kinneson. I be a young man of property, independent means, and respectable family background in search of a female woman companion to share my life and land. Property includes brooks, ponds, extensive views, garden spot and ancestral home built circa 1780. Only lively young women under the age of forty that love good old-fashioned country living and God's great out-of-doors need apply.
>
> Very truly yours,
> Resolvèd Kinneson, Esq.

I handed the clipboard back to Charlie and looked at my cousin. Resolvèd was about fifty, but looked a good ten years older. To the extent that he could be said to resemble anyone at all, he reminded me of the woodcut of old Pap Finn sprawled drunk with the town hogs in my illustrated boyhood edition of *The Adventures of Huckleberry Finn*. To support himself Resolvèd jacked white-tailed deer, held illegal cockfights, and poached big trout, which he kept alive in his barnyard watering trough and sold by the pound, like lobsters, to skunked out-of-state fishermen. His landed estate with its "brooks, ponds, extensive views" consisted of a dozen or so played-out acres of disused sheep pasturage on the ridge above our place. His "ancestral home," where he lived with his look-alike brother Welcome, had been the original homestead of my great-great-great-grandfather and had been going downhill steadily since the day a century and a half ago when our ancestor consigned it to the use of his flock of merino sheep and moved down off the ridge into our present house on the gool.

"Don't seal that up, bub," Resolvèd told Charlie, who had just finished addressing an envelope to *Young Love, True Love*.

Now came a ritual I'd heard about many times but never before been fortunate enough to witness.

Resolvèd, rising somewhat unsteadily to his feet: "How much I owe you, bub?"

Charlie: "Not a cent, Cousin. This was entirely my pleasure."

Resolvèd: "Well, Je-sus! You can't get ahead doing business that-a-way, Charlie Kinneson." (Takes letter.) Then, grimly, as though issuing a thinly veiled threat: "I'll make it up to you, bub. Count on it."

And with a final sneer in my direction he clumped out the door.

No doubt it would be gratifying to report that Resolvèd did from time to time reimburse my brother for Charlie's untold hours of legal and quasi-legal services on his behalf, if not in cold cash, which all Kinnesons have always been notoriously short of, then with presents of produce from his garden spot or freshly killed game, perhaps left discreetly outside Charlie's office door or on the steps of his trailer by the river. It would be gratifying but inaccurate. For to the best of my knowledge Cousin R never paid Charlie one thin dime or brought him anything, either, except more trouble.

No matter. My brother couldn't have been more delighted by a fee in four figures. Collapsing into his chair, he howled with delight.

"Well, 'bub,' " he said when he could finally talk again, "what do you think of our cousin's elegant epistolary style? I can't wait to see if he gets a reply."

"You mean you're really going to let him go ahead and mail that?"

"Absolutely. It's a model of the genre, Jimmy. I don't know what genre, but it's definitely a model. Give me one good reason why he shouldn't mail it. No woman in her right mind could possibly take that letter seriously."

This made sense, and even if it hadn't I probably wouldn't have argued with my big brother. I couldn't have cared less how many ridiculous letters our cousin wrote so long as he left me alone. Resolvèd had a way of suddenly materializing in the woods when I was out alone hunting or fishing that I found extremely disconcerting. I'd be looking up in a black spruce tree for a grouse, say, and suddenly there he'd be standing beside it where a second ago there hadn't been anyone. Or I'd catch a hint of that gamy redolence he carried with himself everywhere and look up from threading a worm on a number-ten trout hook and see him five feet away, already fishing the pool I'd intended to fish. So I told Charlie Dad had invited us to dinner at the hotel to celebrate my birthday, and Charlie said great, he had just time enough for a steak sandwich and a cold one before leaving for his town team basketball playoff game that night in Memphremagog, up on the Canadian border.

Just as my brother reached for the overhead light string, Resolvèd stuck his head back inside the door.

"Say, bub," he said. "You wouldn't have a two-cent stamp laying loose around here somewhere? Post office's closed up tight as Tilly's twat and I want this in the letter box tonight."

Like several other restaurants in Kingdom County in 1952, when the stop signs all said ARRÊT as well as STOP and a third of the farm families still spoke French at home, the dining room of Armand St. Onge's Common Hotel could just as easily have been fifty miles across the line in Quebec. Hand-lettered bilingual notices taped on the walls between mounted deer heads and lunker trout read HOMEMADE CANADIAN COOKING and CHECK YOUR FIREARMS AT THE BAR. Conversations in French were commonplace. Vinegar cruets for french fries sat next to the salt and pepper shakers on every table, and interspersed on the jukebox between country and western numbers were fiddle reels and jigs from north of the border.

Except for Armand, a couple of loggers from Lord Hollow, and my father, who was never late for anything, the dining room was empty when Charlie and I arrived. The half-dozen railroad and mill pensioners who boarded at the hotel had already eaten, and the annual onslaught of downcountry fishermen up for the spring rainbow trout run wouldn't arrive until the weekend.

"*Bon soir*, Har-man," Charlie hollered in his corniest Jacques-the-Voyageur dialect. "Ow har da steak san-weesh tonight, *mon ami*?"

Armand, who after fifty years in the States spoke English with only the faintest wisp of an accent, grinned at my brother. "They're fine, Charlie. The same as every night."

We ordered steak sandwiches and Dad and Charlie ordered a beer before their meal. I asked for a Coke. While we were waiting, Charlie's girlfriend Athena Allen, who also happened to be my eighth-grade grammar teacher and Armand's niece, came in.

"It's the judge's black-eyed daughter!" Charlie shouted, pounding his beer mug on the table. "Come on over and have a cold one with us, sweetie."

Athena sat down next to Charlie but declined his offer of a beer, since in those days schoolteachers couldn't be seen drinking in public. In the meantime one of the Lord Hollow loggers had punched "Your Cheatin' Heart" on the jukebox. Charlie belted out a stanza or two right along with the record, out-twanging Hank Williams himself and pretending to go all to smash at the end, after which he announced in his booming voice that there were only two truly great Americans left and both had the same last name, Williams, and their first names were Hank and Ted.

"Yes," Athena said, winking at me, "ever since the Red Sox passed up their golden opportunity to sign Charlie on a few years ago, he's wanted to be a cowboy singer when he grows up."

My father snorted and I laughed out loud. Athena was referring to a misadventure from my brother's youth that would have made anyone I knew but Charlie wince with embarrassment, though characteristically enough, he seemed actually proud of it. When Charlie was sixteen and made the Northern Border League high school all-star team for the first time, he decided that the Red Sox had struggled along without his services long enough and that it was high time to take Fenway Park by storm. "Gone to catch for Sox," the note my folks discovered one morning on the kitchen table read. It was signed "Your loving son, Charles."

Shrewdly, and with admirable self-restraint, my father waited three full days before embarking from Kingdom Common on the B and M Flyer to retrieve his loving son—whom he found wearing a white cap and selling Cracker Jacks in Fenway's centerfield bleachers.

Athena winked at me again and I winked back. Athena Allen was an extraordinary beauty by local or any other standards. For years I'd been half in love with her myself, and I couldn't understand why Charlie hadn't married her already, though recently I'd overheard my mother telling Dad that Charlie was "somewhat at sixes and sevens" these days. "He can't quite get his own consent to marry Athena or run for the prosecutor's job or make any other really important decision," Mom had said. "He still hasn't completely recovered from being turned down by the Army, you know. Give him a year or two, and see what happens."

Charlie's mysterious inability to get into the service was a sore point in our family. Although there was no way to prove it, my brother couldn't believe that the military had turned him down because of an inner-ear problem and strongly suspected that it was on account of my father's prominent activities as a member of Henry Wallace's Progressive party. As a Vermont delegate to the party's nominating convention in Philadelphia four years ago, dad had called national attention to himself by cosponsoring the so-called Vermont Resolution, which would have put the Progressives on record as not giving blanket approval to any nation's foreign policy—especially Russia's. Unfortunately for both Dad and the party, when he stood up to introduce the resolution it was shouted down, and Dad, ironically enough, was branded by conservative papers and politicians throughout New England and beyond as a Communist sympathizer.

"Charlie," I said to change the subject, "I want to ask you something."

"Shoot, Jimmy."

"Do you think I'll ever grow?"

"Sure you'll grow, buddy. When I was thirteen I grew seven inches in a year."

"I know, but you were already five-nine, five-ten to start with. I'm still shorter than Mom and she isn't even five feet. I'll be in high school in the fall."

"You'll grow," Athena said. "This is *the* spring, Jimmy. I guarantee it."

"Of course you'll grow," my father said. "It would be a physical impossibility at your age not to, a contradiction of the irreversible laws of nature."

"Let's not contradict any of the irreversible laws of nature, Jimmy," Charlie said.

I knew he was trying to get a rise out of my father; but Dad seemed distracted by other thoughts and said nothing in reply, so I turned my attention to my steak sandwich, thankful that an argument had been avoided.

Charlie continued to hum snatches of Hank Williams' songs during dinner, which reminded me of what the Negro boy had said about my brother's country-singer hero at the Ridge Runner Diner that afternoon, which in turn reminded me of the episode with the cook in the dirty apron. When I repeated Dad's advice to him, Charlie howled and pounded the table and said that was exactly what he would have told the son-of-a-bitch.

"The times are all out of joint down there," my father said. "I don't know that matters are appreciably better up here in this neck of the woods, come to think of it. As I was telling James this afternoon, there hasn't been any real law in Kingdom County since I can remember."

"It's a frontier, all right," Charlie happily agreed. "In more ways than one."

So far my birthday supper had gone incredibly smoothly. But I knew from long experience that whenever my father and brother got into a conversation, any conversation, discord was never far away.

It reared its head even sooner than I'd expected.

Looking at me, my father said sternly, "If your brother would spend a little less time playing ball and hunting and fishing, he might have time to run for prosecuting attorney this fall and introduce some law and order into the Kingdom."

"For-get it, buddy," Charlie said to me, and my heart sank like one of Mel Parnell's curve balls. "As you very well know, I did not, repeat not, come back home to sit in the county prosecutor's office all day taking illiterate depositions from Mason White."

"I've often wondered why you did come home," Athena said.

Charlie leaned back in his chair and grinned. "Well, now, sweetie. Use your head. Where else could I put my God-given talents as northern New England's most colorful defense attorney to better use? Where, east of the Mississippi, are there still as many genuine outlaws left in need of defending? Then too, if Zack Barrows gets any older, deafer, or drunker, assuming that's possible, I'll win all my cases against him. I've always wanted to bat a thousand for a year, just to see what it feels like."

"Your brother already does win all his cases against him, James," my father said. "That's the trouble."

"Nope. I hate to contradict your father, Jimmy, but I came out second best in Resolvèd's moose-poaching arraignment just this afternoon. He had to plead nolo and pay a twenty-dollar fine. My fragile ego still hasn't recovered."

"I think his ego has recovered," my father said. "Abraham Lincoln couldn't have won that case after Mason White found the moose's head buried in Resolvèd's manure pile. The point is, James, your brother *shouldn't* have won that case. Besides being illegal, shooting that animal was a despicable act."

"Sure it was," Charlie said. "But as I told Athena's dad just this afternoon, the poor critter was probably dying of brain worm anyway, which is undoubtedly why it stumbled into Cousin R's dooryard in the first place. All he did was put it out of its misery. Then too, there was always the outside chance that if he ate enough of the moose meat, Resolvèd might contract brain worm himself. Think of the savings that would represent to the county judicial system."

"Think of the savings to the county judicial system, James, if your brother ran for prosecutor and slapped the old bastard in jail where he belongs."

Charlie shook his head. "Resolvèd doesn't belong in jail, buddy. Number one, he never hurt anybody, except possibly himself. Number two, he's among the last of that vanishing outlaw breed I mentioned. Recently I've begun to perceive myself as a kind of specialized conservationist preserving a unique threatened species. Like, say, the California condor."

"Preserving vultures?" Athena said.

Charlie whooped with delight; yet he seemed perfectly serious when he said, "Preserving a rapidly dwindling, irreplaceable segment of the population that helps make Kingdom County the frontier it is. Look around. Where's Noël Lord? Where's Quebec Bill Bonhomme? Henry Coville? Gone over the hump, as they say. It's a sad thought."

"They've all been gone for years, James," my father said. "I'd like to know just one thing before I table this discussion and get back to work. I'd like to know what sort of satisfaction there is in beating a guy like Zack Barrows. Can your brother tell me that?"

"None at all," Charlie said in that disarmingly candid manner of his that I think he sometimes used in those days as a perverse sort of justification to bull right ahead on a course he knew himself to be wrongheaded. "None at all. Which is just exactly what I like best about beating him, since it gives me more time for the truly important things in life. To wit, hunting, fishing, and playing ball. Besides, if I did run for that job and somehow managed to land it, I'd have to clap half of my hunting and fishing buddies and three-quarters of my ex-clients behind bars within six months. And that, as a distinguished newspaper editor well known to us both would say, is definitely the beginning and the end of it."

"Not quite," Athena said from the doorway, where she was getting into her boots. "You want to know the *real* reason he won't run, Mr. Kinneson? The real reason is that the prosecutor's job pays five thousand dollars a year. What excuse would old Hank here have left then not to put an end to the longest engagement in the history of Kingdom County and marry me? Right, Mr. Williams?"

"Nope," Charlie said, grinning. "The real reason is I'm pretty sure you'd frown on my diet of rare steak every night and pork chops, cooked extra crisp, for breakfast."

"To each his own," Athena said with a tight smile, and headed out the door.

"I give up, Jimmy," Charlie said. "I give up."

"Happy birthday, James," my father said in a tone of voice not generally employed for such felicitations. "Don't forget that tonight's Production Night. I want you to do the first run."

Without another word he paid the bill and walked out.

"I nearly forgot," Charlie said as we stood up and put on our hunting jackets. "Many happy returns, buddy."

Out of his jacket pocket my brother handed me a baseball. But not just an ordinary baseball. This was a brand-new official American League baseball, inscribed with the signatures of most of the 1951 Boston Red Sox players. Early that morning my folks had given me my first really good catcher's glove. Now with the baseball my day seemed complete, though when I tried to thank him Charlie just laughed and said he'd take it out of my hide if he caught me batting it around the pasture across from the house or so much as tossing it up in the air and playing catch with it.

Outside, we stood on the long porch of the hotel where the pensioners sat on summer evenings watching the trains go by, and listened to the low steady growl of the High Falls behind the hotel—a sound that is so much a part of the village for a month after iceout that you're aware of it only when you've been away for a time. It was dusk now. Across the tracks a woodcock landed on a single bare patch of ground along the north edge of the snowy common and began making its low intermittent buzz. Charlie nudged me and pointed. After a minute the bird flew high over the village rooftops in a series of widening spirals, then tumbled down through the twilight, whistling rapidly.

"He'd better find himself some cover," my brother said. "It's going to snow again tonight. Smell it coming?"

I wasn't sure I did but nodded just as a three-note horn bleated out and a souped-up Fairlane flying Confederate colors came racing over the knoll on the east edge of the village. It bounced across the tracks, headed down along the common, and slewed to a stop beside Charlie's wagon. The horn sounded again, this time the opening bars of "Dixie." Three of the players on Charlie's team piled out, shouting his name: ex-high school standouts, or near-standouts, now mostly in their twenties, who as I look back at them probably would have gladly traded whatever they had—jobs, cars, wives, kids—to have those four glorious years to play over again with what they knew now.

At the time, I was enormously impressed by Charlie's teammates, legendary figures whose names—Stub Poulin, Royce St. Onge, the three Kittredge brothers from Lord Hollow—were embossed with my brother's on a dozen or so Northern Border Town League and five state championship trophies in the lobby case of the Common Academy. I would have given a lot to be allowed to accompany them to Memphremagog to see their playoff game. That, however, was out of the question. Both of my parents felt that certain mistakes had been made in rearing my brother, particularly in the latitude he had been given at an early age to pursue various independent interests—older girls, stock cars, hanging around the village with members of the Folding Chair Club—and both Mom and Dad were determined that these mistakes not be repeated with me.

"See you later, buddy," Charlie said, punching me lightly in the shoulder. "Happy thirteenth."

He jogged across the tracks and down the edge of the common to join his waiting team and I headed over to the *Monitor* for Production Night.

As I burst through the door (in those days it seemed impossible for me to enter a building at anything under a dead run), my father did not even glance up from his typewriter. As usual on Production Night he was pecking out a last-minute story, sitting in his shirtsleeves at right angles to the desk with the typewriter on the side panel and his back to the storefront-sized window with KINGDOM COUNTY MONITOR painted backward on the inside of the glass in chipped and faded black letters.

Dad pointed with one long typing finger toward the Whitlock at the back of the shop to indicate that the first run of the night was already set up and ready to go. To reach the press, however, I would have to pass close by Cousin Elijah Kinneson, Resolvèd and Welcome's ex-brother, who had run the linotype at the *Monitor* since the days of my grandfather.

"Late again, boy," Cousin E said without interrupting his typing. "Where have you been? Scouting 'round the barbershop? Navigating 'round the village? Have you, boy? Eh? Have you?"

The long-handled overhead light on the linotype glinted fiercely off Elijah's green visor, and his inky gray fingers flew over the triple bank of red and blue and black keys as he continued to grill me. I'd always found my cousin's ability to type and talk simultaneously unsettling; but then, nearly everything about Elijah Kinneson unsettled me, from his short-cropped hair, the shade and approximate texture of the grayish lead filings sprinkled over the bottom of Dad's typecase drawers, to his holey shoes and the livid network of scars on his wrists and ankles where they'd been spattered with hot lead over the years.

So far as I was concerned Cousin Elijah was a splenetic old factotum who would be doing my father and the *Monitor* an inestimable service to retire and dedicate himself full-time to his duties as sexton and sometime lay preacher of the United Church. Yet as Dad frequently said, to give our cousin his due, he was close to indispensable around the shop. Besides being an expert linotyper who week in and week out produced a paper with about as many typographical errors as Harold Ross' *New Yorker* magazine, he could fix any machine on the premises from his own mind-bogglingly complex Mergenthaler linotype to the archaic hand-cranked addresser; and he had the uncanny ability to remember by volume number, date, page, and column the principal contents of every issue of the paper printed in the past thirty years.

Except for putting up with my ill-tempered cousin, I liked the hours I spent working for my father at the *Monitor*. I liked sweeping up around the machinery and ancient cabinets filled with tray upon tray of metal and wooden type. I liked the clean odors of well-oiled gears and printer's ink and fresh newsprint just off the Great Northern Paper Company boxcars on the mile-long Boston and Montreal freights. I liked running errands that took me to every nook of the village, from Judge Allen's musty chambers at the courthouse to the telegraph office in the B and M train station, and running off routine job-printing work on the small hand press. Best of all, I liked Production Night, when I got to feed the nine-ton Whitlock.

The Whitlock could print four pages of our eight-page paper at the rapid clip of twelve hundred takes an hour. Then the run was turned over and printed on the opposite side. To print the entire twenty-four-hundred-issue paper required four separate runs of two hours each. I generally took the first shift, then my father took over for a two-hour stint, and Elijah completed the last two runs, usually finishing up well after midnight.

Stashing my autographed birthday baseball on a shelf above the machine, I sat on a high stool and fed one pristine white sheet after another into the inked rollers. Although I could see Elijah jawing from time to time at my father, I couldn't hear him over the clash and rumble of the press. Until quite recently I had liked to pretend that the gigantic Whitlock was the pirate ship of my great-great-great-grandfather, a Scottish freebooter, with me at the helm like a latter-day Jim Hawkins. Now, with the increased self-awareness of adolescence, I was happy just to glance out at the street from time to time and to be seen and (I supposed) admired, not without strong sentiments of envy, by any town boys who happened to look in at me.

Two hours later, as I reached for my red hunting jacket, Elijah was haranguing Dad about a grievance that had been eating at him for the past few weeks. "As I was saying, Cousin, you never, I repeat never, hire a minister until you've interviewed him in person and heard him preach at least one sermon."

My father stopped typing. "Elijah, we have been over this terrain forty-eleven times. How often do I have to tell you that George Quinn and Bill Simpson and I each spoke with the man on the phone for at least fifteen minutes. We checked his credentials and references, and the guy seems to be exactly what we want and have wanted for the past ten years or so."

"Did you hear him preach a sermon over the phone?"

"What the hell sort of question is that? Of course not."

"Then how do you know he can?"

Now my father was really exasperated. "Because, damn it, he has been preaching sermons to Canadian enlisted men and officers for the past sixteen years."

Elijah just shook his head and continued to type. As I tried to sidle past his machine unnoticed he said, "Boy, remember this. You never fill a pulpit until you've interviewed your candidate in person and heard him preach at least one sermon."

It did not seem very likely to me at thirteen that I would soon be in a position to fill a pulpit. I detested church and always had. Now that the trustees had finally landed themselves a full-time minister, Sunday school, which was nearly as bad, would no doubt start back up again too. A night or two ago I'd overheard Dad telling Mom that Elijah's real grievance was that any minister at all had been hired because now my cousin the lay preacher would have to relinquish the pulpit from which he had bored the pants off every last member of the dwindling congregation since the departure of the last resident minister, Reverend Twofoot—who had left Kingdom County nearly two years ago, after suffering a total nervous collapse.

Some members of the congregation felt from the start that Sanford Twofoot was not cut out for the rough-and-tumble demands of a remote border-town pulpit to begin with. He was a high-strung little man in his early sixties, yet it turned out that years ago he'd done a couple of tough missionary stints in the Congo; and though you never would have guessed it to look at him, he had guts and plenty of them. In fact, poor Reverend Twofoot had more guts than common sense. When somebody told him about Resolvèd Kinneson's cockfights, and the gambling and drinking that accompanied them, he marched right up to my outlaw cousin's toting his trusty King James Revised Bible to put a stop to the proceedings. Afterwards, he told Dad that at first the cockfighters just laughed at him. But when he stepped right into the cockpit and began to read them the story of Jesus and the money-changers in the temple, Bumper Stevens, our local cattle auctioneer, threw his prize leghorn fighting rooster on Reverend Twofoot's head. The bird never did get the minister's eyes—it was wearing three-inch steel fighting spurs honed as sharp as a barber's razor—but that was the only luck he had that day. Doc Harrison said he had to use seventy-eight stitches to close him up.

Dad tried to get Reverend Twofoot to press charges, but he wouldn't, and the following Sunday he insisted on preaching as usual. His text was "Love Thy Neighbor as Thyself" but his head and face were bandaged up like King Tut's mummy and you couldn't understand more than half of what he said. The next week he had his collapse and his wife took him away from here. Just a few months ago he'd written to Dad from Africa, where he was doing missionary work again. The heat got to him quicker now that he was older, he told Dad, and the work wasn't easy; but on the whole he found the place considerably more civilized than Kingdom County.

After Reverend Twofoot's abrupt departure, the United Church couldn't find a minister who'd touch the job with a ten-foot pole until, in desperation, the trustees began advertising outside the country. Dad said it was pure luck even then that they'd been able to locate a full-time replacement. Be all this as it may, my cousin Elijah would now have to take down his name from the bulletin board on the front lawn of the church (SERVICES SUNDAY AT 11 O'CLOCK, CONDUCTED BY ELIJAH T. KINNESON, LAY PASTOR) and content himself with his sexton's duties.

He was still running on about the imprudence of hiring a minister sight unseen when I ducked out the door.

By now it must be obvious that my mother was right as rain about the Kinneson family and its "little peculiarities." Nor was I in any way exempt from my own share of these oddities, chief among which was a very real dread of anything related to the supernatural—a fear which was invariably activated whenever I had to walk the half mile home from the village on dark nights past both the cemetery and Mason White's undertaking parlor, not to mention the United Church parsonage.

Unpainted for decades, untenanted off and on for months at a time, its long sagging porch half-concealed by woodbine and bittersweet run crazy, the parsonage was Kingdom County's chief claim to a haunted house. Admittedly, the legend attached to the old place was based on slender evidence. It had been built by one Pliny Templeton, colloquially known in the Kingdom, for reasons I will later explain, as Black Pliny, the founder and first headmaster of the Kingdom County Academy. After a long and distinguished career as an educator, scholar, state legislator, and local historian, Black Pliny was said to have fallen on hard times in his old age and to have shot himself in the downstairs study of the house, just off the porch. Some years before this tragic event, in the philanthropic spirit for which he was renowned, Pliny had willed his house to the Presbyterian (later the United) Church to use as a parsonage; his organs to the medical college at the state university in Burlington; and his bones to the science lab of his beloved Academy, where they had depended from a pole for the past half-century for the elucidation of several generations of senior anatomy students.

According to legend, on the anniversary of Black Pliny's suicide his skeleton would reach up and deftly detach itself from the pole for a walk over to the parsonage, where it rattled up onto the porch and peered into the window of the fateful study to see who was currently living there. So far as I knew no motive apart from an eccentric but entirely benign curiosity was ever ascribed to the old headmaster's bones. Nor did I ever know anyone who actually claimed to have seen the skeleton making its ghostly annual perambulation. But a number of villagers and former tenants averred that they had distinctly *heard* the clattering footsteps on the porch. And whose could they be if not Pliny Templeton's? Whose indeed!

Of course this was exactly the sort of small-town claptrap I thrived on in those days, and I loved to scare myself by racing past the place (during the day), hooting and banging a stick against the broken fence palings in simulation of the ghost's march up to the parsonage veranda. Charlie, however, had immortalized himself in the annals of village pranksters at the age of fifteen with an escapade which, for sheer juvenile bravado and ingenuity, remains unsurpassed in Kingdom County to this day. Entirely by himself one Halloween, when the house had been unoccupied for several weeks, he stole the skeleton from the science lab and hung it from the overhead light fixture in the empty parsonage study, then reported to Cousin Elijah that town rowdies had broken into the place and were raising hell. Although I can't imagine that Elijah was frightened, Charlie always claimed that the crusty old sexton took one look at the skeleton, swaying gently in his flashlight beam, and fainted dead away on the spot.

No tragedy in the parsonage's history was necessary for every kid I knew to give the place a wide berth from sunset on, especially during the intervals when no one dwelt there. In the daylight it might look pretty much like any other big rundown village home. After dark, depending on one's age, it was positively forbidding; and the only reason I had come this way tonight instead of the alternative route by the covered bridge at the west end of the village is that I hated even more to walk through that unlighted and remote portal alone for fear of encountering something rather worse.

Charlie had been right about the snow. As I approached the parsonage, it had already begun, big wet flakes of sugar snow that melted as soon as they touched the street. I wasn't surprised. Up in the Kingdom you can expect plenty of snow throughout April and well on into May.

Tonight, a light was burning in the parsonage study for the first time in nearly a year. Remembering that my mother had been killing herself there all afternoon to prepare the place for the new minister, I gathered courage and walked steadily forward. I knew better than to run. There was nothing like a running boy to excite the least charitable instincts of the ghouls and zombies I strongly suspected took up residence in that house every time the church lost another minister. But as I approached the gate in what remained of the picket fence, the snow suddenly thickened, blotting out the light inside the house and the lights of the village behind me. Within seconds I could see nothing but a yard or two of the macadam road at my feet. It glistened darkly, like a deep river crawling through woods on a starless night.

"Splendid spring weather you chaps have here."

I must have jumped a foot. Someone—I hoped it was someone—was standing just inside the parsonage gate. All I could make out of his presence was the red glow of his cigarette in the snow squall. That, at least, was somewhat reassuring. Though I had no hard evidence that ghosts did not smoke cigarettes, I had never heard that they did.

"Walt Andrews," the voice said. "I just moved in."

I sensed rather than saw him put out his hand. After a couple of false stabs I located it and we shook hands in the dark across the gate. Walt Andrews, whoever he was, had a big hand and a very firm grip, like my father and brother.

"You're the new minister," I said stupidly, and he laughed.

"I plead guilty. But don't hold that against me. What's your name, chum?"

I told him and immediately he said, "The editor's son?"

"I plead guilty," I said, and again he laughed and said he hoped I'd give him time to get his car unloaded before I asked for an interview. Then I laughed, too. But although I was no longer scared I still felt like a base runner caught leaning the wrong way off first. It was a strange experience, to be talking to the disembodied voice of an invisible man less than three feet away.

Stranger still, there was something unaccountably familiar to me about that voice. It was casual and friendly but with an undercurrent of . . . amused irony, I suppose.

A gust of wind hit us. The snow drove faster. When Reverend Andrews flipped his cigarette butt out across the fence, it vanished in the storm before it hit the road.

"Brother!" he said. "This is April in Vermont? Your blooming weather is worse than Korea's."

I knew from the sound of his voice that he'd turned away from the road. A small orange flame spurted up across the gate as he hunched over to light another cigarette. I leaned closer to help block some of the wind, the way I'd seen Charlie and other men do.

And knew where I'd heard Reverend Andrews' voice before.

With a jolt of surprise, I saw in the quivering flame of the lighter that the new minister of the United Church was the black man my father and I had run into earlier that afternoon at the Ridge Runner Diner on our way back to Kingdom County from Burlington.

# 2

Of all the wonderful stories my parents read aloud to me when I was a boy, my favorite of favorites came out of a vast, leatherbound, musty-smelling, ancient-looking tome entitled (unpromisingly enough) *The Ecclesiastical, Natural, Social, and Political History of Kingdom County*, which Dad kept on a long shelf behind his desk at the *Monitor*, along with *The Dictionary of American Newspapers* and his prized 1910 eleventh edition of *The Encyclopedia Britannica*. Written and compiled by the same indefatigable Black Pliny Templeton who founded the Kingdom Common Academy and served nearly fifty years as its headmaster, the *Ecclesiastical History*, besides chronicling local church events, contained whole chapters on such diverse and fascinating subjects as the wild animals and plants native to our corner of New England, the Kingdom's geological evolution and political history, and all kinds of curious legends, anecdotes, diary entries, occasional poems, copies of letters to and from prominent local sons and daughters—even a section of regional recipes like brook trout chowder and partridge pie.

It also included a lively account of the Kinneson family history, beginning with the arrival in the Vermont wilderness of my great-great-great-grandfather, familiarly known in Kinneson family annals as Charles I, which I found endlessly intriguing both in its own right and because, for a number of years in my own early history, I supposed that it had been authored by a skeleton!

To this day what springs to my mind when I think of Charles I's arrival in the Kingdom is not a date, though there is a date attached—it was the fall of 1781—but a picture. It is a picture such as Frederick Remington (with whom my father no doubt would have gone brook trout fishing) might have painted, an autumnal image of a lone man paddling a birch canoe up the Lower Kingdom River from Lake Memphremagog, past pale yellow butternut trees and flaming swamp maples. The paddler's name is Sabattis and he is an Abenaki hunter, trapper, basket weaver, and storyteller, on his annual trek south from his summer home on the upper St. Lawrence to his winter home on the coast of southern New England.

In the picture it is hazy, one of the thirty "smoky" days Pliny claimed always preceded winter in Kingdom County, and getting toward evening. Jay Peak and its sister mountains in the western background are bluish and indistinct and softly contoured, drifting along the horizon more like smoke themselves than a lofty range of northern peaks. But the birch canoe and the amber river, the sparse yellow butternut leaves and the vivid scarlet maples and the lone Abenaki Indian hunter with the single name are as clear to me now as when I was four or five years old and my father read to me from Pliny's big book for the first time. The man is listening, with his head slightly cocked, his lips slightly parted. His paddle is arrested in mid-stroke. A thin stream of droplets slides noiselessly from its cedar blade back onto the motionless surface of the river.

"Imagine our wayfarer's astonishment," Pliny writes, "when he crept up a steep wooded hillside and emerged on a jagged clearing in the wilderness only to behold a towering lean raw-boned man hacking away at a heap of freshly felled spruce logs, attempting to raise a cabin before snowfall in a mountainous fastness where Sabattis had never before seen any sign of another man within fifty miles."

"How is the trout fishing in these parts?" my ancestor is said to have asked Sabattis, who, according to Pliny, was so impressed by his singlemindedness that he stayed on for the rest of the fall to help him complete his cabin and learn his story.

Charles Macphearson Kinneson had been born in the Outer Hebrides Islands, off the western coast of Scotland, in 1730, the eldest son of a Highland salmon poacher and implacable Jacobite put to the sword by the British during the abortive Uprising of '45. After his father's death, young Charles fled to France, where he dedicated himself to a single objective: to fight the British wherever and whenever possible, though never in formal affiliation with another government since as a Reformed Presbyterian bound by the Oath of the Covenant, he was forbidden to swear allegiance to any secular authority whatsoever.

Soon after he arrived in France, Charles took passage on a Marseilles privateer bound for the West Indies to harass the English rum, molasses, and slave trade. In 1766, with the proceeds of his pirate's booty, he established the first printing press in Guadeloupe, on which he composed hundreds of anti-British broadsides and which, a decade later, he moved lock, stock, and barrel to Bath, Maine, to assist the rebelling American colonists with his literary efforts. After the war Charles successfully petitioned President Washington for a pitch of one hundred and sixty acres on the northern slope of the New Hampshire Land Grants (subsequently to become part of Vermont) along the Canadian border. Here in 1786 he wed Sabattis' youngest daughter, the sixteen-year-old Memphremagog (Abenaki for "Beautiful Waters"). The following year he established *The Kingdom Monitor*, which he used chiefly as a vehicle for his undiminished Anglophobia. In 1793 he built the first of six potato-whisky distilleries that would eventually grace the banks of the Lower Kingdom, whose proceeds this strict Scottish teetotaler reserved exclusively for the construction of his crowning accomplishment—the First Reformed Presbyterian Church of Kingdom Common.

On Easter Sunday morning of 1952, as my father and mother and I headed up the slate flagstone walk of the church during the bell's final call to worship for the day, the wind was gusting straight up out of the south, bringing with it a tantalizing intimation of earlier and gentler springs farther downcountry. Everyone lingering in the unseasonably mild sunshine on the church steps that morning knew that despite the advent of mud season and trout season there would be more sudden snow squalls and gray subfreezing Kingdom days and frigid Kingdom nights before warm weather set in to stay. But everyone seemed grateful for the temporary break in the cold and eager to discuss the unusually good weather, the banner early runs of maple sap, the Red Sox' promising start, the upcoming Republican presidential primary, and Charlie's town team's sweep of the Memphremagog Basketball Tournament.

Everyone, that is, but my father, who, besides loathing all small talk, attended church and served on the board of trustees strictly from a sense of community responsibility. "Let's get this show on the road, Ruth," he said as we headed up the steps.

Just inside the door, Cousin Elijah Kinneson, now demoted to usher from his former Sunday morning incarnation as lay preacher, handed my father and mother a program. My father took another one and gave it to me. "Can't tell the players without one," he said.

My mother smiled. I laughed out loud. Cousin Elijah, however, scowled like a constipated parody of his Biblical namesake. Even this morning Elijah emitted a faint sulphurous odor compounded of the hot lead he worked with, stale sweat, and some ineffable but to me quite real essence of universal disapprobation. Yet his unabated disapproval of all boys in general and me in particular was nothing compared to the absolute hatred he bore for his ex-brothers Resolvèd and Welcome, whom he had publicly disowned some years ago with a paid notice in the *Monitor* to the effect that he would no longer acknowledge blood ties with these unregenerate men. Shortly after this unusual announcement, in one of the practical jokes for which he was renowned, Charlie had sneaked into the *Monitor* while Cousin E was enthroned at his linotype and taped to the back of his seat a large placard, visible from the street, which said: RESOLVÈD AND WELCOME KINNESON ARE MY OWN BLOOD BROTHERS AND I'M DAMN PROUD OF IT.

Thinking of Charlie, who at that very moment was fishing the rainbow trout run and maybe already onto a big one, the throbbing tip of his bamboo rod bowed to the river's surface, I trudged morosely up the uncarpeted central aisle of the church behind my folks and turned into the pew five rows back on the left where Kinnesons had planked down for the past century and a half to have their spiritual needs ministered to.

Except for the addition of an organ, the interior of the church had changed very little since the days of Charles I. The windows were plain glass, wavy now and lavendered from time, but without any trace of ornamentation and purposely set too high for the seated congregation to see out of. The wainscoting below them, the pews, the pulpit, and the wooden ceiling were all painted a flat white. On the walls there hung no pictures of any kind. Even the likenesses of Jesus and the disciples had been deemed to smack vaguely of the idolatrous by Charles I and the six other original member families of the church, whose descendants had insisted that this happy tradition be continued to the present day. And although the Presbyterian Church had been a United Protestant Church for sixteen years, with the stipulation that the minister must be an ordained Presbyterian clergyman, not so much as a single small blue crocus brightened its alter this Easter morning as the worshipers trooped in and sat down to the lugubrious strains of Julia "Hefty" Hefner's organ prelude.

The church was by no means full. Still, there were easily one hundred people in attendance today, half again as many as Cousin Elijah had ever drawn in his capacity as lay preacher. Some, no doubt, were there simply because it was Easter. But many must have come to view the curiosity of a minister who was not only the first full-time incumbent in two years but black as well, since no black family had lived in Kingdom County within recent memory.

Anyone who expected Reverend Andrews to say or do much that was out of the ordinary must have been disappointed. He began by thanking the congregation for welcoming him and his son so warmly. (Nathan had slipped in alone and slouched down at the end of the pew across from ours just before the service began.) Reverend Andrews added that if he received one more hot covered dish he'd be able to open a restaurant at the parsonage; this got him a ripple of laughter and broke the ice. I glanced over at Nathan and grinned, but if he noticed me he didn't acknowledge it. He looked as bored now as he had at the Ridge Runner Diner, and as uncomfortable in his jacket and tie as I felt in mine.

Reverend Andrews' sermon was blissfully brief. I can't remember much of what he said, except that he talked about hope and concluded by saying that he personally expected, on this most hopeful of all days, to resurrect the tradition of a minister who would do more than show up in church for an hour on Sunday morning and drink tea in the afternoon with his lady parishioners, which got him another general laugh. Speaking easily in that pleasant and resonant tone that had fascinated me in the diner and again in front of the parsonage during the snowstorm, he enumerated a couple of the goals he hoped to achieve: reestablishing an active youth group and a Bible study class for adults, mounting an organized fundraising drive. Finally, he did one small unexpected thing by inquiring whether anyone in church that morning wished to add to these objectives.

This was many years before young activist Protestant clergymen routinely solicited impromptu participation from their congregations during Sunday services, and there was a brief awkward silence. But before anyone had time to be more than slightly surprised, my father was on his feet. "I think you've covered all the bases yourself, Reverend Andrews," he said in that harsh voice of his that sounded displeased even on those occasions when it wasn't. "Welcome to the Kingdom."

What happened next was totally unprecedented, so far as I know, in the entire history of the church. Spontaneously, the entire congregation stood up as though for a hymn and gave Reverend Andrews a rousing welcoming round of applause. Looking back, I suppose this demonstration of support was meant in part to show both him and ourselves that we had no reservations about having a black man for a minister. Even so, it was a sincere gesture, and I believe that he was genuinely pleased by it, though all he did was smile and nod at Julia, who launched into a gallumphing rendition of "Onward Christian Soldiers."

Five minutes later and no more than fifty minutes after the service had begun, we were back outside in the warm sunshine on the top step of the church, shaking hands with the minister.

"I enjoyed your talk, Reverend," my father said after introducing himself. "As a matter of fact, this is the first time in fifty years that I haven't been bored silly in church."

Reverend Andrews laughed. "That's good. I've always regarded boredom as the eighth deadly sin. By the by, editor, thanks for bailing me out in there. I thought I'd be bombarded by a list of chores as long as my arm."

"Don't be impatient," Dad said. "The bombardment's coming."

My father stayed to visit with Reverend Andrews a minute longer while my mother and I continued down the steps. "Well," Mom said when he caught up with us on the flagstones, "what's your opinion of the new minister, Charles?"

"There are two things I liked about him right off the bat," Dad said as we crossed the street and headed along the heaved slate sidewalk in front of the courthouse. "He isn't afraid to stand up on his two hind feet and say what needs to be done around this place. And he can speak good plain English and get his point across without taking all day about it."

"It sounds as though you might actually go brook trout fishing with him," my mother said mischievously.

"We'll see," my father said. "I just might."

"I wonder what his son's like," I said.

"You can ask him yourself in an hour," Dad said casually. "I've invited the Andrews out to eat Easter dinner with us this afternoon. Afterwards, he's agreed to let me interview him for the paper."

To this day it is a widespread tradition in the Kingdom to have freshly caught baked rainbow trout instead of ham for Easter dinner. Charlie had caught two big ones that morning, and Mom, who had a wonderful recipe for garnishing baked trout with onions and bacon strips that removed every trace of the fishy taste, was humming snatches of that morning's hymns and happily flitting here, there, and everywhere over the prospect of having guests for dinner.

One of the trout had been a female bursting with orange eggs, which made excellent bait. Charlie sat at the big round bird's-eye maple kitchen table tying up the bright spawn in inch-square packets cut out of a discarded pair of mom's nylons. I perched on the lid of the woodbox, inhaling the delicious fragrances of the upcoming feast. I was excited about having the Andrews for dinner, but also a little apprehensive. I had never sat down and talked with a Negro before; above all, I didn't want to make some terrible social blunder.

Since they weren't due to show up for a half an hour, I had some time to compose myself, and there was no better place to do that than right there in our kitchen, where I had spent many of the best hours of my boyhood. There, under Mom's vigilant eye, I did my homework at the table after the dishes were cleared, or read and eavesdropped on the woodbox while Dad held forth on family history or talked politics from his Morris chair. Depending on the season and time of day, the kitchen also served as greenhouse, sugar house, dining room, and parlor, as well as command post for important domestic decisions.

Like most old farmhouse kitchens in northern Vermont, it was easily the biggest room in the house, though the low ceiling gave it a coziness many large rooms lack. It was light, too, with two big windows in the south wall overlooking the dooryard, and two matching windows in the opposite wall looking north up the maple ridge toward our cousins' place. At the windows were bright yellow curtains that caught even the thinnest February sunshine. The walls were papered with a paler yellow wallpaper that invariably started to peel when my mother boiled maple sap on top of the combination wood and oil Home Comfort (wood for winter, oil for summer). The floor was made from the broadest spruce boards I'd ever seen, which Mom kept as polished as the deck of my great-great-great-grandfather's pirate ship.

But the most interesting feature of our kitchen was its doors—all nine of them!

Entering the kitchen from the dooryard, you came through the main door, off the southeast corner of the porch. To your immediate left sat Dad's Morris chair. Moving clockwise, past the chair and the two south windows (now flourishing with tomato sets Mom had started back on Town Meeting Day, the first Tuesday in March), was a second, little-used door giving onto the southwest end of the porch. In the short west wall of the kitchen were two more doors, flanking an oak china cabinet that had belonged to my grandmother Kinneson. As you faced the cabinet, the door to your left led to the woodshed—the first in the straggling train of connected outbuildings linking the house, north-country style, to the barn. Beyond the woodshed were Mom's chicken house, a tool and machinery shed, a horse stable, a grain room, the milking parlor, and the milkhouse. Above the milking parlor rose the shaky old three-story hayloft.

Apart from the psychological comfort of knowing that your livestock, feed, and equipment were all housed safely under the same set of roofs, the practical advantage of this arrangement of attached buildings was that in deep winter when the mercury often dropped to forty degrees below zero, my ancestors had been able to complete their entire round of chores without once stepping outdoors. The corresponding danger, as Dad frequently pointed out to us, was that if a north-country barn were struck by lightning or caught fire from damp hay or faulty electrical wiring, the house generally burned to the ground along with it.

The best feature of the barn was a wonderful leaping brook trout, a full six feet long, that the deaf and mute Dog Cart Man had painted on its road side during my grandfather's time and refurbished several times since. Although the trout was now weathered to a mere outline of itself on the pearly gray, warped old boards, you could still make out its faint orange and blue spots and its handsome white-and-red fin edgings, and, if you knew it was there, the Royal Coachman wet fly fixed delicately in its hooked lower jaw.

To the right of the china cabinet was door number four. It opened onto a steep twisting staircase leading up to my loft bedroom. Early in my boyhood I had discovered that this staircase had remarkable acoustical properties. So long as the door at the bottom was open the slightest crack, I could hear every word spoken in the kitchen below almost as plainly as if I were still sitting on the woodbox, so that even after I was packed off to bed I felt a part of my folks' conversation. An additional distinction of my bedroom was that it contained one of those Vermont farmhouse anomalies called a sideways or coffin window—a narrow slanted window tucked at a forty-five degree angle between my bedroom roof and the roof of the kitchen below.

Set into the long north wall of the kitchen, at each end of the woodbox, were the fifth and sixth doors. One led nowhere at all. It was a false door painted onto the wall some years ago, at my mother's request, by the Dog Cart Man, exclusively for the purpose of balancing off the opposite door on the south wall. It had a painted black iron latch, painted wood panels, and painted iron hinges, and was my favorite door because it was the most unusual, and the subject of several family jokes.

The door on the other side of the woodbox gave onto a square wooden platform of hemlock boards, about ten feet on a side, from which a clothesline on a pulley ran out to an ancient snow apple tree at the foot of the ridge. On the platform, just to the right of the door, sat a circular iron cistern to which a tin eaves spout conducted rainwater off the back roof. Mom used the soft water from the cistern to wash dishes and to wash her lovely ash-blond hair, which she wore shoulder-length and of which she was secretly quite vain, in a girlish way. Underneath the platform dwelt the biggest hoptoad I have ever seen, which in a rare fillip of humor my father had named Zack, after the county prosecutor.

On the east wall of the kitchen were the last three doors. The first led to the pantry; that was a swinging door. The second led to the cellar—a fine big, dim, good-smelling room cool in summer and never really cold in winter, with an immaculate sandy floor, where Mom stored vegetables and preserves from her huge garden in the meadow across the road. The third door in the east wall led to what we referred to as "the other side of the house," most of which had been used very little since the deaths of my grandparents, before I was born—the dining room and parlor and old downstairs bedroom, now a bathroom, and the stairs leading up to three bedrooms, my folks' and two vacant ones.

This, then, was our kitchen, the hub of the house and the center of our family activities, and the way it looked when I was a boy growing up on the gool.

Reverend Andrews and Nathan arrived promptly at one, and we sat down to eat almost immediately. Our new minister, as it turned out, was very interested in Kingdom County and asked numerous questions about its history. This was right up my father's alley. Throughout the meal Dad held forth on Kingdom lore, to the growing exasperation of my brother, who professed to have no interest in local history at all. Still, Charlie restrained himself until Dad launched into his famous anecdote about Pliny Templeton and the yoke of red oxen.

"Pliny Templeton founded the Common Academy, which for many years was the only high school in Kingdom County," my father was saying. "The same school you and James attend today, Nathan. He built it himself, from pink Scotch granite mined up on the ridge above this house. Now granite's an exceptionally heavy stone, so he hauled the blocks for the upper stories up an ingenious series of inclined ramps with a bull wheel powered by a yoke of Red Durham oxen that belonged to my grandfather. The trouble came when the building was nearly completed and the two oxen simply refused to come down. After a week during which every conceivable humane recourse, and some that weren't, had been resorted to by the best drovers in northern Vermont, even my grandfather agreed that the animals would have to be slaughtered and butchered there. Which is exactly what happened."

My father took a sip of his after-dinner java. "There's no question," he continued professorially, "about the importance of the ox's role in the civilization of this part of the country. If the West was tamed with the horse and the gun, northern New England was settled with the ox and the two-headed ax. Just last spring I wrote an open letter in the

*Monitor* recommending in pretty strong terms that the ox replace that sneaking usurper, the Morgan horse, as the official state animal. The ox is superior to the horse in every way."

Here was the opening my brother had been waiting for.

"Reverend," he said, "there aren't two working yokes of oxen left in the Kingdom today. If oxen were really superior to horses, local farmers and loggers would still be working with them. Right, Jimmy?"

"On the contrary, James," my father said, to the minister's puzzlement, "today, everything is hurry hurry hurry. Hardly anybody cares how well a job can be done anymore, only how quickly it can be accomplished. Admittedly, the horse is quicker than the ox. Thus its current popularity. But the ox is more patient. The ox, with its cunning cloven hoof, is more surefooted on ice and snow crust. It's much more resistant to every obscure disease that comes down the pike, hardier in the deep cold and immeasurably more intelligent. The truth is that there's really no comparison at all between the two animals."

"That's right, Jim, there isn't," my brother said vehemently, and began extolling the myriad virtues of horses—about which he knew no more than my father knew about oxen, since so far as I knew neither of them had ever owned a single representative of either species.

As my mortified mother served dessert, the argument intensified. My brother informed me that "stubborn as an ox" was far from an idle figure of speech. My father countered by letting me know in no uncertain terms that horses in general, and especially that Johnny-come-lately the Morgan horse, were a breed of overrated parvenus. By then they were calling me "mister" and "mister man" and I was about as embarrassed as I could ever remember being.

Nathan, sitting beside me, seemed bored by the debate; he hadn't said two words during the entire meal, and neither had I, for that matter. But I thought that Reverend Andrews looked amused. Probably he felt that it was his obligation as our new family minister to intervene before the quarrel ended in bloodshed, though, because when he finally managed to get a word in edgewise he changed the subject.

"How about that interview I promised you, editor? Now that I've totally disgraced myself by eating enough of this wonderful meal for any three men, I'm braced for the ordeal."

My father smiled. "I promise not to make it much of an ordeal. What do you say we walk and visit at the same time? It's too nice an afternoon to sit around inside."

"It's too nice to waste it all talking," my brother said, giving Nathan a friendly tap on the shoulder. "Come on, buddy, I'll show you something out back of the barn you'll be interested in."

It was a lovely afternoon, more like mid-May than late April, and along the gool the speckled gray snow was melting fast. I elected to tag along with Dad and Reverend Andrews, in hopes of finding out more about the minister and Nat. My father took no notes as they visited, but I knew he would remember everything the minister said verbatim.

"How long has your family lived in Canada, Reverend?"

The minister got out a Lucky Strike. "Well, my great-great-grandfather came north from Mississippi on the Underground Railroad about 1840 and established himself in Sorel, Quebec, as a bootmaker. His son and grandson were both master cobblers, and my father was an enlisted man in the Canadian infantry during the First World War."

"Is he still living?"

"No, he was killed in the fighting at Verdun when I was four years old. My mother died when I was eight, and I was packed off by my grandfather to St. Gilbert-on-the-Lake, which is a Presbyterian boarding school just outside Toronto. As you know from my résumé, I took undergraduate studies in history at the University of Toronto and received my divinity degree from the Presbyterian seminary affiliated with that university."

"How did you rank as a student?"

"I was salutatorian of my undergraduate college and first in my class at divinity school."

My father, who had passed up a chance to attend Dartmouth and gone directly into the newspaper business instead, was never one to be much impressed by anyone else's academic credentials. "What prompted you to go into the ministry, Reverend?"

Reverend Andrews laughed. "A bargain. I was inclined to pursue a military career, like my father, but my grandfather the bootmaker agreed to educate me on the condition that I promise to become a minister. He didn't have any objection to my enlisting as a chaplain after I got my divinity degree, so we were able to effect a compromise. But the military would have been my own first choice. I was never so proud as the day I received my RCAF commission. I only regretted that my father wasn't alive to be there."

"Your résumé mentioned that you served on the front in both France and Korea, and that you were decorated more than once for bravery."

The minister laughed. "Almost anyone who was that close to the fighting was decorated. The fact is, editor, I liked nearly everything about military life."

"But you decided to give it up."

"Yes. After fifteen years of charging all over the globe, I wanted a more stable situation for my son. At the time of my decision, I'd been away from Nathan, with the U.N. force in Korea, for more than a year. His mother died from a cancer when he was just three, and I wanted to know our son as something other than long-distance correspondent. Nathan was living with his widowed grandmother, his mother's mother, in Montreal. I felt he was at the age when he needed a full-time father. Under the circumstances, resigning my commission wasn't all that difficult."

We were approaching the covered bridge upriver from the B and M railroad trestle. The river was flowing loud and muddy with snow runoff, and I mentioned to Reverend Andrews that the fly-fishing was especially good in this stretch later in the spring, but rather than shout over the noise, my father turned back along the gool the way we'd come.

"Why did you choose to move to the States, Reverend? There must have been opportunities for you to find a church and settle down in Canada."

"There were, but they all happened to be in or near large cities. I wasn't particularly interested in transplanting my son to yet another city—so here we are, for better or for worse. Which reminds me. There's something I've been meaning to ask you. In church this morning I remarked that half again as many families sat on the left—my right, actually—side of the aisle. Is there some reason for that?"

"Sixteen years ago, Reverend, the old Congregational Church and several other local landmarks burned to the ground in what's since become known as the Great Fire of '36. That's a story in itself, but the upshot of it is that after the smoke cleared, local Congregationalists and Presbyterians decided to unite. Their decision was more the result of economic necessity than interdenominational zeal, since the Congos couldn't afford to rebuild and the Presbyterians had dwindled to the point where they were having difficulties just paying the minister's pittance of a salary. Even so, it took a solid year of haggling back and forth before the two congregations would agree to hold a joint service and share one minister. And then, each faction insisted on maintaining its own board of directors, and by unspoken agreement most of the Congregationalists sat on one side of the aisle and most of the Presbyterians on the other. Of course this arrangement displaced a number of Presbyterians from pews their ancestors had occupied for generations. But it was deemed preferable to full integration. A few years ago the two boards finally merged, with the stipulation that the minister would always be an ordained Presbyterian clergyman; but the seatings have remained the same."

"You and your family sit with the Congregationalists?"

"We sit where the Kinnesons have always sat."

"I see."

Reverend Andrews smoked thoughtfully for a minute. "If you don't mind my presuming to say so, Mr. Kinneson, this tradition strikes me as rather pointless."

"Oh, it's worse than pointless, it's downright asinine. Every minister for the past fifteen years has tried to put a stop to it."

"And?"

"Not one of them's gotten to first base. I'm not telling you how to do your job, Reverend, but if I were you I wouldn't waste an hour of my time on that one. In my opinion you'll have much better luck sticking to your youth groups and fund-raising."

The minister flipped the stub of his cigarette a good ten feet out into the meadow and smiled. "When in Rome," he said. "Where do you suppose your older son spirited my boy off to?"

"I think they're out behind the barn shooting baskets," I said.

"I could use a bit more exercise myself after that Dickensian feast," Reverend Andrews said, winking at me. "Shall we join them?"

As we came around the corner of the barn, Charlie was standing at the foot of the highdrive sloping up to the hayloft, shooting at the netless rim nailed over the huge sliding door. From where he stood at the bottom of the ramp the basket was at least twenty feet away and twelve feet high. Just the same, his graceful two-handed set shots had plenty of loft and spin. One after another, they dropped cleanly through the old iron hoop and bounced back down the drive to him. Nathan stood off to one side, watching. It was the first time that afternoon he'd looked interested in anything.

"That's pretty fair shooting, chum," Reverend Andrews said. "How about a game of HORSE?"

Charlie grinned. "HORSE," he said.

The minister took off his suit jacket, folded it neatly, and laid it over a sawhorse. He removed his cuff links and rolled up his sleeves, revealing arms more like a boxer's than a preacher's. As Charlie flipped the ball to him and he reached out and caught it, he actually looked too strong to be well coordinated.

This was a misconception that Reverend Andrews corrected with his first practice shot. It was a set shot from the base of the highdrive. And although it glanced off the front of the rim and bounced sharply back down the ramp, I knew instantly that our new minister was an athlete.

"Go ahead," he said, tossing the ball back to Charlie.

My brother squared to the basket and made one of his patented set shots—the shot that had been principally responsible for winning three consecutive Class D state basketball championships for the Academy, and more recently, the Memphremagog Town Team Crown for Kingdom Common.

Reverend Andrews made the shot, too.

Charlie sank another one from the same spot; so did the minister.

Charlie moved back three steps and made his third consecutive shot. Reverend Andrews followed suit.

"Two!" Charlie yelled. Now that he had finally found someone who could compete with him, he was ebullient. As the ball skipped back to him, he grabbed it, dribbled hard up the slope, angled off to the right just shy of the basket, and dropped a soft hook shot off the barn wall through the rim. Reverend Andrews duplicated the move exactly, with the same result.

"Hoo!" Charlie hollered. "You've played this game before, Reverend."

"So have you, chum. And not just in a barnyard, I take it."

"Dartmouth, '44 through '48," said my brother, never one to hide any of his many lights under a bushel.

My father frowned. "I thought you came out here to play with Nathan."

"I have been," Charlie said. "He's terrific. Now I know where he gets it from. Next game, guys. You two against us."

As he spoke he took a push shot from the right of the highdrive. It rolled around the rim and spun out.

Reverend Andrews moved to the same spot. He dribbled the ball twice, crouched, leapt suddenly straight up in the air off both feet, and took the first one-handed jump shot I'd ever seen. The ball arched high, spinning beautifully, and fell through the iron hoop as neatly as a swallow settling into one of last summer's mud nests under the barn eaves.

Charlie blinked. "What sort of trick shot was that?"

"No trick to it," Reverend Andrews said. "That, my friend, is the shot that will revolutionize the game of basketball. In two or three years everyone's going to be using it."

My brother shook his head. He turned the ball over in his hands, trying to adjust them right on the seams, then jumped up flat-footed and shot an airball. He not only missed the basket, he literally missed the entire barn door.

For the first time I could remember, my cocky brother, who always managed to seem graceful even when he struck out in baseball, had looked plain awkward.

"*H*," Reverend Andrews said casually, and made the same shot again.

I glanced at Nathan, who was now watching intently.

This time Charlie's shot hit the front rim on a flat hard line and careened all the way back to him in the air.

"*H, O*," Reverend Andrews said, and promptly proceeded to give my brother two more letters. He cradled the ball thoughtfully, as though he was about to polish Charlie off with a fifth jump shot. Instead, he drove up the middle of the ramp, floated high with the ball in his right hand, transferred it to his left in midair, and dropped it neatly over the lip of the rim.

Charlie failed to execute the transfer and the game was over.

"HORSE," he said quickly, to preempt the minister. Although my brother was smiling, I knew he was annoyed. Charlie had never been able to lose graciously at anything in his life.

But Reverend Andrews didn't seem to be gloating. "One of my more secular duties abroad was to set up and manage recreational programs for off-duty airmen. Truth to tell, I've had an abundance of time to practice."

"So have I," Charlie said. "But apparently I haven't been practicing the right shots. Best of three?"

Reverend Andrews shrugged. "If you like."

He looked at me. "You and Nathan want to get in on this one?"

"Look who's coming," my father said before I could answer.

Two men were heading down the lane off the ridge behind the barn. They walked slowly and appeared to be weaving slightly. One wore bib overalls and a black slouch hat like a Tennessee moonshiner's. His companion had on a feed store cap and a tattered wool hunting jacket and held a half-full bottle of Old Duke wine. Trailing away from his other hand was a ratty hank of baling twine eight or ten feet long. Attached to the opposite end of the twine by one stout yellow leg was an enormous red rooster.

It was my outlaw cousin, Resolvèd Kinneson, and his brother Welcome, who could nearly have been his twin, out exercising Resolvèd's prize fighting Rhode Island Red rooster, Ethan Allen Kinneson, for their upcoming Decoration Day cockfight.

When they reached the junction of the lane and the gool, all three members of this singular triumvirate made a sweeping about-face and started back up the ridge at the same zigzagging pace. Not one of them had appeared to so much as glance in our direction, though I was certain that Resolvèd and Welcome had spotted us from their dooryard and come down mainly to get a look at the Negro minister.

"I would have thought cockfights were against the law in Vermont," Reverend Andrews remarked when my brother told him what Resolvèd and Welcome were up to.

"They are," my father said. "That's why they're held up here in the Kingdom. Where there isn't any."

"Any?"

"Law."

"That's intended for my benefit, Reverend," Charlie said. "The crusading editor of the local paper here's been urging me to run for prosecuting attorney this coming fall and clean up Kingdom County single-handedly."

The minister raised his eyebrows. "I had no idea Kingdom County needed to be cleaned up. I've always fancied Vermont to be one of the relatively few remaining places where folks obeyed the law and helped their neighbors in times of need and assiduously minded their own business the rest of the while."

"That's Vermont," my father said. "This is the Kingdom."

"But your 'Kingdom' *is* in Vermont," Reverend Andrews protested.

"Geographically, maybe. I'll tell you a story you'll hear sooner or later anyway. Seeing my cousins and their rooster reminded me of it."

As we walked back around to the dooryard, Dad told Reverend Andrews the sad tale of his predecessor, Reverend Twofoot, and the cockfight, and how Reverend Twofoot left Kingdom County a nervous wreck.

"Good heavens, editor!" Reverend Andrews exclaimed. "I'm beginning to see what you mean about the lawlessness in Kingdom County. No wonder you want your son to run for prosecutor."

He turned to Charlie. "Why on earth don't you, by the way? Not afraid you'll lose, are you?"

For a moment Charlie's black eyes snapped. Then he grinned. "Hell no, Reverend. I'm afraid I'll win."

Reverend Andrews got out another Lucky. "You know, mates, this Kingdom of yours is beginning to put me in mind of what I've read about your southern mountain states. Cockfights, church feuds and factions, a cavalier disregard for the law. My gracious!"

"That's it exactly, Reverend, a southern mountain state—only more so," Charlie said. "Tell you what. The best place to show you some real local color is the annual county fair. No, I take that back. The *best* place is the Smash-up Crash-up Derby, which, by the way, I intend to win this year. The second best place is the fair. No other county fair can hold a candle to it. I'd be delighted to treat you to the night of your life there this summer—if you don't mind being seen in public with a leading member of the notorious Kinneson clan."

Reverend Andrews laughed and said he'd definitely hold Charlie to his promise. "But if this area really does resemble the South," he said in a serious voice, "what about the local attitude toward Negroes? That's not a problem?"

"It never has been," Charlie said.

My father said nothing.

"Might that be because you've never had any Negroes living here?" Reverend Andrews said.

Charlie laughed. "No, because Pliny Templeton, who built the Academy, was an ex-slave. As I'm sure my father'll be all too willing to tell you, my own great-grandfather brought Pliny to Vermont on the Underground Railroad. Oh, there's a certain amount of latent prejudice in these parts, as there is anywhere. You'll hear the same mindless slurs from time to time, especially from the ignoramuses who don't have anything better to do than sit around the commission sales barn and barbershop all day. But Pliny Templeton never ran into any serious difficulty because of his race, and you won't, either."

"That would be a relief for both of us," Reverend Andrews said, looking at Nat. "And I must say that your ex-slave Pliny Templeton sounds most interesting. I intend to look into his history at the first available opportunity. In the meantime, before I leave I'd like a word with Jim."

I was surprised. What could Reverend Andrews possibly want with me?

"I heard you mention something about fly-fishing earlier this afternoon, didn't I, Jim?"

I nodded.

"Well, I'm wondering if you might teach Nathan how to fly-fish? I don't know the first thing about it myself, but I think it's something he'd enjoy."

Glancing quickly at Nathan, I didn't have the impression that fly-fishing, especially with a thirteen-year-old, would be his idea of a good time. But I said I'd be glad to take him any time he wanted to go, and Dad suggested the following Saturday evening, right after supper, when there ought to be a good hatch on the water.

Reverend Andrews stepped inside briefly to thank my mother for the dinner. Just before he and Nathan headed back to town, Charlie suddenly asked him a question, teasingly, the way he'd asked Charlie if he was afraid to run for prosecutor for fear he'd lose. "Reverend, I'm dying to know something. Don't answer this if you don't want to, but what if you'd known in advance about the tragic fate of poor old Reverend Twofoot? Would you still have ventured out into this moral wilderness?"

"Oh, surely," Reverend Andrews said with a smile. "For one thing, I'm not about to go charging up that hill to interfere with your colorful local customs. But just between us, I shall tell you gentlemen something. If I ever do go up there, I won't go packing my Bible."

"You won't?"

"No, sir. For that little outing, I'll be much more apt to tote along my service revolver."

Charlie roared with laughter and slapped Reverend Andrews on the back. "For the roosters, of course!" he said. "Just for the roosters. Right, Reverend?"

Reverend Andrews smiled. "Let's get home, chum," he said to Nat, and gave us a rapid, natty little two-fingered salute, like a World War I flying ace, and headed off along the gool with his quiet son.

"There goes one tough hombre, Jimmy," my brother said approvingly. "I like the guy even if he did beat me at HORSE. If he's just half as good at baseball, I'm going to recruit him for my town team. But I'm curious about something." Charlie turned to my father. "Did Reverend Andrews mention to the church trustees during his phone interview that he was a Negro?"

"No. Why should he have?"

"No reason. I just wondered. But I take it he's had some rough sledding because of his race elsewhere."

"Evidently," my father said. "Does that surprise you?"

"Not at all. But he won't here, will he, Jimmy? Just as I told him, there's been the strongest tradition of racial tolerance in these parts since the days of Pliny Templeton and the Underground Railroad."

"Maybe so, James," my father said. "But keep in mind that there hasn't been a Negro family in the Kingdom since then. At best, it's an untested tolerance we're talking about."

"Come on, Jimmy," Charlie said, gesturing out across the meadow and the river toward the village and the lovely greening hills beyond it, as peaceful-looking on that hazy spring afternoon as the nearly identical scene on the postcards summer people bought at Quinn's Drugstore to send home to their friends and relatives. "This is Vermont in 1952, not Mississippi in 1852. Let's go fishing."

# 3

From the time I turned ten, I worked at the *Monitor* for my father every afternoon after school for an hour or two, with Saturday mornings reserved for chores at home on the gool with Mom. (Dad worked all day Saturday at the newspaper office, just as if it were any other day.) I was no fonder of chores, at home or abroad, than any other kid, but I loved spending time with my lively, youthful-looking mother, and on the Saturday after Easter Sunday (the day I was slated to take Nat Andrews fly-fishing in the evening), Mom and I boiled off the last sap run of the season. Late that week the weather had turned sharply colder again, with two frigid subfreezing nights followed by two sunny windless days, causing the sap to run hard one last time. Although the quality of the maple syrup wouldn't be as high as earlier in the spring, we wouldn't have missed this final "frog run"—so-called because the peeper frogs had already started to sing—for the world.

It was yet another good morning, warmer and hazier than the previous two, and Mom and I spent the first couple of hours gathering sap from the two dozen big maples on the ridge above the farmhouse. As we moved from tree to tree, I wore a wooden yoke that fit snugly down over my shoulders, from whose ends depended two five-gallon pails. My mother poured the sap from the wooden buckets into these pails, and when they were three-quarters full I lugged them down to the house. There we strained the sap through cheesecloth into my grandmother Kinneson's old cream pan, which we used as a boiling-off pan on top of the Home Comfort stove in the kitchen.

One by one, as the kitchen grew hotter and hotter, my mother opened seven of the nine doors to draw off the heat—all except the false door and the door to the "other side of the house," since she didn't want the moisture from the cooking sap to steam off the wallpaper in the dining room and front parlor. I made myself useful by feeding the firebox of the stove with chunks from the woodshed, adding sap to the cream pan, and dashing a sprinkle of Ruthie the Cow's (named by my brother in honor of my mother) cream onto it whenever it simmered too hard and threatened to come to a rolling boil; running a clean rag mop over the ceiling to sponge off the condensing drops of sap; and chattering like a jay to Mom about this and that the entire time.

About ten o'clock there was a loud knock at the door. The first batch of sap had just completed its magical sudden transformation into syrup, and my mother had moved the cream pan to the side of the stove and was ladling the syrup off into one-quart Ball canning jars. I was sitting on the woodbox reading *Oliver Twist* out loud to Mom, who was inordinately proud of my reading and also of the little stories (mostly hunting and fishing tales about dauntless boys who shot huge bucks and caught enormous wary trout, often nobly releasing them after hour-long battles) I'd begun writing recently but showed only to her.

"It's Mr. Resolvèd Kinneson, Jimmy," Mom said. "I think he wants to redeem his bottles. Get my purse and pay him, will you, please?"

I went to the door, and sure enough, there was Cousin R with a bransack of bottles he'd picked up along the roadsides over the past week as the receding snow had exposed them. Although Resolvèd was wonderfully shiftless and improvident, neither he nor his brother Welcome was at all lazy or had ever been "on the town," as the phrase went—meaning neither had ever taken a penny of assistance from that much-maligned precursor of the county welfare commissioner, the overseer of the poor.

As usual Resolvèd looked every bit as rough as a tramp just in off the B and M tracks, though for a wonder he wasn't drunk yet. In fact, he seemed as invigorated from his springtime pursuit as we were from ours.

"Mom said for me to pay you, Resolvèd. She's inside sugaring-off."

"Sugaring-off!" Resolvèd could hardly have sounded more outraged if I'd told him my mother and I were counterfeiting twenty-dollar bills. "It's way too late on into the spring of the year to sugar-off, bub. All's you'll get is Christly blackstrap."

"Blackstrap" was the discolored, buddy-tasting, very late syrup some farmers sealed up in molasses barrels and shipped south to the R. J. Reynolds Company in North Carolina for flavoring chewing tobacco.

"How many you got today, Resolvèd?"

"What? Bottles? Well, now. Let's see here. Let's just have us a little look-see, by God, and tally up."

Resolvèd spilled maybe thirty bottles out of the bransack onto the porch floor. Some were Coke bottles, or Pepsi, worth a cent apiece at the Red and White Store in the Common. A good half of his haul, however, consisted of nonreturnable Old Duke empties, which my mother always scrupulously paid him for anyway, though of course the Red and White wouldn't redeem them. I counted the correct change into his hand from Mom's purse. "Yes, sir," he said, and started down off the porch, making no attempt to bag the bottles back up.

Just then Mom appeared in the doorway with a jar of warm syrup. "Mr. Kinneson!" she called. (She was the only person in the Kingdom who ever called Resolvèd "Mr. Kinneson.")

"Yes, sir," he said again without turning around.

"I wonder if you'd do me the favor of taking this syrup home and sampling it for me? It'll be about the last of the year, I'm afraid."

Resolvèd came back and took the syrup. He held the jar up to the hazy spring sunshine and frowned suspiciously, as though checking for deadly bacteria.

"I don't know as I want a lot of blackstrap around cluttering up my place," he said with his customary graciousness, tucking the jar into his hunting jacket pocket and starting off.

"Resolvèd!" I called after him. "Wait up a minute. You heard anything yet from that letter you wrote?"

"Which letter would that be?" he said, as though he composed several long ones every day.

"That letter you and Charlie wrote, sending away for a mail-order housekeeper."

He was bent over fumbling with something. I hoped it wasn't his fly, with Mom standing right there on the porch!

"That's for me to know and you to find out," he snarled.

I heard the pop of a vacuum-sealed lid coming free. Turning his profile toward us, Resolvèd lifted the quart jar of syrup, tilted back his head, and drained off its entire contents in about six swallows, like a man slugging down his first bottle of cold beer after a long hot day in the hayfield. He wiped off his mouth with the ragged sleeve of his hunting jacket.

"Stomach liner," he said, and tossed the empty Ball jar up to me on the porch. "Add this to your pile, bub. I won't charge you nothing for it."

And he was swinging off in his long-legged woodsman's stride toward the village, no doubt to replenish his supply of Old Duke wine now that his stomach was lined with a quart of maple syrup.

"Boy, Mom!" I said. "You ever see anything like the way old Cousin R just chugged that syrup down? I can't wait to tell Charlie. 'Stomach liner'!"

She had a dreamy look on her face and didn't seem to hear me. "Someday, Jimmy, you'll write wonderful stories about Mr. Resolvèd Kinneson, and Mr. Welcome too. You know, it isn't too soon to begin keeping a journal and recording what they say and do in it."

At the time, I couldn't imagine who except Charlie and maybe Mom herself would want to read about an old drunk and outlaw like Resolvèd. In those days when my mother spoke of my writing "wonderful stories" someday, I automatically assumed she meant newspaper articles for the *Monitor*, like my father's articles and open letters. In fact, though it seemed well-understood that I would follow in my father's footsteps and become a newspaperman when I grew up, Mom had far different ideas when she talked to me about the "wonderful stories" I would write, for in her way, she was as ambitious for me (and Charlie, too) as Dad ever dreamed of being.

We sugared-off the last batch of sap around noon, ate a quick lunch of beans laced with brand-new maple syrup, then gathered up the taps and sap buckets, rinsed them out in the milkhouse, and stored them upside down in the old harness room of the barn. Sugaring was over for another year.

It was still early in the afternoon, and Nat wouldn't show up to go fishing until five or six o'clock. For a while I batted my old taped baseball off the side of the barn, trying to hit line drives at a knothole just below the faded painting of the brook trout. Then I just hung around the dooryard, until Mom appeared on the porch wearing her pink sun hat, in which (as she well knew) she looked no more than about twenty-five years old, and carrying my great-great-great-grandfather's pirate spyglass tucked under her arm.

She stood on the top step, peering off toward the west with the spyglass, looking for all the world like a girl I remembered from a traveling road company's production of *The Pirates of Penzance* she'd taken me to see in the Common the summer before. "It's the right type of day, just hazy enough," she said mysteriously.

"Just hazy enough for what, Mom?"

"For Montreal to be out. Shall we walk up in the gore and see?"

"Sure," I said. I was willing to do almost anything to break up the monotony of the long afternoon ahead, though I didn't have much faith that Montreal would be "out" then or any other day, haze or no haze.

Mom had frequently told me how one mild fall day soon after she had come to Kingdom County to live, my father had taken her up the logging trace to the top of the gore, near where "Russia" was now located, and shown her a wonderful and rare sight, a phenomenon unlike any she had ever seen before. Far to the northwest, hanging suspended in the sky high over the intervening peaks of the Green Mountains, was a splendid mirage of the city of Montreal, nearly a hundred miles away but so sharp and clear she had actually seen a train going over the railroad bridge across the St. Lawrence River. I wasn't skeptical about her seeing the mirage—Dad had seen it several times—only that it would ever recur when I was on hand. But there was always a chance it might be out, and I loved to go to the woods with Mom at any time of the year because she shared my great interest in everything to be found there.

Although Montreal wasn't out, most of the spring flowers to be found in Kingdom County were, and Mom and I had a great afternoon together. Besides painted and red trillium, wild ginger, hepaticas, trout lilies, white and Canada violets, and golden thread, we discovered a good-sized bed of rare yellow lady slippers; sneaked up on a partridge drumming for a mate on a log (something I have seen only twice in my life since); admired a stand of big beech trees scored all along their trunks for fifty feet up with the claw marks of the black bears that had climbed them in the fall to shake down the beechnuts, then slid back down with their claws dug into the smooth gray bark like firemen sliding down a pole; and returned by the disused granite quarry and the wonderful pictograph painted on the cliff above it by the Dog Cart Man of the gypsy stonecutters who once came to Kingdom County each summer.

We didn't get home until nearly five, just in time to have a quick supper before Nathan Andrews showed up to go fly fishing—an event I looked forward to and at the same time, to a degree, dreaded. What would I tell him if the fish refused to strike? Also I still had no earthly idea what the minister's son was really like. It was going to be an interesting evening!

"A dandy hatch was coming on when I crossed the bridge pool," Dad told Nat and me that evening as I got my fly rod down from the wooden pegs on the porch. "You guys ought to do something in the meadow pool tonight. With any luck at all, you both ought to hit for the cycle."

"Hit for the cycle" was my father's baseball metaphor for catching one or more of each of the species of river trout in Kingdom County, a brook, brown, and rainbow. But I knew even before we started down through the meadow toward the big pool across the road that Nat wasn't enthusiastic about our venture.

Except to ask if it was snaky in the meadow (it wasn't), he didn't say a word as we traipsed along past blooming golden cowslips—marsh marigolds, my city-born mother called them, to Dad's amusement—past a pair of scolding killdeer, past brilliant red osiers and clumps of willows just putting out fuzzy lime-tinted catkins.

When I pointed out a woodcock circling high overhead, Nat shrugged. "We don't have those at home," he said.

"What birds have you got?"

"In Montreal, pigeons and gulls, mainly."

"Sea gulls?"

Nat nodded.

"We get sea gulls. They come down off the big lake, Memphremagog, just before a storm. Hundreds of 'em, sometimes. I've always wondered how they know when bad weather's coming, but they do."

"Instinct, I suppose. Come on, Kinneson. Let's get this fly-fishing business over with. I've at least two hours of chemistry problems left to do tonight."

I had a lot of questions I wanted to ask Nat, but his impatient manner and condescending way of calling me by my last name put me off. So we trudged on in silence to the river.

There I simply couldn't contain my excitement. Over the long pool hovered the largest hatch I'd ever seen: thousands upon thousands of the gigantic pale yellow mayflies I called spinners because of the way they twisted down onto the water.

Better yet, the entire surface was boiling with rising trout, feeding voraciously on everything that floated by. Everything, that is, but the flies I had tied to the end of Nathan Andrews' leader. Try as he might, with wet flies and dry flies; with big brightly colored traditional patterns and dun-toned sinking nymphs and garish streamers as long as trout fingerlings—flailing upstream and down, leaving several of my flies in the high limbs of a bankside soft maple tree behind us, several more in the jaws of the hungry trout, and one in the visor of my Red Sox baseball cap, Nathan Andrews did not, under my frustrated tutelage, land a single fish.

The sun sank below the long south shoulder of Jay Peak. The light flattened out; dusk was fast approaching. I was fast approaching tears over my ineptitude as a teacher.

But Nat Andrews didn't seem to care whether he caught a fish or not. He laughed at his own clumsiness and at my feeble pedagogical efforts.

"Shit a goddamn!" a gruff voice behind us said. "What be you boys doing here? A-trying to drive fish down the river?"

I whirled around. Slinking up from the bankside willows with a rusty milkcan in one hand and what looked like a long rolled-up rope hammock in the other, was Cousin Resolvèd Kinneson.

Resolvèd set down the milkcan. He reached out and seized me by the collar of my hunting jacket. "What be you doing here?" he demanded and gave me a good shake, as though to jar loose a reply. "Speak up."

"I'm trying to teach this boy to fly-fish," I blurted. "Only he won't learn."

Resolvèd gave a terrible coughing snort that sounded like a crocodile laughing, and turned to Nat.

"I be!" he said, and thrust his head forward to get a good look at my friend in the twilight. Resolvèd shook his head, as though he couldn't believe what he saw. "You say he's a-fishing?"

I nodded.

"Trout fishing?"

I nodded again.

"Well, Je-sus, that ain't no way to go about her. Tell him to hand that pole here to me."

"Resolvèd says he wants your pole," I told Nat, as though he and my cousin spoke two entirely different languages.

Nat handed him my fly rod. Resolvèd stuck the hammock contraption into the milkcan and stared at the size-twelve Royal Coachman wet fly on the end of Nat's leader. "What's this, a Christly bug?" he said, and ripped off the fly's wings with his three or four remaining side fangs.

From his hunting jacket pocket, Resolvèd removed a lead sinker hefty enough to take any freshwater bait imaginable to the bottom of Lake Memphremagog at its deepest point. He attached this anchor to Nat's leader about a foot above the denuded fly hook. He scowled at the ground for a moment. With the toe of his rubber barn boot, he overturned a dead limb that had dropped off the soft maple tree behind us. He stooped and came up with a nightcrawler as long as a small snake, which he threaded once through its middle onto the hook. He handed the rod back to Nat. From another pocket he produced a pint bottle of Old Duke with only a swallow or two left in the bottom, which he promptly drained off. Closing one eye, he sighted along the neck of the empty bottle at a pinkish granite boulder in the river. "Does he see that rock out there?"

Nat nodded.

"Well, then, goddamn it, tell him to throw in beside it."

For emphasis Resolvèd hurled the bottle end-over-end out into the river, where it smashed to smithereens on the boulder.

Nat threw in. Instantly his bait sank. A minute went by, during which all three of us watched the line intently. Another minute. Then the line began to move downstream.

"Tell him to wait."

Nat lifted the rod tip slightly.

"I said, tell him to wait!" Resolvèd shouted.

"Wait!" I shouted. "He says to wait."

The line, just barely visible in the twilight, continued to cut down and across the current.

"Now!" Resolvèd roared. "Heave her!"

"Heave her!" I roared.

Nat reared back on my rod with both hands. A silvery, shimmering arc flew up out of the sawmill pool toward our heads.

"Good Christ!" Resolvèd shouted and ducked like a man who'd been shot at.

Dangling from a low branch of the soft maple tree eight or ten feet off the ground above us was a thrashing rainbow trout about a foot long.

"Treed!" Resolvèd said with some satisfaction, and picking up the milkcan with the hammock rolled up in it, he continued downstream and faded into the dusk.

Nat seemed amused by the whole episode. While I cleaned his trout, he asked me how Resolvèd and I were related. He didn't see, he said, how anyone as young as me could be cousin to a "bloody ancient codger" like Resolvèd.

"Well," I said, as I slit open the trout's stomach sac to see what he'd been eating, "Resolvèd isn't really our cousin. We just call him that. What he is, is sort of an uncle to my father, I think."

"Sort of an uncle?"

"Sort of a half-uncle, actually. Or a step-uncle. Let's see. If I've got this right, his father was my father's grandfather, old Mad Charlie. Mad Charlie had a second wife, a gypsy woman, and she was Resolvèd's mother. Dad could tell you all about it."

"Mad Charlie!" Nat shook his head. "No wonder your cousin's an outlaw. Is he really an outlaw?"

"You bet he is. And a cockfighter and a moonshiner and the biggest poacher in Kingdom County. Last month he shot a moose through his kitchen window and got caught and fined fifty dollars, and I guess if my brother hadn't paid the fine for him he'd be in jail this minute."

Nat laughed. "I'd never get used to this 'Kingdom' of yours, Kinneson, if I lived here a hundred years. What a place! Let's say we head home, eh? I'll never get to that chemistry at this rate."

It was getting too late to fish, anyway. The spring peeper frogs along the edge of the river were singing like a thousand jingling sleigh bells, and it was almost pitch dark.

Just as we started up through the meadow, a blinding swatch of light illuminated a stretch of river several hundred yards downstream. In it I could see a dark figure bent over something in the water.

"Stop right there, Resolvèd Kinneson!" a high-pitched voice commanded. "You're under—"

The figure in the river straightened up fast. A dark arm shot out toward the source of the beam. The light swept crazily across the night sky, looped over and over, and vanished. From downriver we heard loud splashings, grunts, curses.

Seconds later someone went crashing up through the bankside alders into the meadow.

Just downriver, Sheriff White—for that was undoubtedly who the high voice belonged to—now lightless, wallowed noisily back to the opposite shore.

"I saw you, poacher boy," he shouted. "I saw you and I've got your net and your trout. You're under arrest for poaching and for assaulting an elected officer of the law.

"Go ahead and run," the sheriff hollered. "Run to the woods, run to the hills, run to Charlie Kinneson. Run all the way to the Supreme Court, damn you. You're as good as behind bars already."

But as Nat and I stole back up toward the farmhouse on the gool, trying to suppress our laughter, I was certain that I heard low chuckling near us in the puckerbrush.

*Plunged in the battery smoke*
*Right through the line they broke.*

I stared at the stern block letters on the blackboard. Unhelpfully, the letters stared back at me.

"We're waiting for you to diagram and parse that sentence, James Kinneson. We'll wait as long as we have to."

Of that I had absolutely no doubt at all. Although school had officially ended for the day five minutes ago, not a student in Athena Allen's eighth-grade grammar class had budged one inch. Every set of eyes was on the poetic jewel on the blackboard, which I had been selected to diagram and parse. Parse! I had no earthly idea what the quotation even meant, much less how to break it down into its component parts of speech by means of arcane lines more suitable to a geometry exercise.

Ordinarily, I very much looked forward to Athena's end-of-the-day English class. She was a crackerjack teacher, every kid's favorite, full of fun and great stories: "Tell us the one about the Great White Whale, Miss Allen!" "Read us how old Huck meets up with the King and the Duke!" And because Athena had learned to fish and hunt with her father the judge long before she was our age, and still regularly fished and hunted with him and with Charlie, she was genuinely interested in our tiresomely predictable compositions about trout and grouse and deer and read them with genuine appreciation.

But as Charlie had often said, Athena Allen was a "high-toned woman," and you definitely did not want to get on her wrong side. Not very often—just frequently enough to keep us on our toes—she would lose patience with the whole class and keep us after school for an hour or more, to "hammer the grammar" into our thick young heads (as Charlie said) and to show us that even though she was young and pretty and funny and sympathetic, she was still the boss.

I must say that those sessions were quite apt to follow close on the heels of Athena's fights with Charlie. And since I knew from my brother that they had just had a real donnybrook two days ago over Charlie standing her up the past Saturday night to go drinking in Canada with his basketball teammates, I was not surprised that lovely Athena was up on her high horse with us today.

I hated to be called on at those times, and I especially dreaded having to go to the front of the room. Even under ordinary circumstances this onerous pilgrimage was a real trial by fire in Athena's class, partly because Nathan Andrews and half a dozen other upperclassmen had a silent study period in the back of the room and so were on hand to witness my humiliation, and partly because when I returned to my seat I was invariably favored by a veritable barrage of kicks, jabs, punches, and missiles from Frenchy LaMott, who sat next to me, and who had the well-earned reputation of the worst boy in town.

The illegitimate son of Bumper Stevens, the commission sales auctioneer, Frenchy lived with his mother, Ida LaMott, and his two younger half-brothers at his uncle Hook LaMott's slaughterhouse out on the River Road. He was a good two years older than anyone else in our class and he hated Athena Allen with a passion because, although she was sympathetic to his circumstances and more than willing to give him extra help, she did not believe in social promotion and had flunked him twice already. Frenchy also resented Athena because two years ago her father, the judge, had sent him to the state reform school at Vergennes for several months. Suffice it to say that by the spring of 1952 Frenchy's single academic goal was to turn sixteen and "do for" Athena Allen once and for all, then quit school in a burst of glorious notoriety, an event to which he looked forward with more relish than any honor student ever anticipated delivering a valedictory.

But like it or not, I had been chosen to parse those idiotic lines on the board, and parse them I knew I must before any of us left that room. Worse yet, of all the days to be detained, today was one of the worst because this afternoon Resolvèd was slated to be arraigned at the courthouse for the trout-poaching episode Nat and I had witnessed. Of course Charlie would be representing him, and I desperately wanted to be on hand to see the fun.

Athena was looking out the window of her second-floor classroom, down onto the common. "What is so rare as a day in June?" she said. "I shall tell you, ladies and gentlemen: a day in May. A warm, pleasant day in May, like this day," she continued. "A very pleasant day. A pleasant day to play baseball. Or go fishing. Or to parse sentences."

Something hit the back of my head and bounced off onto the floor beside my desk. With a quick glance at Athena, who was still looking out the window and extolling spring, I bent over and picked up a tightly wadded piece of paper. At first I thought that this missive was a conventional spitball thrown at me by Frenchy. But at the back of the room Nat, who had stayed late to finish some homework, was signaling to me. "Read it," his lips said silently.

I unfolded the paper, which just fit into the palm of my hand. On it I saw:

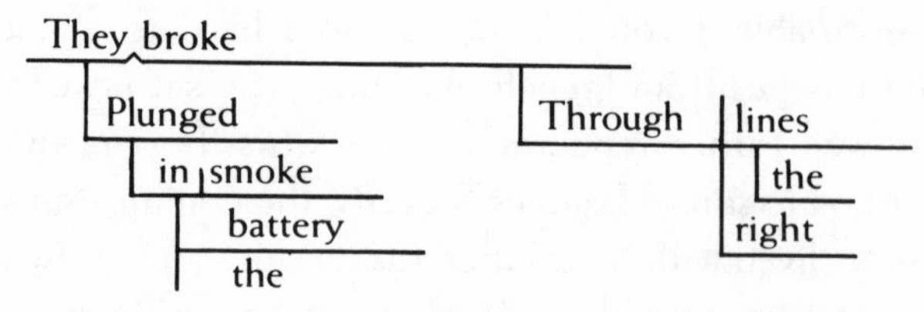


As quickly as possible, with several furtive glances at the crib sheet, I got up, transposed this marvel to the blackboard, and sat back down again.

Slowly, ever so slowly, Athena Allen turned away from the window and loomed down upon me. A yard away from my desk she stopped and turned to the blackboard. "Who wrote that, James Kinneson?"

"I wrote it, Ath—Miss Allen."

Ever so softly she said, "You wrote it."

It was neither question nor statement. I cannot in fact say what it was. But its implications were dreadful.

"Yes, Miss Allen."

"Then, James, let us parse. What, pray, is the subject?"

"The subject?"

"Yes. The subject."

At that moment I could not have told the good woman what subject we were studying, much less the subject of that involuted sentence. She might as well have asked me to render the thing into Greek.

Dazed as I was, I vaguely recollected that the subject of a sentence was quite apt to come first. Looking hurriedly at the lines on the board, I said, " 'Plunged.' "

From nearby came a nasty snicker.

"Who was that?" demanded Athena.

"Me," said Frenchy LaMott. "What you going to do about it?"

Athena's eyes blazed angrily. I wouldn't have changed places with Frenchy at that moment for anything in the world. Then, to my amazement, Athena burst into laughter. "Frenchy," she said, "you may not know much grammar, but you get an A-plus for honesty.

"Class," she announced, "just this once, we will celebrate Mr. LaMott's honesty with an undeserved dismissal. Enjoy your afternoon in May."

. . .

"Working hard, James?"

I was on my way up the courthouse steps two at a time, hoping to catch at least the tail end of Resolvèd's poaching arraignment, when Plug Johnson, self-appointed president of the Folding Chair Club, hailed me from the top step.

Plug was standing near the main door of the courthouse with half a dozen other pensioners retired from the B and M Railroad and American Heritage Mill. There was no way for me to get by them without stopping.

Although none of these savants was noted for an altruistic concern for local youth, except to predict grimly that most of us would come to no good end because we did not know the meaning of the word "work" (all members of the Folding Chair Club having apparently gone to work full-time at the age of eight or nine), they indulged me in a patronizing and badgering sort of way because they liked and admired my brother. Also, as the local editor's son I was regarded as a potential pump for news and information, though I was under the strictest injunction from both my parents never to mention a word of anything I heard at the *Monitor* or at home to these nosy old gossips.

Besides, next to reassuring themselves that everyone else was working hard, the Folding Chair boys, as the half-dozen charter members of the club referred to themselves (though their cumulative age totaled upward of five hundred), were in fact much more interested in manufacturing and dispensing news than in acquiring it.

"Heard the latest, James?"

"No, Mr. Johnson. What's that?"

"You mean to say you ain't heard about the hotshot lawyer in town this afternoon?"

"You mean Charlie?"

"*No*, I don't mean Charlie. I mean that slick downcountry lawyer name of Moulton Charlie's imported up here to help him defend Cousin Resolvèd. Tall fella? Pale as a trout's belly in January? Distinguished-looking? Pulled up in front of the courthouse in a taxicab about an hour ago. You ain't heard about him, James?"

I shook my head.

"You'll know about him shortly, then," Plug said. "Ain't that right now, boys?"

The boys duly agreed that it was right.

"Best defense lawyer in Vermont, is all Moulton is. You ask Farlow upstairs—he'll tell you all about him. And James."

"Yes, Mr. Johnson?"

"Don't overdo, now."

"I won't, Mr. Johnson. Aren't you coming inside to watch the hotshot lawyer?"

"Court's recessed until three forty-five, James. I guess old Charlie's meeting with him right now."

I was puzzled by Plug's news. This was the first I'd heard of Charlie bringing in an out-of-town lawyer. Charlie was the hotshot, wasn't he? It seemed out of character for my brash big brother to resort to outside help, especially in a run-of-the-mill poaching case. By now I was really curious to see my cousin arraigned. But just inside the door I paused. Something about the name Moulton rang a bell.

Then it came to me. Moulton was the Montpelier prosecutor who had handled the infamous Ordney Gilson lynching case, which also happened to be Charlie's first important case and the making of my brother's own reputation.

Even today the Ordney Gilson case is well remembered in Vermont. Back in January, just after Charlie graduated from law school, a well-to-do farmer known locally as Ornery Ordney Gilson went out to his barn to milk at his usual ungodly time of 3:30 A.M. A few hours later he was found bound in a bizarre way, with his wrists tied to his ankles beneath his thighs, and hanging by the heels from an elm on the village green—frozen stiff as a side of beef.

Somehow, what had apparently started out as a weird practical joke had turned into a murder.

The subsequent investigation revealed what everyone in the Kingdom knew anyway, that Ordney Gilson had a reputation as a hard man to work for. Over the years he had gone through more than a dozen hired men, and just that past Christmas Eve he had lost yet another employee. The man, Sheriff White's brother Titman White, who drifted from farm to farm and was considered throughout the Kingdom to be shiftless and a little softheaded, had evidently come to the barn that evening drunk. As he was wheeling two forty-quart milkcans down a short ramp to the milkhouse, he tripped and lost the entire load. According to Titman (so-called because he was the runt of the White litter), Gilson had flown into a towering rage and kicked him, "just the way the miserable son-of-a-bitch kicked his cows."

Titman quit on the spot, moved out of the hired man's trailer across the road, and spent the next several days telling his story to anyone and everyone in the Common who'd listen, particularly the crowd that hung around Bumper Stevens' commission sales barn.

During the week between Christmas and New Year's, Gilson received several anonymous threatening notes and telephone calls. His wife was worried. He apparently was not. Not, at least, until the early morning of January 1st when he found himself trussed up like a New Year's turkey and dangling from an elm tree in thirty-degree-below-zero weather on the village green.

Titman White had an alibi for his whereabouts on New Year's Eve and early the following morning; he had been at a party at the commission sales barn, with ten or twelve other local roughnecks, all of whom confirmed his story. But Sheriff White, who had no love for his brother, had been able to prove that the rope Gilson had been tied up with had come from the overhead hayforks in Gilson's own barn, where Titman had worked for several months prior to the Christmas Eve blow-up. Murder charges were brought against Titman, who promptly engaged Charlie to defend him.

Technically, the trial should have been held in the Kingdom County Courthouse with Judge Allen presiding and Zack Barrows acting as prosecutor. But Zack had just gotten out of the Memphremagog hospital for his chronic drinking and was convalescing at home; and because of the tremendous publicity the case was receiving, Judge Allen ordered a change of venue to Montpelier, where one Sigurd Moulton served as prosecutor before a judge and jury from that area.

The trial was covered by every major paper in New England, and by the end of the first day two things were obvious to everyone. First, that in all probability Titman White had, at the very least, had a hand in Ordney Gilson's murder. Second, that he could not possibly have acted alone.

In a brilliant and melodramatic defense, Charlie paraded Farmer Gilson's myriad enemies through the witness box one after another, demonstrating that he was a hated man, the very antithesis of a good Vermont neighbor. Nor did my brother put Titman himself on the stand for Moulton to grill and confuse, though the prosecutor, who had never before lost a case, ruthlessly cross-examined each of Charlie's other witnesses.

The courtroom battle raged for two weeks. Then in his summary speech Charlie stunned everyone by requesting that the judge issue a little-used "directed verdict" of innocent to the jury, on the basis that not a shred of real evidence existed to link White with the murder. Astonishingly, the judge complied—a decision which, however reluctantly, two courts of appeal and the Vermont Supreme Court ultimately upheld. White and his accomplices, whoever they were, went scot-free, and virtually overnight Charlie earned a reputation as a no-holds-barred, silver-tongued advocate who could win big cases.

Still, why would my brother need this Moulton, of all people, to help him in the most routine of poaching cases?

As I bounded upstairs toward the courtroom, which occupied most of the second floor of the building, I caught a spicy whiff of bay rum after-shave lotion and clove-scented hair tonic. Farlow Blake, Kingdom County's part-time bailiff and full-time barber, and a veritable walking barbershop of aromatic suffusions himself, buttonholed me on the landing. "Greetings, young James," he said in his portentous courtroom tones. "Big doings this P. of M. *Very* big doings."

Farlow gave me a canny wink. Moving like a blocking back in slow motion, he expertly steered me into a corner of the landing where he could impart his news in secrecy, though we were the only two persons within sight or earshot. Popping a wintergreen breath sweetener into his mouth and offering one to me (it was such small acts of thoughtfulness that made Farlow a universally popular man in Kingdom County; Charlie said he was the only bailiff in Vermont and probably all New England who could serve you a court summons and make you feel like a recipient of a Nobel Prize), he said in a near-whisper: "Brother Charlie's hailed in a ringer. Best lawyer in Vermont, James, name of Moulton. Just resigned from being prosecutor down to Most Peculiar to set up his own firm."

"Most Peculiar" was Farlow's standard way of referring to Montpelier, the capital of all Vermont except possibly Kingdom County.

"Why would Charlie do that?" I asked in a foolish near-whisper.

"I'll tell you why, James, if you won't breathe a word to another soul. Honor bright, now? Not a word?"

Having received my solemn pledge, Farlow said, "Because for the past two days, old Zack's been telling it all 'round town that he's got

Resolvèd dead to rights on this latest fish poaching business and for once Cousin R's going straight to jail. No extenuating circumstances. No plea bargaining. No *nothing*, James. They say Zachariah intends to show the voting public that he can still win a case, no matter what Dad K writes in the *Monitor* about him. They say that's why Brother Charlie's hailed in this ringer from Most Peculiar to help him—tall, pale, distinguished-looking fella they say never's lost a case in open court except once before—and that one to Charlie!"

Perhaps I should point out here that although Farlow Blake's principal responsibilities as courtroom officer consisted of announcing "All rise" when Judge Forrest Allen came out of his chambers and "Please be seated" after the judge sat down, he was also widely acknowledged to be unsurpassed at the subtle arts of swearing in witnesses, pampering bored juries in civil-suit cases by entertaining them with the latest magazines, newspapers, barbershop gossip, and Frenchman jokes, and maintaining the courtroom in spick and span condition. Yet in addition to being a sort of informal personification of the dignity and orderliness of the court, Farlow was a receptacle of all kinds of behind-the-scene information (much of which he had gleaned in his less glamorous capacity as town barber and some of which had actually been known to be accurate), which he dispensed in a conspiratorial and oracular manner to absolutely everyone who walked through the courthouse door, while simultaneously giving the impression of selecting his confidants only after enormous deliberation.

Like a good veteran newspaperman, Farlow never revealed his sources, attributing all of his inside lore to a mysterious entity known only as "they say." Depending on the circumstances, "they say" could be anyone from Judge Allen to Sir William Blackstone, whose venerable tomes Farlow studied in slack times at the barbershop with all the assiduity of an apprentice attorney preparing for his bar exams. In this instance, however, I strongly suspected that "they say" was Charlie himself, since during my school lunch hour that day when I'd gone over to the *Monitor* to run an errand for Dad I'd seen my brother and Farlow coming back from the hotel cheek and jowl together, with my brother laughing and doing all the talking.

Farlow checked quickly over his shoulder to make sure the coast was clear. "When I—when Zack got wind of what Charlie was up to, he was so mad he didn't know whether he was afoot or on horseback. They say he swore not to budge one inch this time, Most Peculiar lawyer or no. Catch you later, James, here come the Folding Chair boys. Dad K's sitting in the press area."

Farlow glided toward the head of the stairs to waylay Plug Johnson and his cronies. I went inside the courtroom and sat down beside my father in what he called the press area, the back row of chairs nearest the door, where he could get up and leave whenever he felt like it without attracting undue attention to himself.

Dad looked up briefly from the northern New England edition of the *Boston Globe*. He nodded once, as though greeting a junior colleague, and returned to a front-page story headlined, NO PROGRESS AT KOREAN PEACE TALKS.

Charlie was sitting at the defense table in front of the judge's bench, on the left side of the aisle. As I sat down he turned around and grinned and gave me a thumbs-up high sign. He was wearing gray dress slacks and an L. L. Bean green-and-blue-checked flannel shirt, and looked as relaxed as though he were sitting in his cluttered office sipping a cold one and listening to the Red Sox trounce the Yankees. Beside him at the table sat my outlaw cousin, who as usual was wearing his torn red hunting jacket and wool pants and rubber boots.

In the first row of chairs behind them was a well-dressed stranger who I assumed must be Moulton, the Most Peculiar lawyer. He had dark hair, slicked straight back, and even from the rear he looked formidable.

Across the aisle from the defense table, Zack Barrows and High Sheriff Mason White were looking through some papers at the prosecutor's table. Zack wore an ancient bottle-green sports jacket and a wide crimson tie. Mason was dressed in his sheriff's uniform. The only other person in the room was Julia Hefner, who in addition to her duties as church organist was Kingdom County's court clerk and stenographer and all-time number one purveyor of half-baked local scuttlebutt. She sat at a small desk directly below the judge's bench, painting her nails. As I shifted in my chair to get comfortable, she looked up and shot me a frown.

My father handed me the sports section of the *Globe*. I'd just started a story describing the festivities planned at Fenway Park for Ted Williams Day—for the second time in his career, the Thumper was leaving the Sox for the Marines and active duty as a fighter pilot, this time in Korea—when Farlow ushered in the Folding Chair Club. As usual they sat in the second row back from the front, behind the prosecutor, so that they would have the best angle for watching Charlie's performance at the defense table. Farlow made sure all the water glasses were full, then took his seat beside the empty jury box.

Almost immediately Judge Allen came out of his chambers, heralded by Farlow's solemn "All rise, please."

The judge sat down, glanced once quickly out the window, and without any further preliminaries said, "*The County* vs. *Resolvèd Kinneson*."

More to himself than the court he added, "Again."

If, over the years, Farlow Blake had cultivated the carriage and demeanor of a rather pompous judge, Forrest Allen had come to resemble nothing so much as a rangy, weather-beaten hunting and fishing guide. The last local direct descendant of Ethan Allen's nephew Ira, who had come north to Kingdom County soon after my own great-great-great-grandfather, Judge Allen had once confided to my father that since the death of his wife ten years ago, his chief satisfactions in life were sitting at home reading in the evening with his daughter Athena, landing a large trout on light tackle, hunting with his Brittany spaniel Frank James on a blue day in October, and hearing a well-argued brief—presumably in that order.

On two occasions Forrest Allen had turned down federal judgeships elsewhere in Vermont in order to remain in the Kingdom, where he could hunt and fish to his heart's content; and more than once on certain soft spring days at the peak of the mayfly hatch he had been observed wearing waders in court under his judicial robes in order not to waste precious seconds getting onto his beloved river. There was no doubt, however, that he was highly regarded as a shrewd and fair, if mildly eccentric, judge by everyone who knew him.

"*The County* vs. *Resolvèd Kinneson*," Judge Allen said in a louder voice.

Zack Barrows, who was deaf as a cedar post, continued to shuffle through the papers on his table. Farlow Blake looked expectantly at the judge, who scowled and nodded. The bailiff stood up. Silent and smooth as a blacksnake, he glided toward the prosecutor's table. Placing his mouth about six inches from Zack's bent white head, he roared in the voice of a Roman stentor: "*THE COUNTY* VS. *RESOLVÈD KINNESON*."

The elderly prosecutor gave a terrific start. But after fumbling through his papers for a good half minute, he stood up and read a deposition to the effect that on the evening of May fourth, High Sheriff Mason White did apprehend Resolvèd Kinneson in the process of removing a gamefish from a gill net strung across the Lower Kingdom River in a section known locally as the old Kinneson meadow pool. According to Sheriff White's statement Resolvèd had fled into a nearby swamp, leaving behind the net and fish and a milkcan half full of water containing a second large fish. The County was charging him with three violations: taking a protected species of fish by illegal means, transporting a live game fish for illegal purposes, and evading an officer of the law.

"Resolvèd, do you understand the charges against you?" Judge Allen said.

"He does," Charlie said.

"Defendant is requested to answer yes or no in person," Stenographer Hefner said in an officious tone of voice.

All three men—Charlie, Resolvèd, and the Most Peculiar lawyer—said yes.

My father looked up briefly from an account of the impending nationwide steel strike, then resumed reading.

"Is your client prepared to enter a plea, Charles?"

"Yes, your honor. Not guilty. Zack's indicated that he's planning to request a jail sentence for Resolvèd regardless of how he pleads," Charlie explained.

"I see," Judge Allen said, though it was apparent that he did not, entirely.

Charlie stood up. "May I approach the bench, your honor?"

Judge Allen glanced outside at the fading afternoon, scowled again, and nodded curtly. He and Charlie conferred briefly; then Charlie returned to the defense table and sat down. Judge Allen looked at Zack. Then he looked at the Folding Chair Club, who to a man were as attentive as if viewing the aftermath of a serious train wreck. The judge then looked at Charlie and Resolvèd, and finally he looked at the Most Peculiar lawyer, whom he seemed to notice for the first time. Except for the intermittent hissing of the ancient steam radiators along the walls, the courtroom was very still. The overhead globe lights suspended by steel rods from the stamped tin ceiling had not yet been turned on. Outside, the sun had gone under a heavy bank of clouds.

"Zachariah," Judge Allen said loudly, "would you object to having Sheriff White clarify a few points in his deposition before we put the county to the expense of a jury trial? Charles has assured me that it won't take more than fifteen minutes—so that those of us who pursue the piscatorial arts ourselves, within the strict confines of Vermont's fish and game regulations, of course, won't miss more than the beginning of this evening's hatch."

Zack looked from the judge to Farlow, who, getting the green light from the bench, approached the prosecutor's table again and bellowed out in a voice loud enough to wake the dead in the United Church cemetery, "JUDGE A WANTS MACE TO ANSWER TWO, THREE QUESTIONS SO'S HE CAN CLEAR THE HANG OUT OF HERE AND GO FISHING."

None too nimbly, Zack got to his feet again. His left hand continued to shuffle spasmodically through his papers, reminding me of the way a dead partridge continues to jerk for a second or two after you've shot it. People who knew him far better than I did had thought so before and been wrong, but the boozing old prosecutor really did look as though he was on his last legs.

"Just who is going to put these questions to Sheriff White, your honor?"

Farlow turned to the judge. "JUST WHO—"

He stopped in midsentence and a foolish expression crossed his face.

Charlie looked back at me and grinned.

"I am," my brother said, pointing to himself for Zack's benefit.

Zack looked relieved. Obviously, he didn't want the hotshot Most Peculiar lawyer grilling his flunky the sheriff.

"All right, Forrest," he said after a moment's deliberation. "But I'm certain that deposition's in perfectly good order. I helped Sheriff White prepare it myself."

At the judge's request Mason White went up to the witness stand, where Farlow swore him in with as much pomp as though he were inducting a new Chief Justice of the Supreme Court, and the sheriff folded his elongated frame into the witness chair.

Mason White was one of the few men in Kingdom County who were taller than my father and brother. For years in my early boyhood, in fact, I had assumed that his title as high sheriff referred to his stature. It was not just that he was treetop tall. Everything about the man was high: his hips, his neck, his high, narrow hunching shoulders, his forehead, even his voice. And though his long arms and legs were as skinny as fence rails, he was oddly flabby in spots, with a red double chin like a turkey gobbler and a tidy little potbelly over which his holster belt, all a-gleam with ordnance enough for a half-day shootout, was drawn at a rakish angle like some sort of outlandish decorative truss.

Personally, the high sheriff had an ingratiating and at times condescending manner, which he had cultivated during his years as assistant to his uncle C. V. White, the local undertaker, whose business Mason had recently taken over.

To my brother, who referred to Mason as Uriah Heep White, he was a caricature of a caricature. My father, on the other hand, regarded the sheriff as one more blight on the diseased legal system of Kingdom County. And although Mason pandered to me as a means of insinuating himself into the good graces of our family, I was somewhat leery of him myself, partly because he patrolled the village streets and county roads in his long black undertaker's hearse, on whose roof he had mounted a set of blue police flashers.

Adjusting himself in the ordinary-sized witness chair as comfortably as a six-foot eight-inch beanpole in full-dress law enforcement regalia could, Mason smiled out over his bony knees and squeaked, "Yes, sir, Brother Charlie. Just what was it you wished to bring before the court this P. of M.?"

"I'll oversee the county's judicial proceedings today, thank you, Sheriff," Judge Allen said. "And let me caution you, Charles. These questions of yours had better justify the time and deviation from standard procedure."

"They'll be worth a limit of good trout, your honor," my brother said to an appreciative chorus of guffaws from the Folding Chair contingent.

Charlie remained seated while he talked to Mason. He used no notes and did not appear to have a copy of the sheriff's deposition in front of him. He spoke in an amiable, conversational tone of voice, though unlike Zack he never affected a northern New England dialect when questioning witnesses or talking to juries. He did not speak especially loudly but enunciated every word carefully for the deaf prosecutor's benefit.

"What time was it when you went down to the river to look for poachers, Mason? I don't believe your deposition specified, except to mention that it was evening."

"Well, now, Brother Charlie. I'd say it was getting on toward dusk, or maybe a tad later."

"Which?"

"Which what?"

"Was it dusk, or later?"

"There wasn't what you could call a whole bunch of daylight left," Mason admitted. "You don't poach fish at noon, do you?"

"I don't poach them at all," Charlie said good-naturedly.

Another chuckle rippled through the gallery of old men. But Judge Allen scowled again. At the mention of fish and daylight, he had looked intently out the window. Although it was perceptibly darker than when I'd first come in, once the fishing season was under way Farlow Blake had standing orders from the judge not to switch on the lights until, as the saying went, it was too dark to see under the table—as though leaving them off would somehow retard the onset of night.

"Did you have a light with you, Mason?"

"Yes, indeed, Brother Charlie. I had my long-handled Big Shooter Battery Beam that I always carry with me in the patrol hearse. The subject was standing in the water taking up his net when I arrived. I crept out and when I got about as close as I am to you, I switched on the Big Shooter and played it right full in his face. You never saw such a surprised-looking fella in your life, if I do say so."

"So you'd call yourself a pretty good shot, Sheriff? I mean with the Big Shooter?"

More laughter.

Judge Allen was unamused. "Charles Kinneson, I'm serving notice to you to get to your point, if you have one, right this instant, or I'll slap you with a cool hundred-dollar fine, payable on the spot."

Although I'd never heard of Judge Allen's actually slapping anyone with such a fine, this warning was invariably effective.

"Where's the flashlight now, Mason?"

"That particular light? Well sir, that particular light would no doubt be somewhere at the bottom of the river between here and Memphremagog, on account of when I got out in the water to where he was standing, the subject knocked it out of my hand and took off for the puckerbrush. *After* I positively identified him. Which, frankly, I could have done with no light at all on the darkest night of the year. He's as rank as a pile of old burning tires, Charlie, and everybody knows it."

The Folding Chair Club laughed out loud, but Judge Allen said in a voice like river ice breaking up in the spring, "Sheriff, I won't have defendants or anyone else in this courtroom demeaned by such gratuitous aspersions. Watch your remarks, sir."

My father, who had the unusual faculty of hearing and remembering long skeins of courtroom dialogue while simultaneously reading the newspaper, interrupted his perusal of the *Globe* long enough to write in his notebook, "See what I mean, James?"—which I supposed to be a reference to the general lack of law and order in the Kingdom.

Mason began to apologize profusely. The judge cut him off and told my brother to get on with matters.

"What did you do after the subject took to the puckerbrush?" Charlie said.

"Well, I picked up the gill net with the fish still caught in it, and I confiscated that fish and the net and the milkcan with the other fish in it."

"How big were the fish?"

"How big? Oh, about ye big." Mason spread his great splay-fingered hands apart about twenty-five inches. Judge Allen leaned forward slightly, looking interested in the afternoon's proceedings for the first time.

"Those were dandies, all right," my brother said. "What kind were they?"

"What kind?"

"Yes. Several different species of fish come up the Lower Kingdom in the spring to spawn, Sheriff. Suckers. Wall-eyed pike. Bullpout. Salmon. Trout. What kind were these two babies?"

"They were trout, Charlie. Gamefish, protected by the State of Vermont. We're prepared to produce them for the upcoming trial. They're home in the wife's Frigidaire this minute."

"What kind of trout were they? Your deposition, otherwise unimpeachable except for the minor omissions of the time of day and the Big Shooter Battery Beam, didn't specify."

No outdoorsman, Mason shrugged. "What the Sam Hill difference does it make? A trout's a trout, isn't it? They're all gamefish. They were trout-trout."

Charlie looked back at me and grinned again, but Judge Allen was by now really irritated. "A trout is not just a trout, Mason. There are several species of trout native to this area, and to a trout fisherman it makes a considerable difference." The judge glanced back at my father, now sketching a fish on the notepad on which he seemed to write everything but notes, and said, "To some trout fishermen, it makes a big difference. I strongly suspect that these in question were spawning rainbow trout. But for the purposes of this court all trout are gamefish and in this state it happens to be against the law to take gamefish of any kind with a net unless they have been hooked by rod and line and duly played into one and *don't* you lay a finger on that light switch, Mr. Blake, or I'll fine you a cool hundred dollars, payable on the spot."

Farlow, who'd been gliding along the wall toward the switch, jumped as though he'd brushed up against a weed-chopper electric fence.

Charlie must have sensed that a summary adjournment was at hand. Quickly he said, "Mason, you said a trout's a trout. Is a subject a subject?"

Zack stood up at this point. "See here, your honor. These questions are preposterous. Young Kinneson is leading Sheriff White clear 'round Robin Hood's barn. He's laying snares for the sheriff and I won't have it. We'll go to jury and take our chances there."

"If that's an objection, it's sustained. Charles, this is a court arraignment, not a seminar on the taxonomy of fish. You have sixty seconds by my watch to make your point, assuming you have one, before I conclude these proceedings for what little's left of the day."

"Thank you, your honor. That's all I need."

Charlie turned around and whispered something to the Most Peculiar lawyer, who nodded.

"Mason," my brother said in a brisk businesslike manner, "is the subject you identified netting fish on the evening of May fourth here in this courtroom today?"

"Present and accounted for, Charlie. He's sitting right beside you."

"Will you please describe him?"

"Fella wearing the ratty old lumber jacket. Long hair hanging down in his face."

"What about the man I just spoke to, sitting directly behind me? Have you ever seen him before?"

"No, Brother Charlie, I'm sorry to say I've never made that distinguished gentleman's acquaintance. But I do believe I know of Mr. Moulton by reputation."

"Will the man Sheriff White identified as Resolvèd Kinneson please stand up and state his name?" Charlie said.

The man beside him at the defense table stood up. "My name be Welcome Kinneson, brother to Resolvèd Kinneson, and I never poached nothing but a hen's egg in my entire life."

There was a moment of stunned silence; then Zack was on his feet. "Objection!" he shouted. "Objection, your honor. All those damn Kinnesons look alike—"

"Like trout," Charlie interrupted. "Excuse me, Judge Allen. I believe I've still got fifteen seconds of my allotted time left. Will the distinguished gentleman sitting behind me, whom Sheriff White identified as Mr. Moulton, please stand up and state his name."

The scholarly-looking man in the front row got to his feet. Leering straight at Zachariah Barrows and revealing a mouth destitute of all but two or three broken side fangs, he said, "Resolvèd T. Kinneson, goddamn it. Esquire."

Mason White's neck and face turned bright red. He began to sputter. The sheriff flailed his long arms but couldn't seem to spit out his words. Zack continued to roar objections. The Folding Chair Club was hooting like a gang of bad boys at the Saturday matinee in the Academy auditorium. Judge Allen hammered steadily on his desk with the heel of his hand, and Farlow was calling for silence, silence in the courtroom.

At the height of this wonderful commotion, I noticed my father staring past me across the aisle. I turned and looked straight into the amused countenance of the Reverend Andrews. How long the minister had been there I had no idea; but on his face was a broad, unmistakable smile.

By degrees the uproar subsided. The judge's blows decreased in frequency and volume until at last he was tapping his forefinger at five-second intervals. "Mason," he said when the room was perfectly silent, "you may step down. Zachariah, sit down and compose yourself. Unfortunately, you don't have much of a case left."

Judge Allen pointed at my brother. "You," he said, crooking his finger. "In my chambers."

"All rise," said Farlow Blake in the ensuing hush. But for once he was late on the draw. Before the words were out of his mouth the door had already closed behind the departing judge, and although my brother gave me another jaunty grin over his shoulder just before following, I would not have changed places with him that moment for all the trout in Kingdom County.

■ ■ ■

"Shag ass," Resolvèd growled at Welcome. "I got to slide on over to the post office before she closes."

Despite Resolvèd's Brooks Brothers suit, which I now recognized as Charlie's, and freshly pressed white shirt and conservative dark tie and polished shoes, despite his close shave and what was probably the first barbershop haircut of his life, he now looked exactly like himself again as he and his look-alike brother slouched out of the courtroom together.

My father and I walked downstairs with Reverend Andrews. "Give my congratulations to Charles the Younger, if you will," he told Dad. "Assure him that if I ever need a good advocate, I'll know where to find one."

Outside it was noticeably colder. Reverend Andrews lit a Lucky Strike and he and Dad stood on the top step of the courthouse and visited about the arraignment. Resolvèd and Welcome cut across the common toward the post office, taking long swinging strides. The Folding Chair Club came straggling outside, buzzing like a bee tree on a hot afternoon in haying time.

"Yes, sir, editor," Plug Johnson said. "That Charlie of yours is some old Charlie. Ain't that so now, boys?"

The boys in the Folding Chair Club unanimously agreed that my brother was some old Charlie.

"Evening, Reverend," Plug said. "How you like it so far up here in God's Kingdom?"

Reverend Andrews said he liked the Kingdom very well and expected to like it even better when and if spring ever arrived. The Folding Chair Club laughed heartily. To a man, they took a strong proprietary interest in the local weather and considerable credit for its notorious severity.

"That's good," Plug said. "That's real good. Just watch the company you keep and you'll make out fine. I ain't telling you what to do, Reverend, but if I was you I'd steer clear of that whole Kinneson outfit. One side of that family is outlaws and the other's mainly radicals and Socialists. Ain't that right now, editor?"

"If you say so, Plug."

Laughing mightily at his own witticism, winking at my father and

Reverend Andrews, and not neglecting to enjoin me to keep working hard, Plug hobbled down the courthouse steps with his venerable coterie and up the street toward the hotel. In the meantime, Hefty Hefner and Farlow Blake joined us on the steps.

"Reverend Andrews, I believe you look thinner than the last time I saw you," Hefty said in a tone of mock rebuke. "Are you still batching it over there in that drafty old barn of a parsonage? You hire yourself a housekeeper to start fixing you and your boy three proper meals a day or I'm going to come over and do it myself. We've lost enough ministers around here without having one up and starve to death on our hands."

"Stop bullying the man, Julia," Farlow said. In his light spring overcoat and stylish fedora he looked more magisterial than ever. He sidled close to my father and checked over his shoulder. "I thought all along there was something fishy about that out-of-town attorney, editor."

"You were right about his being a most peculiar lawyer," my father said.

Farlow, who had absolutely no sense of irony, nodded in solemn agreement. After asking Reverend Andrews how he liked God's Kingdom, he headed up the street with Julia, who was still nattering on about the minister's diet and threatening to take matters into her own hands if he didn't hire a housekeeper.

"Talk about baptism into small-town life by fire," my father said. "You're getting it, my friend."

Reverend Andrews grinned. "I take it Julia likes to josh."

"She likes to mind everybody's business but her own. She'll be going through your desk to see how much you've been spending for postage stamps if you let her. She's been a thorn in the side of every minister in this town for the past twenty years. That's one you want to put in her place right off the bat."

Reverend Andrews shrugged. "I fancied her to be the mother-hen type, well-meaning enough."

"Fancy again. She eats ministers up for breakfast, and I'm not fooling. Plug Johnson is a scholar and gentleman compared to—"

The courthouse door opened and Zack Barrows and Mason White stepped out onto the portico. "Well, Charles," Zack said. "I hope you aren't going to splash this latest fiasco all over the front page of the paper."

"What happened up there is news, Zachariah."

"What happened may be news, but it's hardly fit to print. One of these times that smart-aleck son of yours is going to go too far. Tell him I said so."

I knew my father was very angry with Charlie for his latest courtroom shenanigans. But I also knew he would not stand for anyone else, particularly the old prosecutor, criticizing my brother.

"Tell him yourself," Dad said sharply.

"You there, Reverend," Mason White said in his incongruously high voice. "What's so funny?"

Quickly my father said, "Mason, this is Walter Andrews, the new minister. Reverend Andrews, Sheriff Mason White."

"I know perfectly well who the fella is, editor," Mason said. "He came waltzing in right after I took the stand upstairs. He was smiling all through my testimony, just the way he is now. All I asked him is what's so all-fire comical?"

"Come on," Zack told his toady, who loomed over him like Jeff over Mutt in the comic strip. "Let's get over to the hotel. I could use a stiff drink, and so could you."

But Mason was determined to salvage some part of his self-esteem. "I asked this man a question, Zacker. I'm still waiting for an answer."

"Do you really want me to answer it?" Reverend Andrews said, still smiling.

"Come on," Zack told Mason, starting down the steps. "This has gone far enough for one afternoon."

Mason gave the minister a hard stare and then followed the prosecutor. When he reached the sidewalk he turned and called back, "I'll give you a friendly tip, Reverend. I don't know about where you come from, but up here in the Kingdom we don't like being laughed at in our faces. And while I'm on the topic, up here ministers don't stand around smoking in public, either. Not if they expect to last long."

Reverend Andrews exhaled a cloud of smoke; still smiling, he nodded. "I appreciate the tip, Sheriff," he said, and flicked his cigarette butt out into the street. The butt did not come especially close to Mason. Perhaps ten feet away. But it came close enough to be an ambiguous gesture, and Mason stood on the sidewalk for another second or two, staring up at the minister, before turning to follow Zack.

"Not that I blame you much," my father said. "But you just made your first enemy."

"I don't completely trust a chap who doesn't have any enemies. I take it from your editorials that you aren't reluctant to make a few yourself, eh?"

"I can afford to. You can't."

The minister shrugged. After thanking me for taking Nat fishing, and asking if I'd take him again sometime soon, Reverend Andrews gave us his jaunty two-fingered salute and said goodnight.

I'm not sure just how much longer Dad and I waited in front of the courthouse. Maybe ten minutes. Maybe longer. The supper-hour Montreal highball went by, cutting off the hotel and the entire north end of the village from the common. I counted one, two, three, four diesel engines, doing the work a single steam locomotive had accomplished just two years ago. It was too dark now to read the names on the sides of the cars, but I could guess at their contents accurately enough by their shapes, and as usual I felt that nagging restlessness, that urge to go somewhere, to see what lay on the other side of the hills, which would eventually take me away from Kingdom County for a time before I returned, like my father, to settle down at the *Monitor*.

" 'SHE CAME DOWN FROM BIRMINGHAM ON THE WABASH CANNONBALL . . .' "

If Charlie was any the worse for his session with Judge Allen, you wouldn't have guessed it from his unsubdued appearance, singing at the top of his lungs and laughing and jabbing me out of my reverie of faraway places with a thumb in the ribs.

"Well?" Dad said.

"Well, what? You want the whole number? 'From the wide Atlantic Ocean to the far . . .' "

"What did he say?"

"Old Uncle Forrest? About what you'd expect. It was a cheap trick. 'Cheap, Charles.' I compromised the integrity of his court. And my profession. And my family. And if I ever do anything remotely like it again, he'll personally haul me up in front of the state Law Review Board."

"Is that all?"

"As a matter of fact, it wasn't. When he finally finished raking me over the coals, he tried to persuade me to run for county prosecutor."

"And?"

"And, right this minute, I'm going over to the hotel for a cold one. You guys want to come along?"

To my surprise, my father agreed. Just as we walked into the hotel, we met Resolvèd and Welcome coming out, and at Charlie's suggestion Dad took his picture standing with his arms draped over the shoulders of my two cousins under the fourteen-point buck's rack mounted just over the inside of the door.

"Well, bub," Resolvèd started to say to Charlie after the photo session. "How much I—"

"Cousin," my brother said, holding up his hand, "at long last you and I are even. You don't owe me anything. I don't owe you anything. We'll leave it there. Okay?"

I think Charlie said this at least as much for my father's benefit as for Resolvèd's. Maybe something Judge Allen told him had actually given him pause. Or maybe he was just tired of defending our cousin for nothing. I don't know. But neither he nor Dad mentioned anything else that evening about the arraignment.

Later that week I was surprised again when my father ran the shot of my brother and cousins, standing under the deer head, in the paper, along with the arraignment story and two open letters. The first was to Zack Barrows, strongly recommending that he resign immediately and devote himself to his prizewinning perennial garden. The second was to my brother, urging Charlie to run for Zack's job before the attorney general in Montpelier came up and took matters into his own hands.

But the biggest surprise of all was when my father came home the night after the issue appeared and said that Resolvèd was so pleased with the way the picture turned out that he dropped by the *Monitor* and cadged two free extra copies, without insulting anyone once—not even his ex-brother, Elijah!

# 4

COCK FIGHTS TODAY, the sign said. NO WOMEN NO DOGS NO KIDS.

It was Memorial Day, garden-planting time in Kingdom County. All morning my mother and I had worked together in the large plot across the road in the meadow, where over the centuries ton upon ton of rich alluvial soil had been deposited by the flooding and receding river.

And all morning, as we planted peas and potatoes, early sweet corn, and the tomato sets Mom had started weeks ago on the kitchen windowsills, cars and pickups and battered three-quarter-ton farm trucks had jounced past us along the gool and turned off onto the lane by Welcome's hand-lettered sign announcing my cousins' traditional Decoration Day cockfights.

Many of those vehicles had out-of-state plates and were occupied by strangers who had come to bet on the day's matches. But every fourth or fifth truck carried fighting roosters in portable pens or slatted crates. There were big flashy Rhode Island Reds, like Resolvèd's Ethan Allen. There were even bigger and gaudier Golden Buff Orpingtons, a variety my mother sometimes raised for eggs. There were White Leghorns with dazzling snowy breasts and wings and ferocious-looking clipped red combs, and numerous other varieties I didn't know the names of, some of which crowed all the way up the lane to my cousins' like bloodthirsty little gladiators.

I had never witnessed a cockfight; like the commission sales barn and the abandoned granite quarry up in the gore, my cousins' place on the ridge was strictly off-limits for me. But I was determined someday to see what went on there on cockfight holidays.

By noon, when my father came home for lunch, parked cars and trucks were strung all the way down the lane to the gool like vehicles at an all-day farm auction. Mom had fixed us sandwiches, which we ate picnic-style on the porch in the warm sunshine, but as the spectators continued to arrive, now parking along the gool itself, Dad grew angrier and angrier—angry with Zack Barrows, mainly, for failing to put a stop to the cockfights, but also with my brother for refusing to run for prosecutor and do it himself.

"I know this is killing you, Ruth," he was saying, when a large pink car came roaring down the gool from the red iron bridge and slued into the dooryard beside our DeSoto. It was Bumper Stevens in his new Cadillac with the words KINGDOM COUNTY COMMISSION SALES emblazoned across the driver's door in powder-blue letters. Frenchy LaMott, Bumper's son, was hunkered inside the open trunk holding his father's mammoth leghorn fighting rooster, the Great White Hope, in a fruit crate.

"Yes, sir, editor," Bumper called out his window. "I'll pay you two bucks to park my rig here in your dooryard where some Christly foreigner from York State or Canady won't sideswipe her."

My father stood up. "Get off my property," he said.

"Make that five," Bumper said and started to open the car door.

Moving very quickly for a man in his fifties, or anyone else, for that matter, my father was off the porch and across the dooryard before I knew it.

"I'll give you five," he said, slamming the door shut in Bumper's face. "Five seconds to clear off these premises."

Bumper cursed fiercely; but in considerably less time than the allotted five seconds, the big pink car was out of our dooryard. As it tore down the road past the collapsing barn, Frenchy hung onto the Great White Hope with one hand and fended the jouncing lid of the car trunk off his head with the other. The bird gave a long derisive-sounding crow.

My father returned to the porch, where he remarked that ten years ago he would have muckled onto Bumper Stevens and thrown him into the biggest snowbank south of Labrador instead of just ordering him off the property.

"I'm glad it's not ten years ago," my mother ventured with a smile at me, but I wished it was; at thirteen I would have loved to see the old man muckle onto Bumper and clean his clock.

"Walt Andrews is coming out this afternoon," Dad told us. "He wants to talk over some more local history with me."

"He seems almost as interested in local history as you are, Charles."

"He is at that. Now he tells me that he's got some sort of grand idea involving local history for a big church fundraiser. It's still in the planning stages, he says. He wants to sound me out about it before he brings it up in front of the other trustees. I don't have the slightest notion what he's got in mind, except that he confided to me that this shindig, whatever it is, is going to replace the church's annual minstrel show."

"I've thought for years that the minstrel show was in poor taste," my mother said. "I doubt that Reverend Andrews is going to have a very easy time replacing it, though. The Ladies' Auxiliary looks forward to that all year long."

"I don't," Dad said. "It's worse than in poor taste. If I have to write one more story about Julia Hefner getting up on the Academy stage in blackface and singing 'Mammie,' I'm going to throw up. Not to mention Bumper Stevens and Mason White making pure fools out of themselves with that idiotic Rastus and Remus routine. Whatever Andrews has up his sleeve has got to be an improvement on that nonsense. What's more, this is the right time for him to make his move. He and his congregation are still in their honeymoon period, and if he wants to make some changes, he'd better strike while the iron's hot. Soon enough the nitpicking's bound to begin. When that happens, look out."

"Reverend Andrews strikes me as the type of man who doesn't back down easily," Mom said.

"Good. The trustees wanted a go-getter. Now they've got one. But

Andrews is pretty quick on his feet. It wouldn't surprise me at all to see him stay here for two or three years, say until Nathan graduates from the Academy, get this hidebound outfit halfway shaped up, then move on before they really start to make life miserable for him."

At thirteen, I had less than no interest in church politics. But even I knew that Reverend Andrews was doing a first-rate job of getting the church back on its feet again. His sermons continued to be mercifully concise and to the point and, in my father's assessment, both literate and thoughtful. He got out and visited elderly people and shut-ins, whose stories about old times, like my father's, he seemed to relish. Earlier in the month old Coach Whitcomb, who had taught at the Academy for forty years, had sustained a mild stroke while playing a trophy-sized rainbow trout below the High Falls behind the hotel, and Reverend Andrews had volunteered to coach the school's baseball team, even though Nat wasn't playing on it. And though he needn't have troubled himself on my account, the new minister had already reestablished the defunct Sunday school and choir.

"Walt's going to bring Nathan along this afternoon, James," my father remarked. "Why don't you take him fishing again?"

I said I'd be glad to take Nat fishing if he wanted to go, but I doubted if he would. I'd asked him a couple of times the week before and he'd seemed lukewarm about the proposal, at best. I liked Nat fine and so did most of the other kids at the Academy, though no one seemed to understand why he didn't want to play baseball; we knew from our pickup games at recess that he had a blazing fastball and a wicked curve. But I didn't feel I could ask because Nathan was a junior, and I was still in eighth grade and reticent around the high school kids, and besides being an inveterate city kid, Nat was evidently somewhat of a loner. I didn't quite know what to make of him, and I strongly suspected that the puzzlement was mutual.

Nat did show up with his father that afternoon. He wanted no part at all of fishing, even though I assured him that this time we'd use garden worms instead of flies and go up the burn, as my father called the small stream that ran out of the gore, where no doubt the brook trout would be biting like crazy this time of year.

For a while we shot baskets out behind the barn, but I was no match for Nat at this and I could tell that his heart wasn't in it, either; so after a few minutes we went inside the hayloft where it was dim and cool and sat down on an old horse-drawn hayrake and Nat talked in a bored way about this and that, but mainly about how little there was to do in the Kingdom.

"So what would you be doing this afternoon if you were back in Montreal, Nat?"

"Don't I wish I were! Let's see, what would I be doing? Well, I imagine I'd ride the bus downtown, say down to St. Catherine Street, and take in a horror movie. Dracula or Frankenstein or something along those lines."

This intrigued me. Despite my fear of anything having to do with the supernatural, I had a keen interest in horror stories, Poe's especially, and in spooky movies too, though I hadn't seen very many. But before I could pursue the subject, Nat brought up something more interesting still.

"If I couldn't find a good Dracula or Frankenstein, I'd probably settle for a blue movie, eh? St. Catherine Street's lined with them from one end to the other."

"A blue movie? What's that? Like Technicolor?"

Nat laughed. "You are the naive one, Kinneson, meaning no offense. A blue movie is what you'd call a dirty picture. You know, fellows and their girls having sex together."

I jumped up. "Wait a minute," I said. "Hold on here just a minute. You mean to tell me there are movies, in Montreal, where guys and girls go at it right up there on the screen?"

Nat laughed so hard he nearly fell off the hayrake. "You could jolly well put it that way, Kinneson. But truth to tell, blue movies are fairly boring too after you've seen a dozen or so, and I probably wouldn't waste my time or money on one more anyway. So assuming I couldn't find a horror show, I'd probably just walk the streets joshing with the whores. Or maybe I'd go up to the fine arts museum on Sherbrooke Street and visit the Egyptian wing. They've got real mummies there, artifacts dating back five thousand years and more. Now that's something I'd like to go into—archeology. I'd have given about anything to be along on the Carnarvon expedition. Can you imagine how Howard Carter must have felt when he broke through that last seal and realized he was in Tut's tomb at last? Thrill of a lifetime, eh?"

I remembered reading about the King Tut expedition in the Boston *Globe*, and from what I knew about it, I could imagine wanting to be anyplace on earth other than inside that dreadful tomb. "Didn't all those guys die violent mysterious deaths after they broke in there, Nat?"

Nat laughed. "That's a lot of hooey, Kinneson. Now you're confusing the movie with the reality. No, they didn't die violent deaths."

He was silent for a moment. A gloomy expression had suddenly come across his face. "Oh, what the hell," he said. "I wish we'd never gotten onto the subject."

"Of Egypt?"

"Of Montreal."

"You wish you were still there, don't you, Nat?"

"What I wish doesn't make the slightest difference. I'm not there. I'm stuck in an end-of-the line little burg where the nearest thing to an artifact is this bloody piece of farm junk I'm sitting on."

I didn't know how to respond. What Nat said about the Kingdom hurt my feelings, yet I couldn't help sympathizing with him. I knew how I'd feel if I woke up in the middle of downtown Montreal without a friend to my name or anywhere to fish or hunt.

But I was curious.

"Nat, how long did you live with your grandparents?"

"Oh, off and on for about ten years. My grandfather died when I was five, not very long after my mother, so Gram and I sort of took care of each other after that. She pretty much let me do as I pleased, the way grandparents do, you know, and I was always good about getting my schoolwork done and helping out around the place. We were . . . well, friends, I suppose, Gram and I. A couple of times Dad tried having me stay with him on an air force base, once in Vancouver and once for a short while in Germany, but I didn't like it and it wasn't a good setup, without any mother and all."

"What did your grandfather do before he died?"

"He was a professor at McGill."

"McGill?"

"The University in Montreal. Let's drop it, shall we, Kinneson? If I think about it much more, I'll take the next train back."

We drifted outside, and Nat took a halfhearted shot at the basket and didn't bother to retrieve the ball as it bounced back down the ramp. "Say, Kinneson," he said, "what's going on up there on that hill? Where all the cars and trucks are parked?"

"That's my cousin Resolvèd's cockfight," I said. "He has one every

Decoration Day. People come up here from all over to bet on the roosters."

"You ever go?"

"Well, not exactly."

Nat laughed, not in a mean way. "What do you mean, not exactly? Have you been to a cockfight?"

"Look," I said, "you want to see what goes on there?"

He shrugged. "I wouldn't mind."

"Fine," I said in my best Huck Finn style. "Follow me, I'll be glad to show you."

Dad often referred to my cousins' place as the Kingdom's own Congress of Wonders, and as Nat and I came into their dooryard, it was obvious why. At first sight, it looked like a parody of a roadside animal farm. Two half-wild raccoons growled at us from the top of a Model A Ford sitting on wood blocks. In a makeshift coop converted from the shell of an ancient bread truck were four or five partridges, which Resolvèd snared live in the woods and kept on hand for his prize fighting rooster, Ethan Allen Kinneson, to practice his martial arts on. A feral-looking hog rutted in the beginning (and end) of the most wretched garden I'd ever seen.

The dooryard contained a number of antiquated farm implements, a quantity of chicken wire, several handleless tools, and a watering trough where half a dozen large rainbow trout hung finning near an inlet pipe that kept a steady flow of icy spring water bubbling in. TROUT 4 SAIL, read a sign propped against the trough.

At one time a barn had been attached to the house, but my cousins had cannibalized it for firewood over the years until all that remained was the squat silo, itself canting off at an angle that made pictures I'd seen of the Leaning Tower of Pisa seem absolutely plumb. In recent years, Welcome had converted this edifice into an impromptu automobile body shop and observatory, from whose top he watched for flying saucers and other extraterrestrial objects with my great-great-great-grandfather's pirate's telescope.

Besides his body shop in the old silo-observatory, Cousin Welcome maintained a junkyard on the edge of the woods running up into the gore, where for ten or fifteen dollars you could purchase a vehicle that he guaranteed would "run good." ("I never said how far," he would tell the dispirited and sometimes enraged teenaged boys who made up most of his fifteen-dollar-and-under clientele as they trudged back up the lane from the gool, where their crippled clunkers had stalled out for good. "Buy her back from you for five bucks?") It was from Welcome's junkyard, too, that many local boys and men purchased their entries for Kingdom County's annual end-of-July Smash-up Crash-up Derby.

Welcome's junkyard covered about five acres. It was an incredible mechanical hodgepodge, not just of old dead cars of all makes and vintages going back to Model T's, but of dump trucks, logging trucks, tractors, stoves, old-fashioned iceboxes, console radios, a Brink's armored car, and an operating steam crane on crawler treads with which Welcome moved vehicles around and stacked and unstacked them with unflagging gusto, making of his wrecks the most marvelous pentagons, Druid circles, and fleurs-de-lis, designed to attract visitors from outer space.

Cousin W's masterwork was a totem of car shells twenty vehicles high, resembling a surpassingly outlandish multicolored windmill tower. Sticking out of the top of this structure was the point of an old white pine, which Welcome had used to steady his automobile abacus. In a high wind, the whole shebang whipped back and forth with fearsome groans and clatters of protesting metal that could be heard as far away as the village common. My cousin's car totem was one of the wonders of Kingdom County and something to see—from a distance.

As we came into the dooryard, Welcome was grilling the day's losers over a blazing fire in the old sunken vat once used to keep cans of milk cool. Stuck in his slouch hat was a small American flag in honor of Decoration Day. The neck of an Old Duke bottle protruded from his hunting jacket pocket. At his feet was a great heap of dead roosters of every color, which Frenchy LaMott was plucking and cleaning.

"So where is everybody?" Nat asked me.

"Down cellar. They have the fights in the house cellar."

I was afraid Welcome would send us packing, but instead he beckoned us forward. "Hurry up, boys," he called. "You're just in time for the finale."

As we approached the old slab of concrete, Frenchy ripped the innards out of a limp, gray-speckled bird and threw them in the direction of the two raccoons, who scrambled down off the Model A, snarling ferociously. "I thought that sign said no kids," Frenchy said.

"Family," Welcome said, meaning that I was related and so exempt from the no-kids rule. To me he said, "You're just in time. Ethan Allen's about to be put up against Bumper's Great White for the championship."

Frenchy, in the meantime, had been staring at Nathan. "Say, preacher boy. Old Bumper says your daddy ain't going to last out the summer. Bumper says he don't like the idea of your daddy preaching in that church."

"Why not?" Nathan did not seem angry, just curious.

"You know why not," Frenchy said. "You know damn well why not. You'd better tell your daddy to watch his step."

"Bumper Stevens ain't been in that church since the night he got blind drunk and mistaken it for the hotel and went in to order more beer and tripped over the pulpit and knocked himself out cold, Frenchy," Welcome said. "He don't have no say what goes on over there. Now shut up and finish plucking them roosters."

Welcome shoved the first mess of roasting chickens to the far end of the grill where they wouldn't burn and said, "I got to get down to that finale now. You two boys go along the side of the house to the cellar window past the kitchen. You can look in there and view the proceedings. Don't say I sent you if you get caught."

Nathan and I started around the corner of the house, which listed off toward the east, where for years my cousins had banked up the foundation with dirt and the sills had rotted away. The kitchen door hung partway off its hinges, revealing a room unlike any I have ever seen since. Everywhere, on the table and counters, kitchen shelves and windowsills, were stacks of dishes encrusted with the unidentifiable remains of long-forgotten meals. Even the wood stove was piled high with plates and saucers. Stuffed into a gaping hole in the floor were burlap sacks overflowing with bottles and Campbell's bean cans. Fly-specked calendars with faded pictures of cowgirls and bathing beauties sporting heavily waved hairstyles were tacked askew on the walls. A rank odor resembling that of rotten potatoes drifted out the door, though in the south window sat three of the biggest and reddest geraniums I'd ever seen, which Welcome had somehow managed to conjure into bloom under conditions that should have wilted the hardiest houseplant within a week.

"Right out of *Better Homes and Gardens*," Nat said.

He put his finger to his lips and pointed to the cellar window just ahead of us. He dropped to his hands and knees. So did I, and we crawled forward through the debris of broken planks and tarpaper with which my cousins covered the opening during cold weather. Motioning for me to stay where I was, Nat rose to a crouch, sprinted past the window, flattened himself on his belly and looked back around into the cellar. Very cautiously, with my heart beating fast, I eased into position and peered into the cellar from my side.

A rush of cool air hit my face. I caught the scent of damp earth, cigarette smoke, and the sweaty press of hard-drinking men crowded together in a small area.

All I could see at first was a single naked lightbulb hanging from the cellar ceiling. By degrees, as my eyes adjusted to the dimness, I made out a ring of shadowy figures. Above them, on all four sides, rose the gigantic unmortared granite boulders my great-great-great-grandfather had somehow levered into place with the intention of using this redoubt as an ammunition and powder magazine for his projected invasion of Canada.

The hundred or so men crowded below us were squatting around a shallow pit directly under the lightbulb in the center of the floor. The pit was about as large as a batter's box and strewn with sawdust. Kneeling on opposite sides of it and facing one another like two troglodytes were Bumper Stevens and my cousin Resolvèd. Each man was holding his rooster by the tail feathers and the birds were lunging at each other across the pit. Just to one side sat a water bucket with a long-handled dipper.

At first I thought the championship fight had already started, but after a minute I realized this was some sort of preliminary exercise to the serious bloodletting, since the birds were allowed to come only within a foot or so of each other, then were drawn back. Welcome, in the meantime, was elbowing his way through the crowd, recording bets on a pad and collecting money.

Bumper and Resolvèd stood up and held their birds out over the pit. Both roosters let out shrill war cries. They slashed the air with their spurred feet and the light from the overhead bulb glinted fiercely off the honed steel rowels of the spurs.

"Yes sir, gentlemen," Welcome announced. "All wagers should be in, the championship bout of the day is about to commence. Be them birds ready?"

"You bet your hairy ass!" Bumper Stevens roared.

"Hold your water," Resolvèd said. "Which regulations is it to be here, Albany or Boston?"

"Albany, by the Jesus," Bumper growled.

The crowd murmured approval.

"I don't know about Albany," Resolvèd said. "Ethan Allen's six years old. He's won what, four fights already today? He's tired. Besides, I intend to put him out to pasture with two, three good-looking young hens after this bout."

"I and the Great White shall put him out to pasture for you," Bumper said. "We'll put him six foot under your Christly pasture."

"Old Ethan's going to a bar-b-que, Cousin R," yelled a stumblebum in a dirty white cowboy hat.

"I ain't just determined on no Albany regulations, Bumper," Resolvèd said. "This was to be Ethan's last go-round before retirement."

"It will be," Bumper said. "I guarantee it."

"Albany rules, brother," Welcome said briskly. "These good folk didn't journey clear up here into God's Kingdom to watch no sparring match. Ready?"

"Ready!" Bumper hollered.

Resolvèd said nothing.

"Commence," said Welcome, and the men tossed their birds into the ring.

What happened next was not pretty. Before they hit the sawdust the two roosters were locked together. They spun over and over in a whirling blur of red and white feathers. They landed, disengaged momentarily, leapt high, and came together again.

"Break," Welcome said when the birds parted for the second time.

Resolvèd and Bumper snatched up their roosters. The leghorn seemed to be unhurt, but Ethan Allen had been raked along the neck. How badly I couldn't tell, because of the bird's dark red plumage, but blood was dripping steadily off Ethan into the sawdust.

Resolvèd stretched the red rooster's neck out between his fingers and ran his tongue over the wound. He turned his head aside, spat, and repeated the process, like a man giving first aid to a snakebite victim. I was amazed. This was the first humane act I'd ever seen my outlaw cousin perform.

Resolvèd reached for the water dipper. "Open your trap," he said to Ethan, not ungently.

Incredibly, Ethan Allen gaped his beak wide as a hungry nestling. Cousin R sipped from the dipper, tilted his head sideways, and allowed a few drops of water to trickle out of the corner of his mouth and down the rooster's throat.

Across the pit, Bumper Stevens flapped the leghorn's wings up and down to ventilate its body. Someone handed him a bottle of beer, which he drank in three or four gulps, pouring the last small swallow directly down his rooster's throat. Exultingly, he roared, "We got you now, poacher boy. I and Great White have got your ass in a rhinestone sling, by the cockfighting Jesus Christ."

"Commence," said Welcome.

This time Bumper released his bird before Resolvèd was ready. The leghorn gave a great fluttering spring and landed on Ethan's back.

Fast as a fighting tomcat, Ethan Allen executed a barrel roll in midair. The Great White Hope hit the sawdust. Before the Hope could turn aside, Ethan was astride its head and had driven a spur deep into its left eye. A jet of blood spurted up into Bumper's face. The onlookers roared and surged forward in a body. Bumper cursed viciously.

"My God," Nathan said softly.

"Break," Welcome shouted.

Bumper grabbed his bird, whose eye was dangling from its socket by a single thin filament.

"Jesus!" Bumper said, and bit off the ruined eye and spit it out into the sawdust.

The Great White Hope was bleeding profusely. Swearing steadily, Bumper dashed an entire dipperful of water over its head. Meanwhile, Resolvèd was blowing air into Ethan's nose and mouth. Time and again the red rooster twisted in my cousin's hands, trying to free itself and finish off its opponent. Ethan was enraged, beyond any human or animal rage I had ever witnessed, by the steady flow of blood running out of the leghorn's eye socket and down over its snowy neck and breast.

"Albany rules," Welcome said. "Commence."

With a final curse Bumper booted his rooster back into the pit. Blinded by pain and blood, it turned away from Ethan Allen, who leaped high and came down squarely on its neck with both spurred feet extended, like a chicken hawk I'd once seen swoop out of nowhere and pick up one of my mother's pullets.

The Great White Hope sagged into the sawdust. He jerked twice. Then, mercifully, he was dead. Ethan Allen Kinneson gave a single long triumphant cry. Depending on how they'd bet, the spectators cheered or groaned.

Bumper reached down, unbuckled the dead rooster's spurs, and dropped them into his shirt pocket. He picked up the limp carcass by its yellow legs. "Go fry, goddamn you," he said, and flung it straight through the open window where we were watching.

Nathan and I jumped to our feet, whirled around, and found ourselves staring smack into the grim faces of my father and Reverend Andrews.

"How was the show, boys?" Dad said. "Bloody enough for you?"

"It's all my fault," I blurted. "It was my idea, I got him to come here—"

"He's old enough to know better," Reverend Andrews said.

The minister got out a cigarette and stepped into the shelter of the house wall to light it. Nathan sighed, gave me that fatalistic glance kids exchange when they've been caught doing something they shouldn't, and headed around the corner of the house with me at his heels.

Just as Nathan passed the kitchen doorway Bumper Stevens came slamming through it, colliding with my friend and nearly knocking him over. The auctioneer cursed. Then he saw who he'd run into.

"Well, if it ain't young Step'n Fetch, the new preacher's boy. Did your daddy send you up here to pray over us, sonny? Or was you going to perform a little cakewalk for the boys?"

Bumper, who was facing Nathan, had not yet seen Reverend Andrews. The minister looked at my father. "Is this the man who threw the rooster on Reverend Twofoot?"

Before Dad could reply, Bumper whirled around. "None other," he snarled. "What do you intend to do about it?"

Then he added, in the most slurring manner imaginable, that word my father would punish Charlie and me more for using, if we'd ever used it, than any other in the language: "Nigger."

Reverend Andrews did not seem to hit Bumper Stevens especially hard. Just very, very fast. And it was not a haymaker punch. It appeared to be more of a jab, though it landed squarely on Bumper's jaw with every bit of the force of another man's haymaker.

Bumper reeled back. He looked like a circus clown riding a bicycle backward. His peddling legs were having difficulty keeping pace with his upper body. He came up against the horse trough where Resolvèd kept his trout and sat down in the water the way an exhausted man plops into an armchair. Bumper did not make a large splash; a little water sloshed over the rim of the trough. Except that his jaw was twisted off at an odd angle to the rest of his face, Bumper looked more surprised than hurt and only mildly surprised, at that.

By this time half a dozen men had emerged from the kitchen, blinking like men who had spent hours in a cave. Among them was Welcome Kinneson, who glanced at Bumper.

"Soaked through," my cousin said without breaking stride.

Reverend Andrews flexed his hand. He gave his quick two-fingered salute to the men in the yard.

"Let's go home, old son," he said to Nat. "You've seen enough low-life for one day."

# 5

So far, the spring of 1952 had been a banner one. After the cockfight episode, my father had issued several ominous threats involving "trips to the woodshed" and "boys who were never too big to muckle onto." Then my mother had quietly and firmly confined me to our premises on the gool for the rest of the school year. But the river ran smack through the middle of our property, a whole glorious half mile of it, and with Mom to come along with me (she did not fish, but just enjoyed walking on the bank and seeing the birds and whatever else we happened across), I had all the freedom and company I needed.

Mom was not only the main companion, but also the chief confidante of my boyhood on the gool. Charlie, of course, was my idol; but Charlie had been off at college and law school for years, showing up only on vacations, and then spending much of his time with Athena

Allen. To my father, I stood in the relationship of pupil to mentor, apprentice to master, novice to expert. The very happiest hours of my early childhood were the ones I spent in the company of my youthful-looking mother.

Ruth Emerson Kinneson was the daughter of a prominent Boston Salvation Army officer, one Captain George Emerson, who along with his wife and fellow soldier in the battle against poverty and infidelism, my grandmother Louisa, departed this earthly vale in the line of duty during the great typhoid epidemic of 1927—the year after my mother was married. My grandfather had been educated at Harvard and came from an old Beacon Hill family, which, my mother rather vainly gave me to understand, had a "slight distant connection" to the celebrated Concord Emersons. He and my grandmother had married late—he was past forty, she in her late thirties. And this is the sum of my knowledge about my maternal grandparents, except that in addition to his professional duties, "the poor captain," as Mom invariably referred to her father—though whether because he was impoverished, which given his Harvard education and Beacon Hill background I doubt, or in reference to his untimely demise in the typhoid epidemic, or from some oblique association with her own strange situation as the daughter of not one but two Salvation Army officers, I have no idea—the "poor captain" was an elder of the Methodist Church and an amateur botanist of some renown.

"I didn't have the most ordinary of childhoods, Jimmy," my mother used to say with a smile. "But I had an interesting one."

Certainly the first part of her statement is true. Growing up with the poor captain and Louisa in the by then rather dilapidated family mansion, my mother divided her time between serving tea to her father's botanical associates and playing the piano for the "unfortunates" who frequented the captain's waterfront mission. What those sad devils must have thought of the blue-eyed beauty who at fifteen and sixteen and seventeen hammered out hymns and doled out soup in the prim matching navy skirt and blazer of the Boston School for Young Methodist Ladies is anyone's guess. But the tall, skinny young Boston *Post* reporter who stuck his head into the mission one dreary November evening during the second verse of "Shall We Gather by The River" was as close to astounded by her as he ever permitted himself to come.

"I'm Charlie Kinneson and I'm doing a story for the *Post*," he said a few minutes later as he came through the soup line behind an octogenarian still beating time to "Shall We Gather" with his spoon. "What in the name of Ethan Allen and the First Continental Congress is a good-looking dame like you doing in a joint like this?"

When my mother, who was just seventeen, laughed and brushed a thick strand of her beautiful blond hair away from her face and said she'd wondered exactly the same thing herself a hundred times, my father was smitten. They eloped to Kingdom County six months later, on the day after my mother's valedictory speech at the School for Young Methodist Ladies, arriving at our farm on the gool in the early summer of 1926, and my mother not only fell in love with northern Vermont instantly, but fell in love with it at its loveliest. From the day she arrived she loved the tall woods and quick streams, the jumbled mountains and icy green lakes, the brilliant falls and uncertain springs—even mud season; even the interminable winters.

On the other hand, she didn't much like the village or anything about it. She served on the Ladies Auxiliary from a sense of community responsibility but she was at least as frustrated with its hypocrisies as my father. She helped out sometimes at the *Monitor* but shared little of my father's keen interest in local, state, and national politics. And though she always admired dad's stories in the *Monitor* and those he told us at home, her own stories to me, and before me to Charlie, were entirely different and had few sharp edges and no "points." My father's tales were exemplums, allegories, "news" old and new. My mother, for her part, loved to tell about going up into the gore by sleigh to get the Christmas tree with my grandfather that first winter she spent on the gool, going with him on the great snowroller to pack down the roads after a blizzard, and shoveling snow for sleigh runners onto the covered bridge. Like the books she read me—*Little Men, Grimms' Fairy Tales, Around the World in Eighty Days*—my mother's stories were meant to entertain and delight rather than instruct me.

And, best of all, we almost never got into an argument.

Still, I was more than ready for a change of scenery by the Saturday morning in mid-June after school let out for the summer—the day my restriction was lifted. I grabbed my new catcher's mitt and made straight for the parsonage.

• • •

At the junction of the east end of the gool and the county road, I struck boldly off onto a detour through the cemetery. On such a splendid morning, with not a cloud over the mountains and the fringe of the gravel path through the cemetery bright with daisies and red and yellow Indian paintbrushes and the village suffused from end to end with the heady fragrance of varnish from the American Heritage furniture mill, even the graveyard seemed a friendly spot. I gave Black Pliny's tall obelisk a smart-alecky salute as I passed it, wondering idly for the hundredth time why under the sun his students had bothered to erect such an imposing monument to him when Pliny's remains did not repose here at all but dangled from the metal pole in the Academy. And I shot an insouciant high sign to the substantial pink granite markers of my ancestors, sparkling almost cheerfully in the June sunshine. Even the so-called pauper's corner off under the north boundary row of cedars looked less forlorn and somber this morning.

"Scat!" said a sharp voice.

Cousin Elijah Kinneson materialized from the cemetery toolshed. In his hand he held a spade, with which he made several jerky sweeping motions in my direction, like an old woman shooing a stray tomcat off her porch. As he did so, the great ring of keys at his belt seemed to jingle angrily.

"Scat," Elijah said again. "What are you up to, James Kinneson, navigating around here where you don't belong? Go along! I won't have boys navigating and prowling and spying and prying in my cemetery."

I was never entirely certain what my cranky old cousin the sexton-linotypist meant by accusing me of "prowling and spying and prying," except that, next to the absolutely unforgivable (and equally obscure) offense of "navigating," these crimes were among the most heinous any boy could commit. Even in broad daylight, there was a certain ghoulish quality about Elijah, a quality enhanced this morning by the shovel with which he intended to perform heaven knew what gruesome task.

The previous summer he had offered Frenchy LaMott two dollars to assist him in moving the graves of a young woman named Craft and her infant daughter to the cemetery in Memphremagog. According to Frenchy, after they had exhumed the coffins, nothing would do but that Elijah must positively identify their grisly contents. Frenchy said that no sooner were the remains exposed to the air than the wispy hair of both mother and child disintegrated almost instantly, a Poe-like image that haunted me for years to come. Frenchy also said that when he refused to touch the coffins again, Elijah never paid him a cent for reopening the graves, for which Frenchy had vowed to "do for" him someday when he least expected it.

"Scat," Elijah repeated, and I hurried off along the path to the parsonage.

"Cheerio, Jim," Reverend Andrews said. He smiled in a friendly, ironical way that I didn't quite know what to make of, almost as if he and I shared a good joke. "Your chum's up in his room, reading funny books, no doubt. Kindly pry him away from there if you can. It's too fine a day to stay indoors."

I couldn't imagine anyone wanting to be shut up in a dim old house on a day like this. I was sure I could coax Nat into playing ball with me.

"First door on the left at the top of the stairs," Reverend Andrews called after me.

That was the room directly above the minister's study, looking out over the porch roof onto the street and Cousin Elijah's sexton's cottage across the way. The door was partly ajar, and Nat was sitting Indian-fashion on his unmade bed, surrounded by old comic books. Loose comic books were strewn across the floor, and cardboard boxes of comics were stacked in the corners and heaped up on the dresser.

Never in my life had I seen so many comics together in one place. There were hundreds of them, representing every genre from fighting-men-at-war to gothic horror to classics.

"So, what are you up to, Kinneson?"

"I thought you might want to play some ball on the common, Nat."

"Maybe later this afternoon."

"We can't then. At one o'clock, Charlie's town team has it for the rest of the day."

Nat shrugged.

I went over to see what he was reading. It turned out to be a coverless old issue of *Beyond the Grave*.

"Great stuff, eh?" Nat said, flipping it to me and flopping across his bed as though he intended to stay there for the rest of the summer.

I loved comics of all kinds, partly because they had always been strictly proscribed in my Presbyterian household. This one was so horrifying that it brought out goose bumps on my arms. To the best of my recollection, it chronicled a murderous rampage through Merry Olde England of the walking corpse of a mad miller, well-dusted with his own poisonous flour.

"Your father lets you read these?"

"Sure. Why shouldn't he?"

"I don't know. I'm not allowed to. Doesn't it give you the creeps?"

Nat groaned and stuck his head under a caseless pillow.

"There's just one thing, Nathan."

"I know. Baseball."

"Yeah, but what I was going to say was I wouldn't read these alone in this house after dark if I was you."

"I don't imagine you would," he said in a muffled voice with his head still under the pillow.

"What I mean is, with the ghost here and all."

Nat sat up, still holding the pillow to his head. "What ghost?"

"Old Pliny Templeton's," I said casually. "You know. The guy that built this house and the Academy? The fella whose bones are up in the science room closet, hanging from the pole? Once a year he comes back here, or his bones do anyway, to sort of check up on things. You can't see him, but you can hear his footsteps on the porch. They say that if you could ever grab him on that night and wrestle him down and bury the bones, his soul would be put to rest."

Nat threw the pillow at me. "Come on, Kinneson. You don't believe that bloody crap. Have you ever heard these footsteps?"

"I haven't," I admitted. "But I know somebody who has. Last summer Bumper Stevens said he'd give Frenchy LaMott five dollars if he'd stay here in the parsonage alone all night. It was August fourth, I think. That's the night old Pliny committed suicide, when he's supposed to come back."

Nat looked at me skeptically. "And?"

"And if you knew Frenchy, you'd know he's crazy enough to do almost anything for a dare, especially if there's money involved. Bumper and Plug Johnson and that bunch are always bribing him into trying dumb stuff. Like going over the High Falls behind the hotel in a truck inner tube when the water's high in the spring. Or fighting some big rugged farm boy in the auction ring over at the commission sales barn. Stupid stuff like that. Anyway, nobody was living here in the house then, so Frenchy sneaked in and hid in the study and he heard those footsteps off and on all night. At first he figured it was Bumper and Plug scaring him, because he looked out the window and saw shadows on the porch. Even Frenchy knows ghosts don't throw a shadow. And once he heard old Bumper say in that low raspy voice of his, 'This'll roust him out, boys.' Then a big loud Canadian salute firecracker went off right under the window. But way later on, after Bumper and the others got drunk and went home, Frenchy swore he heard footsteps again, tramping up and down right outside the study."

"And you believe him?"

"Yes, I do. You would too if you'd lived in the Kingdom all your life."

"No, I wouldn't. That's the last thing I'd believe. Especially from this Frenchy character."

"Well, Nat, I don't want to argue with you, but if you'd lived here as long as me, you'd know one thing. Those LaMotts are a rough bunch, but there's one thing about a LaMott that everybody who lives in Kingdom County knows; they always tell the truth. A LaMott won't lie, no matter what."

"And that's the beginning and the end of it, right?" Nat said in that bored way of his, as though he couldn't even quite muster the energy to make fun of me. "Well, I'll be listening this coming August fourth. But I doubt I'll hear anything."

An idea occurred to me. "You mind if I come over and listen with you? I've always wanted—"

"Are you chaps going to spend all morning jabbering up there?" Reverend Andrews called from the foot of the stairs. "I've got a meeting at the newspaper office with Jim's father. I'm taking off."

Nat rolled his eyes and sighed. "All right," he told me. "All right. Yes, you can listen with me if it'll make you happy. Now come on. Let's get this bloody baseball game over with."

Baseball was still *the* game in Kingdom Common and a hundred other New England villages like it during the early fifties. In northern Vermont when I was growing up, every four-corner hamlet with a filling station and a general store seemed to have its own team. Naturally, this fervor spilled over to us kids, and although Kingdom Common was too remote from other Vermont towns to join a Little League or Pony League network, our Saturday morning pickup games on the diamond at the south end of the green were as fiercely contested as any intertown rivalry.

It was still early when we arrived, just past nine-thirty on the courthouse clock. For half an hour or so, as the sun burned the dew off the outfield grass and we waited for more boys to show up, Nat and I played flies and grounders with my old taped baseball. Nat was exceptionally good at this game. Except for fly-fishing, I can't think of a sport he wasn't good at; and with his speed and ball sense he made even hard catches look easy. What sticks in my mind is that he was the first kid I ever saw catch fly balls basket-style, like Willie Mays, circling under the ball and letting it drop into his lap instead of reaching up for it.

Gradually other boys drifted in, town boys mostly, though a sprinkling of country kids, too, in the village with their folks for the morning. By about ten we had a gang of a dozen or so. Al Quinn and Justin LaBounty, both of whom played on the Academy's team, chose up sides. As the youngest kid there, I was picked last; but I was playing on Nat's team, and gratified just to *be* playing instead of relegated to shag foul balls on the United Church lawn across the street from the backstop.

Our team took the field first, with Nat pitching for us. Al dispatched me to pick daisies in deep center, near the monument of Ethan Allen taking Fort Ticonderoga, where I promptly tried to make a basket catch with my catcher's glove on the first hit of the game, a towering fly ball. I misjudged it entirely and gave up a home run on a play that should have been an out.

"Good show, Kinneson!" Bobby Hefner jeered from first base. "There's a water bucket over at the Academy locker room that'll have your name on it for the next four years."

"You'll be riding the pine, all right, if you try that fancy stuff in high school, Jimmy," Al Quinn called out to me from shortstop. "Leave that to Nat, here. He knows what he's doing."

"Just give me a shot at catching," I yelled in to him, thumping my mitt; but Bobby Hefner gave me a long raspberry.

At the plate I did better. Justin LaBounty was pitching for the other team, and I had to grit my teeth to keep my foot from going in the bucket. But I had learned years ago, batting against Charlie and my father in front of the barn, to hang in there against a fastball. First time up I got a soft opposite-field single, and later that same inning I beat out a drag bunt down the third base line that Al said was a beauty. Even old Plug Johnson, who'd come over from the hotel and was watching from the third-base bleachers with three or four of his cronies, croaked out "Good job."

Nat batted three times in our half of the inning, and hit three long line-drive home runs.

"I don't know why Nathan wouldn't play for the Academy, especially with his father coaching," Al Quinn said to me in a low voice as Nathan rounded third base on his third consecutive homer. "A bunch of us boys even went up to his house to try to talk him into it."

On my third time up I beat out an infield hit to shortstop.

"Hey, Nat," Justin called out, "your little buddy here can motor."

"He's had lots of practice, running away from Frenchy LaMott and his brothers," Bobby said, and again everyone had a good laugh at my expense.

Something stuck in my mind, though. Justin had called me Nat's buddy, so word must have gotten around that he and I were friends. That, at least, made me happy; and around eleven o'clock, when our catcher had to leave to mow a lawn, I had my big opportunity.

"Okay, Kinneson," Nat said, "how about calling signals for me for an inning or two?"

I didn't need to be told twice. All the catcher's equipment we had was one old face mask with a single strap, but I clamped it loosely over my head, stuck my hand as far into the recesses of my new catcher's glove as it would go, and squatted down behind the plate.

The first batter up that inning was Billy Kittredge, who was just a year older than me. Nat wound up easily and threw him a medium-speed pitch. Billy swung from the heels and missed. He swung and missed at the next one, and the next one, too, but I dropped the third strike and Billy ran down to first.

The next two batters flied out, and Justin was up. He grinned at Nat and waggled his big Louisville Slugger. "Put some mustard on it, Andrews."

Nat grinned. He wrapped his long fingers around the ball, then hid it in his glove. He pumped, kicked high, and blazed one right in there. All I saw was a white streak.

Justin swung way late, I jumped to the side, and the ball whizzed by and whanged into the backstop.

"Don't quail away from those pitches, mister," a harsh voice from behind me barked out.

I whirled around. My father, who could no more stay away from a baseball game than ignore a good story, was standing just behind the backstop. Beside him stood Reverend Andrews.

Worse yet, Charlie was now approaching the bleachers with Royce St. Onge and Stub Poulin. "Yes, James," he called over, laughing. "Let's not quail away."

This was wonderful. Half the town and two-thirds of my own family were on hand to witness my latest humiliation!

"Give me another one of those," Justin told Nat as I retrieved the ball from where it had lodged deep in the chickenwire mesh of the backstop. "I'll catch up with it this time."

But he didn't, and neither did I. This time Nat's fastball went clean through the wire screen and across the street into the church lawn, rolling all the way to the foot of the bulletin board, where Elijah Kinneson was putting up a new message for the coming week. Elijah glanced down at the ball but made no move to pick it up and throw it back.

"Watch your arm, son," Reverend Andrews said, then walked across the road to retrieve the ball.

"I'll tell you something, mister man," my father said to me. "You've got to learn to keep your body behind that ball."

I returned to the plate, with my father still lecturing me. Squinting out at Nat, fighting back tears, I caught the words "mister" and "muckle onto it."

I braced myself, praying I wouldn't quail away from Nat's next pitch, knowing I would.

But this time he pulled the string on everybody. Instead of his fastball he threw a big slow looping curve that the bottom dropped completely out of when it reached the plate. Justin missed it by a good six inches, the ball bounced in front of me, and in a single motion, I swept it out of the sandy dirt and tagged Justin, ending the inning.

My father nodded his approval. Charlie whistled, and Reverend Andrews came over to where I was swinging my bat in the on-deck circle. "Good scoop, Jim. Let me ask you a question. Have you ever played any infield positions? Second base, shortstop?"

I shook my head. "Nope. I'm a catcher, just like Charlie."

The minister smiled. "No offense, chum, but with your quick hands and speed, I'd have you playing shortstop on my team. We've got a good catcher coming back next year, but with Al Quinn graduating, short's an open position. We could use somebody there who knows how to throw some leather. Think it over."

I did, and the next inning I got Al Quinn to switch positions and gloves with me. The second batter hit a scorcher along the grasstop to my right. I backhanded it and threw the runner out by three steps.

"Good job, Phil Rizzuto!" Charlie yelled.

From behind the backstop Reverend Andrews gave me his small salute and headed back across the street to the church. I couldn't have been more pleased by a standing ovation at Fenway Park; I knew right then and there that I had found my position. Never again, at least when it came to baseball, would I think of myself just as Charlie Kinneson's kid brother.

By now the brick shopping block was lined with vehicles. A long freight was unloading lumber cars in the mill yard behind the courthouse, and the air was filled with the shunting of the cars, the steady whir of the big dust blowers on top of the American Heritage Mill, the clang and clatter of cattle trucks being loaded and unloaded at the Saturday morning commission sales auction, and the bellow of cattle, interspersed with snatches of Bumper Stevens' singsong voice over an outdoor microphone.

Across the street from the south end of the common, Reverend Andrews and Elijah Kinneson seemed to be having some sort of disagreement over the bulletin board, where Elijah had just spelled out this comforting message: IN THE HANDS OF THE LORD THERE IS A CUP, BUT THE DREGS THEREOF, ALL THE WICKED OF THE EARTH SHALL WRING THEM OUT AND DRINK THEM. Elijah was waving his hands, the minister was shaking his head. Abruptly Elijah turned away and stalked over to the *Monitor*. Reverend Andrews watched him cross the street, then began taking down the letters.

By now several more of Charlie's teammates had arrived and were playing catch along the sidelines. Charlie squatted down and began warming up big Harlan Kittredge. "One more half-inning, guys," he called to us.

As the game continued, I glanced over my shoulder and noticed

Frenchy LaMott and his two younger half-brothers, Emile and Jeanie, slouching across the outfield from the direction of the commission sales.

"Hold up a minute, Nat."

Frenchy and his brothers continued to take their own sweet time crossing the field. And they seemed to be chanting something, like an auctioneer's pitch of some kind.

"Go ahead and throw the ball," Bobby Hefner urged Nat. "Those morons'll get out of the way."

Nat wound up and threw. By now the LaMott boys were just behind me on the infield dirt, still chanting. I began to catch some of the words. Then more words.

I sucked in my breath sharply. At the risk of taking a line drive in the back of the head, I spun around. They continued to chant:

*Nig-ger monkeypaw, laid an egg in our straw,*
*Egg was rotten, long forgotten,*
*Nig-ger monkeypaw.*

"What's that you're saying?" Justin LaBounty yelled to the LaMotts from the on-deck circle.

Frenchy halted near third base. "I weren't talking to you, LaBounty."

"Who were you talking to?"

"Only see one monkeypaw out there," Frenchy said, and Emile gave a long laugh exactly like a turkey's gobble. Not to be outdone, Jeanie hooted like a loon, inspiring Emile to let out a shrill crow I couldn't have told from Ethan Allen's regular five A.M. reveille. To the delight of the Folding Chair Club, Jeanie began to honk and hiss like a mad gander, hunching his shoulders forward, jutting out his neck at Nat, and swaying his close-cropped round head from side to side.

"Look at his hands, long as a frigging ape's," Frenchy said.

Nat ignored him and got ready to pitch; but Justin took several steps toward Frenchy. "You say one more word, boy, and Nat's going to clean your clock good."

Frenchy laughed and began again to chant, "Nig-ger monkeypaw, laid an egg—"

"End of game," Nat said, and flipped Justin the baseball and headed off the diamond on the first-base side.

"Nat! You going to let him call you that?" Bobby Hefner hollered.

As usual Bobby was spoiling for someone else to fight; but I felt the same way. I caught up to my friend and grabbed his sleeve.

"Come on, Nat. Go back and kick Frenchy's ass for him. Otherwise you'll never hear the end of that monkeypaw stuff."

"Egg was rotten, long forgotten," Frenchy and his brothers chanted. They kept looking toward the church lawn, ready to bolt if the minister started to cross the street. But Reverend Andrews made no move to interfere. Clearly, he intended to let Nat fight this battle himself.

I looked at Charlie, who had not even stopped playing catch with Harlan.

"Nig-ger monkeypaw, nig-ger monkeypaw," the LaMott boys chanted.

Nat continued up the common with his back to them.

"Nig-ger monkeypaw . . ."

I had heard enough. Rushing up to Justin LaBounty, I grabbed the Louisville Slugger out of his hands and started toward Frenchy. Instantly Al Quinn intercepted me and yanked away the bat. "No," he said quietly. "Nat has to do this himself. You butt out."

I looked at Justin, who nodded. "He's right, Jimmy. I've wrestled with Nat in the locker room. He could make mincemeat out of Frenchy if he wanted to."

What on earth was wrong with Nat? I wondered. He was the best ball player at the Academy since Charlie's days, yet he wouldn't play on the team even after his father began coaching it. He probably was the best wrestler in school, too, but he wouldn't stand up to Frenchy LaMott.

Of one thing I was certain, though. Nathan Andrews had not heard the last from Frenchy and his two half-brothers.

"I'm not going, Kinneson. You can suppose that I'm afraid of your local bully or whatever you want to suppose. In time it'll blow over. Or it won't. I don't know or care."

Nat sank back on his bed and stared at the ceiling. It was two evenings after the terrible name-calling episode on the ballfield. Just that afternoon Frenchy had confronted Nat on the common again, this time challenging him to a fistfight that night at the commission sales barn—and here my friend was holed up in his bedroom as though he was scared for his life!

"I know you aren't scared, Nat," I told him pleadingly. "I know you could kick Frenchy's ass from here to Canada. But you've got to prove that to Frenchy. Otherwise he'll never let up. He'll lay for you and torment you with that stupid song from now until the cows come home. You've got to stop him."

"Not tonight, I don't. Tonight I've got to write to my grandmother."

"Come on, Nat. He's waiting now. All it'll take you is about ten sec—"

Before I knew what was happening, I found myself sprawled on the bed, with Nat standing over me.

He jerked me to my feet. "Go away," he said wearily, and shoved me toward the door. "Just go away."

I was nearly crying with frustration. It was past nine o'clock already, the time Frenchy had challenged Nat to fight him.

"Nat, you've got to go. Otherwise they really will think you're scared."

"They?"

"The other guys. Justin and Al and Bobby and them. The town boys."

"I don't give a hoot what your town boys think. The trouble with you, Kinneson, is you're far too much swayed by other people. Justin and most of the guys know I'm not afraid of Frenchy. But even if they didn't, I wouldn't fight him. Would you?"

"I would if I were you."

Nat grinned tiredly. "In fact, you wouldn't if you were me, because then you'd have the same reason not to that I have."

"But wouldn't you like to?"

"Of course."

"Then for God's sake, why don't you? You can tell *me*, Nat."

Nat sighed. He tossed his comic book aside in an abrupt impatient motion, and I jumped back for fear that he was going to muckle onto me again. But he didn't. "Kinneson, if I tell you why I won't fight Frenchy, will you promise me two things?"

"I'll promise anything. I just have to understand this, that's all. So I can tell—"

"No! That's the first thing I want you to promise. I want you to promise not to *tell* anyone anything. Number two, I want your word that you won't pester me about the matter ever again."

"You've got it. Cross my heart and hope to die if I breathe a word to anyone or ever bring it up again."

"Let's not be quite so melodramatic, Kinneson. You probably will tell somebody; but I'll take a chance, just to get you off my back."

Nat went over to the window and looked out into the twilight. "The reason I won't fight Frenchy LaMott, or anyone else for that matter, is I gave someone my word that I wouldn't."

"Your dad?"

"Hardly. Dad's the one who started me in with boxing lessons about the time I was five. He'd back me up one hundred percent if I went after Frenchy. I think he wishes I would, in fact. You can bet *he* would, in my shoes. But Dad doesn't know about this promise I made.

"You see, Kinneson, I promised my grandmother that I would never under any circumstances short of absolute necessity, say if my life was at stake, get into a fight. Gram's always been like a mother to me, and I've never broken that promise, nor intend to."

"I'm sorry, Nat. I didn't know. I mean, I didn't understand."

"You still don't."

Although I wasn't sure, I thought I saw Nat's shoulders shaking. Thirty seconds or so passed, during which neither of us spoke. Then he turned around and sat back down in the welter of coverless comic books on his unmade bed. "About two years ago I got into a bad scrape up in Montreal. It was down on the lower part of what's called The Main, St. Lawrence Street, in a pretty rough district of town I used to cut through sometimes on my way home from school. Actually it was one of my favorite parts of the city, what with the river and port being nearby, and big freighters coming in from all over the world. A few of my school chums and I used to go swimming there in the summer, though Gram would have had a fit if she'd known. And there were all kinds of curious little hole-in-the-wall shops—Polish butcher shops and Greek candy and cigarette shops and Asian fish markets and I don't know what all. That was where the calèche drivers kept their calèches, too. And in good weather there was an open-air market where people came to buy vegetables and fruit and stuff."

"What's a calèche, Nat?"

"It's a little one-horse tourist buggy. If you ever go up there, you'll see 'em all over the place, especially down in Old Montreal, pulled around by these terribly broken-down old horses about ready for the glue factory. Once in the wintertime I even came on a bunch of people cooking one of those horses whole right in the street over a big fire, like an ox. Anyway, I liked it down there. It was a lively place, just like St. Catherine Street. Until I had the trouble."

"So what was the trouble?"

"I'm coming to that. One fall evening when I'd stayed on after school for soccer practice, I was coming back through that market about dusk. The street was full of cornhusks and cabbage leaves and broken pieces of wooden crates, and I was just ambling along when I felt this squishy thing hit the back of my neck and slide down between my shoulders. When I turned around, here was this gang of boys on the corner in front of a candy store, smoking cigarettes and laughing. One boy, who was a good deal bigger and older than the rest, stepped out and yelled something to me. I'd seen him around before, that one. He was their ringleader, a big hulking boy with a clubfoot. Instead of a shoe he wore this horrible black boxlike affair on his bad foot. I don't know what his real name was but I'd heard him called *Ti Chevaux*. In French that means Little Horse, and he was about as big as a horse, too. I think he was slow-witted, to tell you the truth. Anyway, he shouted something and threw another tomato, and this one hit me square on the front of my school uniform jacket, right above the crest. That really made me mad.

"I was scared, too. There were half a dozen or so boys in that gang, and I was alone. But as scared as I was of *Ti Chevaux*, I was more scared of being thought a coward, or thinking myself one. So I did a stupid thing. I went back and challenged him to fight. Right there in front of his gang."

"Oh, boy, Nat. That *was* stupid, if I do say so. And he cleaned your clock, right? This *Ti* got you down and put that big black box to you and that's why you don't want to fight Frenchy."

Nat shook his head impatiently. "Stop interrupting, Kinneson. Of course he didn't clean my clock. Didn't I tell you Dad had taught me to box? He was a heavyweight Olympic boxer, in case you didn't know, and he saw to it I could use my hands, too. He said the time would probably come when I'd need to. And I figured this was the time so I mopped up the street with that boy. The problem was, he just wouldn't quit. Every time I knocked him down he got back up and came at me again, kicking and punching and roaring, with that gang of his yelling

'*Ti! Ti! Ti!*' to spur him on, don't you know. Finally a policeman came along and stopped it, but that was after I'd broken the boy's nose and shut one eye and done who knows what other damage to the poor devil."

"So why don't you just clean Frenchy's clock too, then? I don't understand, Nat."

"I haven't told you the worst part."

"What, did the cop take you home to your grandmother?"

"No, he didn't seem to mind seeing *Ti* get his comeuppance. The worst part was that I *enjoyed* beating that boy. I *wanted* him to keep getting up so I could keep hitting him. I wanted to put him in hospital, or worse. It didn't matter to me that he was crippled or slow-witted or what. I was like . . . like an animal. It was as though I was taking out all my frustrations on that poor chap—all the times I'd been called a name and my mother's death and Dad's being away and everything. Afterwards I told Gram and she made me promise I'd never fight again. I was very willing to promise, too, because after I'd had a chance to think about it, the one I was really most scared of was myself. Now do you see why I won't fight Frenchy?"

I nodded. But at the time, all I understood for certain was that Nat Andrews was my friend and his life had been infinitely more complicated and difficult than mine, and I had been too quick, far too quick, to assume that because I would react a certain way in a certain situation, he should react the same way.

"I'm tired, Kinneson. I'd like for you to go home now. No more explanations. No more stories from the dark past. Just go home and keep your mouth shut, if that's remotely possible."

Running hard, I swerved into the lane between the hotel and the commission sales barn, past Bumper Stevens' Cadillac and dark cattle truck, into forbidden precincts, where men traded cattle, as they had done for a hundred years, told obscene jokes, and gambled late at night; where, it was darkly rumored, whole farms had sometimes changed hands over the turn of a card; where, when the place was otherwise empty, town boys sometimes took "wild" girls; where (I would learn later) certain poor women outcasts had actually been auctioned off for the night, like cattle, to the highest bidder after the regular sale ended; and where Frenchy LaMott had grown up brawling with anyone who would fight him in the ring while the after-hours crowd bet on winners, exactly as they did on Resolvèd's cockfights.

To the right and left, penned calves bleated continually. From somewhere in the barn's recesses, a bull roared. Fleeting thoughts of Ordney Gilson and that fateful New Year's Eve murder crossed my mind.

A single lighted bulb hung at the end of the aisle that sloped toward the auction ring. It was slick as ice from cattle urine and manure and I skidded and nearly fell. I kept running, knowing that if I paused for so much as a second I would lose my nerve.

Murmuring voices. Dark bulky forms crowded around a wooden ring. The smells of whiskey and tobacco. Older town boys, some I didn't know by name, sprawled in the rickety bleachers. And lounging shirtless in his filthy jeans and battered engineer boots on a hay bale in the ring, his dark shaggy hair hanging over his eyes, was Frenchy LaMott.

As I vaulted over the wooden sideboards he stood up. "So where you monkey pal, Kin—"

I never stopped. It was absolutely essential that I get in the first one or two punches if I was to punch at all. But instead of hitting Frenchy LaMott I surprised both him and myself by lowering my head like a ram and butting him right in the pit of the stomach. To my astonishment, I knocked him over the hay bale and up against the slats at the rear of the ring. I must have knocked his breath out, too; although he was still half-standing, he was bent over gasping and grabbing his stomach. Here was my golden opportunity.

I hit him just once, squarely on the nose. I swung again, a wild haymaker, but he had already covered his head with his forearms. The second punch glanced off his bony elbows and stung my hand. Then he was swarming all over me, punching, kicking, kneeing, fighting the way he had fought far bigger and stronger boys from the time he was eight or nine years old and Bumper first put him in the ring.

Blood was everywhere; some was Frenchy's, most was mine. I fell backward over the bale and tried to roll away. There was no place to go. Frenchy was driving his steel-toed engineer boots into my arms and legs. I rolled into a corner, and he had me at his mercy. I actually thought he might kill me.

"GET OFF HIM."

Through the blood on my face I caught a glimpse of a yellow shirt and black baseball pants. The fearful kicking stopped.

"What the hell's going on here?" Charlie roared.

He was holding Frenchy with one hand by the back of the neck, and as big a boy as Frenchy was, he looked like a puppet thrashing in my brother's grip.

Bumper Stevens said, "Just a couple of young bucks duking it out, Charlie. Nothing serious."

"Bullshit!" Charlie said.

"Go wash up," he told Frenchy, and half threw him toward the gate in the ring. He pulled me to my feet and turned to face the crowd of older boys and men in the grandstand.

"If this is your idea of a good time, you're all bent. Pitting two kids against each other gives you your thrills? I can't believe it!"

He paused, spat into the straw and manure at our feet, then turned back and roared, "All right, assholes. You want to see a fight? I'll take on any three of you. Come on," my brother said coaxingly, ominously, beckoning with his finger. "How about you, Stevens? You haven't had your jaw broken yet this month. Pick any two of these rummies to bring in with you. Pick three or four."

"We don't want no trouble with you, Charlie K," Bumper said. "Settle down, now. No call to get all het up with your own good friends and gentle neighbors."

"No," Charlie said, "let's get along with our own good friends and gentle neighbors and just persecute strangers, especially if they aren't the same color we are, right, Bumper?"

Charlie whirled back to point at the retreating figures in the grandstand, now clearing out like Athena Allen's eighth graders on Friday afternoon.

My brother spat again in disgust and called after them, "If I ever hear of any of you bothering my brother or any of his friends, including the Andrews, in any way at all, or putting young LaMott or anyone else up to bothering them, you won't travel so far that I won't find you. Then you know who I'll be defending over in that courthouse? Myself, that's who, for aggravated assault with two deadly weapons. These two."

Charlie held up his fists; but by now the grandstand was empty.

He looked at me and grinned. "Come on, Sugar Ray," he said. "Let's go get you cleaned up."

"Hi, sweetie," Charlie said into the phone. "Jimmy got in a little fracas with another kid tonight. He needs some motherly medical attention."

Charlie looked over at me, sitting at his cluttered kitchen table with an ice pack over my left eye, and winked as he listened to Athena's reply. "It won't take three minutes, hon. Just to check and make sure he doesn't have any broken bones or loose teeth."

Again Charlie listened. With my good eye, I read his statistics from the Outlaws' first fifteen games of the season, which he'd posted up on his old-fashioned refrigerator, the kind with a round motor on top. He was currently batting .434.

"All *right*!" Charlie said and hung up. "She's coming, buddy! This should work out well for both of us."

It would work out well for me, at least. I would a hundred times rather be examined by Athena than by Painless Doc Harrison, who had not come by his sobriquet because of any inclination toward or expertise in humane medical methods. I was scared to death of him and enormously grateful to my brother for calling Athena, whatever ulterior motives he might have.

She arrived in the judge's black Lincoln within two or three minutes and began by carefully checking inside my mouth to see if I still had all my teeth. She didn't say "Open wide" or condescend to me in any other way, just very gently tried to wobble my teeth.

She bent back my head to look at my swollen lips and nose. Her dark hair brushed my face and I caught a scent of some faint clean-smelling perfume. A thrill shot through me as she carefully pressed the bridge of my nose, checking for broken bones. My face got red and Charlie laughed.

"Relax and enjoy it, buddy. It isn't every young blade that's lucky enough to have the fair and frolicsome Athena Allen hold him in her arms for five minutes."

"Quit picking on him, Charlie," Athena said. Then she gave a little jump and scream. "Damn you! Cut that out."

I suspected that Charlie had given her a pinch on the fanny. He was always doing that when he thought no one was watching, that or putting his hand up her leg or inside her sweater, which to my bafflement seemed to embarrass her and please her at the same time.

"That eye looks pretty bad to me," Charlie said. "You get any licks in before Frenchy went to town on you?"

I nodded. "One. I made his nose bleed all over."

"Good. But what in the world possessed you to go in there in the first place?"

"Well, he wanted to fight Nat, but Nat wouldn't go, so I thought —I don't know what I thought, that I ought to stand up for my friend, I guess."

I desperately wanted to explain to Charlie and Athena why Nat wouldn't fight Frenchy. But I'd given my word to Nat not to breathe a word of what he'd told me.

Charlie reached into his refrigerator and got out two bottles of beer, opened them, and handed one to Athena. She took a long drink. I liked the way that, instead of sipping, she drank like Charlie, taking two or three swallows at a time.

Charlie shook his head. "I appreciate what you were trying to do for your friend, Jimmy, but I can tell you right now that it won't work. What Al Quinn and Justin and those guys were saying on the common Saturday is the truth. Nat's got to fight his own battles."

"Probably Nat thinks it wouldn't do much good to fight Frenchy," Athena said as she checked my sore ribs. "It might even make things worse. I imagine he's heard these slurs off and on all his life. It must bother him, but he may actually have come to expect it."

"His old man almost seems to enjoy a good row," Charlie said. "But I'm sure you're right about why Nat won't fight. He didn't act afraid when Frenchy braced him over on the common. In fact, I think you'll see that when and if the time comes when Nat's back is to the wall, Frenchy'll rue the day he ever laid eyes on him. In the meantime, Jim, just try to be his friend. Don't fight any more of his battles for him. Old Painless Doc doesn't need business that badly. Right, sweetie?"

Athena took another long swallow of beer. "Charlie's right, Jim. And don't blame Frenchy too much. No doubt Bumper Stevens is putting him up to all of this. My uncle Armand told me that the day Doctor H unwired Bumper's jaw, he came in the hotel and made some pretty nasty threats about getting the Andrews out of town before the summer's over. Uncle Armand said he knows Bumper's a big blowhard, but the more he thought about what Bumper said, the more it bothered him. He actually went over to see Zack Barrows about it, but Zack just laughed and said that Bumper was all talk and wouldn't do anything."

"I hope not, for Bumper's sake," Charlie said, laughing. "Reverend Andrews can take care of himself. My only reservation about the fella is that he says he's too busy this summer to play on my town team. Who ever heard of somebody being too busy to play baseball?

"Now that we know you aren't dead, kiddo, go curl up on the couch in the other room and go to sleep," Charlie told me. "I'll call old finely tuned Ruthie and explain that you're okay and going to spend the night. This girl"—draping his arm around Athena's shoulder as though she were one of his baseball buddies—"and I have to have a long, serious talk."

I lay down on the couch in Charlie's tiny living room, and Athena put a blanket over me and tucked it in around my shoulders. Then she and Charlie drank some more beer in the kitchen while I tried to sleep. But my eye throbbed like crazy and my side ached where Frenchy had kicked me.

I looked up at the wall. In the dim light from the kitchen I could just make out the pinups that Charlie had literally papered the inside of his living room with. Even the ceiling was covered with magazine cut-outs of tough-looking gun molls from *True Detective* and sultry-eyed young lovelies from *Argosy* and *Esquire* and calendars advertising automobile parts and farm machinery. Despite my discomfort, I felt a vague but powerful longing for . . . I wasn't sure what.

I must have fallen asleep. The next thing I knew, I heard a thump, like someone tripping, and people laughing softly like laughter in a dream.

"Stop it, Charlie!"

The trailer was totally dark now, but there was enough moonlight coming through the window for me to make out two forms in the doorway to Charlie's tiny bedroom.

"Stop it!" Athena said again in a breathless half-whisper. "Not with Jimmy here. What if he wakes up?"

"He isn't going to wake up. He's dead beat, so to speak. Come on, hon. I need an experienced teacher. One with your impeccable credentials."

Athena giggled. "You need a bath, preferably a cold one, and a few cups of black coffee. We aren't even officially engaged anymore, remember?"

"We'll be engaged in five minutes, I promise," Charlie said. "Come on. What is it with you recently?"

"I said, not with Jimmy here. Don't you have any common sense at all?"

"You sound like my father. 'Grow up.' 'Run for county attorney.' 'Use some common sense.' It'll be more fun with Jim there. We'll have to be extra quiet, like the old days."

"The old days are gone," Athena said, and I saw the smaller form twist away and out the door, followed closely by my brother, still talking, almost pleading with her now.

Outside a car door slammed, then a second or two later an engine came to life and Athena's car sped off down the county road toward the village—leaving me with more to think about than my fight with Frenchy or the buxom Miss February, smiling coyly down from the wall above me.

# 6

Charlie must have forewarned my parents about my battered condition and its causes, because the next morning when I limped home after he fed me a loggers' breakfast of eggs and pancakes and pork chops cooked extra crisp, just the way he loved them, Mom told me to stay away from Frenchy LaMott and the commission sales barn in the future. My father, I think, was secretly proud of my loyalty to Nat, misguided though it was. But all he said was that I ought to use a hay hook on Frenchy the next time I tackled him, because he was probably impervious to anything less lethal.

Dad had a church trustees' meeting at the parsonage that morning, at which Reverend Andrews intended to announce his plans for the big church fundraiser. "What are you going to do today, Ezzard Charles?" he asked me.

Although it hurt, I had to laugh through my swollen lips. I told him I'd planned to take Nat crawfishing this morning but in view of the way I looked I'd rather wait a couple of days before going overstreet.

"Get your crawfish trap," Dad said. "We'll walk over to the parsonage together."

"Dad," I said, "I really don't—"

"Get your trap," he said. "You don't have a thing in the world to be ashamed of."

But Nat's reaction was altogether different, as I'd known it would be.

"Oh, no!" he groaned when I appeared in his room. "Aren't you the sight for sore eyes! What gets into you, Kinneson? You look as though you got run over by a bloody streetcar."

"A French Canadian one," I said. "Okay, it was a dumb thing to do. Let's just forget it. How about coming crawdadding with me this morning?"

"Crawdadding? What do you do with those buggers?"

"Well, for one thing, you can use them for bait. Trout love crawdads. Mainly, though, we eat 'em, boil 'em right up in a kettle. They're terrific, just like lobster or better."

Nat was sitting cross-legged on the foot of his bed. Suddenly he put his finger to his lips and bent forward, cocking his head. Through the round heat grate in the bedroom floor, voices were floating up from the parsonage study, where the church finance committee meeting was getting under way.

Nat beckoned me to come over and pointed down through the swirled iron filigrees of the grate. Below, besides my father and the minister, I recognized George Quinn, Julia Hefner, and old Prof Chadburn, the Academy headmaster. Dad was sitting at the minister's desk. Prof sat on a folding wooden chair borrowed from the church Sunday school, and Julia had plopped herself down next to the minister on a worn horsehair couch that set my teeth on edge just to look at it, like the steel wool Mom used to scrub her frying pans.

"About this idea of yours, Reverend," George Quinn was saying in his prissy voice. "I'm not saying it's not a good one, it's just that we hate to see anything replace the annual church bazaar and minstrel show. They're traditions, you know, going back forty or fifty years."

"Minstrel show?" Reverend Andrews sounded amused.

"Oh, it's all in good fun, Walter," Julia said, giving Reverend Andrews a proprietary little pat on the arm. "With your grand sense of humor, you'd love it."

It was hard to tell from our angle, but I thought that Reverend Andrews and Dad exchanged glances quickly.

"Let the man finish presenting his idea, Julia," Dad said.

"Yes, by all means." Prof Chadburn said. "I must say that from what I've heard so far, it sounds most intriguing."

"Intriguing" was Prof's favorite word. If a boy was sent to his office at the Academy for sassing a teacher, he invariably found that boy's behavior intriguing. In his own Latin classes Prof never failed to introduce a new verb as "intriguing," and he was equally intrigued by his students' more comical misapprehensions of, successively, Caesar, Cicero, and Virgil, our winning (or losing) an important baseball game, and any and all of the ideas of his own board or staff.

"Yes, go ahead, Reverend," George Quinn said unenthusiastically. "Let's hear your idea."

"Well, as you folks all know, 1952 is the one hundred and fiftieth anniversary of the founding of the church. Almost since the week I arrived, I've been thinking that we ought to commemorate the event in some appropriate way. At the same time, we need to build up the coffers of our treasury, which are pretty sadly depleted."

"In a nutshell, here's my idea," Reverend Andrews continued. "What I'd like to propose is that we combine a celebration of the church sesquicentennial with an Old Home Day on the common. We can establish the history of Kingdom County as our theme and focus on the history of the church. We'll continue the tradition of the church bazaar by holding it right on the common along with game booths and skits, and we'll culminate the day with a grand historical cavalcade around the common. If the celebration's a success, and I'll vouchsafe that with everyone's united efforts it will be, Old Home Day can become an annual event with a different theme each year."

For a few moments the committee was silent. Then Dad said, "I like the idea. In fact, I like it a lot. I move we go ahead with the first annual Old Home Day and Sesquicentennial Celebration."

"I second that motion," Prof said.

"Discussion," George said.

"Oh come on, George," Dad said. "What is there to discuss?"

"Change."

"Change?" Reverend Andrews said.

"Yes. You see, Reverend, we have to be cautious here. We have to be cautious not to change too much too fast, for fear of losing what we've already got."

"How's that?"

"Well, I mean the congregation. Membership has been decreasing over the past several years—until recently, at least. Now that we're on the upswing, we don't want to risk upsetting the apple cart by doing anything so radical that the congregation won't go along with it."

"What's radical about a sesquicentennial celebration?"

"Nothing, really," Julia chimed in. "But we've got the minstrel show committee to consider. There are a lot of people on that committee who'd be mighty upset to learn we'd just ruled out their show for an idea we haven't ever tried before."

"We're not saying we're against all change, Reverend," George said. "You've done a heck of a job here already in making changes that were long overdue. The Sunday school enrollment is up nearly two hundred percent. The youth group, the choir, the men's Bible study club—those are good changes, and we appreciate them. We appreciate you. But this Old Home Day—well, I just don't know if we can move quite that quickly. Besides, the bazaar and the minstrel show are our main annual fundraisers. Without the income from them we'd really be in the hole."

"Just out of curiosity, how much do they bring in?"

George cleared his throat. "If memory serves me correctly, the two fundraisers combined last year brought in a total of six hundred and seventy-eight dollars and seventeen cents."

"That's good," Reverend Andrews said. "I wouldn't have guessed that high. With the Old Home Day celebration, I propose to generate a total of between twenty-five hundred and three thousand dollars."

Except for my father, who was staring out the window with his Ted Williams expression, the finance committee let out a gasp of surprise. Nat looked at me and grinned, as though the money were already safely ensconced in the church's account at the First Farmers' and Lumberers' Savings Bank.

"My word!" George said. "Are you sure? That's hard to believe, Reverend."

"For one thing," Reverend Andrews said, "we'll not only incorporate the blooming bazaar right into the celebration, we'll highlight it and sell two or three times as much as usual. And the historical pageant will give our local thespians more opportunity to display their talents than the minstrel show ever afforded. The game booths alone ought to bring in close to a thousand dollars. I've done similar things on military bases, and I'm virtually certain that we can raise twenty-five hundred as an absolute minimum. With a good day, we may well exceed thirty-five hundred dollars."

As he spoke, Reverend Andrews lit a cigarette. "Folks, let's face the facts. The church needs money. The parsonage is falling down around our ears. We need a new furnace, some of the plumbing doesn't work, the wiring's bare in places, the sills are rotting out. The church needs repairs as well. I'm told it hasn't been painted in more than a decade. And it's humiliating to all of us not to be able to afford to send even five dollars a week to the World Missionary Fund."

"Not to mention being unable to pay the minister mileage for home visits, or close to a living wage," my father said. "Look here. If the Old Home Day doesn't go over, we're under no obligation to do it again. But let's at least try it. I move the question."

After a brief pause, George, whose misgivings had evidently been somewhat allayed by Reverend Andrews' fiscal projections, said, "All in favor of holding an Old Home Day to celebrate the sesquicentennial of the church say aye."

My father and Prof said aye. After a brief pause, so did Julia Hefner.

"The ayes have it," George said, and Nat grinned at me again.

"I just hope it doesn't rain that day," George said on his way out.

"It won't," Dad said. "Walt here has connections."

As Dad, Prof, and George left, Julia remained seated. "Walter, if you have another sec, I'd like a word more with you about the bazaar," she said.

"Surely," he said, and stood waiting by his desk.

Julia crossed her legs; if she had not been forty years old and a widow, I would have said that she actually did this in a coy way. "I'm certain that it will be a great success, actually. I mean Old Home Day. What I really wanted to say, Walt, is a bit more personal. If you've absolutely decided that you're not going to get yourself a housekeeper, I've made up my mind to take matters into my own hands. I'm going to have you over to my house for at least one decent meal. I'm considered to be a very capable cook. Maybe a tad too capable for my own waistline at times, though before he died, Fred—he was a great joker, Fred was—always said that most men *prefer* women with a little flesh on them. Anyway, I'd like to have you come over this Wednesday, say around seven o'clock. Bobby'll be gone to his cousin's in Memphremagog all next week and we should have the chance for a quiet little chat and a few brandies together."

"Well, thank you very much, Julia," Reverend Andrews said. He got a small black appointment book out of his back pocket. "That's a very kind invitation and I'm delighted to accept. What time shall we plan to come?"

"We?"

"Nathan and I."

"Nathan?" Julia said. "Oh, Nathan! Actually, Reverend, I was thinking more of a kind of *business* meeting over dinner, just between you and me. With Bobby gone, off visiting his cousin, I'm afraid Nathan would be bored stiff."

"Well, frankly, Julia, since coming here to Kingdom Common, I've tried to include Nathan in my own social schedule whenever possible," the minister said smoothly. "The fact is I don't really like to leave him alone at mealtime. Would you rather I come another night? Sometime when Bobby's going to be around?"

"No," Julia said in a petulant voice. "No, that's perfectly all right. Whatever you say. If Nathan gets bored after supper, he can always come back home again."

"Well, thank you very much," Reverend Andrews said as he escorted Julia out toward the porch. "We'll be looking forward to Wednesday night, then."

Nat slapped his forehead. "This is bloody great. Now I've got to chaperon my old man."

"They said you could leave after supper, Nat."

"Don't you know anything at all, Kinneson? My father doesn't want to be alone with that old walrus. Not that I blame him. She'd probably jump him the minute I left. Damn! Let's get the hell out of here for a while. Even crawdadding would be better than sitting around this warped burg."

"So where have you been catching these delicacies?" Nat inquired as we headed north out of town on the River Road with my bait trap and feed sack.

"You know that big pool out past LaMott's slaughterhouse, under the railroad trestle? It's crawling with them. Charlie and I used to go there a lot together. I'm not allowed to go alone."

"Why's that?"

I explained to Nathan that in warm weather railroad tramps sometimes jungled up on the sandbar below the trestle. Several times a summer we could see the reflections of their fires from our farmhouse on the gool. Like the entourage of gypsies who had come to town in my great-grandfather's time, these roving men were reputed to be an untrustworthy lot. Every boy I knew had strict orders to steer clear of them.

"Yes, but why?"

"I guess if they caught you out there alone, they might do something bad to you."

"Like what?"

"I don't know what," I said, though I did, or half knew.

"Did you ever personally know anybody the tramps did something bad to?"

"No. Well, yes. Sort of. Al Quinn. He was bullpout fishing off the trestle once and a tramp stepped out from beneath and whipped out his thing and showed it to him. Al said it was about as long as old Mason White's nightstick. It made him pretty sick to look at it but for a minute he couldn't not look."

"I shouldn't think it the most appetizing sight in the world myself," Nat said. "What did Al do?"

"He hightailed it home. What would any kid do? But I've been out there plenty of times with Charlie and other friends, and I've never seen any tramps myself."

"I hope we see one," Nat said. "It would break up the monotony."

Except for a single neat set of raccoon tracks on the sandbar beneath the trestle, there was only an ancient pile of blackened logs left over from a bonfire to indicate that anyone had been there before us. The smell of decaying fish hung on the air. From up at LaMott's slaughterhouse I heard the whine of a meat saw. Otherwise it was quiet.

The trestle pool was deep and well over my head in the middle. It was a choice spot to catch big crawdads, though I suspect that their unusual size and abundance was accounted for by the fact that the small brook that trickled through the slaughterhouse dump emptied into the river just upstream, bringing who knew what rich nutrients to the local crustacean population.

Catching them was simple. We baited the minnow trap with a couple of half-rotten bullpout heads we found on the bank and tossed it out into the pool on a rope. After letting it sit on the bottom for ten minutes or so, we hauled it up with a dozen or so scrabbling crawdads inside. They had shiny bluish claws and were handsome, in their way, though Nat didn't seem much impressed by them.

We shook the crawdads out into my burlap sack, which I'd soaked in the river first to keep them from drying out. Then we heaved the trap back out in the pool and waited for another batch to come swarming in. It was plenty warm enough to go swimming but neither of us wanted to swim near that polluted brook, so we sprawled on the sand in the sunshine, visiting in a desultory way about this and that.

I mentioned that older boys from town were rumored to come here late at night with wild girls who allowed themselves to be undressed. Nat laughed and said I wouldn't know what to do if a girl ever did let me undress her. I told him he might be surprised, and he said there was no might about it, he'd be astonished. I asked him if he'd ever had a girlfriend. He said he'd known a few girls he liked, but that was in school back in Montreal.

"Maybe you'll get a girlfriend here, too, Nat."

"Maybe the moon's made of green cheese. You don't think for a minute that a local girl would go out with me, do you?"

"Why not?" I knew what he meant, but I really didn't see why not. Since I had stopped consciously thinking of Nat as a Negro weeks ago, I assumed the same was true for most of his classmates at the Academy.

"You know very well why not," he said quietly and flopped back onto the sand and shut his eyes, exactly the way he flopped onto his bed at home whenever he was disgruntled.

That was when an idea occurred to me.

"Nat," I said in a low conspiratorial voice, "how would you like to see three or four naked girls?"

Nat laughed. "Assembled your own private harem, have you, Kinneson?"

"Come on, be serious."

"You be serious."

"I am," I said. "Every year at Kingdom Fair they have these girlie shows, where the girls strip right down to their birthday suits. They've got tents, see, way down at the far end of the midway, with names like Club California and Paris Revue. The girls do stripteases inside the tents."

Nat propped himself up on his elbow and looked at me.

"Now, I don't know about this next for sure, because I've never seen it myself. But Frenchy LaMott told Justin LaBounty and Justin told me that way late at night, after the rest of the midway's all shut down, they take down the ropes on the stage inside those tents and anybody who wants to can pay five dollars and go right at it with the girls."

Nat grinned. "You have it on good authority, all right. Third-hand, by way of Frenchy LaMott."

"Laugh if you want to, but I told you the LaMotts never lie, and they don't. Anyway, here's my idea. The fair's this week. On Friday, you tell your dad you're staying over with me the next night, and I'll tell my folks I'm staying over with you. Saturday evening we'll go to the fair and slide on down to the midway and hang around until it shuts down. Then we'll sneak in one of those shows under the tent and see for ourselves. It'll work out great. Dad's spending that weekend up at Judge Allen's fishing camp with the judge, and Mom always lets me do about what I want when he isn't around to worry about her worrying about me."

Nat sat up straight. "I've heard rumors of such goings-on on St. Catherine Street up home, but I never really believed it, even there. What you're describing sounds more like Sodom and Gomorrah. Not that it doesn't fit right in with everything else I know about your town, come to think of it."

"Lay off the Kingdom, will you, Nat? Why did you come here, if you think it's such a dump?"

"I didn't have any choice, remember?"

"Didn't you want to be with your father?"

Nat didn't reply immediately. "Yes," he said finally. "I did, and I still do. He's pretty strict with me, and he expects a lot. Sometimes I get the idea he expects me to be about perfect. He was pretty mad, in his own way, about that cockfight business. He even threatened to send me back up to my grandmother and my Montreal school if I ever pulled anything like that again, though I don't think he really meant it. And he was a little mad at me at first when I decided not to play baseball, too."

"Why don't you play baseball, Nat? You're the best player in school. Charlie told me you're the best player he's seen in the Common in years."

Nat shrugged. "I don't know why I don't play," he said. "I guess it just doesn't mean as much to me as it does to you and some of the other boys—to get back to my father, I've told him I can't be perfect, and he even agreed and said probably every minister's son has felt the same way. Then he said he and I both live in a glass house, so to speak. He wants me to be a sterling representative of our race,' something he's always been big on. But I still think he expects a lot."

Now I had a revelation to make. "I know how you feel. Sometimes I think my father expects me to be perfect. Only in my case, I get the idea that because Charlie was so wild when he was my age, I have to make up for all the things he did."

"Well, is it decided?" Nat said.

"Is what decided?"

"Are we going to the public orgy at the fair this Saturday night?"

"What do *you* think?"

"I don't see any reason why not, to tell you the truth. We aren't perfect and neither one of us can be expected to be, so we'll prove it by going to the show. But instead of lying about staying over at each other's places we'll say we're going camping, and we will—after the tent show. Maybe old Julia Hefner will be moonlighting there. I hope so."

I laughed hysterically, fell over, and rolled on the sand. At the same time, I felt a little tremor of apprehension. I had no real idea what we'd see at the girlie show or how I'd react, and what if we got caught? The restrictions placed on me after the cockfight would be nothing compared to what would happen if Mom and Dad ever got wind that I'd been to one of those shows.

Nat flopped back down on the sand and said sleepily, "Wake me up if it starts to rain, Kinneson. I'm tired."

"You're always tired," I said.

But he was asleep already.

After a while I got up to check the bait trap. Out of the corner of my eye I caught a fleeting glimpse of movement on the bank above us. Standing not fifteen feet away was Frenchy LaMott, hefting a good-sized rock in a calculating way I did not like one bit.

"Nat, wake up."

"I am awake."

"Frenchy's here. He's got rocks."

Nat rolled over and looked up at Frenchy, who was tossing the stone up in the air a few inches and catching it.

"What you boys trespassing out here for?" Frenchy said.

"We're on our way," Nat said mildly.

I quickly pulled in the minnow trap and emptied the fresh batch of crawdads into the sack.

"Say, monkeypaw, you catching crawdads?" Frenchy said in a surprised voice. "Well, now, you just pack up and clear on out of here. That way."

He pointed across the trestle. "Because you ain't crossing them frigging tracks and coming up on my premises again."

I wondered when Frenchy had acquired the right of way to the Boston and Montreal railroad, but thought better of inquiring.

Nathan stood up. "Come on, Kinneson."

He picked up the sack of crawfish and headed at a slant up the bank, away from Frenchy and out onto the trestle.

"Step on it, monkeypaw," Frenchy said, and threw a handful of ballast from the railbed at Nat's heels. The stones bounced off the ties and rails and rained down through the spaces between the ties into the river far below. It made me dizzy to see them hit the water.

"Monkeypaw Andrews. Crawdad Andrews," Frenchy hollered. "Looks like a crawdad, acts like a crawdad. Backs away every time. NOW, BOYS!"

That is when Frenchy's two half-brothers, Emile and Jeanie, scrambled up over the far end of the trestle and stationed themselves directly in our path. We were trapped!

"Where you going now, crawdad?" Frenchy started out onto the trestle behind us.

"Only one place *to* go," Frenchy said. "Down."

Frenchy LaMott reached into the pocket of his filthy denim jacket.

He brought out another handful of ballast and flung it at us. As I turned to shield my face with my arms, a rock thrown by Jeanie or Emile grazed my head. It stung fiercely, transforming my fear into rage.

I lowered my head and charged Emile and Jeanie, who looked at me for a moment, then turned tail and broke for safety. They jumped down onto the bank and disappeared into the alders, where they thrashed around like two moose calves.

I had assumed Nat was right behind me. But when I turned around, he was standing in the middle of the trestle, facing Frenchy LaMott. He had set down the crawdad sack. His hands were at his side and there was an indefinable looseness about the way they hung there and the way he was standing, waiting for Frenchy, who looked suddenly uncertain.

"Go on back, Frenchy," Nat said. "Don't come any closer to me."

"You going in the river, crawdad," Frenchy said. "Down in the slime with you friends."

But he didn't sound so sure of himself anymore.

Nat shook his head. "Go back."

"Frenchy!" someone screamed. "You get down off there and leave that preacher boy alone."

It was Ida LaMott. She was coming down the road from the slaughterhouse, wearing a blood-smeared rubber apron. She screamed something at her son in French just as he aimed a tremendous roundhouse at my friend's head. Nat stepped back, moved his head fast to one side, reached out, and slapped Frenchy with his open hand. Frenchy swung again, missing by a good foot. Again Nat slapped him. Frenchy came at him, roaring. Nat held him at arm's length and slapped him once, twice, three times.

It was no fight at all. Frenchy hadn't laid a hand on him.

Ida LaMott was screaming in French. Now Hook LaMott was coming down the road. "What da hell going on here?" he bellowed.

On the trestle Frenchy lashed out at Nat with his boot. Nat stepped back and at the same time swatted Frenchy to hold him off. Frenchy gave a great enraged shout and charged. Nat hit him again with his open hand and Frenchy tripped and fell off the trestle thirty feet into the river below.

"No!" Ida LaMott screamed as her son fell. "No, no, no!"

Frenchy hit the water feet first with a tremendous splash and sank like a stone. I ran out beside Nathan and we looked down into the murky pool, waiting for Frenchy to surface. I had little doubt that he would be up at any moment. More than once I'd seen him jump off the trestle just in front of the Montreal Highball, its airbrakes and whistle shrieking.

But this time Frenchy LaMott did not reappear.

"Oh, brother," Nat said, and dived into the pool. I don't know how long he was under, but it seemed like a very long time. When he came up he was well below the trestle, swimming slowly and towing Frenchy with his chin just above the water. I ran down the bank and helped Nat drag Frenchy out, and we turned him face-down on the sand. By the time Ida and Hook arrived, Frenchy was breathing again, up on his hands and knees and gasping. Ida screamed at him in French and shrieked in French at Hook. Hook was laughing.

"Get da hell up on you feet," Hook said, and assisted Frenchy with a boot in the behind.

Hook turned to Nat. "Let him drownd next time, you," he said. "He ain't wort hauling out."

Somewhere behind us, Emile and Jeanie were still thrashing in the alders.

"Haw," Hook LaMott said. "Look for dem dummies tomorrow, next day, up Memph'magog."

Sending Frenchy reeling in the direction of the trestle with another well-aimed kick, Hook went back to work.

"Thank you, boy, thank you," Ida LaMott kept telling Nat. "You save my Frenchy life."

Nat shrugged. He got the sack of crawdad and he and I headed back to town.

"You won't have any more trouble with him, Nat," I said excitedly. "Or from anybody else around here. This'll be all over town within an hour. You're a hero."

But I was amazed to see that Nathan Andrews was nearly crying.

I wanted to console him, but what could I say? I was beginning to see that being a Negro was different and harder than being white, whether you lived in Canada or Europe or Kingdom County, Vermont.

That night was Production Night at the *Monitor*. Around nine o'clock, as I was coming down the stretch with the second run, Reverend Andrews came into the shop with a notepad. He gave me his two-finger salute, then conferred briefly with my father. I was afraid Nat's father might be mad at me for taking Nat out to the trestle that morning. But after a minute the minister went downstairs to the basement, where my father stored the back issues of the papers. Shortly afterwards I finished the run.

At about the same time, Cousin Elijah shut off his linotype and stalked across the room and down into the basement. "That preacher," he said when he reappeared, "is ransacking through back issues. What's he after, I'd like to know, prying and spying and navigating around down there?"

"He isn't spying on anyone, Elijah," my father said. "He's researching local history for the church sesquicentennial. What's more, he has my express permission to come in here and do that anytime he wants."

"Does he have your express permission to set fire to the building?"

"For God's sake, Elijah, what do you mean?"

"Don't blaspheme, cousin. I just apprehended him smoking a cigarette down there. I made him extinguish it. Very likely that's how the Great Fire of '36 started. Some tramp smoking a cigarette and navigating around where he shouldn't have been."

"His vigilance has prevented another local Armageddon," my father told the framed photograph of H. L. Mencken on the wall above the addressing machine.

From the cellar I heard a chortle. A minute later Reverend Andrews emerged and wandered over to the shelf behind my father's desk, where Dad kept Pliny Templeton's *Ecclesiastical History*.

"This looks most fascinating," he said. "Useful for my research, as well. Would you mind if I borrowed it?"

"Not at all," Dad said. "But guard it with your life. That's the only copy of the book in existence."

"Hold on here a—" Elijah started to say, but Reverend Andrews had already given us another quick salute, thanked my father, and gone out the door.

Now Elijah was really angry.

"I can't believe you let him just walk off with that, Cousin. As you very well know, it's irreplaceable. I wouldn't trust that fella with it for a minute."

"I trust him with it," Dad said. "And since it belongs to me and is mine to lend if I choose to, that's the beginning and the end of it."

"I'll tell you this straight out, Cousin Charles, and you'll do well to listen. Your friend the new minister is not what he appears to be. He may hoodwink you and the trustees, and he may hoodwink the congregation. But he's never bamboozled me for a minute. He is not what he appears to be. Why did he want to leave a good job in the service? Why did he want to leave Canada? What happened to that wife of his?"

"She died," my father said. "What happened to yours?"

This so enraged our peevish cousin, who had even less use for women than for boys, that just before I headed out the door, he stamped off into the night.

Outside, the evening had cooled off noticeably. As I headed diagonally across the common, it started to rain. Hurrying along under the big elms, I wondered what Elijah meant by saying that Reverend Andrews wasn't what he seemed to be. As nearly as I could tell, he was exactly what he seemed to be: a minister, and a good one, who wanted to bring up his son in the country. To me, the real mystery was Elijah's suspicious nature. How my father had ever put up with him for all these years was beyond me.

As I crossed the tracks at the north end of the common, a long dark vehicle slid out of the driveway between the commission sales barn and the undertaking parlor and pulled up beside me. The driver rolled down his window. "That you, Jimbo?"

Instantly my heart began to beat faster. It was Sheriff Mason White in his patrol hearse.

"You on your way home, are you? Hop in. Seeing it's raining, I'll run you out to the gool."

I was desperate to think up some excuse not to get into that frightful vehicle. "That's all right, Sheriff. I—I like to walk in the rain."

"Yes, sir," he said with a knowing laugh. Then, in an altogether different tone, "Get in. I've been waiting for you."

Scared nearly out of my wits, I got into the front seat of the hearse, keeping my eyes unswervingly ahead. I had no reason to think that there was a corpse in the back at that particular moment, but I wasn't taking any chances.

"Jimbo," the Sheriff said in a stern voice as we eased away from the curb, "I got a bad report on you this P. of M. Word is, you and young Andrews was up to some serious mischief out to the high trestle."

"We were not," I said, nearly crying. "We went for crawdads and Frenchy LaMott came along and shagged us out on the trestle with rocks. He took a swing at Nathan and Nathan slapped him. Then Frenchy fell off the trestle into the river, and if Nathan hadn't dived in and pulled him out, Frenchy would have drowned."

"That ain't quite the way I heard it, Jimbo. According to my reports, the Andrews boy suckered Frenchy out on the trestle and knocked him off a-purpose."

"That's not true!" I shouted. Now that my dander was up, I didn't care who or what Mason White had in the back of that hearse. Dracula himself could have been back there, for all I cared.

"Talk to Ida LaMott if you don't believe me," I said.

"Calling me a liar, are you, Jimbo?" Mason said as we headed slowly east out of the village. "I reckon we'll just have to see what Mother and Dad Kinneson have to say about a boy that talks back to an elected officer of the law and calls him a liar."

"That's right, we will."

"Mother and Dad K know you were out there by that trestle today, Jimbo?"

When I didn't reply, Mason chuckled. "Mom and Dad K are going to be pret-ty upset, seeing you brought home in the patrol hearse and all."

To my relief, instead of turning left over the red iron bridge onto the gool, Mason pulled into the turnoff just across from Charlie's trailer, where the woods had been logged off the previous summer. The trailer was dark. No doubt Charlie was off with his team.

Leaving the motor running, Mason said, "Well, Jimbo, I and you can come to an understanding between us yet. Tell you what. According to my reports, you weren't really the one to blame out there this afternoon anyway. Any more than you were to blame for that ruckus at Bumper's barn last evening. So I'd be more than satisfied if you were to retract that allegation you made back there about me not telling the truth."

"I apologize for calling you a liar," I mumbled. "But Nathan and I—"

"That's good, that's real good," Mason said. "Now just one more thing, Jimbo. You really ought to be a little choosier about the company you keep, now that you're getting older."

When I started to object, he held up his hand. "I don't mean I have anything against the colored fella and his boy. Some of the finest people I've ever known were colored folks. You're just better off sticking closer to your own kind, the folks you grew up with, if you know what I mean."

I did know what he meant and it made me sick to my stomach. But I also knew that Mason had no way to keep me from associating with Nathan Andrews or Nathan's father or anyone else I wanted to associate with.

"Okay, skeedaddle," the sheriff said, revving his engine. "Oh, one more thing. Say hello to Mom and Dad K for me, will you, and tell that big brother of yours hello, too, if you can ever find him."

Just before I shut the hearse door, Mason leaned over toward me and lowered his voice. "I don't care what old Zacker thinks, Jimbo. Brother Charlie's one smart cookie. I wouldn't mind working with him one day. Tell him I said so, will you? Tell him I might be in to see him about the matter myself in a day or two."

# 7

"All right, gents, here we go. The cow in first place has a tad more overall *dairyness* than the others. We've got a very close placing here between number two and number three, but two walks more correct on her hind legs. Four has a more refined head than five, five's udder is firmer attached than six's. Six has an ab-so-lute-ly *classic* neck. . . ."

Bumper Stevens, decked out in a cowboy hat and a pink shirt and a black string tie, strutted slowly along the row of handsome Jersey cows, the long cord of his microphone trailing behind him over the dewy grass. After every sentence or two, he paused so that Armand St. Onge, sitting up in the judge's stand with a second microphone, could translate what he said into French. It was still so early that the brand new American and Vermont flags high above the white cattle barns hung limp with dew; but already several hundred spectators were crowded along the freshly whitewashed board fence surrounding the open-air grass ring, listening intently to the results of the first cattle class of the day.

It was judging day—Saturday, the last day of the Kingdom Fair—and the day Nat Andrews and I had been planning for since the afternoon the previous week when we lay in the sand near the B and M trestle and decided that we would sneak into the girlie show.

Kingdom Fair, in the early 1950s, had what my father called a split personality—a bucolic and wholesome daytime personality, and a tawdry but equally marvelous nighttime personality. Toward midmorning, after the family milker class of the Jersey judging, at which Bumper grudgingly awarded another blue ribbon to Kingdom Gool Ruthie, Nat and I joined my mother to tour one of my favorite daytime purlieus, the long dairy barns. Each barn—Jersey, Ayrshire, Holstein, Guernsey—had a welcoming festive atmosphere, with gaudy bunting tacked above stalls emblazoned with the names of farms, and displays of intertwined cedar boughs and sap buckets crammed with black-eyed Susans and buttercups. Outside, the temperature was already up in the seventies. But the animal barns remained as cool as our root cellar at home.

From the dairy barns we ambled over to the horse stables to see the nervous, slender-legged sulky pacers and the treetop-tall workhorses with gigantic feathered feet as big around as peach baskets. From there we went to the cacophonous fowl shed, where Mom's huge gander Leroy had already been designated Grand Fowl of the '52 fair. Then we spent a whole hour in my favorite building of all, Floral Hall, which was a cornucopia of color and fragrance containing every conceivable kind of early-summer garden and farm produce that can be grown in northern Vermont, in addition to a three-tiered baker's window display of homemade breads and pies, strained clover honey and comb honey, rectangular blond blocks of pure maple sugar, quilts and comforters as bright as an October hillside, paintings by local artists, and more than one hundred categories of cut flowers.

"You know, James," Mom said with a conspiratorial laugh, "I'm so happy you and Nathan are willing to indulge me in this little excursion. Your father would come here with me if he absolutely had to. But he really hates anything that has to do with farming, and I couldn't bear to ask him."

"Well, I like all this," I said truthfully enough, though I think what

I liked best about the daytime fair was being with my mother, who never made educational seminars out of our small expeditions, but just enjoyed them. I even felt somewhat conspiratorial myself; and when I thought of that other secret, the secret Nat and I shared, and our "camping trip," a scary thrill went up my spine.

Around noon we climbed up to a sparsely occupied section high in the grandstand and opened the wicker picnic basket Mom had packed the night before: boiled ham sandwiches on homemade bread, a fresh garden salad, baked beans, pickles, sharp cheese and crackers, raspberry pie, and chocolate cake!

"Have you noticed?" Nat said with his mouth full. "This is the only place on the grounds where everyone seems to be just sitting still?"

My mother nodded and smiled. "Time doesn't entirely seem to stop here, Nat, but everything slows down in a way I like. I could sit here all afternoon."

"Me too," Nat and I said together.

I had never seen my friend so relaxed. Maybe, in the crowd, he found an anonymity he'd been looking for. Maybe the bustle reminded him of Montreal, or maybe the old-fashioned exhibits and events coincided with his idea of the way authentic country ought to be. Whatever it was, Nat, like my mother and me, loved the fair at first sight, belittled nothing, couldn't get enough of it. Yet reflecting now, I wonder if it might not have been being with my mother, or any gentle, motherly woman, that Nat really liked.

Except for the loudspeakers announcing the intermittent sulky races it could almost have been a hundred years ago. In between the trotters and pacers, the workhorses were brought out of the barns to pull buckboards and high old delivery wagons with elegant stenciled lettering. Then the track was swept smooth by a farm truck trailing a half dozen freshly cut birch saplings with their leaves still on, an outlandish broom of the woods that amused us all to no end.

Around three, Mom told us to have a good time camping out and left to get ready for her part in the Grand Saturday Cavalcade, in which most of the animals shown at the fair were led or driven by their owners in a wondrous procession twice around the racetrack in front of the grandstand—hundreds of dairy cattle, scores of riding horses with richly tooled saddles and working horses with great hammered silver harness trappings and jingly brass bells, strutting tom turkeys, herds of sheep caparisoned in brilliant yellow and blue and red mantles like miniature medieval war steeds, flocks of chickens and ducks, and yes, Leroy the Gander, the Grand Fowl of the Show, being led on a string by my proud, pretty mother.

By the time the cavalcade ended, the afternoon was well advanced. "Well, Nat," I said, "how about hitting the midway?"

"Okay," he said. "Excelsior!"

Despite all the wonderful things we'd done and seen so far on that wonderful day, despite the far more exciting thrills we anticipated for the night ahead, I was as eager as a ten-year-old to get over to the rides and games. For at Kingdom Fair or any fair, the midway is the one place where you don't just see the events. There, with luck and a receptive frame of mind, you can temporarily become a part of them.

Early dusk was the best time to walk along the midway. The strings of colored lights glowed softly and invitingly, and looking in at the game booths always reminded me of strolling home through the village with my father at Christmastime and looking in house windows at the beautifully lighted trees. Fried food smells clung agreeably to the cooling air. The pitchmen had their second wind after the heat of the day but weren't frazzled and irritable yet, the way they'd be at the end of the night.

"Step right up and give it a try, you can't win a prize by walking by," they chanted over the blaring midway music. Of course Nat and I couldn't win anything by playing those age-old rigged midway games, either, but that didn't keep us from trying. We tossed a lopsided baseball into a slanted bushel basket that bounced it back out every time. After five attempts, Nat finally managed to knock over three weighted milk bottles with a softball. I tried twice to cover up a red circle with five silver disks and left plenty of red showing both times. Nat had his palm read by a gypsy woman with a monstrous gold hoop in one ear, and we rode the Tilt-A-Whirl and octopus until the whole fair began to spin slowly away from me and I barely escaped being sick.

Then Charlie showed up with Reverend Andrews, whom he was giving his long-promised grand tour of the fair, and insisted that Nat and I join them on a battered old carousel with a glorious menagerie of carved wooden circus animals with chipped and faded trappings but an eternal stately prance. Next we visited the Freaks and Wonders of the World Show. Here, for fifty cents apiece, we saw a tattooed lady sticking pins up her nose, a sword swallower and fire eater, a contortionist who nonchalantly folded his legs behind his head and smoked a cigarette, and for an extra quarter, a real live geek who turned out to be none other than Titman White, whom Charlie had gotten off the hook in Ornery Ordney Gilson's murder trial. He was sittting in a torn burlap loincloth, painted all over his body with stripes like a zebra, in a pen with a few sick-looking garter snakes draped around his bare feet. Every so often he would grab one of them and stick its head in his mouth and pretend to bite it off. Nat took one look and left the tent, but Reverend Andrews kindly told Titman that if he was looking for part-time work, he'd hire him to cut the cemetery grass on a weekly basis.

Bumper Stevens and Mason White were standing nearby and overheard the minister's offer.

"Say, Mr. White, which would you ruther be, a Presbyterium preacher or a stud horse?" Bumper said loudly in his stagy minstrel-show voice.

"Why, I don't rightly know, Mr. Stevens," said Mason, who always played Bumper's straight man at the annual blackface show. "Which would *you* rather be?"

"I'd much ruther be a Presbyterium preacher, Mr. White."

"Why's that, Mr. Stevens?"

"Use your head, Mr. White. Breeding season's longer for the preacher."

"Let's clear the hell out of here, Reverend," Charlie said angrily. "Not all the freaks seem to be in the freak show."

On the way out of the tent we met Royce St. Onge, Stub Poulin, and two or three other players from Charlie's team on their way in, laughing and drinking beer. Stub yelled, "Hey, here's Charlie K!"

When we brushed by fast, Stub turned and called after us, "What's the matter, Charlie? Ain't you got time for us white folks tonight?"

We rejoined Nat outside the tent and started back up the midway the way we'd come. But before we'd taken five steps a gong began to clang. Simultaneously a siren shrieked out. Thirty feet above our heads a sparkling burst of colored lights erupted.

For a moment I thought a ride had blown up; but it was nothing of the kind. All this uproar was only my cousin Welcome's latest invention, which he'd just unveiled: the tallest and strangest high striker I'd ever seen, announcing the first winner of the evening.

Every country fair has a high striker—also known as a hammer-and-bell—the strength-testing machine where young huskies try to impress one another and their girlfriends by ringing a bell at the top of a sort of gigantic vertical yardstick by sending an iron weight shooting up it with a post mall. But no other fair I've ever seen has boasted a high striker remotely like the one my cousin had been working on in secret that summer. Besides its spectacular pyrotechnics and fire-engine sound effects, it was twice as high as most others and equipped with more elaborate lights and mirrors and slogans than a cross-country eighteen-wheeler. Astraddle the top was a life-size tin replica of an alien-looking green girl with two green antennae, called Marsha the Martian, between whose shapely emerald legs the iron weight momentarily disappeared when a customer rang the bell.

Reverend Andrews laughed and shook his head. "Only here," he said.

"My lord!" Charlie said in genuine awe. "Welcome, you have outdone yourself with this gorgeous artifact. She's a true work of art."

"I imagine she is, Cousin," Welcome said as a crowd gathered around the high striker. "Have a whack, Jimmy?"

I hefted the mall. It was heavier than it looked, but I heaved it up over my head and let fly at the spring-weighted platform. The weight zipped up to the line on Marsha's knees marked "Sissy Boy." She made a rude noise, the crowd laughed, and I retreated in ignominy.

"That's not very polite," Welcome said to the green girl. "You were little once too."

"I'll give her a go," said Royce St. Onge. Royce sent the weight speeding up to her thigh—"He-Man"—but no farther.

"Judas priest, will you look at this contraption, now, Mr. Stevens," said Sheriff White, who had come to see what the noises were about. "Only a Kinneson could come up with something this outlandish." He peered up at the slot between Marsha's legs. "Why, this is ob-scene, to boot!"

"I bet you could ring the bell, High Sheriff," Welcome said. "Give her a whirl."

"Try her out, Mace," an onlooker chimed in. "Big tall fella like you ought to drive that bell clear up in her gullet."

"Nope, boys, not when I'm in uniform. Hat and gun here would get in the way."

"Take them off," Charlie said in a needling voice.

Standing back in the crowd beside Reverend Andrews in his baseball cap and sweatshirt, holding a half-full bottle of beer, my brother looked like any other fairgoing workingman.

"Come on, Sheriff," Royce said. "I'll hold your hat and gun for ya."

"Well, now."

"All in good fun, Sheriff. Might get you an extra vote or two this fall."

"All right, all right." Mason took off his hat and gunbelt and handed them to Bumper. "You hold on to these, Mr. Stevens, if you will. Reach me that mallet, there, Welcome."

Now, although Mason White was as skinny and awkward-looking as Ichabod Crane, no one who'd ever seen him wrestle a big bulky farmer's corpse into a bag and down a winding back stairway doubted his raw strength. His length of arm alone was enough, I thought, to ring that bell. Up shot the weight and up and up, triggering lights and sirens and bells, all the way to "Almost But Not Quite."

"Tee-hee," said the green girl. "Close. But close don't count except in horseshoes."

"Don't speak to High Sheriff that way," Welcome told her sternly. "Can't you recognize an elected official of the county when you see one?"

"Rigged piece of crap," the sheriff sputtered. "He's got it fixed so's that weight won't go all the way to the top."

"You think Mr. Kinneson's invention here is rigged, Sheriff White?" Reverend Andrews said.

"Certainly it is. You don't know these outlaws around here the way I do, Andrews. They're so crooked they can't lay straight in bed."

The minister looked at Welcome. "Is this machine rigged, Mr. Kinneson?"

"It's a rig-put-together," Welcome said obscurely. Then, to clarify, "From spare parts."

"I see," Reverend Andrews said, taking the mall and ringing the bell so quickly yet with such apparent effortlessness that it was a moment before I realized that he had done it one-handed!

Sheriff White scowled, took his gunbelt and hat from Bumper, and melted into the crowd moving down the midway. "Jesum Crow!" Royce St. Onge said. "I want to shake your hand, Rev. Why the hell—I mean, why the *heck*—ain't you playing ball for us this summer?"

"He probably thought the team was just for 'white folks,' " Charlie said sarcastically.

"Shoot, Charlie K, Stub didn't mean nothing by that," Royce said. "Old Rev here *knows* we didn't mean nothing by that, don't you, Rev? Shake hands with the man, boys."

Stub Poulin was so drunk he could hardly stand up. He reeled and staggered and held up his hand. "Shake hands with Rev, boys," he hollered. "I just did. See? The black don't come off."

"Come on," Royce said to Stub, and pulled him off down the midway. "He's drunk, Reverend. He don't mean nothing."

"He was drunk," Charlie said lamely to the minister.

But Reverend Andrews only shrugged and said in that faintly ironical way, "Maybe so. But as an old air force friend of mine used to say, he was sober before he got drunk, wasn't he? I've seen enough of your fair, Charles. I'm going home."

"Hey, hey, hey, Paris comes to New Hampshire," yelled the barker, a fat, bald, one-eyed man in a filthy T-shirt.

"This ain't New Hampshire, dummy. It's Vermont," Bumper Stevens shouted from the crowd of men pushing up near the platform in front of the tent.

"It ain't Vermont, neither," somebody else yelled. "It's Kingdom County."

The one-eyed barker seemed to enjoy this repartee. "Paris comes to King's County, then, boys. It don't matter. Inside of that tent you'll think you've died and went straight to heaven. Speaking of which, here she is right now, the star of the Paris Revue, Heaven Fontaine. Step out here, honey, and show these boys what you got. Don't be shy, now."

Heaven Fontaine, when she appeared on the rickety platform in front of the Paris Revue tent at the far end of the Kingdom Fair midway, did not appear to suffer from shyness. She was a big, strapping, hard-featured, middle-aged woman in a red bathrobe slit all the way up her thigh. With her was a somewhat younger version of herself, whom the barker introduced to the crowd as Heaven's sixteen-year-old sister, A Little Piece of Heaven, though even from the back of the crowd I could tell that this chunky little tart was closer to thirty than sixteen.

"And inside the tent, boys, we've got something very special tonight, which except to say her name is Saint Catherine and she's hot off the streets of downtown Montreal where she got her grammar school, high school, and college, I won't say another word."

Heaven Fontaine swayed mechanically to the blaring burlesque music. Little Piece jounced and bounced beside her like a stout wind-up doll with a perpetual grin, not even pausing in her vigorous gyrations when she brushed her hair away from her sweaty face.

In the meantime the adjacent Club California was making a competitive bid for business with a younger barker and two skinny blondes in spangled scanty costumes. "Red-hot ramble, long and strong," the barker snarled into his microphone, strutting up and down the platform in front of the girls in his shiny black leather jacket and dusty engineer boots. "They strip to please and not to tease."

"Hey, hey, hey, Paris comes to King's County, Ver-mont," chanted the barker of my show, though a man in the middle of the crowd yelled that the closest Heaven Fontaine and Little Piece had ever been to Paris was Paris, Maine.

This was what Nat and I had been waiting for. This was the show we intended to see. But how? We'd already determined that sneaking in through the back of the tent was next to impossible. It was pegged down every foot or so to prevent just such incursions.

To complicate matters, Elijah Kinneson was standing off to the side of the crowd, handing out religious tracts he'd printed up the previous week at the shop. If he saw me "navigating" around, he'd certainly report me to my father and there would be hell to pay.

"Say, what youse two up to?"

It was Little Piece, standing just behind us in the shadows. "You boys want to see what-all goes on inside?" she said in a teasing voice. "Five bucks apiece and I sneak you in through the truck."

I was flat broke, had been within twenty minutes of hitting the midway earlier that evening.

My heart fell as Nat shook his head. "Don't have it," he said.

Little Piece shrugged. "How much do you got?"

Nat grinned. "Five dollars for us both."

Little Piece licked her bright red lips thoughtfully. "Tell youse what. For that, one can see the show. Hurry up and decide which. I got to get in there."

"No deal," Nat said. "Both of us or neither of us. Double or nothing."

"Gimme the fiver," Little Piece said quickly.

I would have forked the money over before she had a chance to change her mind. Nat knew better. "When we get there," he told her.

"Okay, smartie. Follow me."

We detoured out around the crowd of men now lining up in front of the barker's stand for tickets. As we passed Elijah, I scrunched down, but I was quite sure he saw me anyway.

We slipped in between the side of the Paris Revue tent and the adjacent Club California, and Little Piece led us up a set of portable steps and through the side door of the show truck. We followed her into a narrow passage between a tiny gas stove and sink, past a cot and two bunkbeds, and past a curtained-off section where Little Piece paused to shout, "Show's about ready, honey," she turned to us and hissed, "*Saint* Catherine. She ain't no saint, I'll tell you that, and she ain't from no ritzy Montreal nightclub. We picked her up by the side of the road last night on our way down here from Canada, walking the roads like a common tramp. Hollywood! That's all she talks about. Hollywood and being in the movies. Dumb little French bitch! Says she's a performer, though, and that's good enough for us. Gimme that five-spot now."

We had pushed through another curtain into the rear section of the truck. The wide metal tailgate jutted out into the tent, forming an impromptu stage illuminated by two or three harsh spotlights fastened to the tent poles. Nat gave Little Piece the five-dollar bill and she gave us a shove.

"Get down there, in under the tail," she said. "Them johns'll be pouring inside in a minute. Wait two, three more minutes till they all in. Then slip out and stand off to the edge. Old One-eye, he'll be too busy up here to see youse. Just watch out for that cattle prod, zap youse right on youse asses."

"She doesn't seem to like that new girl much," I said to Nat as we scuttled in under the tailgate and hunkered down onto the stubbly ground.

"She's probably jealous of her," Nathan explained. "Afraid the new girl will replace her."

After a minute he laughed softly. "Kinneson, tell me something. What in the bloody hell are you and I doing here?"

I began to laugh too. This was so totally different from anything I'd expected or ever could have predicted. And at that moment, laughing together in the darkness under that battered show truck at the far end of the midway of Kingdom Fair, I think Nat and I were as close as we would ever be.

"Alley oop!" the barker yelled from the entrance. "Show time!"

In swarmed the paying customers, though all we could see of them was a shuffling forest of denimed legs from the knees down. Brass burlesque music blared out inside the tent. The tailgate above us vibrated furiously and a rousing cheer went up. The trousers and boots and sneakers pressed closer. I could smell the manure on a pair of barn boots scant inches from where I lay, and I had to fight back a trapped sensation. The tempo of the music increased. The men cheered again.

"Okay, Kinneson. You sure you're ready for this?"

"Damn right," I said, though my face felt unnaturally hot, as though I were coming down with summer flu, and my stomach was queasier than when I'd gotten off the octopus an hour ago. But the die was cast.

Edging along crab-fashion on our knees and elbows, we sneaked out from under the tailgate, scurried back toward the dim recesses along the sidewall of the tent and looked up at the stage. Heaven and Little Piece were grinding and bumping away as naked as jaybirds!

After a minute or so the two women plunked down and draped their legs over the tailgate. Yet another cheer went up as the one-eyed barker climbed onto the stage.

"All right, boys," he yelled. "Just two at a time, now, or I'll give you a thrill you didn't come in for."

As he brandished his electric cattle prod, the men pressed forward and began to lick and fondle those two great bovine women. Except to say that I was about equally shocked and fascinated, I cannot accurately describe my sensations. Outside, watching the girls' come-ons, especially those of the limber young pros at the Club California, I had been aroused and excited. Now I was scared and confused. There was a brutal quality about the men and a dreadful grim yet cheery resignation in the submission of the women.

"Okay, Kinneson," Nathan said. "This is bloody disgusting. It's the most disgusting thing I've ever seen in my life. Let's get the hell out of this hogpen."

I was more than ready. By now I was afraid I was going to be sick right inside the tent. But the surging crowd of men had completely blocked the entranceway. For the moment, at least, we were trapped in the place we'd most wanted to be.

At this point Bumper Stevens, who was pushing in behind us, spotted me. "Say now," he said, "what have we got here. A young buck that ain't had a chance at the ladies yet. Don't be shy, Jimmy. Don't hang back, now. That ain't no way to get what you come here for."

Bumper seized my upper arm and began to steer me straight through the reeking crowd.

"Let go of him," Nat said, grabbing the old fool.

Bumper shook him off. "Your turn next, Sambo," he said and hauled me straight toward Little Heaven, who was spread-eagled on her back on the hard metal tailgate.

I have no idea what effect this intended initiation might have had on me, then or later, had not the one-eyed barker chosen that moment to announce, "And now, gentlemen, what you've all been waiting for, the star of the Paris Revue, a girl not yet seventeen years old, in town for a one-night performance only, Saint Catherine of downtown Montreal!"

On the stage above us, trembling like a frightened kitten, appeared a girl who seemed no more than two or three years older than me. Her rain-colored eyes were glazed over, as though in terror, and she had on a long red and blue and yellow dress, like some sort of costume, with a tear halfway up the side. Through the rent in her dress I could see one slender white leg, and it was shaking too, and not with the music.

"Jesus!" Bumper said, letting go of me. "That's just a kid!"

At that moment a strong hand gripped my shoulder from behind and began propelling me toward the entrance. I twisted around and looked up into Charlie's face. "Let's go, boys," he said. "I trust you've already seen what you came for."

Cousin Elijah must have told him that we had sneaked into the tent!

As we moved through the crowd the barker made a grab at Saint Catherine, missed, grabbed again, and tore her dress down off her shoulder and front, revealing one small breast, which she instantly covered with her hands. She tried to retreat back into the truck, but the barker blocked her path and seized her arm.

Charlie had stopped to watch what was happening on the stage. The young girl in the torn dress twisted and cringed away from the barker, who yanked her roughly toward the press of men.

"LET GO OF HER, YOU SON-OF-A-BITCH!"

My infuriated brother was up on the stage like a shot. The barker jabbed at him with the cattle prod. Charlie kicked it out of his hand. The barker grinned and swung at him and Charlie kicked him squarely between the legs as hard as a man can kick.

At the same time that the barker went down, Saint Catherine flung herself into Charlie's arms and screamed, "Monsieur Kinneson! Monsieur Kinneson!"

I had never seen Charlie look so surprised. But before he could say a word, a whistle blasted out. It was followed instantly by two pistol shots.

"It's a raid!" somebody yelled. "We're being raided, boys!"

Sure enough, in the entranceway of the tent, not far from where Nat and I were being jostled back and forth by the excited crowd, his head nearly scraping the canvas tent roof, his revolver drawn and pointed upward, was High Sheriff Mason White, and beside him his deputy Pine Benson. Instantly Bumper Stevens grabbed Little Piece by the hair and yelled, "You're under arrest, whore! I've got her, Mace. This one won't get far."

The crowd was in an uproar. Heaven tried to bull past Pine Benson. Pine muckled onto her arm. She swung at him and missed. She swung at Mason and smacked him squarely in the stomach. Still holding the pistol, he bent over and gasped for breath like a stranded sucker.

In the meantime the crowd was pouring through a gap in the rear of the tent, spilling outside into the midway. Nat and I were swept along with them, fighting to stay on our feet to keep from being trampled. Charlie overtook us, and before we were swept out into the night I looked back onto the stage, which was empty except for the supine barker. Saint Catherine, it seemed, had escaped through the truck.

"All rise, please. This court is in session."

It was two-thirty in the morning. Judge Allen, as he strode into the courtroom for the arraignment of the Paris Revue outfit, looked as angry as I'd ever seen him. Above all, the judge hated to be disturbed when he was at his fishing camp, where he and my father had gone to spend the weekend. Hunkered down in the front row of the gallery above the room, where Charlie had agreed to let us watch the proceedings, Nat and I were still shaking.

My father, who looked as little amused as the judge, sat in his customary spot in the back row nearest the door. (It seemed strange to see him in public in his fishing clothes.) Heaven, Little Piece, and the one-eyed barker stood at the defense table next to my brother as Zack Barrows read Mason's affidavit. They were being charged with lewd and lascivious conduct in a public place, which carried a maximum fine of one hundred dollars and a sentence of up to thirty days. Zack was asking for a fine of fifty dollars apiece for the Misses Fontaine, one hundred dollars for Mr. One-eye Billy Carbonneau, and five days in jail for all three of them.

"Misses Fontaine and Mr. One-eye Billy, how do you plead to these charges?" the judge inquired with ominous irony.

"Innocent, your honor," said all three.

"Ah," Judge Allen said, looking back toward my father as though to indicate that he should have expected this, too. "Innocent. Do your clients deny, then, Mr. Kinneson, that they were in that tent last night performing the antics alleged in Sheriff White's affidavit?"

"No, your honor. They were there, all right, along with what looked like about half of the male population of Kingdom County. They don't deny that. What they deny is that they were performing in public. The Paris Revue is a private business, conducted out of the public view, with the full knowledge and blessing of the Kingdom Fair Board of Trustees, I might add. To read from the contract signed on June twentieth, 1952, between the board and Mr. Carbonneau: '. . . for the sum of three hundred dollars per night, we hereby grant the Paris Revue Shows, Inc., owned and operated by William Carbonneau, the right to present a private dance exhibition on a leased section of the fairground's midway.' "

"Fine!" roared Zack Barrows, his face as red as a turkey gobbler's. "I shall concede that the contract is in good order. Nevertheless, as the affidavit states, the 'dancers' of this show were apprehended in the act of performing lewd and lascivious acts that according to Vermont statutes are illegal in any setting, public or private, and are punishable by the fines and incarceration cited in the affidavit."

"You agree that the Paris Revue Show is a private enterprise?" Charlie said.

"Whatever you say. Public or private. The act itself is illegal."

"May I see the signed writ of entry authorizing this raid on the agreed-upon private premises?"

"Signed writ of entry?" Zack roared. "What do you mean, 'signed writ of entry'?"

"Perhaps Judge Allen would prefer to explain," Charlie said.

When the judge said nothing, Charlie added, "You've agreed, Zack, that the Paris Revue tent was private property. You and I and Sheriff White all know that you can't just barge into someone's private home or business, even if it's a tent, without an entry warrant or search warrant signed by a judge."

"The judge was off fishing," Zack shouted. "He wasn't available."

"It's my understanding," Charlie said, "that in the absence of a judge, the local justice of the peace has the authority to sign entry warrants. Is that correct, your honor?"

"Yes," Judge Allen said wearily.

"Well, the justice of the peace wasn't available either," Zack said. "I looked for him and he wasn't available."

Judge Allen actually smiled. "This case is dismissed," he said, and no more than five minutes later he and Dad were on their way back to the lake to fish the early morning rise, and Heaven, Little Piece, and One-eye Billy were on their way back to the fairgrounds and thence to their next engagement.

It rained hard all the rest of that day. I took a long nap in the afternoon and spent most of the evening reading and visiting with my mother in the kitchen. Like Charlie before me, I had always been quicker to confide certain thornier kinds of problems to Mom than to Dad, yet I could hardly confess that I'd actually been inside the girlie tent when it was raided. When I told her that Nat and I had run into Charlie and attended the arraignment, she listened attentively, then said that the fair people were much more to be sympathized with than condemned. To my surprise, she was glad that Charlie had gotten them off the hook.

The driving summer rainstorm continued, and we left the porch light on for my father, who was covering a late meeting in the village. Just before I went up to bed in my loft chamber, Mom said, "I hope the Dog Cart Man's warm and dry tonight, Jimmy."

I could barely remember the Dog Cart Man, though I had a fairly distinct recollection of his mongrel companions. It had been at least seven years, maybe eight or nine, since he'd come to the Kingdom but voicing concern for his well-being had become a family ritual on stormy nights.

"What's he look like?" I asked. "The Dog Cart Man, I mean."

"Well, he looks like the Pied Piper, I guess, all spattered with paint of every imaginable color. He doesn't talk at all, of course, and can't hear, either. I suppose that's why he learned how to paint. Painting's his special way of making himself understood."

My mother was an accomplished amateur watercolorist herself, but when I asked if the Dog Cart Man's murals were as good as her nature scenes and portraits of Charlie and me when we were little kids, she laughed a little self-deprecatory, pleased laugh and said oh, my yes, he was a *real* painter.

"I'll never forget the first time I saw him, Jimmy. It was the summer your dad and I were married, and everything about Kingdom County was fresh and marvelous to me. One morning he just appeared in the dooryard. At first I actually thought he was a hobo. I was going to take him coffee and sandwiches. But your grandfather explained that he was a painter and was getting ready to paint a picture for us.

"For a long time, he stood and stared at that faded old mural of the trout on the barn. Then before you could say Jack Robinson he began to paint, very fast, just slapping those amazingly bright colors up on the side of the barn. It didn't take him an hour from start to finish!

"Of course, I was terribly fascinated. I'd never seen anything remotely like him or his dogs, and I would have given a great deal to tag along with him for a day or two. I'll tell you what, Jimmy. If he comes again, and I'm pretty sure he will, I hope you'll spend some time with him. He's the last of a kind, you know—sort of like Cousin Resolvèd and Cousin Welcome. When he's gone, his like won't be seen again in these parts or anywhere else. And if you get to know all these folks now, someday you'll be able to write wonderful stories about them that won't be like the stories anyone else is writing. So we'll keep our eyes peeled and hope he shows up soon."

My own concerns on that rainy night in 1952 kept returning to the fair and the tent show and the scared girl on the stage. Something about her rain-colored eyes and the frightened way she'd looked at the audience haunted me. I hoped she was all right and safely away from One-eye and his rough bunch, but other thoughts kept crowding into my mind, too, fantasies of rescuing her from her plight myself and spiriting her off to some sequestered spot to console and . . . I was not sure what.

After being up nearly all night the night before, I should have been exhausted. But for some reason, maybe because of my nap that day, I wasn't. For a long time I lay awake listening to the rain on the metal roof just outside my coffin window, and hoping it would blow over in time for Charlie's ballgame the following evening in Memphremagog, which he'd promised to take me to see.

When I finally drifted off to sleep, however, I did not dream of Saint Catherine but of the lunatic miller from Nat's comic book. In my nightmare the miller was chasing me and I jumped onto the Dog Cart Man's cart and he whipped up his dogs and off we sped along the River Road. The madman gained on us steadily, and when I turned to look at him, all white and floury, he bore a terrible resemblance to Frenchy LaMott. The dogs hitched to the cart howled like a ravening pack of wolves, and suddenly I was awake and someone was pounding on the kitchen door.

It was pitch dark. The rain had stopped but the river was up and roaring. The knocking continued. Wearing just my pajama bottoms, I trotted down the loft stairs into the kitchen and opened the door.

Standing on the top step of the porch, drenched from head to toe, was Saint Catherine from the Paris Revue girlie show.

"This is the home of Monsieur Kinneson?" she said in a strong French Canadian accent.

"Yes," I said, barely able to believe that she was standing at our kitchen door.

"I am Claire. Claire LaRiviere?"

At first I thought she might not be sure of her own name. Then from the way she was looking at me it dawned on me that she expected me to know why she was there.

Unfortunately, I did not.

"Well," I said, "come in. Come in out of the wet, Claire."

Claire LaRiviere came inside and went immediately to the stove while I grabbed some kindling out of the woodbox and began to build the fire back up. As soon as it caught, I perched on the woodbox lid and stared at our strange guest with open curiosity.

She looked a little older than she had looked at the fair. She had long hair, too wet to tell what color. Her rain-colored eyes had huge craters beneath them. A coffee-colored stain shaped uncannily like the state of Maine ran over the right shoulder and down the front of her colorful dress, which was badly torn and splashed with bluish mud all along the fringe, so that I knew she had been walking the back roads of Kingdom County. Where the dress was torn, material had been gathered into huge safety-pins. Despite the mud I could see that it was a very elegant, old-fashioned dress with lacework on the front and sleeves and hem. On her feet she wore sneakers that might once have been white. Clutched to her chest she held a black handbag as large as my camping knapsack. Her face was small and oval-shaped, her chattering teeth were small, and although she was taller than me by inches, she was slender nearly to the point of emaciation. Only her eyes were large, preternaturally so, and they looked terrifically tired and somewhat confused yet oddly determined as she examined her surroundings with a peculiar slow, exhausted intensity.

"Here at last," she said.

"Would you like some coffee?"

She shook her head emphatically, shaking more water into the puddle forming around her sneakers. "No coffee, thank you. Coffee is make me shake. You have tea?"

I nodded. I filled the tea kettle and set it on the stove just as my father padded into the kitchen in his slippers and bathrobe.

"Can't you be a little quiet—" He never finished the sentence. "Mister Baby Johnson! Who in thunder is this, James?"

"It's Claire LaRiviere," I said, as though I'd known her for years.

"This is my father," I said to Claire. "Mr. Kinneson."

A puzzled frown appeared on the girl's oval face. "He is not Monsieur Kinneson," she said.

My father looked at me. "Well, if I'm not, then I've been strangely mistaken for the past half century or so. The question is, James, who is this young woman and where is she from?"

The girl continued to frown at my father. "You resemble the photo of Monsieur Kinneson perhaps a little. But most certainly you are not Monsieur Kinneson."

To judge from the expression on his face, my father did not seem pleased to be informed by a perfect stranger standing in his kitchen in the middle of the night that he was not who he had thought he was.

"Do you know this girl, James?"

"Well, not really," I said, unwilling to admit where I had seen her before.

"I will show you the photo," Claire LaRiviere said.

She set the huge black handbag on the table. Very deliberately, she began to remove the contents. "It will be right here, of course."

One by one the drenched girl took out several Hershey wrappers, an empty Good & Plenty box, a crumpled box of Dots, a broad pink comb with several missing teeth, three or four colored ticket stubs, and a timetable like the one on the counter at the railroad station in the Common—the detritus, I suddenly realized, of some kind of journey.

In the meantime, my father pulled the belt of his bathrobe tighter around his waist; no doubt he was ill at ease to be caught out of his suitcoat and tie, even in his own kitchen at one fifteen in the morning.

"Who is the little boy who greets me at the door?" Claire asked him out of the blue, without turning to look at me on the woodbox.

"That's my son James."

"And Monsieur Kinneson? Where is he?"

Now my father, the two-fisted newspaperman who with good reason prided himself on getting a line on the shiftiest politician within five minutes of meeting him; who did not hesitate to tender detailed and ungentle advice in the form of open letters in the *Monitor* to governors, senators, managers of professional baseball teams, and even presidents; whose letters and columns were frequently reprinted by papers as far away from Kingdom County as Idaho and Louisiana; who had already served once and would twice serve again as president of the American Association of Independent Weekly Newspapers—my father, the reporter's reporter and editor's editor, was totally at a loss when it came to dealing with almost any crisis on the home front that could not be remedied by fixing someone a cup of java.

So I anticipated what was coming next.

"James," my father said, beckoning me into the hallway. *"Go get your mother."*

"How distressing," Mom said, without appearing to be especially distressed, when I woke her up and told her the news. "It's that poor girl, I'm afraid."

She put on her robe and hurried down to the kitchen to set matters straight.

Claire LaRiviere was still sorting through her bag.

"Hello, dear," my mother said. "There's been a small misunderstanding."

"Oh yes," my father said, retreating toward the bathroom.

"At last!" the girl said, and held up a picture that looked as though it had been clipped out of a newspaper.

In fact, it *had* come from a newspaper. It was torn almost in half and faded and smudged. Unmistakably, however, the man smiling out of the photograph at us was my brother Charlie!

It was the photograph my father had taken of him, flanked by our two cousins, standing under the deer head inside the door of the Common Hotel several weeks ago, just after Resolvèd's triumphant poaching arraignment.

Someone—it was not hard to guess who—had cut Resolvèd and Welcome out of the picture and scrawled above my brother's handsome face, "ME. RESOLVÈD T KINNESON."

"The man who is come to my rescue at the show, eh?" Claire said proudly.

"You're the girl Resolvèd sent away for in that silly magazine, aren't you, dear?" my mother said. "I'm afraid that he's played a very mean trick on you. Unfortunately, the man in this picture isn't who you think he is."

Over more tea, after the misunderstanding of the picture was straightened out, Claire LaRiviere gave us a sketchy outline of her life in Canada. She had been born and brought up in Quebec City, the daughter of a boulevard mime and traditional French Canadian fiddler. She told us proudly that she had acquired much of her English from the movies, which she loved, and that from the earliest age she had longed to go to Hollywood and act in a movie herself. Her father, Etienne LaRiviere, had encouraged her in this ambition and had taken her with him from the time she was five years old to stepdance to his fiddle reels on the street corners and to mime celebrities. At this point Claire gave us several demonstrations of her talent, including one of Winston Churchill and one of Charlie Chaplin in *City Lights* that delighted my mother and me so much we clapped.

Then a tragedy had occurred. Two winters ago Etienne LaRiviere had contracted pneumonia from working outdoors in the frigid Canadian streets and died. After Etienne's death there had been a succession of men in their home, the most recent of whom had repeatedly tried to violate Claire's honor.

"Etienne LaRiviere carried a knife in his shoe, a knife made of the sharpest steel. He would have slit this fellow's throat the first time he so much as glanced at me," Claire said haughtily. "But Etienne, the most celebrated mime in all French Canada, was gone, poof!, like the cold wind that blow off the ice on the river and kill him. My mother is not a strong woman. What are we to do? We are at this bad man's mercy!

"So I make up my mind, me. 'Claire,' I say, 'you must leave this house and this city.' Fine. But where will I go? The States, most certainly. Holly-wood!"

At about this time Claire had run across Resolvèd's letter in the Montreal tabloid. She had responded, and to her surprise, Resolvèd had written back (probably with Welcome's assistance), enclosing the spurious picture of himself from the *Monitor* and thirty dollars for bus fare to Kingdom County. On the day the letter arrived she gathered together her few belongings, including her colorful stepdancing dress, stuffed them into a paper sack, and caught the morning bus south to Sherbrooke.

At this point in Claire's tale my father reappeared, now shaved and fully attired in white shirt, suit, and tie. To his great embarrassment she immediately singled him out to address exclusively, much the way a cat in a roomful of people will jump up into the lap of the one person in the room who is uneasy with cats. This discomposed my father so much that he began vigorously polishing his shoes on the lid of the woodbox.

Since the bus for Vermont and Memphremagog would not leave Sherbrooke until early evening, Claire had spent the afternoon watching *Under the Big Top* in a downtown theater. She sat through two complete showings, she said. Back at the bus station she discovered that she had made a miscalculation. After the movie, she did not have enough money left for her ticket to Vermont.

Undaunted, she immediately started walking. After getting lost several times, she reached the Sherbrooke city limits about dusk, where she was picked up by the Paris Revue entourage, who offered her a ride to Vermont in exchange for a night's dancing in the show.

"I imagine this Revue is dancing only, like my performances with the celebrated Etienne on the boulevards of Quebec," Claire told us.

"In fact, it is a bad show with a very bad director. Who knows what might have happened to me if the Kinneson in the photograph and the police had not arrived."

After Mason's raid Claire had run off the fairgrounds into the woods, where she'd hidden in an old maple sugar camp. The following night, tonight, she found the gool, but in the rain and darkness she missed my cousins' turnoff and walked far up the logging road into the gore before realizing her mistake. Retracing her steps, she mistook our light for Resolvèd's.

"Already it has been a long journey," she said, shaking her head. "And yet I have come only a little way if I am ever to get to Hollywood. At times I begin to think I am watching myself in a movie. Or perhaps a dream. The kind of dream where one knows one is asleep but cannot wake up? To say the truth, I am becoming weary of all this traveling. Now I shall work as housekeeper for this man Resolvèd for a time before continuing my trip."

"I should think you might be tired, Claire," my mother said. "You're welcome to stay here with us as long as you like."

"Yes," said my father. "If it hadn't been for one of us, you wouldn't be in this jam in the first place."

Claire looked gravely at my father. "So the man in the photograph is not the Monsieur Kinneson who writes the letter?"

"Definitely not," my father said. "Though they have a lot in common."

"Is all right," Claire said, though it was obvious that she was very disappointed. "I must find the right one, then."

One by one she replaced the candy wrappers and ticket stubs and timetable in her gigantic handbag. Last of all she folded the mutilated picture of my brother and tucked it in with the rest.

"I thank you, my friends, for the warm fire and the tea," she said. "Now, this other Monsieur Kinneson, this Resolvèd—the one that sends for a housekeeper. He lives nearby?"

"She can't go up there, Ruth," Dad said. "She doesn't have the faintest idea what that place is like."

"My husband's right, Claire. The man who sent you that picture isn't who or what you think."

"He's the worst outlaw in the county," Dad said. "He lives in a pigpen with his lunatic brother."

"I'll tell you what, dear," my mother said. "I'll make up the daybed in the spare room for you. Just for tonight. In the morning we'll talk some more."

Claire looked at my mother carefully. Then she nodded. "Very well. But I prefer to sleep here by the stove. This is possible?"

My mother said it was possible. She got a blanket and a pillow, but by the time she was back Claire had curled up on the woodbox in her multicolored dress and had fallen asleep with her head on her pocketbook.

My father was getting into his topcoat.

"Where are you going, Dad?"

"To see your brother," he said on his way out the door. "I don't want him around here for a few days. Then I'm going to work."

It was two o'clock on the nose.

I was exhausted, but once again when I got back upstairs I lay awake for a time, thinking about the mysterious daughter of Etienne LaRiviere, the girl who had learned English from the movies and fallen in love with my brother's picture and come to Kingdom County with a show and who was now sleeping in the kitchen below me.

It was broad daylight when I awoke. The sun was shining brightly in a clear blue sky, and I knew even before going downstairs that Claire LaRiviere would be gone.

I was furious with myself for missing Claire, who despite all my mother's protests had left for Resolvèd's an hour ago. I was tempted to sneak up there and check on her; but something told me not to. Instead, I got my fly rod and walked down to the river, hoping to while away a few hours on the stream until it was time to go to Charlie's ballgame.

The water was up a foot from the rain and the color of a freshly plowed field. Even the meadow pool was too fast to fish, so I started up the burn into the gore. The burn was high, too, and as roily as Huck Finn's Mississippi. If the big trout were up here, they were already full and had stopped feeding. By the time I reached the brook's source at the disused granite quarry, I was ready to quit.

"Hello, James."

I froze. Suspended in midair, high over the natural ledge dam where the brook spilled out of the quarry, was a filmy white shroud, partially obscured by leaves dancing lightly in the morning breeze. Suddenly it laughed a genuinely amused laugh. "Here," a voice said. "Down here."

Claire LaRiviere was sitting with her back against a gigantic yellow birch tree near the corner of the ledge dam. The "ghost" was her white slip hanging from a branch of the tree and drying in the sun. Her dress of many colors was spread out neatly beside her on the ledge.

Suddenly I found myself extremely embarrassed because Claire was wearing nothing but her underpants and bra. I looked away fast and she laughed again. Only by degrees could I look back at her, and then only at her face. Nathan Andrews had teased me that I wouldn't know what to do with a naked girl if I found one. To my chagrin, he had been absolutely right!

Her hair was still slightly damp but no longer matted and stringy. She was combing it with her broken pink comb and it shone softly in the morning sunlight falling down through the small yellow birch leaves. It was the color of light maple sugar and her eyes were no longer the color of rain but of the burn on a summer day where it ran over a blue slate ledge a few hundred feet below the quarry. Her oval face was at repose. The fatigue and confusion of the night before were gone. And she did not seem at all self-conscious to be considerably more than half undressed with me six feet away, trying not to look at her.

"Any luck?" she said.

I shook my head.

She laughed again. "The same for me, James. I have had no luck at all this morning."

I climbed up the bank, leaned my fly rod against the yellow birch tree, and sat down on a flat granite rock a few feet away from her. "Well," I said, trying not to look at her slim white legs, "I guess you missed Resolvèd's place again."

"By no means, James! I have met both him and the brother."

"And?"

"It is not really so very bad there. At first it resembles to me a kind of farm. All the animals! The chickens, the fish, the raccoon, even. It makes me think of the farm of Ma and Pa Kettle, yes? In the comical movie?

"I approach the house, thinking that Resolvèd Kinneson will still be sleeping. But no! The door of the kitchen is open and the Resolvèd and the brother are sitting at the table drinking red wine from a bottle.

Also on the table, eating small pieces of grain from a dish, is a large red he-chicken. The brother is reading from a magazine. The Resolvèd is cleaning a long gun. The kind that resembles two guns made into one gun, which the coach drivers carry in cowboy pictures?"

"A shotgun," I said, trying to envision Ethan Allen Kinneson dining on the table with my cousins.

"Certainly. When I see this shot-gun I am afraid to go inside. But to myself I say, 'Claire, you have come a great way to Ver-mont. You must try this arrangement for a little while. At least until you repay the Resolvèd for the bus ticket.'

"Very well! I enter. I announce my name. I make a polite curtsy. Are they surprised? No! The brother continues to read. The Resolvèd says only, 'It has taken you long enough to get here. What held you up?' "

Claire tilted her head and leered at me sideways, out from under an imaginary feed store cap. It was the best imitation of Resolvèd I had ever seen, even better than Charlie's. Effortlessly, she had captured his pompous surliness, his broad accent, the entire outlandish absurdity about the man. Not only did I all but see Resolvèd there in front of me, I forgot all about my own embarrassment. In another year, or year and a half, this would not have happened. But from that moment on I might as well have been talking to my own sister, if I'd had one, or another boy my age, instead of to a nearly naked girl of seventeen or eighteen.

"Now, James, this Resolvèd who writes the letters to me, he says he will present me to his household. 'This is my brother,' he tells me. 'He has got a screw loose in his head.' The brother continues to read. 'This is E. A. Kinneson,' the Resolvèd says, and points at the he-chicken eating from the dish on the table. 'This is Duke, the poor man's best friend,' he tells me next. I look here, there, everywhere, for a dog or perhaps a little cat. But no! He is holding up the bottle of red wine! 'And this is Duke's wife, Betsy,' the Resolvèd says, and he aims the shotgun straight at my head and laughs like a crazy man."

Laughing exactly like my cousin, she drew such a convincing bead on me with an imaginary shotgun that I flinched.

"How did you get away from there, Claire?"

"Oh! It was not difficult. But first the Resolvèd instructs me to begin my housekeeping duties by cleaning the dishes. When the sink becomes too full for him to pee in, he informs me, it is time to 'hoe out.' Excellent! Here is something I can accomplish. I get a bucket and some rags. I make a fire in the stove. I heat some water. All the time, the Resolvèd is watching me. I inquire about soap. There is no soap. He tells me he will travel to the village for it and at the same time pick up some more of his friend the Old Duke. He says now he is 'hot,' but by and by he will drink himself cold sober and then we will sit down together and have a good long talk, and off he goes, with Betsy.

"As soon as the Resolvèd is gone, the brother with the screw loose shows me a picture in the magazine he is reading. It shows a great flying covered dinner platter with tiny green mens climbing in and out. 'Do you have these up in Canady?' the brother says to me. But I have seen such strange sights only in the movies and I do not know what to reply.

"I tell the brother that now I must go and wash my clothes, and I will be back soon. I take my pocketbook and come here and wash first my dress and slip, then myself. That is when you come, James. In the words of the celebrated Etienne LaRiviere concluding a performance on the great wooden promenade of Chateau Frontenac: 'The end.' "

She stood up and got into her slip and dress as unselfconsciously as though she'd been alone.

"What are you going to do now, Claire?"

"Well, I cannot go back to Quebec. That is out of the question. I must think. This Holly-wood, where the movies are made? Is far?"

"Hollywood's a long ways. Why don't you come back home with me? I know my folks can help you."

"I think of that already, James. But I cannot do it. The Resolvèd will certainly know I am there and come searching for me with Duke's wife Betsy."

"No, he won't. Resolvèd's an awful piece of work, but he isn't going to kill you or anyone else."

"Then perhaps I should go back there and try once more. After all, there are many dishes to do and there is still the matter of the bus ticket. Etienne LaRiviere did not bring up his daughter to ignore her debts!"

An idea occurred to me. "Claire, there's one more thing you could do. You know my older brother Charlie? The guy whose picture Resolvèd sent you, who jumped up on the stage and sort of came to your rescue at the fair? Well, he's a lawyer and smart as a whip. Plus he wrote that— Well, let's just say he'd help you. You can bet on it."

Claire thought a minute. "Where does this man with the face like a cowboy star live, James? This brother of yours?"

"You know the bridge you came over to get to our place and Resolvèd's? Right there on the riverbank in a little green trailer—"

"You!"

I spun around. Not ten feet away, standing on the far end of the ledge, up to his ankles in the brook, his shotgun crooked over his arm, was Resolvèd Kinneson!

"Down to the house," he said to Claire, and jerked his head in that direction.

She looked at me significantly, as though she'd known all along that this would happen.

"You don't have to go anywhere with him, Claire. Not anywhere."

"I believe it is for the best, James."

"You don't have to go."

Claire just shrugged again and headed off through the second-growth woods toward Resolvèd's.

My cousin remained where he was until she was out of sight. Quite deliberately he shifted the gun so that it was pointed at the ledge between us. "I'm a-going to tell you a thing, young boy," he said. "One thing, just once. Keep away from my housekeeper."

I stared at him and did not reply.

For a moment Resolvèd stared back. Then he turned and sloshed down the burn and blended into the trees.

# 8

I arrived at Charlie's trailer at five o'clock on the dot. He was sitting in his underwear at the kitchen table with the red-and-yellow-patterned linoleum top, thumbing through the July issue of *Argosy*.

Charlie had recently returned from a fishing trip to Canada with Royce St. Onge, and the trailer reeked of mildew, fish scales, overripe live bait, and wet canvas. Besides the usual clutter, the wadded-up uniform parts slung here and there, the empty quart beer bottles, the batting statistics taped on the refrigerator door, and the girlie calendars on the wall, the room was strewn with fishing and camping gear: damp smelly sleeping bags, drying fly lines strung back and forth from one end of the kitchen to the other, greasy frying pans and tin plates and cups, boxes of leftover cans of corned beef hash and baked beans and evaporated milk, and slung over the top of the refrigerator, a rank-smelling two-man pup tent.

"It's Jim Kinneson, the next All-State shortstop to come out of the Common Academy!" Charlie hollered in his great booming voice as I came through the door. "You ready to see the Memphremagog Loggers get whipped within an inch of their worthless lives under the lights tonight?"

I was ready, all right. I'd never seen a night game before, and I'd been looking forward to going on this trip with Charlie and his Outlaws for days. But there was something else I had to discuss with my brother before I could concentrate on baseball.

"Charlie? You know that girl from the fair, Saint Catherine? The one that knew you?"

Charlie covered his head with the magazine. "Your father's filled me in on the situation, buddy. He wasn't overjoyed, to say the least. I never in this world believed that anybody would answer that ad I helped Cousin R write. Question is, what the hell are we going to do with her? Is she still at home?"

Quickly I brought Charlie up to date on the events of the day, how Claire had gone up to Resolvèd's early that morning and met him and Welcome and Ethan Allen, and my encounter with her and Resolvèd at the quarry.

My brother didn't seem particularly distressed by her predicament. "Well, chances are that after two or three days she'll go back to Quebec or wherever she came from, buddy. In the meantime, you and I have got a baseball game to go to."

He rolled up the magazine, went into his batting stance, and hit an imaginary home run. "I intend to go four for four or five for five tonight. Plus I'm going to put one over the centerfield fence into the lake. You'll love it, let's get going."

We met the rest of Charlie's team in the Common and headed up old Route Five toward the little Canadian border city of Memphremagog, on the south end of the big lake of the same name. Memphremagog was Kingdom Common's longtime traditional rival. The two teams were tied for first place in the Northern Vermont Border League, and we had the makings of a convoy tonight. Charlie led the way in his woody. Royce St. Onge and Stub Poulin and I rode with him. The three wild Kittredge brothers from Lord Hollow came next, followed by Pine Benson and Johnny Quinn and several others.

I rode in front between Charlie and Royce. As we bounced along over the heaved macadam with grass growing up in the middle, Royce and Stub teased my brother mercilessly. The story of Claire LaRiviere and how she had come to Kingdom County was all over town by now, and worse yet, it turned out that Stub had been in the Paris Revue tent when Charlie had rescued Claire and she'd called him by name.

"I'd hate to think what your cousin Athena would do to Charlie if she ever got wind of that tent show business, Royce," Stub said.

"She'd divorce him, that's what she'd do," Royce said, opening a beer. "Old Athena don't put up with no two-timers, I'm here to tell you."

Stub was notoriously slow on the uptake. "How can she divorce him, Royce? They ain't even married."

"You explain it, Charlie," Royce said. "You're the lawyer." And he laughed uproariously.

"Crack me open a cold one, Royce," Stub said.

"Who the hell you think I am, anyway, your nigger waiter?" Royce said.

"Speaking of which," Royce said as he opened Stub's beer, "how you coming on getting your buddy the new preacher to play ball for us, Charlie K?"

Charlie shrugged. "He says he can't this summer. He's too busy."

"Poor excuse," Royce said. "You know what they say about fishing. When you're too busy to go fishing, you're too busy. Same's true about playing baseball. High school boys say he's quite a ball player, too. Hit the ball a ton, and a curve ball they couldn't none of them touch."

"This ain't high school ball," Stub said. "In case you hadn't noticed. The day that nigger walks onto the field with us is the day I walk off. I don't want to tell you how to run your business, Charlie, but you and some others in your family is getting the name around these parts of nigger lovers."

"That's right, Stub, you don't want to tell me how to run my business," Charlie said. "So don't."

"Don't get all hot under the collar, now, Charlie," Royce said. "Stub don't mean nothing by all that. Hell, until Andrews hit town I doubt Stub'd ever even seen a colored fella. Did you, Stub?"

"I seen a few," Stub said. "Enough to know I don't like 'em."

"Why's that, Stub?" Charlie said.

"Well, for one thing, you can't trust them around your women.

Christ, once a woman's been with one, she don't want nothing more to do with a white man."

"To put it politely, Stub, that's bullshit."

"I don't know," Royce said. "I ain't saying what Stub says is true in all cases, Charlie, but did you ever see one in the shower? I did once. I think there might be something to it. Another thing. I don't know if I should be saying this in front of young Jim here, but when I was over across in France I went with a colored woman once, and hoo boy, was she something!"

"So why would a Negro man want to go with a white woman, then?" Charlie said.

"They do, though," Stub said. "They all do."

Charlie laughed. "You guys are so ignorant on this subject you don't know how ignorant you are. But what if a Negro man did want to go out with a white woman? So Christly what?"

"You want old Athena dating Andrews, do you?" Stub said.

"I don't want old Athena dating anybody except me, but I'll tell you something right now. If and when the Reverend Walter Andrews ever decides to play for this team, he's going to—and that's the beginning and the end of it."

The Memphremagog baseball field was over on the northeast side of town, across the bay and behind the big paper mill where most of the Loggers team worked during the day. There was a night shift at the factory, and you could find the factory by following your nose; the stench was terrific.

The field was a poor excuse for a ball diamond, with a gravelly infield and a few clumps of brown grass here and there in the cindery outfield, where the local high school team played soccer in the fall. I sat on the third base line behind the Outlaws' dugout. The Loggers drifted onto the field and took batting practice and then infield. Afterwards the Outlaws took batting practice, and when Charlie came up he pounded one ball after another deep over the outfield fence. The last ball Charlie hit knocked out a light on the center field light pole, which the Memphremagog manager tried to get him to pay for. Charlie laughed and some sharp words were exchanged, much to the amusement of the rest of the Outlaws.

In the first inning, Charlie hit a home run so far over the fence it landed in the bay. As he trotted around third, he winked at me, on my feet and clapping like crazy.

In the Loggers' half of the inning, my brother threw out two base runners with perfect pegs. One tried to steal second and Stub Poulin didn't move his glove three inches to slap on the tag. Charlie caught the other runner napping off first base and nailed him with a bullet.

Stub led off in the third inning with a single. Big Harlan Kittredge was up next, and the Loggers' pitcher reared back and threw the first pitch straight at Harlan's head. Batting helmets were unknown in those days, and Harlan got down in the dirt just in time. But when it happened again on the very next pitch, Big Harlan charged the mound so fast he was halfway there before I realized what he was doing. I think he got at least one good lick in, because the next thing I knew the pitcher was sitting on the pitching rubber and holding his glove over his head. But then the Memphremagog catcher ran out and gave Harlan a rabbit punch in the back of the neck, and all hell broke loose as both benches cleared, and the umpire called the game on the spot.

"Can I ask you something, Charlie?" I said an hour later, after we'd dropped Stub and Royce off in the Common. "Remember what you said to Dad back on Easter Sunday? That there wasn't that much prejudice in Kingdom County? What about Stub, what he said about not playing for the Outlaws anymore if Reverend Andrews played? Isn't he prejudiced?"

"You bet he is, buddy. So's Bumper Stevens, so's Frenchy LaMott, so's that flaming asshole Mason White."

"Well, old Mason did tell me that some of the nicest folks he ever met were colored people."

"Bull. Nine out of ten bigots will tell you the same thing."

"How about Royce? He doesn't seem to dislike Reverend Andrews, but what about that business about seeing Negroes in the shower and all?"

"That's just ignorance on Royce's part. Which of course defines all prejudice. Ignorance and fear of what's strange and different."

I shook my head. "I guess I just don't understand. Stub's prejudiced, Bumper and Mason are prejudiced, Frenchy's prejudiced, even Royce is prejudiced. They can't all be exceptions to the rule, can they? I'm not trying to start an argument, Charlie, but wouldn't you say Dad's right, that there's as much prejudice here as anywhere else?"

"Look, Jimmy, prejudice exists in Kingdom County the same as it does everywhere else, including Dartmouth College and Harvard Law School. And I have to admit that I've been surprised by the extent of it here, and by its casualness. I've heard all those mindless slurs for as long as I can remember; but truth to tell, I never paid much attention to them until recently. It's funny, but you never really see your hometown all that clearly until you go away and come back."

"So how come you hang around with these guys, then, Charlie?"

"Not hanging around with 'em isn't any solution. That would be prejudiced on my part. I don't have to agree with them to be friends with them, and I don't have to give up my friendship with them to be friends with Walt Andrews. Understand?"

I wasn't at all sure that I did, but I didn't say so. Another question had been bothering me. "So just how much prejudice is there up in the Kingdom, do you suppose?"

Charlie frowned. "Maybe it's time we asked ourselves that question."

"But what's the answer?"

For once my brother seemed to be stymied. "I don't know," he said seriously. "Time will tell, I guess."

"Oh, no. Oh, *no*. There's trouble ahead at the pass!"

Every light was on inside Charlie's trailer, and in the bright headlights of the woody, Claire LaRiviere was sitting in her dress of many colors in the dooryard on an enormous pile of bedding and chairs and clothes, tents and sleeping bags, fishing and hunting gear, beer bottles and broken china, and magazines and books. Off to the side sat Judge Allen's black Lincoln Continental.

Charlie didn't even bother to shut off his headlights before leaping out of the woody.

"WHAT IN THE HELL—"

Claire scrambled down off the pile and rushed headlong into my brother's arms. "Monsieur Kin'son!" she yelped. "Oh, Monsieur Kin'son, I am so glad you arrive at last. A crazy woman is destroy your house!"

At that exact moment a kitchen chair flew through the trailer's screen door. It was followed immediately by Athena Allen, dressed in the sheerest and briefest lavender-colored nightgown. In her arms was a stack of outdoor and girlie magazines, which she flung in Charlie's direction.

"Athena!" Charlie yelled. "What's going—"

Athena vanished inside the trailer again. Claire gave another shriek and clung to Charlie's neck like a frightened puppet. He couldn't shake her off to save his life. Athena reappeared, staggering under the weight of a cardboard box containing Charlie's country and western albums, which she slammed down on top of the pile of household furnishings.

Athena smiled at my brother, who was still trying to disengage himself from Claire. "Hello, Charlie," she said. "How'd you guys do tonight? Did you win?"

Athena did not appear to be especially upset. She didn't raise her voice at all, but went briskly back inside, reemerging seconds later with Charlie's two-foot-high MVP trophy from last winter's basketball play-offs, which she casually hurled over the top of the trailer and out into the dark river.

"Monsieur Kin'son wants a cute little housekeeper, Jimmy, so we'll give him one," my ex-grammar teacher said with another sweet smile. She was quite calm, quite serene as she stepped back inside, administering en route a kick to the screen door and knocking it completely off its hinges into the bull thistles beside the stoop.

Charlie finally managed to disentangle Claire's arms from around his neck and was holding her off by the wrists when Athena next appeared in the trailer doorway. This time she was carrying a volume of considerable size and weight. I realized with horror that it was Charlie's treasured scrapbook chronicling his athletic accomplishments from his most recent town team exploits all the way back through his glory years at Dartmouth to his heyday as a three-sport star at the Academy.

"KINGDOM COMMON TAKES THIRD CONSECUTIVE STATE HARDBALL TITLE: KINNESON WALLOPS WINNING HOME RUN," Athena read in her most pleasant school-marm style, and hurled the scrapbook galley west.

Precious, irreplaceable clippings and photographs dating back more than a decade rained down all over the dooryard. Claire shrieked.

"Jim, get this girl the hell out of here," Charlie roared. "Take her home. Take her anyplace—but *get her out of here.*"

I grabbed Claire's hand and we took off together, out of the dooryard and back down the county road toward the red iron bridge. The last thing I heard from the trailer was shattering glass and then Athena's voice, quite calm and reasonable, saying, ". . . and two leftover pork chops in a number-ten frying pan, fried crisp just the way Monsieur Kin'son prefers them. We're through, you two-timing son-of-a-bitch!"

When the misunderstanding was finally straightened out, to the degree that it ever was straightened out that summer, this is what we discovered had happened. While Charlie and I were in Memphremagog Claire had run into an unexpected problem at Resolvèd's, which she explained to me after we sought temporary refuge under the red iron bridge downriver from Charlie's trailer.

Claire said that soon after supper Resolvèd had actually proposed to her. When she recovered from her astonishment and told him that marriage was definitely out of the question for her, citing her plan to go to Hollywood and try for a part in the movies, he had flown into a towering rage.

"You are familiar with the great red he-chicken, James?"

"Ethan Allen? Sure."

"Very well. As you know, this Ethan dwells in the house with the Resolvèd and the brother. Tonight when the Resolvèd becomes angry with me because I will not agree to marry him, he gets out his shotgun, Betsy, and tells me he will show me something very entertaining. He goes out and a moment later he returns. Under his arm he is holding a wild brown bird. I have heard my father's mother from the Laurentian Mountains call this bird 'chicken of the woods.' I do not know what you call it here in Ver-mont."

"A partridge," I said.

"Yes? Well, I am thinking he will want me to kill this part-ridge and cook it. Fine, I am willing. But no, he closes the door of the room. He shows the part-ridge to the great red he-chicken, Ethan, on the table. Then he releases her and she begins to fly like mad with the red chicken pursuing. All the while the brother is reading his flying-platter magazine and paying no attention.

"I duck! The part-ridge, she is hit the wall, the roof, the window. Once she knocks off the reading brother's black hat. Twice the he-chicken catches her. Both times she escapes. Blood! There is blood over everything.

"At last I can endure no more. I run to the door and open it. The brown bird flies for the opening. BANG! Before I know it, the Resolvèd has shoot the poor bird dead. Next he points his Betsy at me. His mouth is going, he is very angry, but I have no idea what he is saying because my ears are singing so."

Claire paused. "This is when I make up my mind, James."

"You mean to leave?"

She shook her head. "No. This is when I make up my mind that the farm of the Resolvèd does not much resemble the farm of Ma and Pa Kettle."

"You could safely say so," I said. "What happened next?"

"The Resolvèd continues to drink until his friend Old Duke is gone. Then he begins to clean Betsy again, and look at me, sideways from under his cap and say by and by we will see who is boss of his house and who opens doors without his consent and who does not. But at last he goes to sleep with his head in a dish of chicken feed on the table.

"As soon as the Resolvèd is sleeping, the brother gets five dollars out of his purse and hands it to me and tells me to go home to Canady. He says be sure to write him a letter if I see any flying platters or green mens. Very good! I take the money and thank him and walk here to the village, already with my mind made up to work as the housekeeper of your brother, the true Monsieur Kin'son of the picture. After all, he has help me once, perhaps he will help again. And I do not think the Resolvèd will dare harm me there."

Arriving at the trailer about nine o'clock and finding the place dark and empty, Claire had gone inside and decided to make herself immediately useful, while awaiting my brother's return, by cleaning up the kitchen.

In the meantime, as I would learn later, Athena Allen was waiting up at home for her father the judge, who had been off with my father on an all-day fishing trip to the Upper Connecticut River. Judge Allen arrived around nine and remarked that when he and Dad had passed Charlie's trailer, the kitchen light had been on but Charlie's woody was gone. This gave Athena an inspiration.

After the trout had been put away and the judge had drunk his bourbon nightcap and gone to bed, Athena slipped into the lavender baby-doll nightie Charlie had bought her in Montreal a year ago, threw the judge's red wool hunting jacket over her shoulders, and drove over to Charlie's trailer in her father's Continental, intending to treat my brother to an intimate little two-person surprise party when he returned from his ballgame.

When she arrived, she discovered to her amazement a good-looking young woman washing my brother's breakfast dishes. Apparently Claire was equally surprised by the sight of a beautiful woman whom she had never laid eyes on before, clad only in the filmiest and most provocative nightwear, standing open-mouthed in the trailer door.

"Who are you?" they'd said simultaneously.

Athena never did identify herself. But finally Claire had said, "I am Claire LaRiviere. Monsieur Kin'son's new housekeeper. From Quebec City, in Canada."

Athena nodded slowly. After a pretty long pause, she said, "So you're the young woman from the fair?"

Claire had said yes and had begun to try to explain everything, but by then Athena had started her acts of destruction. She was in the first flush of her outrage, not hurrying, but smiling and saying "I see" and hurling clothes and fishing gear and guns and magazines out the door. Working unhurriedly and thoroughly, telling Claire to sit down and take a break while at the same time, picking up the nearest kitchen chair and tossing it through the screen door. Telling Claire if she wanted to be useful she could warm up the two leftover pork chops in the pan on the stove, only to be sure to get them crisp. And all the time Claire was wanting to explain but she was too frightened to think of the English words. Finally Athena tried to pick up Charlie's squat old refrigerator but she couldn't budge it, so she opened it up and began methodically throwing beer and meat and vegetables and eggs and other perishables out the door. At this point Claire fled to the dooryard because she'd made up her mind that the woman in the lavender lace nightie was as crazy as Resolvèd.

It took me a while, but eventually I managed to explain to Claire that Athena Allen wasn't crazy, only jealous over Charlie. She had undoubtedly gotten the wrong impression when she'd walked into the trailer and discovered a pretty girl who announced out of the blue that she was Charlie's new housekeeper.

"Oh!" Claire said, putting her hand to her mouth. "This woman, this Athena. She and your brother, they are lovers?"

"You could say that," I said, thinking of the night I'd stayed over at Charlie's after my fight with Frenchy. "Some of the time, anyway."

"Then I understand. The Athena is very passionate, very jealous!

Oh, James! I believe I am fortunate she does not take a knife and slit my throat. You did not inform me your brother had a lover! Now surely I must leave Vermont. I would rather run the risk of meeting the Resolvèd again than this fierce lover of your brother's. Did you see her eyes? Never have I seen such a fine anger. Will she kill him now?"

I laughed and told Claire not to worry, that Charlie and Athena had had fights before, plenty of them, and everything could be explained. In the meantime, we desperately needed to find somewhere for her to stay. Once again I suggested my folks' place. But she wouldn't hear of it.

"Look, Claire, if you won't stay with us, why not stay with—" With whom? Who would help this engaging girl I had half-fallen in love with myself?

Suddenly I had an inspiration. Ministers were supposed to help people. And Reverend Andrews had lots of room at the parsonage. What's more, he needed a housekeeper, if only to get Hefty Hefner off his back. And when and if Resolvèd did find out where Claire was, he wouldn't dare go near the parsonage after what Reverend Andrews had done to Bumper Stevens on the day of the cockfight. Also, I could see her there as often as I wanted.

It seemed like the perfect solution.

"I've got it!" I said excitedly. "There's this minister in the village. He's really nice, and his son's my best friend. I'm about positive you can stay there."

Claire thought for a moment. Then she reached out and grabbed my hand and squeezed it. "Good! The matter is settled. You will tell me how to get there."

"I'll do better than that, Claire. I'll take you there myself."

I was quite sure that Resolvèd would never harm Claire when he was sober, but it occurred to me that even now my outlaw cousin might be out hunting for her with his bosom friends and fellow troublemakers Old Duke and Betsy. Moreover, as we approached the village I began to have misgivings about my proposal. Despite my earlier assurances to Claire, I didn't really know Reverend Andrews well enough to be sure he'd take her in.

As we started up the knoll on the east end of town, another doubt crossed my mind. "Claire? There's something I forgot to tell you. The minister we're going to see? He's a Negro."

"A Negro? You mean a colored man?"

"Yes. Like I said, he's a really nice man. Everybody likes him a lot. Well, the cattle auctioneer doesn't, but he doesn't count, he's just an old drunk. Everybody else does. Nobody even thinks of him as being a Negro, actually. I just wanted you to know ahead of time so you wouldn't be surprised."

"I do not care about that, James. I see many black mens, black womens, too, in Quebec. Just so I can remain there a little."

We walked faster. Moving lights appeared, illuminating the mist ahead like a will-o'-the-wisp. We dodged into the ditch and the local milk truck rumbled by. Sheepishly, my heart still pounding, I helped Claire back onto the shoulder.

At the top of the knoll, across the road from the parsonage, Elijah Kinneson's cottage squatted darkly in the fog. For all I knew the sour old sexton might be out navigating around in the nearby cemetery. It was a well-known fact, at least to us local boys, that my weird cousin often went walking about the village and surrounding countryside alone at night, for heaven knew what strange, private purposes.

I wasn't surprised to see a light in Reverend Andrews' study window. I knew that the minister habitually stayed up until all hours reading or writing his sermons or doing research for the upcoming Old Home Day celebration. Nathan's room above the study was dark.

"This is the house," I whispered when we reached the edge of the yard. "The minister's still up. You wait here and I'll go ask."

"No, James. You should not be involved in this. I will go alone."

Claire squeezed my hand hard and headed up toward the house. I ran along the broken-down fence and slipped in behind an old topless maple tree at the corner of the lot, where I could hide and watch what happened.

Claire walked up the steps and crossed the rickety porch to the door. There she hesitated, a pale form, just visible, looking as evanescent as the ghost that was rumored to parade there once a year. I thought she waved to me once. At least I saw a faint blur that might have been a wave. Then she knocked softly, three times.

After a few seconds the porch light came on and the door opened.

"Hello! What have we here?" Reverend Andrews said.

"You are the preacher?"

Already Claire's voice sounded different, interrogatory and uncertain again, pitched higher than when she talked to me.

"Yes, I'm a minister," I heard Reverend Andrews say.

"I am—Claire? Claire LaRiviere?"

After a moment's hesitation, Reverend Andrews said in a surprised tone of sudden recognition, "Oh! You're the Canadian girl who's been staying out in that shack with Charles Kinneson's relatives. Well, well. What on earth are you doing out at this time of night, Claire? Are you in some sort of difficulty?"

Claire murmured something I didn't catch, and then to my great relief the minister asked her in, and the porch light went off. At the same time, I thought I heard a noise across the street at Elijah's cottage; but when I looked over his place was as dark as ever.

To avoid having to pass near Charlie's trailer again—despite my reassurances to Claire, the fight between my brother and Athena had disconcerted me terribly—I decided to go home by way of the village and the covered bridge. As usual late at night, the deserted Common looked like a totally different spot from the bustling daytime hub of activity for the county. The hotel and commission sales barn were totally dark. The courthouse and Academy were dark. Except for the single nightlight reflected in the *Monitor*'s window, the entire brick business block was dark.

As I approached the covered bridge, I was tempted to keep right on going and cross to the gool on the B and M trestle. But I didn't relish the idea of feeling my way over the ties high above the river in the dark, so, taking a deep breath, I started through the pitch-black portal at a fast walk.

Miraculously, I made it to the other side of the bridge intact. The mist was much thicker now. It clung wetly to my face and hands and cut visibility down to almost nothing. I had to feel for the road with my feet, which suddenly went completely out from under me. I was overpowered by the odor of Old Duke wine as I reached into the darkness to break my fall, clutching first a boot and then the cold steel of a gun barrel.

I had tripped over Resolvèd Kinneson, sprawled dead drunk by the side of the road with his beloved Betsy cradled in his arms.

# 9

"Just now she's up in Nathan's room, regaling him with the tale of her odyssey to Vermont," Reverend Andrews said with one of his wry chuckles. "She's already told me the saga half a dozen times in the past couple of weeks. It puts me in mind of a Frenchified version of *The Perils of Pauline*."

It was early evening, mid-July. The minister and my father were sitting in two kitchen chairs Reverend Andrews had brought onto the veranda for summer porch furniture, looking out through the great tangled bittersweet vine that ran from railing to roof. I sprawled gloomily on the porch steps.

For the past couple of weeks, since Claire had moved in with the Andrewses, Nathan had been more aloof than ever. I didn't know whether he blamed me for getting him entangled in the raid at the

Paris Revue tent or was still upset over the episode with Frenchy at the trestle; but for days on end he'd been denned up inside the parsonage, doing what I had no idea. Once or twice we'd gone over to the ball field together and played Twenty-seven Outs, an ingenious and endlessly fascinating game of Nat's devising in which we batted, pitched, and fielded our way through a simulated nine-inning game between my Red Sox and his team, the Brooklyn Dodgers; but for the most part he seemed not to want to hang around with a kid three years younger than he was, or with any other kid for that matter. The fact is that Nat Andrews simply wasn't interested in most of my rural pursuits and had been more or less miserable since the day he arrived in Kingdom County. I'd sensed his dissatisfaction from the minute I first laid eyes on him at the Ridge Runner Diner, and nothing had happened to change his outlook since then.

Claire, on the other hand, was always happy to see me; but she was busy with her new "housekeeping" duties at the parsonage, and had little time on her hands.

Across the street from the parsonage, Elijah Kinneson was out on his porch working on his single hobby, a four-foot peeled and polished pine log on sawhorses, which for as long as I could recall he had been carving into a wooden chain with no beginning and no end. He called this dizzying oddity his "Endless Maze of the Kingdom," and by the time I was thirteen it was already many hundreds of links long and one of my father's "Seven Man-made and Natural Wonders of the Kingdom"—the others being Pliny Templeton's *Ecclesiastical History*, the Dog Cart Man's pictograph on the cliff above the disused quarry of the gypsies who once came annually to Kingdom County, the leaping brook trout on the side of our burn, and Elijah, Resolvèd, and Welcome themselves—though as nearly as I could see, Elijah's Endless Maze served absolutely no purpose at all. Like my weird cousin himself, it was a conundrum to me.

Carving away with his long shiny knife, Elijah didn't ever seem to glance over at us. But I had no doubt that my cousin had seen every move Dad and I had made since we'd arrived at the parsonage fifteen minutes ago.

Reverend Andrews shook his head. "That bloke across the street's been over twice in the last couple of days to tell me that I ought to send the LaRiviere waif packing. The second time was this afternoon, and I all but sent *him* packing.

"At least I don't have to worry about his brother the outlaw for a while," Reverend Andrews added. "That's a relief."

I laughed and looked at my father, who actually smiled. After coming across Resolvèd passed out on the gool the night Claire had gone to stay at the minister's, I'd run right past our house and back across the red iron bridge to Charlie's trailer to report my discovery; Athena was long gone by the time I arrived, but far from being dejected by the outcome of her visit, my irrepressible brother had told me to hop into his woody if I wanted to see something new and wonderful happen. Charlie then proceeded to play what may well have been the crowning practical joke of his career. We'd driven back out to the gool, geehawed my cousin's insensible carcass into the woody, and taken it straight to Painless Doc Harrison's house on Anderson Hill. There Charlie had recruited the doctor, a famous practical joker in his own right, to put Resolvèd out of commission for several weeks by clapping my cousin's entire left leg into a cast. When Resolvèd came to, Painless solemnly told him that he'd fallen off a culvert and broken his leg in four places, and if he didn't lie still in bed for a solid month he'd never walk again.

"Elijah's not the only busybody who's been hectoring me about the girl," Reverend Andrews was saying to my father. "The reason I asked you to stop by this evening is that I'm under a considerable amount of pressure to ship her out. Julia Hefner dropped by this afternoon and read me a regular lecture on the matter. She began by telling me that it's been bruited about town that Claire was originally with those strip shows at the fair and that she just spelled trouble. 'To put it plainly, Reverend,' she said, 'speaking on behalf of some concerned ladies of the church, we'd very much like you to find another place for her immediately.' "

My father snorted. "That's Julia for you all over again. She and I went to school together. There's no one anywhere who's better at finding a pious reason to do a mean thing than that old biddy. What does she want you to do, kick the poor kid out in the street?"

"Well, I probably shouldn't have done this, but having just heard the same line from our friend the sexton earlier in the day, I was pretty vexed. So I said, fine, which of the concerned ladies of the church would be willing to put Claire up for a few days?"

"That's calling the old bat's bluff. What did she say to that?"

"She asked if I couldn't just put the girl on a bus back to Canada or wherever. I told her I supposed I could. Don't think the thought hasn't crossed my mind more than once. But I can't quite bring myself to do that. Claire doesn't want to go back to Canada, and as I understand it, for very good reasons.

"I told Julia as tactfully as I could that I was at least as uncomfortable about the situation as anyone in town, but I couldn't just wash my hands of the girl. I resisted the temptation to cite the story of Jesus and the fallen woman about to be stoned, by the by. I don't suppose Julia would approve of how He handled that, either. I did make bold to tell her that I didn't for a minute believe that the ladies of the church would want a minister who turned his back on this type of responsibility, though."

"Sure they would," Dad said. "Julia may or may not have been officially representing the ladies of the church; Ruth hasn't mentioned any such meeting to me and I tend to doubt it ever took place. But the sad fact is that the vast majority of the entire congregation would agree with her."

"Perhaps so. Because the next thing she said was that the church ladies believed my first responsibility was to my own congregation. 'So do I,' I said. 'You let me know when I begin to neglect them. In the meantime, I'll do all I can to find an appropriate alternative for the LaRiviere girl. That's the best I can do.' "

"Good for you," Dad said. "I'm glad that at last we've got a minister who isn't afraid to stand up to that old crow. I told you back last spring that she ate preachers for breakfast, and I wasn't fooling. Give her as good as you get; it's the only way to deal with her. Just be sure to cover your flank, because she won't forget this. In the meantime I'm going to help you do whatever's necessary to find a proper home for that girl."

Reverend Andrews laughed. "That reminds me. Before Julia left she harangued me for a good ten minutes about getting a bona fide housekeeper and threatened to come in afternoons herself to do our wash and straighten up if I don't. It's not that bad an idea, you know, hiring a housekeeper. Claire LaRiviere won't be here forever. At least I hope she won't. I can't begin to do all the cooking and washing and cleaning myself and still do my job, and it's unfair to Nat not to have a better home situation. You wouldn't know of a good reliable woman I could hire three or four days a week?"

"I'll ask Ruth. Anything to spare you Julia's blandishments."

Reverend Andrews laughed. "Small towns! I could live in one for fifty years and never cease to be amazed."

My father stood up. "Let's go for a stroll in the cemetery, Reverend. Want to come, James?"

It was a lovely summer evening, cool and still and peaceful, and in the reassuring company of my father and Reverend Andrews, I didn't mind walking through the dusky graveyard in the least. The air was sweet with the scent of new-cut grass and the resinous odor of cedars. As we walked along the narrow gravel paths, my father talked to us about small towns.

"I'll concede that a small town can be as nosy and sometimes as downright cruel as any place on the face of the earth, Walter. You know Ring Lardner's story 'Haircut'? Read it and weep. But what it all boils down to is this. Small towns can be extremely sympathetic, in a rough-hewn sort of way—if you *belong*—but the Lord help strangers who wander in needing help, from the hobo out on the B and M tracks who freezes his foot in the wintertime and needs emergency medical attention to the residents of the next town down the line."

We had arrived at Pliny Templeton's tall pink granite monument.

"Speaking of outsiders," Reverend Andrews said, "I'd like to ask you a question or two about this old fellow. I've been poring over that marvelous *Ecclesiastical History* of his nearly every night since I borrowed it. The more I read, the more intriguing he and your Kingdom both seem. But he doesn't seem to write much about himself in his book. Where did he hail from originally? I'd like to do some sort of skit on him at the sesquicentennial celebration."

"Tell the story, Dad! Tell the story about Pliny Templeton and Mad Charlie and Satan Smithfield!"

"Mad Charlie! Satan Smithfield!" Reverend Andrews laughed. "They sound like characters straight from Dickens!"

"Pliny Templeton grew up on a Georgia plantation," Dad began, leaning against the soaring monument of the subject of his story. "He was a genius, I suppose, or the very next thing to one. So far as I know he was a total autodidact, who at thirteen or fourteen had mastered both Greek and Latin and read widely in classical literature and history and the natural sciences and mathematics. My grandfather told my father that Pliny could recite whole skeins from Shakespeare, as well as Virgil and Cicero and Sophocles and Aeschylus. By the time he was sixteen Pliny was tutoring white children from plantations for twenty miles around."

"How under the sun did such a fellow ever land in Kingdom County?"

"Now we're getting to the story. Despite his favored status on the plantation, Pliny's desire for freedom was an overriding passion. He ran away and was caught and fetched back five different times before he was twenty years old. Once he got all the way to Pennsylvania before they nabbed him. Evidently the plantation owner did everything possible to keep him happy short of emancipating him. But Pliny didn't care about being happy; all he wanted was to be free. So finally the owner lost patience and told him that the next time he went on the lam, he intended to put Satan Smithfield on his trail and wash his hands of him entirely.

"Well, Reverend, this Smithfield was the bane of runaway slaves all over the Deep South. Slave owners who wanted to make an example of inveterate runaways would hire Smithfield to track them down. But he didn't just find slaves and return them. He hunted them like animals and murdered them, as examples. His motto was that for the right price he'd harry a runaway back to Africa and exterminate him there. He was so feared by Negroes and so detested by Underground Railroad organizers that they'd conferred the sobriquet 'Satan' upon him, which he was said to be proud of. And it was well deserved. Smithfield was reported to have murdered more than one hundred fugitive Negroes in cities as distant as Boston and Montreal. The Underground had put a price on his head, but he had his own network of paid spies and informers and nobody could catch him.

"Now my grandfather Charlie—Mad Charlie—was a close friend and later a son-in-law of the abolishionist John Brown. At the time, Brown lived just a hundred miles or so from here, over in upstate New York's Adirondack Mountains. Together they set up the eastern-Vermont-to-Montreal leg of the Underground. My cousins' present-day house on the ridge above our place was the final stopover on that route before Canada. Hundreds of fugitive slaves spent a day or two in that cellar before crossing the border. Anyway, Brown and my grandfather knew all about Satan Smithfield. They had put a price on his head—quietly, of course—but it seems that this maniac was a master of disguises and accents, and no one knew exactly what he looked like in his own incarnation. So Mad Charlie set a trap to kill the slave killer. And he used young Pliny Templeton as bait.

"First, Charlie sent word to Pliny urging him to run away again. This was in 1860, the year after John Brown was hanged for his part in the raid on Harper's Ferry, which my grandfather was in on too, though he was lucky enough to get away.

"Anyway, Pliny split the coop. True to his word, the plantation owner contacted Smithfield and the hunt was on. Pliny had been told to avoid most of the traditional Underground stations, and leave only enough clues for Smithfield to suspect that he was headed here, to Kingdom County. In fact, my grandfather had arranged for Pliny to take the eastern route up Lake Champlain toward Brown's old homestead in the mountains of northern New York, where the plan was for Pliny to lie low until my grandfather came for him."

As he continued his story, my father walked slowly from Pliny's monument toward the paupers' section under the cedars.

"I'm going to jump ahead, now," Dad said. "Early one morning in the fall of 1860, while Pliny was still working his way north, a dour-looking Scotsman named Reverend Cluney MacDougal got off a northbound train in Kingdom Common and took a room at the hotel. Within a day or two word had spread that MacDougal was a missionary recently back from the Belgian Congo, with a magic lantern show depicting his work and travels. Of course there was talk, speculation that he might somehow be allied with my grandfather, who had a wide and curious assortment of acquaintances. But if he knew Mad Charlie, who at the time was across the border in Canada on special business related to Smithfield, MacDougal didn't let on. In the meantime, the good reverend was invited to display his magic lantern pictures in church the following Sunday afternoon, which he did, to a good-sized and enthusiastic crowd.

"Midway through the show, there was a terrific clatter outside. The front door burst open and my grandfather Charlie charged inside on his Morgan mare and rode straight down the central aisle to the pulpit.

" 'Be you Cluney MacDougal?' he roared out to the missionary without dismounting or identifying himself.

" 'Aye,' said the man. 'No other.'

"And to the utter astonishment and horror of the assembled congregation, MacDougal produced a gun from under his clergyman's frock coat. But even as he was cocking it, my grandfather pulled out the

United States Army government-issue horse pistol he'd confiscated in the raid on Harper's Ferry the previous year and shot the man point-blank in the heart. Then before anyone could stop him, he seized the dead man, threw him across his horse, and galloped out of the church and across the common to the courthouse, where the twelve Negro witnesses he'd brought into the Kingdom the night before from Canada and hidden in the cellar of the house in the gore were waiting in the jury box.

"No doubt the twelve Negroes were as terrified as the rest of the villagers; but my grandfather propped MacDougal's corpse at the defense table and asked each witness in turn to identify it—which they promptly all did. Satan Smithfield, the man who had slaughtered their relatives and fellow fugitives in cold blood for the past twenty years, was finally brought to justice.

"The whole proceeding took less than ten minutes. As soon as it was over my grandfather hauled the body unceremoniously back downstairs and over to the cemetery, where he buried it himself—right here."

Dad pointed to a small worn wooden marker at our feet. There was just enough light left to read the epitaph Mad Charlie had carved on it:

*Here lies Satan Smithfield*
*For whom no bell will knell.*
*His cursed remains beneath your feet*
*His soul in deepest Hell.*

"My Lord!" Reverend Andrews exclaimed. "This Reverend MacDougal was actually Smithfield?"

"You bet he was," Dad said. "Pliny Templeton arrived here a week later. With my grandfather's help he attended Middlebury College, then returned to the Common and built the Academy and stayed on and taught here for forty years."

"I'm beginning to understand why your grandfather was called Mad Charlie," Reverend Andrews said. "But at least Pliny's story had a happy ending."

"No."

"No?"

"No. At the end, there was a schism between Pliny and my grandfather. A schism that has a direct bearing on some of the trouble in the church that's lingered on to this day."

"Schism is a strong word, Charles. What was Pliny's part in this?"

"Well, from the days of Charles I, our place of worship was a Reformed Presbyterian Church. After Pliny built the Academy, the school was operated under the church's auspices as a private Presbyterian institution, with the same board of trustees as the church itself. As you know, in those days Reformed Presbyterians disavowed all worldly authority, including that of the United States government. But as the decades went by and Pliny continued to teach in the school, and to write and lecture, he drifted away from strict RP dogma. He still considered himself a Presbyterian. But he made it known that he saw no harm in taking an oath to serve in the military or testify in court or hold public office. He served several terms in the Vermont State Legislature himself, and with distinction. As he put it, he saw no contradiction between being a good Presbyterian and being a good citizen. Naturally, he didn't condone drinking or gambling, but he eventually went so far as to propose introducing dancing lessons and a piano at the Academy, to which my grandfather and the other RPs strenuously objected.

"Finally, in 1900, when Pliny and my grandfather were both old men, Pliny declared himself a United Presbyterian and tried to disaffiliate the Academy from the church, partly in order to get that piano into his school. A number of the trustees supported him. An equal number didn't. They met to vote in closed session and Pliny cast the decisive ballot to break from the church. Afterwards, my grandfather came over to the parsonage and there was a terrible row between the two old friends. The upshot of it was that poor Pliny Templeton shot himself that very evening, after which my grandfather went totally insane and spent the last two years of his life in the state lunatic asylum at Waterbury."

"Good heavens!" Reverend Andrews said. "I had no idea. What about his family? Pliny's, I mean. Whatever became of them?"

"He never had one, or a wife either. My grandfather, though, was like a brother to him. Which, I suppose, explains his despair when the old man repudiated him at the end."

Reverend Andrews shook his head. He got out one of his patented

Luckies, lit it, and looked off across the village—as peaceful-looking in the July twilight as a Currier and Ives lithograph. He smoked quietly for a moment. "So your grandfather just cut himself off completely from his lifelong friend, whom he'd brought up out of slavery and had formally educated and established as headmaster? Just like that? Over a piano? A minor point of doctrine?"

"Nobody thought it was a minor point of doctrine at the time, Walter. Those were life-and-death issues, the dancing and the piano, with the integrity of Reformed Presbyterianism and the secession of the Academy at stake. The fact is that to this day a number of older mossbacks in the church, beginning with your esteemed sexton and my linotype operator, Elijah Kinneson, still consider themselves to be Reformed Presbyterians."

Reverend Andrews took a long drag on his cigarette, and exhaled the smoke slowly. "So what do you think we need to bring everybody together, Charles?"

"A miracle," my father said grimly. "You've got your work cut out for you, Reverend. Good luck with the Old Home Day. It's a start, at least."

On the way back to the parsonage through the twilit cemetery, Reverend Andrews paused at the Kinneson family plot. He looked around at the dim outlines of the gravestones: Charles I's, Charles' son James, and my great-grandfather Charlie's flanked by the smaller stones of my great-grandmother, John Brown's daughter, and my great-step-grandmother.

"Blood ties!" Reverend Andrews said. "Who's related to whom. That's such an interesting part of the history of small towns. Just one more question, Charles. How on earth are those cousins of yours, Elijah, Resolvèd, and Welcome, related to the rest of your clan?"

My father walked over to Mad Charlie's plot and touched the stone of my great-stepgrandmother. "When he was well on into his seventies, my grandfather married a gypsy girl after his first wife died. This is her stone. Elijah, Resolvèd, and Welcome were her sons. That's yet another story, Reverend. Read the chapter in Pliny's *History* called 'Strangers in the Kingdom.' It's all there—and Pliny himself does a much better job with that tale than I could."

■ ■ ■

From Pliny Templeton's *Ecclesiastical, Natural, Social, and Political History of Kingdom County*, the chapter "Strangers in the Kingdom":

"The gypsies are coming! The gypsies are coming!"

Often and often over the years have I heard this exclamation, half-thrilled, half-frightened, echoing across white picket fences from dooryard to dooryard, over the elm-strewn common and even up and down the hallways and through the classrooms of my academy. No matter then the importance of the task at hand or the lesson under consideration! The sternest headmaster could hardly in good conscience deny young scholars the pleasure of crowding to the windows to witness the gypsies' wild tintinnabulation as they swirled into the town like so many bright autumn leaves, beating on pots and pans and hawking mirrors and glass jewelry, their under-fed and half-tamed nags tied to gaily painted carts, on their way to their traditional tenting ground in Charles Kinneson's meadow on Kingdom gool. There they pitched three tents, one green, one blue, one red, and the women conducted a lively week-long bartering-fair (besides certain racier nighttime entertainments connected with the Romany tribe since time immemorial), while on high in the quarry in Kingdom Gore the men cut out and carved fine pink "Scotch" granite tombstones for Kingdom residents who had died over the past twelve months.

Now it came to pass not many years ago, on an unusually warm evening for September in the Kingdom, in high fall foliage time when the hills were solid banks of reds and oranges and yellows, the gypsies and certain men from the village convened on the east end of the gool by the new iron bridge. There the head gypsy, a vigorous gray-headed man in his late middle years, had by prearrangement with the townsmen agreed to race one of his wild plugs against the pride of Kingdom horseflesh: a full-blooded Morgan stallion named Capering Cy, owned by Captain Jehoshophat Allen. After viewing Capering Cy, the gypsy chieftain gave a harsh laugh and told his youngest daughter, Mari, to fetch one of the gypsy nags, any one she could catch.

This Mari was a limber-limbed raven-haired smoky-eyed girl in her mid-teens, manifestly swollen in the belly, though I have it on sound authority that her premature rotundity did not prevent her from discharging with particular gusto her dancing in the gypsy tents (dancing of neither the ballroom or ballet variety). In fact, some venerable and hoary members of the church congregation who had caught wind of this entertainment had made up a party and visited my friend Charles Kinneson just the previous evening in order to object to his allowing the dancing on his property; but my friend refused to see them, having been afflicted with depressed spirits since the death that past winter of his wife, the former Belinda Brown, daughter of the Abolitionist John Brown.

Yet when Charles learned from a gypsy lad whom the wench Mari had sent up to his house to borrow a carrot and some alum, that a race was to be held, he bestirred himself and went onto the porch to watch. No sooner had he stepped out, he informed me later, than he saw the gypsy girl catch a prancing young black mare and lead her into a willow brake by the river, from which she emerged some minutes later with a broken-winded sway-backed swag-bellied mud-smeared hobbling ancient nag, all bedecked with wild cucumber vine and woodbine and docks and vetch, which the girl half-led and half-hauled down the gool to the starting point for the race. By now dusk was fast approaching, and a hundred or more townspeople had gathered by the bridge to watch and to lay bets on the outcome.

"Gentlemen, I would na cast wager wi' this gypsy mon," cried my friend to the assemblage. "The wages of all wagers is trouble." And indeed, Charles knew for whom, since even as the townsfolk were laughing and jeering at the spavined old nag hobbling up the gool with rheumy eyes and a drooling frothing mouth, he had seen the wench force the last of the carrot laced with alum between its long teeth.

And the gray-headed gypsy bet on his animal with any and all, while my friend intoned darkly, "He who casts wager casts his lot wi' the old horned de'il." But the multitude heeded not this warning, and one after another bet on Capering Cy.

The horses were placed side by side facing west into the crimson afterglow above the mountains. They would run in an elliptical circuit, down the gool and across the covered bridge and back through the village to the starting point. Captain Allen's young nephew Forrest, a boy of considerable mettle, mounted Capering Cy; and the chieftain turned to the girl Mari with the swollen round belly and said something to her in the strange guttural gypsy tongue and instantly she leapt upon the nag's back. Some of the people protested for fear she should fall from the horse while great with child; only my friend Charles Kinneson observed that no sooner did she mount the crippled nag than it pricked up its ears and stood straighter, and stamped its lame foot twice.

"On your mark!" came the cry. "Get set. Race!" At which the girl leaned forward slightly and the nag, all bestrewn with wild cucumbers and the vines of the wild bluegrape, sprang from a dead standstill a good six feet through the air. She landed in a thundering gallop with her mane and burred tail streaming. She passed Charles Kinneson's place a full five lengths ahead of the celebrated Cy and increased the lead to ten lengths by the time she reached the covered bridge. In the village the people who had remained, the white-headed old people of the church and some of the young women of the church, heard the girl shouting in the gypsy tongue over the thundering hoofs and then the horse appeared in a swirl of dust, dusky-colored in the lowering dusk, with the girl-woman Mari stretched out on its back all low in her wide-belled gypsy trousers and wide-sleeved embroidered gypsy blouse, shouting encouragement in the language only the horse understood and urging it forward with a whisking motion with the flat of her hand. "Like someone sharpening a scythe with a whetstone," one of the venerable old churchmen said. But another ancient, who had not been to church for years, said afterwards that he heard two voices crying in the outlandish tongue, and those few who believed him said the second voice was the voice of a demon inside the horse itself, which even they knew was foolishness, until the old reprobate said, no, it was the voice of the babe in the womb of the gypsy girl, which likewise everyone knew was foolishness, though a small boy also insisted that he heard the high shrill muffled voice of a second person exhorting the horse as it raced back across the new bridge where the race had begun and over the finish line well before Capering Cy was even within earshot.

The astonished multitude scattered fast. But the gypsy woman wheeled the horse about in the dusk and came charging back at them again, reining hard into the meadow and riding full-tilt into the pool below the bridge and across the river, where the horse seemed to undergo an Ovidian metamorphosis, emerging onto the far bank and back over the bridge again as an entirely different horse, a beautiful strong black pacing mare. Again the woman shouted, this time a great lusty triumphant shout in the Romany tongue, and this time there was no doubt at all that with her shouted a shrill triumphant babe's voice in the same tongue, so although the people knew very well that this must be some gypsy trick of ventriloquism, many of them were horrified and appalled. And the jet-black horse, as black as the girl Mari's hair, pranced high and proud in its victory, and although the people who had bet on Capering Cy, who was just now coming into sight in the twilight, were in an uproar and furious, they had no choice but to acknowledge they had lost their wagers.

Whose misbegotten inspiration the tarring-and-feathering party was has never been entirely clear, though a man named Zeke Stevens, a dealer in cattle and horses himself who had bet and lost heavily on Capering Cy, was said to be in the vanguard of the mob that marched on the gypsy encampment later that night. My friend Charles Kinneson heard the trampling of their feet on the bridge at about half-past-twelve. He was not surprised. He was sitting in his kitchen watching the low fires of the gypsies flicker in the meadow across the gool, with the great U.S. Army horse pistol across his lap that he had brought back from Harper's Ferry and used to shoot the slave-killer Satan Smithfield in the church pulpit, and he knew even before he went into his dooryard and saw the pine-knot torches and dark-lanterns and the glimmer of white hoods, that it was a mob. He met them partway down the gool between the gypsy camp and the bridge.

He did not ask them what they wanted, but shrewdly inquired who was in charge. To which no one replied a word, though the mob was murmuring one to another behind their hoods.

"I asked, who is in charge here?" Charles Kinneson repeated. Again there was no reply.

"Aye," he said. "I thought as much. Home, dogs, to kennel! I'll send a lead ball through the heart of the first coward amongst you who takes another step this way."

"Don't be interfering, Charlie Kinneson," said a voice resembling that of the estimable horsetrader Stevens. "This isn't nothing to do with you."

BANG! A ball from the purloined Army pistol knocked out Stevens' dark-lantern. BANG! A second ball whistled a foot above the rabble's heads. BANG! A third ball struck the road scant inches from Stevens' boots. The mob gave back fast, turned, and rushed back over the bridge toward the village.

And lo! the next morning in the thin early light before the sunrise, when Charles Kinneson went to the barn with his lantern to discharge his morning chores, the gypsies were gone, leaving only the spent embers of their campfires and three circles of trampled brown grass where their three tents had been pitched. But in the horse stable—where as payment for allowing them to camp in his meadow and supplying them free of charge with eggs and milk and vegetables the gypsies were wont to leave their friend perhaps a horse, or peradventure a spotted cow, and once an endless maze carved from wood which the gypsy chieftain had begun carving years ago and lugged from place to place until abruptly, gypsy-fashion, he had lost interest in it after completing several hundred links—in that stable were two granite monuments. One bore the name of Charles's deceased wife: "Belinda Brown Kinneson, Daughter of the Abolitionist John Brown. Born Mineville, New York, January 4, 1843, Died Kingdom County, Vermont, February 23, 1897." And upon the other was written: "Replacement Mari Kinneson, Born Bucharest, Romania, November 8, 1886," with the rest blank.

My friend held the lantern high, and once again read the words on each stone, the one he had bespoken and the other he had not, when in the dimness behind him he heard the same shrill harsh cry that seemed to come from the gypsy woman's belly the evening before, only this time there were no words, Romany or otherwise, only the sharp insistent and unmistakably hungry outcry of a newly born infant. He turned and saw in the lantern light the smoky-eyed gypsy girl, Replacement Mari, reclined on the stable straw like that other Mary from long ago, and holding up to him proudly and even a little defiantly a newborn man-child.

"Aye," Charles Kinneson said in the determined manner I have come to know so well over the years. "I see." And he took the babe in his hands and held it aloft and said, "We name this child Elijah, for it has prophesied from the womb, and given utterance to its pure thoughts." And returning the man-child back to the arms of its mother, he said, pointing at it, "Elijah!"

"Elijah," she said in her harsh guttural accent. "Elijah."

And my friend said to the woman, Replacement, "Aye. Elijah."

And he led her into his house and wed her that very afternoon. And to them the following year was born a second son, Resolvèd, and the year after that a third, Welcome. So ends my historical account of Charles Kinneson and the gypsies."

# 10

More than half a century later, under a clear morning sky, my mother and I walked down the gool by the meadow where the gypsies had set up their tents and my great-stepgrandmother, Replacement Mari, had won the race the night before she gave birth to Elijah; past the faded leaping brook trout on our dilapidated barn; and past the lane leading up to my cousins' place, until we came to the covered bridge. In the bright July sunshine, accompanied by my mother, I wondered how I could ever have been afraid of the place. The trestle downriver where Nat and Frenchy had fought looked just as innocuous—an ordinary wooden railroad trestle like any other.

We crossed the bridge, pausing as usual to read the faded patent medicine ads inscribed on the inside timbers, and followed the River Road to the dooryard of Hook LaMott's slaughterhouse.

Nobody seemed to be home. The house, which was surrounded by Canadian bull thistles as high as Mom's hollyhocks and was still banked with rotting hay bales from the previous winter, had an unoccupied air. So did the long adjacent slaughtering shed and the concrete freezer locker. Even the towering mountain of cow skulls and rotting hides out of which the stygian brook that polluted the river just above the railroad trestle seeped like pus out of a festering wound looked oddly deserted by the purple-headed cowbirds and scrawny cats that usually prowled its perimeter, though it was buzzing with a veritable Egyptian pestilence of bluebottle flies.

We picked our way through the debris to the foot of the wooden ramp slanting up to the shed and peered inside. In spots the floor planks showed through the sawdust, and I could see bloodstains on them. Along one wall ran a conveyer track with hooks hanging down at intervals of several feet. Over the past winter Athena Allen had read *A Tale of Two Cities* to my eighth-grade grammar class, and the slaughtering shed and massive heap of offal outside it reminded me of Dickens' grislier descriptions of Robespierre's Reign of Terror.

"You looking for somebody, you?"

Frenchy LaMott appeared in the doorway. He had a large dirty bandage around his left thumb and a big filthy black toe was sticking out of a hole in one of his engineer boots. He was wielding a lethal-looking stick with a rusty spike jutting out of the end. Strapped to his waist was a .22 revolver.

How did my finely tuned mother and I happen to be standing that morning in the place of all places in the Kingdom that I most dreaded? After Dad and I had gotten home from the minister's the evening before, my folks had spent a long time discussing Julia Hefner's meddling visit to Reverend Andrews. Mom had confirmed our suspicion that in fact Hefty Hefner was operating strictly on her own and had not been commissioned by the Ladies Auxiliary to deliver a message to the minister. But both my parents agreed that he needed a part-time housekeeper as soon as possible. The reverend had declined Claire's offer to become his permanent housekeeper because he felt there were decisions she had to make about her life. He feared that employment would give her the opportunity to postpone these and I'm sure he was right. But that left him with the troublesome Hefty.

"He certainly doesn't want that old moose snooping around over there and giving him the eye," Dad said. "And he doesn't need a live-in housekeeper. Just somebody to come by two or three times a week and do the wash, throw together a few casseroles, swamp out the kitchen. I told him you'd probably know of somebody, Ruth."

"As a matter of fact I do," Mom said. "Somebody who's efficient and completely trustworthy and could certainly use the extra income."

"Who's that?"

"Ida LaMott. Jimmy and I can drop by and see her in the morning."

"Come on, Mom. Frenchy'll just beat me up. You know what he tried to do to Nat out at the trestle."

"We'll go about eight-thirty," my mother said. "As for Frenchy, it's really time for you to see him in his own element, Jimmy. Until you've stood in somebody else's shoes, you can't really judge that person fairly."

"Frenchy doesn't even own a pair of shoes. He wears engineer boots with holes in them. Besides, I'm not judging him. I just don't want to get pounded up."

"You won't, I promise. Eight-thirty tomorrow, son. We'll make it a nice little outing."

How my mother could conceive of a visit to the slaughterhouse as a nice little outing was beyond me. To me, Hook LaMott's gory precincts were horrible and repulsive, partly because of their connection with death, partly because of my fear of Frenchy.

But that day at the LaMotts' I learned something important about my mother, which I had not suspected before. I learned that she possessed not only remarkable resilience and endurance but real physical courage as well.

"Hello, Frenchy," Mom said as he came down the ramp toward us. "Is your mother home?"

"Up the house," Frenchy said sullenly, pointing with his stick. "Up there with little dummies making headcheese. Ought to grind dummies right up in Christly grinder along with pig brain. Wouldn't be no great loss."

I laughed, and Frenchy, inspired by the felicitous thought of grinding up his two half-brothers for headcheese, swaggered down off the blood-encrusted ramp to escort us to the house.

"That's all right, Frenchy, I'll find my way. Jimmy can stay here and help you with your chores."

"Don't need no help, missus," Frenchy said, but Mom was already on her way up to the house, and he and I were left standing toe to toe, like Tom Sawyer and the new boy in town, with me feeling very much in the role of the new boy.

So of course I did the stupidest thing possible. "Well, Claude, what kind of work do you do here, anyway?"

"What that you called me?"

"Claude," I said innocently. "Isn't that your name?"

"Be careful, you," Frenchy said angrily. "You know my name. You friend ain't here to defend you now, Kinneson. You big brother ain't here, neither. I make you into sausage, you call me that frigging school name again."

Frenchy underscored this threat by expectorating a solid amber jet of tobacco juice onto the ground by my sneaker, where it glistened and quivered momentarily like something that had crawled out of the offal heap.

Suddenly he grinned. "You want to know what I do here? Come on, I show you."

Frenchy marched back up the ramp, with me trailing reluctantly along behind. "Here the way we do it, Kinneson. Old Bumper, he takes and brings cows down here from sales barn overstreet. Sometimes one or two, sometimes whole Christly herd. Sometimes he let me drive, too. That if he in a good mood or I just tune his Christly truck engine or he too drunk to drive himself.

"Anyway, big goddamn truck comes tearing in. First I drive cows down ramp out of truck, then I drive'em up ramp into shed. They don't move fast enough, I hit'em with this." He made a menacing jab in my general direction with the homemade cattle prod with the rusty nail impaled in the end.

"All right. Now say I got to kill a little veal calf, weigh about what you do, Kinneson."

Frenchy gleefully jabbed an imaginary little veal calf of about my size up the ramp toward imminent doom.

"Now, by God, once I get veal in shed, I grab it by the ear, throw it down, and shoot it with this old peashooter."

Frenchy drew the .22 pistol from his holster, and fired a real bullet directly into the floor of the shed. I was scared half to death that he might dispatch me next; but to my relief he stuck the gun back in his holster and continued his lecture.

"Veal calf dead as knob on a door, eh? So I grab old dead veal by hind legs and lift it up and tie it on hook and slit it throat and skin with skinning knife. Then I go back and get next one while Hook, he butcher veal up, all with one hand, too, cause that all he got, the old bastard. How you like be that veal on the hook, Kinneson?"

"I guess I wouldn't," I said in all truthfulness. But I was impressed. An outcast whom I'd feared and hated for years had just revealed to me that he could efficiently slaughter and skin an animal I could only eat, not to mention drive an enormous cattle truck whose engine he had just tuned, all the while enduring the miserable suzerainty of bad-tempered old rips like Bumper Stevens and Hook LaMott, and not without a certain grim sense of humor.

A thought my mother would have been pleased with flashed through my mind. I wondered, as we headed back down the ramp, if all these years *I* might have been prejudiced against Frenchy LaMott.

But he quickly redeemed himself in my opinion. "Say, Kinneson, who that French girl hanging 'round the preacher's place? True what going 'round 'bout her, she that little hoor from girlie show?"

"Nah," I replied, "that's a damn lie that Fatty Hefner and those old church busybodies are spreading around town. She's just a poor kid from up in Canada with no place else to go."

"They say she been up at Christly Resolvèd's for a few days letting him and Welcome put the britches to her every goddamn night. Old Bumper tell me. He tell me I ought to get her down under goddamn trestle and put the britches to her myself, me. Just a little French tramp is all, Bumper say. He say he like to get her in commission sales barn some night himself, by Christ.

"Say, Kinneson. You know her, you? I give you a dollar you get her out to trestle for me. Plus when I finish up you can have a go at her."

"You've got a filthy mind, Frenchy LaMott, and that's a damn lie about her being a tramp! Her father was a famous actor up in Quebec, and she's going to be in the movies someday. You just wait. You don't know what you're talking about."

Frenchy laughed. "How 'bout I give you two dollars?"

"How about you go to hell?"

But Frenchy LaMott did not hear my rejoinder. Frenchy was flying through the air. Then he was sprawled on all fours on the ground at the foot of the ramp and Hook LaMott, all six feet, six inches of him, was shouting angrily at him from the entrance of the slaughterhouse, where he'd come silently up behind us and, with no warning at all, booted Frenchy off the ramp.

"What da hell you doing, firing off guns 'round here, you crazy French bastard?" Hook yelled.

Down the ramp Hook came, swinging his great iron homemade prosthetic device menacingly. "Give me dat gun, you wort'less little shit."

Frenchy scrambled to his feet. He clapped his hand over the pistol butt. "Come get it, you one-clawed old son-of-a-bitch."

Just then Ida called Hook's name. She and my mother were hurrying down through the bull thistles from the house. "Hook! I got three more day a week work, me. Housekeeper work!"

Hook looked from Frenchy, standing crouched with his hand on the .22 in a weird parody of a western gunslinger, to his sister Ida. He frowned. "Over there?" he said, pointing across the river toward our farmhouse.

"No, overstreet in village. Madame K here tell me new preacher fella need a housekeeper three day a week. Well, we need money, us. Frenchy got to have new pair boots soon. Just last night I say three extra Hail Marys for Frenchy boots and today, job pop up! God is good, eh?"

Hook frowned and rubbed his hook. Or maybe he was rubbing his hand with his hook. It was hard to tell. "What Bumper say?"

"Bumper don't have no say. I ain't Bumper's nigger servant, excuse me, missus. Bumper ain't my boss, him. Bumper ain't nothing to me one way or other no more. You the one I work for, Hook. You got the say-so here."

"I don' know," Hook said.

"What you don't know?"

"Don' know if I want you keep house for dat colored fella."

"He ain't no ordinary colored fella, Hook. He a Christly preacher. Speak the best goddamn English in the Kingdom next to Editor K. What more you want, you? Want me to get a job keeping house for the frigging Queen Mother?"

"I don' know as I want you traipsing all over da Christly Kingdom keeping up colored preachers' houses when you got sausage to grind here, by da bald-headed Christ."

"Let her go, *mon oncle*," Frenchy said in a surly voice. "I grind you frigging sausage for you."

"I told you shut you trap!" Hook said, and kicked Frenchy hard in the leg with his steel-toed workshoe.

Howling in pain, Frenchy drew his pistol and pointed it straight at Hook's chest. "You had it, you Canuck bastard," he shouted. "You going to die!"

Hook laughed and took a step toward him. Frenchy fired, and a jagged splinter ripped off the frame of the shed entrance beyond Hook's head. Hook laughed again and took another step. Frenchy fired past him twice more.

When, to my total astonishment, my mother stepped quickly between Hook LaMott and Frenchy.

"Hand me that revolver, Frenchy," she said. "Someone's going to get hurt if this keeps up. Give it here, please."

My mother's voice was quiet and businesslike, as though she were removing a sharp instrument from the hands of a young child.

"Hand it here," she said again. "We've had quite enough gunplay for one morning. I'll give it to your mother and she'll give it back to you again after everyone's simmered down."

"Give her gun, Frenchy!" Ida screamed. "Give her gun, quick, 'fore you do something can't be undone."

Mom held out her hand. "Give me the gun, please, Frenchy."

Miraculously, Frenchy handed the revolver to my mother, who in turn gave it to Ida.

"I kill you later, Canuck," Frenchy yelled at Hook. But his uncle just laughed again and went back up the ramp into the shed.

"Well, then," Mom said to Ida. "Shall I tell Reverend Andrews you'll be there at nine Monday morning?"

"You bet, missus," Ida said, beaming. "You bet I be there. With, how it go? With bells on, eh? You tell that preacher man I be there with Christly bells on. And if Ida LaMott say she do something, you know she do it. Thank you, missus. And thank you for keeping Frenchy from killing old Hook and going jail, then Ida go to poorhouse."

"I don't think he really intended to harm his uncle," my mother said.

"Yes, he did," Ida said. "Some day he going to, too. You mistreat a dog long enough, he turn on you, eh? But not today maybe. Thank you, missus."

"Yes, indeed, Mrs. LaMott. Thank you. Good morning."

"Good morning, missus. See you later, Jimmy. Come again, you. Come anytime. God is good!"

"Boy, Mom!" I said over and over again on the way home. "Boy oh boy oh boy. I loved the way you got that gun away from Frenchy. That was terrific. Dad couldn't have done any better himself."

My mother smiled. "Speaking of your father, Jimmy, let's just keep this little episode at the LaMotts' a secret between us two, shall we? You know how he worries about me. This might upset him more than would be good for him."

"You got it, Mom. Mum's the word. Say, where did you ever get all those guts? Weren't you scared Frenchy was going to shoot you?"

"Oh, no. Your grandfather the poor captain was forever disarming his unfortunate gentlemen at the mission. You'd be amazed at what he'd confiscate just in a month—broken bottles, homemade knives, homemade guns, even. I was the only student at the Boston School for Young Methodist Ladies with a souvenir collection of lethal weapons in her bedroom."

I laughed, but I couldn't stop thinking about the events of the morning. "You think Ida'll really show up at the minister's, Mom?"

"Absolutely. If the LaMotts say they'll do something, why, they will. And that's the—"

"—beginning and the end of it," I said, and we both laughed.

It had rained hard on the night in late June that Claire LaRiviere arrived on the gool. Then it did not rain again for more than a month. Day after day the filmy dawn mist above the river burned off to reveal the clearest of blue summer skies.

I spent many afternoons that month haying for Ben Currier, and hated nearly every minute of it; haying is the hottest and hardest farm work there is. Mornings, I worked for Dad at the *Monitor*, and in the evening I kept Mom company out in the garden or fished with Dad or Charlie, though as the drought continued and the river and burn dropped, the trout fishing got spotty. I had to master some of the finer points of handling a dry fly to get any action at all.

I saw all of Charlie's home ballgames, and by mid-July he was batting over .600. Once again he was talking about trying out for

Montreal in the Triple A International League and maybe "going all the way to the top"—though not before he won the annual Smash-up Crash-up Derby, for which he'd hired Welcome Kinneson to fix up the old Brink's armored car for him to enter in the big event. Dad told him bluntly that he ought to forget about the derby and concentrate on getting to the top of his own business, which in case he'd forgotten happened to be practicing law, but Charlie just laughed and said he could practice law anytime, but the derby came just once a year and this year he was determined to win it.

Then later in July, with the derby just two weeks away, something happened that not only brought Charlie back to his office and responsibilities with a thunderous jolt but became the talk of the county and, for a time, the entire state—while simultaneously bearing out my father's most vitriolic jeremiads on the lack of law and order in Kingdom County.

Late one morning while I was at the *Monitor* cranking out handbills advertising Reverend Andrews' upcoming Old Home Day, three large men in green Men from Mars masks with foot-long wavering antennae walked into the First Farmers' and Lumberers' Savings Bank of Kingdom Common and heisted $29,348.16 at shotgun-point while the mile-long 11:03 A.M. Montreal freight lumbered by just outside, effectively cutting off the bank and the robbers from most of the village. They were inside the building for less than three minutes, no shots were fired, no one was hurt, and they escaped in Welcome's Brink's car, which they'd stolen earlier that same morning, along with the Men from Mars masks, from my cousin's junkyard. Later that day the armored car was found abandoned up in the gore near Russia. But to the ill-concealed delight of nearly everyone in Kingdom County, there was absolutely no trace of the bandits or their loot.

Over the next several days, countless conjectures about the identity of the bank robbers were advanced on the sidewalk in front of the brick shopping block, in the post office and stores, in the courthouse offices, and in farm kitchens and dooryards and barns throughout the county. Gradually two very different theories emerged. The first, which at the time my father and Charlie both seemed to think quite probable, was that like three or four other bank robberies in remote towns along the Canadian-Vermont border over the past couple of years, the hit on the First Farmers' and Lumberers' was very likely the handiwork of Montreal pros. It had all the earmarks of the other recent jobs, from the stolen local getaway car abandoned on an unwatched back road near the border to the use of shotguns—though the Martian masks were a new and inspired twist.

The second (and more generally favored) theory about the robbery was that the three wild Kittredge boys from Lord Hollow—Harlan, Hiram, and Hen—had pulled off the heist, shrewdly timing it to coincide with both payroll day at the American Heritage Furniture Mill and the arrival of the B and M freight. Proponents of this theory held that after abandoning the Brink's car at Russia, the Kittredge boys had cut cross-country over two mountains and through a big cedar swamp to their father's place, where they promptly buried the money for disbursement at a more fit season.

Unfortunately for Sheriff White and the five or six solemn and embarrassed FBI. agents who swarmed out over the countryside along the border for the next week or so, every shred of evidence against the Kittredge boys turned out to be highly circumstantial, a point my brother stressed repeatedly during the federal inquest that occupied every minute of his working time during the rest of that month. True, Charlie conceded, old Whiskeyjack Kittredge had marched into the Farmers' and Lumberers' the previous week and requested a loan of five hundred dollars to erect a cedar-oil still at the junction of the Lord Hollow brook and the Upper Kingdom River, and when asked about his credit said it must be A-number-one because he had never borrowed a cent from anyone before in all his life. True, when he'd been turned down flat he had sung out in the presence of eight customers, two tellers, the lending officer, and the bank vice president that he intended to have his loan one way or another. Yet that was no proof that he had put his boys up to robbing the bank.

Nor, Charlie was quick to point out, was the Kittredge boys' long record of bar fights, motor vehicle violations, moonshining, whiskey-running, and infractions perpetrated against the wild four-footed, winged and finny populations of Kingdom County any indication that they would go so far as to hold up a bank at gunpoint. And of course the reputation of Big Harlan Kittredge as a man who, for a modest commission, would burn down your barn for the insurance was only that—a reputation, based on rumor. After all, Charlie had already gotten him off the hook for just such a charge back in March.

So in the absence of witnesses who could identify the bandits, and since no trace of the stolen money ever did come to light (though Big

Harlan and his younger brother Hen motored south to attend Hank Williams' funeral the following January and stopped in New York City on the way home, where they were reported to have spent thousands of dollars on booze and girls during a monumental twenty-eight day binge), the United States attorney who convened the inquest in St. Johnsbury that July simply didn't have a case he could take to a jury. Once again, as with the Ordney Gilson trial, Charlie's name was bruited about the state in the newspapers, and Kingdom County was reconfirmed in the eyes of the rest of Vermont as a place where any type of law at all was a joke—an anomalous fragment of a wild and wooly frontier generally associated with territory twenty-five hundred miles further west a century ago. And once again, Attorney Charlie Kinneson was something of an outlaw-hero in the eyes of almost the entire Kingdom.

The goings-on did preclude Charlie from any involvement in the smash-up derby; a fact that made him pretty ornery for a few days, but he vowed to win big the following summer, and I, for one, had no doubt that he would.

Now that the misunderstanding of Claire's nocturnal visit to my brother's trailer had been cleared up, Charlie and Athena Allen were on good terms again. They were even talking about getting married in the fall, though Athena said she wouldn't live in a trailer, especially one papered with cutouts of Marilyn Monroe and Jayne Mansfield and smelling like a baseball clubhouse, and Charlie would have to get a place in the village first.

As for Claire, after Ida LaMott came to work at the parsonage, she began taking long afternoon walks out into the countryside. One day when she passed our place I trailed along behind her, partly out of curiosity to find out where she went on these solitary excursions and partly to have an opportunity to see her alone and warn her about Frenchy's designs.

Instead of continuing along the gool and crossing back over the river by way of the covered bridge, she headed up the twisty woods road into the gore. For a minute I actually thought she might be returning to Resolvèd's place. But she passed his lane with a single apprehensive glance toward the dilapidated old house and kept climbing up the mountain.

About halfway to the top, she ducked off the gore road and struck out along the burn toward the abandoned quarry. I was surprised to see that there was a pretty well beaten path here. Apparently she'd been coming this way regularly.

If Claire was going skinny-dipping, I didn't want to startle her when she was in the water. So as soon as she reached the quarry, where I'd discovered her the first morning she went to Resolvèd's, I hurried out of the woods and called her name.

"Nathan?"

"No, Claire, it's Jimmy Kinneson. I didn't mean to scare you."

"Oh, by no means. You did not scare me, James."

Claire waded out into the brook and began to wash her hair in the little falls that dropped over the lip of the quarry.

When she was through we sat together under the yellow birch tree at the corner of the granite ledge above the pool.

"So, James. You are having a pleasant summer holiday from school?"

"Yeah, it's been okay. How about you? You doing all right over at the Andrews'?"

"Oh, yes, I like it there very much, though of course now that Monsieur Andrews has hire Madame LaMott to keep house for him, there is really very little for me to do."

"That reminds me of something, Claire. You know Frenchy LaMott? Ida's boy? You've got to watch out for him. The other day he offered to pay me two dollars to get you down under the old railroad trestle out of town, where he could . . . you know, attack you. If I were you I wouldn't go out on any more walks alone."

"Bah! This Frenchy. Who is he that I should fear him? A dirty butcher's boy. He is the least of my worries. If he attempts an offense, he will wish he never heard the name Claire LaRiviere, daughter of Etienne."

Claire looked off down over the tops of the trees along the burn. In the summertime from here, when the leaves were thick, you could just make out the top of the courthouse clock tower and the white church steeple. But the hills beyond and the varied greens of the farms and woodlots running up their sides stood out sharply under the clear blue sky.

"Your Kingdom is very beautiful, James, do you not agree? It is every bit as beautiful as the small farm of my Laurentian grandmother. And you and your mother and father and your brother, the first Monsieur Kin'son of the photograph, and Monsieur Andrew and Nathan too, you have all been very good to me. Do you know what I wish? I wish I could stay here forever."

"Well, Claire, maybe you can. Maybe you can stay right here and go to school in the fall."

"It would be a fine thing to think so, James. But that is out of the question. Surely the Resolvèd will not be in bed with the sick leg much longer. When the leg is well again, he will come looking for me and there is bound to be trouble—trouble Monsieur Andrew and Nathan must not be involve in. I must tell you that Monsieur Andrews, he is very good to me, like a father, but it is clear that he too wishes me to leave. Why else would he hire Madame LaMott to be housekeeper when I am already doing a satisfactory job?

"Also, there is the matter of Holly-wood and the movies. Do not imagine that I have forgotten that. After Etienne LaRiviere is get sick I am promise him that I will someday be a famous star in the movies and put to good use all he taught me when we work together in the streets of Quebec. I will never break that promise to Etienne.

"Look, James. Here in my purse I have ten dollars. When I have twenty more, I will repay the Resolvèd for the bus fare he sends me and then I will save the sixty necessary for the ticket to Holly-wood, and be on my way. I do not expect it to be easy. But Etienne LaRiviere is train me well, and with hard work and a bit of luck, I will be a star yet. I am certain of it!"

"Claire, I wasn't going to tell you this. But my brother Charlie, he's already paid Resolvèd for that bus ticket, and Resolvèd took the money, too, to keep himself in Old Duke while his leg's in the cast. You don't need to worry about that."

"Then I will repay Monsieur Charlie Kin'son!"

"You don't have to do that, either. Charlie wouldn't take your money if you tried to give it to him. He feels sort of responsible for your being here, see, 'cause he helped Resolvèd write that letter to the magazine in the first place."

"Is not his fault, James. I will repay him soon. Then I will go to Holly-wood if I must walk there. I am determined!"

"Well, if you are, I suppose you'll get there all right. But promise me one thing. If anything happens, anything at all, and you do decide to leave right away, meet me here first. I've got over a hundred dollars in the bank that I could get out and—"

"James, I can never take your money. But I will promise you this, that before I depart, when the time to depart comes, I will certainly not go without saying goodbye to you. This I promise. What is that?"

"What's what?"

"In the bush down the brook. You did not notice?"

I stood up and looked down along the alders. "I don't see anything."

"I am sure I see the bush move, James, and a green flash."

"I think we'd better get out of here, Claire. Resolvèd's 'bad leg' isn't as bad as you might think."

We headed quickly out around the alders where she'd seen the movement and along the path to the trace. We were both relieved to arrive there safely.

"I don't like that quarry much," I admitted on our way down to the gool. "It gives me the jim-jams, like the cemetery at night. That first morning I met you up there after the big rain? I thought your slip hanging in the tree was a ghost! Pretty silly of me, I guess."

"By no means," Claire said solemnly. "It is well-known in the Laurentian Mountains that the terrible loup-garou, the creature with the body of a man and head of a wolf, frequently lies in wait in a tree for children who have strayed from home."

Abruptly Claire twisted her oval face slightly, made her eyes go crazy, lifted a hand like a claw, and gave an eerie little howl. Effortlessly she had turned into the dreaded loup-garou of the wild northern forest. I jumped back, and she laughed.

"As a young girl visiting my grandmother, I am very much frightd of the loup-garou, and other ghosts besides. It is only right to beware of such things at that age. Then as I grow older I am find that men like the bad man who is come to live with my mother after my father dies and the man with one eye at the Paris Revue and even perhaps the Resolvèd, with his green shirt and Betsy, are more to be frighten of than the Laurentian were-wolf even."

I walked Claire back down the gool and over the red iron bridge to the parsonage. Nat was sitting out on the porch, in behind the bittersweet vines, and he gave me a start.

"What's the matter, Kinneson? Did you think I was old Pliny's ghost?"

"Do not make jokes of James' ghost, Nathan," Claire said. "In my grandmother's mountains there were many of them, all very real indeed.

"I go in now, eh? Thank you, James, for keeping me company this evening and walking home with me. Your father is out, Nathan?"

"He'll be back any minute," Nathan said shortly. "There he is now—nope. It's just that weird bloke across the street."

Elijah Kinneson, coming from the direction of town, turned into his walk and went fast up his steps and inside his tiny sexton's cottage.

"Well, then," Claire said. "We will visit later, eh?"

I told Claire so long, but Nathan continued to sit out for a while, so I sat with him.

"Let me ask you something, Kinneson. Do you really believe in ghosts?"

"Well, to tell you the truth I don't always. But the funny thing is, I'm afraid of them anyway."

He laughed. "I know how to break you of that."

"You do? How?"

"Remember that tale you told me about old Pliny's bones coming here every year on the date of his suicide?"

"Sure. Everybody in town knows about that."

"And if you can surprise the bones while they're walking, grab 'em, and bury 'em, his soul'll be put to rest? That's how it goes?"

"That's right."

"Let's do it."

"Oh, boy. I don't know, Nat. You really mean it?"

"Why not? If Pliny doesn't put in an appearance, well then you don't ever need to be afraid of ghosts again, right? You can write the whole tale off as a lot of crap. If he does show, why not do the old guy a favor and bury what's left of him? It can't be that hard just to grab him. If you ask me, those bones ought to be buried anyway. It's almost sacrilegious to have 'em hanging over there in the science closet like something in a museum. What's the date when they're supposed to walk?"

"August fourth. The same day as your dad's big celebration."

"What do you say, are you game? At least it'll give us something to look forward to besides that stupid Old Home Day. Keep me from going crazy in this burg."

I shrugged. "What the hell. I'm not scared if you're not."

"Yes you are," Nat said with a good-natured laugh. "Me too, a little. Let's do it anyway. We'll flip a coin to see who holds the lantern and who grabs him. Deal?"

I thought for a minute. Then I grinned. "Deal," I said, already thinking how amused Charlie would be when I told him about our plans. Maybe he'd even join us, which would be just fine with me.

Except for the bank robbery, July was a welcome hiatus in an otherwise all-too-eventful summer. After the initial grumbling, plans for the big Old Home Day celebration were coming along swimmingly, as Reverend Andrews put it. Every day and again most evenings, committees met at the church or parsonage to plan the floats, skits, food, and entertainment booths, a big grudge baseball rematch between Charlie's Outlaws and the Memphremagog Loggers, and a Grand Historical Cavalcade and Pageant. With the exception of the commission sales crowd and Cousin Elijah Kinneson, who flatly refused to participate in the celebration because of the "gaming booths," everyone in town was excited about Old Home Day, though Castor Oil Quinn and a few of the older people in the church periodically shook their heads and looked at the cloudless sky and perversely predicted rain.

And sure enough, on the evening of August third, as Mom and Dad and I were coming down out of the gore after listening to a Sox game on the car radio, it did begin to rain, first lightly, then a steady drenching downpour.

"Mister Baby Johnson!" Dad said, as we sat in the car in the dooryard, watching the rain stream across the windshield. "Wouldn't you just know. Well, now we're going to see what sort of stuff our minister friend is made of."

As soon as we stepped into the kitchen, the phone rang. It was Reverend Andrews for Dad.

"Well, Walt," Dad said into the phone, "you did the best you could with this one. We'll just have to start over again."

Then the minister talked some more, and finally Dad said "All right, fine," and hung up.

"That answers my question," he told us. "It's supposed to rain hard all night tonight and most of the day tomorrow. He wants us to get on the horn right now and start calling everybody we can think of."

"To postpone the celebration?" Mom said, disappointed.

"Hell no, Ruth. To spread the word that it's on, rain or shine!"

# 11

Soon after the first gray light illuminated the dripping red-and-gray slate roofs of the courthouse and Academy, vehicles began nosing in against the long east and west sides of the village common, their windshield wipers slapping ineffectually in the downpour. A dozen or so town boys were already loitering on the courthouse portico, though the first major event of the celebration, the Grand Cavalcade and Pageant of historical floats, would not start until one o'clock.

"I thought you had connections in high places, reverend," Julia Hefner said.

"I do," he said with a grin at me. "It isn't snowing, is it?"

The rain showed no signs at all of letting up, but around nine o'clock my mother dragooned me into lugging umpteen cardboard boxes of secondhand clothes from the church basement, where they had been stored, over to the rummage sale tables on the green. There, under a jury-rigged canvas awning, Mom was immediately caught between two factions of the rummage committee, which my father, in the following week's issue of the *Monitor*, facetiously dubbed "the savers and the chuckers." The chuckers were all for throwing out stained and torn apparel, worn-out shoes, mismatched mittens, and clothes so laughably out of fashion that no one would ever wear them, much less buy them. These chuckers were disgusted by the frugality of the savers, who in turn were horrified by the prodigality of the chuckers. As Dad pointed out in his write-up, the chuckers and savers had formed ranks along more or less denominational lines, with the Presbyterians, led by Julia Hefner, salvaging what Mrs. Ben Currier and the Congregationalists had relegated to the throwaway boxes.

By ten, when I trudged across the green in the drilling rain with the last box of used babies' clothing, double-breasted jackets, striped suspenders, and ridiculously wide ties, there had already been a blow-up. All the chuckers and most of the savers had stalked off in anger, leaving Hefty Hefner and my mother to work the tables alone.

"I don't want you squirreling away prize items for yourself, now, Ruth," I overheard Julia tell my mother. "On the other hand, we couldn't be blamed for setting aside any especially choice little items we come across. You know as well as I do that the ones that really need these things for their families won't buy here anyway because they're on the town and so live better than you and I do— Why *won't* that dawdling boy of yours step on it! I could have run those boxes over here in half the time he's taken."

I felt like telling old H.H. to get her boyfriend Zack Barrows to do it if she wasn't satisfied (for according to local scuttlebutt she and Zack had been keeping company at least as long as Fred Hefner had been gone). But my mother tipped me a wink and mouthed the word "story," meaning someday I'd be able to put Julia in one, and flicked her fingers slightly to signal me to get away from the aborted clothing bazaar while the getting was good.

For the next hour or so I wandered around the common, marveling at the huge crowd that continued to pour into town despite the rain. Men in yellow volunteer fire department raincoats and high black hip boots rushed here and there spreading awnings over food and game booths. Farmers in barn boots and slickers stood quietly in groups of twos and threes, smoking under the dripping elms. Elderly ladies with umbrellas tottered along the edge of the common, and Reverend Andrews, in a long blue Royal Canadian Air Force raincoat, seemed to be everywhere.

"It's us against the weather, folks," the minister kept saying, clapping people on the back and encouraging everyone to have a good time. And because he kept his spirits high, everyone else's seemed high as well.

Everyone who lived or ever had lived in the Kingdom seemed to be convening on the common that day. By noon cars and trucks were lined all the way up Anderson Hill, and out past the church to U.S. Route 5, and along both sides of the county road east of the village. At Reverend Andrews' request, the Academy and courthouse had been opened up so that people could get in out of the rain; but it was a warm rain and no one wanted to stay inside for long. All over the village there was an air of small kids playing in the rain, a little defiant and silly, laughing, having a good time in an unexpected way, the good time coming from inside themselves and from the spirit of togetherness that Reverend Andrews had inspired in everyone.

I helped Seth McCormick set up his pony-ride ring on the north end of the common, near the statue of Ethan Allen taking Fort Ti. Then for the rest of the morning, as the crowd continued to swell, I filled in at various food and game booths. (Nathan showed up briefly about noon to help Welcome Kinneson in the barbecue pit.) Two booths down from the baseball throw, where I was working at the time, Athena Allen's kissing booth was doing a booming business. Athena was wearing a green blouse and a red skirt and had done her hair in gypsy ringlets and hung a great gold hoop from her right ear. Although she was sopping wet, every male in the Kingdom from sixteen to eighty seemed to want to give her a kiss—though I noticed that when Julia Hefner spelled Athena around noon so she could help her father the judge set up tables on the hotel porch for the barbecue, business at the Bower of Romance fell off considerably.

The cavalcade started promptly at one, despite an even fiercer spate of rain just before it, which Reverend Andrews said was doubtlessly the clearing shower. The minister narrated the procession from the bandstand. There were floats representing my great-great-great-grandfather's trip up across the White Mountains with the Revere church bell, my great-great-grandfather James' ill-conceived attacks on Canada with the Irish Fenians in 1856 and 1860, and my great-grandfather

Mad Charlie's secret meetings with John Brown. There were floats with elaborate tableaux depicting the history of agriculture and maple sugaring in Kingdom County and floats on fishing and hunting in the Kingdom, not to mention the Sunday School float, which I had just barely been able to talk my way out of participating in on the basis of being a teenager now, in which Caster Oil Quinn, dressed in black clerical robes, enacted the part of Headmaster Pliny Templeton teaching a class of students at the Academy with a McGuffey's Reader in one hand and a Civil War sword in the other.

"In those days," Reverend Andrews quipped, "they learned or else."

There were the obligatory dozen or so antique cars brought out for every parade in Kingdom County that I can ever remember, the village's two ancient hook-and-ladders with hand pumpers, earnest 4-H and Grange floats, and floats with contradancers and square dancers skidding around through their intricate maneuvers like drunks at a barn dance.

"First place was awarded to a motorized pantomime entitled 'The Whiskey Runners,'" my father wrote in that week's *Monitor*, "in which High Sheriff Mason White, dressed in official regalia and piloting his redoubtable patrol hearse, chased a '29 Ford driven by Auctioneer Bumper Stevens twice around the common. In keeping with a long-established local tradition, no arrests were made."

And then, miraculously, as Reverend Andrews was handing out the prizes, long after almost everyone had given up hope, a dome of blue sky opened up over the bandstand and a minute later the sun came out, and everyone cheered, though whether for the break in the weather or just from their collective good spirits, I couldn't say. It reminded me of Reverend Andrews' first Sunday in church, Easter Sunday, when the entire congregation had stood up and applauded him.

As the clouds continued to sail away and the blue expanded, a dozen of us boys made a bucket brigade on the baseball field and with pails and brooms and snow shovels and three truckloads of sawdust, we began to get the infield in playing shape for the big game between Charlie's Outlaws and Memphremagog, which was slated to start at four o'clock.

During the rain an ineffable goodwill had spread over the crowd. People ate even more, laughed even more, were even more convivial than they would have been on a sunny day, shaking hands with strangers they turned out to have gone to school with, renewing old acquaintances with neglected friends. And the storm was a great equalizer. The class differences so insidiously entrenched in any small town seemed to melt away with the rain. Bobby Hefner was seen hobnobbing with Frenchy LaMott. George Quinn and Bumper Stevens teamed up in the horseshoe championship doubles match against Zack Barrows and my father. And when the sun came out the goodwill metamorphosed into a festive euphoria unlike any I have ever experienced since, with the big ball-game still to come.

Kingdom Common's baseball diamond was probably the best in northern Vermont. The infield, which drained faster after a rain than any other in the area, was laid out at the south end of the green, with the left field foul post located directly across the street from the *Monitor*. Once I had seen Charlie wallop a home run through the plate-glass window of Quinn's Drugstore, a good four hundred and fifty feet from home plate. But it was a rare event for even the strongest local hitters to put a ball in the street, much less up against the brick block.

By three-thirty the newly painted green bleachers along the first and third base lines were packed. Hundreds of additional spectators stood behind the backstop and along both outfield foul lines, and more fans were strung all the way around the fenced-off outfield. I had been accorded the honor of serving as water boy for the Outlaws. My job was to keep two sap buckets appropriated from my mother's sugaring operation full of cold water from the outside faucet on the church and, more importantly, to replenish as often as necessary a third pail just behind the Outlaws' bench from a mammoth keg of beer in the back of Charlie's woody.

It had turned into a grand afternoon for baseball, with a good fresh breeze to dry the grass and base paths after the long rain. As usual in Kingdom County fair weather was coming in from the northwest, but twice during the Outlaws' warm-ups Charlie fungoed towering fly balls directly into the teeth of the wind and clean over the street onto the sidewalk in front of the brick shopping block. Each time the huge crowd responded with an ovation.

"Play ball!" barked my father, who was umpiring behind the plate; and the big grudge game, the highlight of the celebration and the highlight of my summer to date, was underway.

I knew by the end of the first inning that it was going to be a contest. Our pitcher, Big Harlan Kittredge, was in top form. Over the first three innings, four or five Memphremagog batters managed to topple weak grounders that Royce and Stub scooped up and tossed over to Pine Benson. But nobody hit a ball out of the infield.

The Outlaws couldn't seem to do much better at the plate themselves. Memphremagog had one of the best pitchers I'd ever seen, a fireballing young Frenchman with long stringy black hair who Charlie said was a ringer brought in from the Canadian Semi-pro League to beat us in front of our home crowd. The ringer didn't seem to have much of a curve, but he threw so hard that the ball kept popping out of their catcher's glove and dribbling into the dirt in the batter's box. Even Charlie couldn't seem to connect. Except for one tremendous foul fly ball that bounced off the cab of Royce's pickup truck parked just south of the *Monitor,* he didn't get his bat on the ball once in his first two trips to the plate.

After my brother's second strikeout my father took off his face mask and shook his head. "Why does he try to pull everything, James? Of course he's going to strike out if he does that against a speedball pitcher."

"That's Charlie for you, Dad. Just wait until he gets hold of one. Then you'll see something. Ted Williams doesn't go with the pitches, either."

"Ted doesn't need to go with the pitches."

The game was still scoreless after six innings. The huge throng of spectators had grown quieter and quieter, and by midway through the seventh inning they were so absorbed in the pitching duel between Harlan and the Canadian ringer that only a smattering of people stood up to stretch, a ritual that Kingdom Common fans scrupulously prided themselves on observing.

In the top of the ninth, the Memphremagog crowd came to life, stomping and cheering like madmen. But Big Harlan, who was throwing as well as I'd ever seen him, struck out the Loggers' lead-off man on three consecutive fastballs. That quieted their rooters and sent ours into a frenzy.

The Canadian pitcher was up next. He menaced with his bat and gave Harlan a snaggletoothed grin.

"You'd better start swinging right now if you want to hit this one, Jacques," Charlie said in his needling catcher's voice.

Harlan double-pumped, triple-pumped, pumped yet again. His long arm swung back and up and came whipping down past his cap like a big striking snake, and the Canadian stepped into the pitch and lined it into the gap in deepest right-center, far over the snow fence, for a home run.

As the Frenchman rounded the bases to a tremendous ovation, I noticed that Big Harlan was holding his pitching arm. Harlan threw just one pitch to the next batter. It hit the dirt several feet in front of the plate, and that was that. He was through for the rest of the day, and everyone knew it. And everyone knew as well that with Carter Pike—Harlan's only backup pitcher—out of town, the Outlaws were in serious trouble.

As Harlan left the field and Charlie conferred excitedly with Royce St. Onge and Stub at home plate, Reverend Andrews walked over from the third-base bleachers. "Maybe I can help you chaps out," he said. "I used to pitch some in college. If you don't have any objection, I'd be willing to try my hand at it again."

Charlie just smiled like the cat that swallowed the canary and tossed him the baseball; but as the minister headed out toward the mound Stub Poulin, true to his word, stalked off the field without a word.

"You walk off this team now, you're never coming back, Stub," Charlie called after him. "Stub Poulin! You hear?"

Stub kept going.

Charlie shrugged. "Okay, have it your way, buddy."

He beckoned to Pine Benson's younger brother, Robbie, the Outlaws' utility infielder, who ran eagerly onto the field.

The Memphremagog fans continued to scream and hoot; but Reverend Andrews, still in his street clothes, began taking his six allotted warm-up pitches and paid no attention to them at all.

"Looky, pa!" a little kid in the first-base bleachers shouted. "There's Jackie Robinson!"

This broke the tension, and everyone within earshot, including Reverend Andrews, now finishing his warm-ups, laughed.

"Hush up," the kid's father said. "That man's the preacher at the church across the street. You hush, now."

But the boy waved and shouted out to the mound, "Hi, Jackie!"

By now everyone was laughing—some, I think, to see how slowly Reverend Andrews threw for such a big man. His pitches just drifted in, though I noticed that the last two or three acted oddly. Charlie grinned and winked at me. He closed the fist of his throwing hand and tapped his knuckles. Then he opened his fingers and fluttered them up and down like a trapped bird.

So that was it. Reverend Andrews was a knuckleball pitcher!

There was not much laughing on the Memphremagog bench or in their bleachers for the next five minutes as the minister set down their next three men on seven pitches. The first two struck out on what looked like six consecutive knucklers and the third lifted a high foul into the sunset, which my brother pulled out of the third-base bleachers in the best running catch of the day.

"Two runs!" Charlie shouted over and over again to the Outlaws as they came running in for their last at-bat. "Two runs are all we need. The order is: Benson for Poulin, St. Onge, Kinneson, Andrews for Kittredge. If you want to bat, that is, Walt."

The minister shrugged. "That's up to you, Charles. It's your team."

"If Royce or Robbie gets on, you won't have to anyway," Charlie said. "I guarantee it. This time, boys, old Charlie K is going to put one out of here. I mean I am going to *park* it. That imported Frenchman started running out of gas two innings ago. Last time up I was way out in front of him. Besides, the keg's empty. We've got to win this inning or parch to death."

With these and similar exhortations, my determined big brother revved up his team, walking up and down in front of the bench, clapping and laughing and joking so that you'd have thought we were ten runs ahead instead of behind by one and going into the last half of the last inning.

Robbie Benson grounded out weakly to second on the first pitch. That left the Outlaws two outs away from only their third defeat of the season.

Royce St. Onge, pie-eyed from beer, headed toward the batter's box. Charlie grabbed his arm. "Listen, buddy. Get on base. I don't care how you do it, but do it. Then camp there."

Royce looked at my brother through glazed eyes. He swayed a little and finally he nodded. He crowded the plate more than usual, and on the second pitch he laid down a perfect bunt, catching the third baseman flat-footed. Boozed up as he was, though, Royce couldn't beat the throw and was out by a step. That brought Charlie to the plate and the crowd to its feet.

The great crowd was thundering. The Folding Chair boys were up, Plug Johnson was pounding on his trusty leather cushion, and Athena Allen was jumping up and down on the bleachers and screaming for Charlie to hit a home run. I could think of nothing but how desperately I wanted my brother to park one in the street or, better yet, up against the brick block and tie the game for his team and our good friend the minister and our town.

Charlie gave the crowd a cocky grin and stepped into the batter's box. Just as the big rangy Frenchman got set, my brother theatrically raised one hand over his head to call time. He shifted his feet, tapped his spikes with his thirty-eight-inch Louisville Slugger, and grinned again, this time at the pitcher. He stepped back in the batter's box, and the Canadian threw a fastball straight at Charlie's head.

The next two pitches were let-ups over the outside corner. Charlie tried to murder them, and fouled each pitch back into the screen. My father shook his head. The Kingdom crowd fell deadly still.

Again Charlie backed out of the box. Again he smiled at the pitcher. He stepped back in and leveled his big bat belt-high across the plate and wagged it slowly, once. I dare you, he was saying. I dare you to put one right there, right down the center of the old platter. To me at that moment, my big brother looked invincible. But the Frenchman apparently thought differently. He just smiled that contemptuous smile, kicked high, uncoiled, threw.

It was the pitch my brother had been waiting for all afternoon, and he swung from the heels as hard as I have ever seen a batter swing, and he missed the ball completely.

The Memphremagog crowd was screaming so loudly I barely heard Reverend Andrews shouting. The minister ran up to the batter's box, where Charlie was still down on one knee from the momentum of his tremendous whiff.

"Run!" shouted the minister. And from our bleachers came shouts of "Run! Run!"

Charlie leapt to his feet and spun around. The catcher was racing toward the backstop, where the baseball lay at the foot of a support post. My brother dropped his bat and tore down the baseline, crossing the bag a split second before the ball smacked into the first baseman's mitt, and the Outlaws had a life after all.

Now it was up to Reverend Andrews.

I knew that our minister could handle a baseball bat. I'd seen him hit fielding practice for the Academy team, one-handed, with a glove on his left hand. I'd seen him drive balls deep into the outfield with one hand. But that was with the leaded fungo bat. And I also knew that he batted cross-handed. He had learned that unorthodox technique playing stickball as a boy, Nat had told me. So I was not surprised when he stepped into the batter's box and gripped the bat with his left hand on top of his right hand. The crowd did not appear to notice, because Charlie was dancing around wildly off first and clapping his hands to draw the pitcher's attention.

You might think that my brother, after the ignominy of reaching first on a dropped third strike, and in view of the Outlaws' back-to-the-wall situation, would have taken a more conservative lead. (A maxim of my father's comes to mind: "Three steps off first, six off second, four off third on the grass.")

But Charlie was now a good *five steps* off first base, dancing and jeering. My heart was in my mouth; he was bound to get himself picked off and run his team right out of the ballgame. The pitcher, still in his set position, looked in at his catcher. My father crouched over the catcher intensely. Reverend Andrews was bent over slightly, his broad shoulders bulging out of the too-small uniform top he'd put on at the last minute.

Quick as lightning the pitcher whirled and made a perfect throw to first base, catching Charlie a good six steps off the bag.

It was exactly what my brother had been waiting for.

Instead of sliding back into the first baseman's tag, the instant the Frenchman's back foot moved off the rubber Charlie broke toward second. The first baseman swiped his glove down at nothing, then panicked and threw the ball into left field. Charlie never stopped running. He rounded second and was three quarters of the way to third by the time the Memphremagog outfielder had the ball.

Later, replaying the game, as they replayed every game, my father and Charlie disagreed about what the outfielder should have done. Charlie said he should have run the ball in himself, all the way home if necessary. Dad said he should have thrown it to the pitcher. But whatever the fielder should have done, he should *not* have tried to peg my brother out at third, because even a good throw wouldn't have gotten him, and the throw the fielder made, far from being a good one, sailed ten feet over the third-baseman's head into the bleachers.

Charlie never broke stride. He crossed home with the tying run to a tremendous ovation from a thousand or more fans. Somehow, my flamboyant big brother had managed to go from goat to hero in less than a minute!

But the Frenchman was furious. The first pitch to the minister was straight at him. He hit the dirt, and the cheering of our crowd changed to a rumble of outrage. My father strode out to the mound and said something to the pitcher, who merely shrugged and turned away as Dad returned to his station behind the plate.

Dad looked at the ball, which the catcher had retrieved from the screen. He tossed it to me. It had a deep gash in it from where it had smacked into the wire backstop. Dad fished in his ball bag and came up with another.

Reverend Andrews got set again. He did not seem perturbed over the beanball. He adjusted his inverted hands and adjusted his feet, still in his street shoes. The Canadian kicked high and pitched. . . .

"The crack of good straight-grained ashwood meeting horsehide squarely is a unique sound," my father ended his article on the game in that week's *Monitor*. "No matter how many thousands of times you have heard it, it still comes with the suddenness and something of the inexorable violence of lightning. Yet the crack of the Reverend Walter Andrews' bat was not especially loud. And the ball did not seem to travel particularly fast. It rose out of the infield almost leisurely, and continued to rise, catching the last rays of the setting sun, in a great soaring parabola—the kind of ball experienced outfielders merely shrug at as it goes over. Those of us who have seen long balls hit before on the common waited for it to strike the brick front or carved upper facade of the shopping block and rebound back into the street. We waited in vain. The ball was still climbing when it passed out of sight over that building. . . ."

"Mister Baby Johnson!" Dad said as the Reverend Andrews rounded first base.

And then, as the minister touched second, "Fair ball."

Sheer pandemonium broke out as the Outlaws and hundreds of their fans rushed toward home plate to greet Reverend Andrews.

It was one of the happiest moments of my life to that point, as happy as if my brother himself had clouted the already legendary home run.

It was the last truly happy moment I can remember from the summer of 1952.

. . .

"Wake up, Kinneson."

Someone was shaking me. For a panicky moment, I didn't know where I was.

"It's after midnight," Nat said, giving my shoulder another shake.

I must have been sleeping very hard because I still felt fuzzy-headed. When I'd arrived at the parsonage around nine o'clock for our appointment with Pliny's ghost, Nat was nowhere to be found and the house was totally dark. I hadn't dared wait on the haunted porch, so I sneaked up to my friend's room, where somehow I'd managed to fall asleep while waiting by the window.

"Where were you, Nat?"

"Out with Claire. Keep your voice down, my father's working in his study. What are you doing here?"

"Don't you remember? Tonight's the night we're supposed to wait for Pliny's ghost."

"Come on, Kinneson. You don't really believe that story, do you?"

Something, I had no idea what, had happened to change Nat's mind about catching Pliny's skeleton and burying it. But why hadn't he told me? I was bewildered and annoyed.

"Well, one thing's for sure. It'll never show up if we don't believe in it."

"Like Peter Pan, eh?"

Crouched beside the bedroom window, Nat and I could see all the way down the street to the north end of the common. Except for one short string of colored lights left on by mistake over a game booth and the dim reflection of Reverend Andrews' study light on the slate flagstones leading up to the parsonage porch steps, the village was totally dark.

The only sound was the low throb of the tin dust blowers, hunkered like invisible gargoyles on the roof of the American Heritage furniture mill. Even the falls behind the hotel were almost still, a thin inaudible ripple over the granite flume that had been a raging torrent just three months ago. Kingdom Common was as quiet as only a small town after a big event can be.

Then off in the distance, faintly yet distinctly, came the long mournful wail of the 12:45 A.M. southbound highball, hooting at the trestle north of town. A few seconds later we both started. As the train approached the crossing between the hotel and the north end of the common, a siren blasted into the night. Mason White's patrol hearse shot out of the driveway of the undertaker's parlor at the foot of the knoll and bounced over the railroad tracks scant seconds in front of the hurtling freight.

The hearse accelerated like a stock car on a straightaway. The blinking reflection of its blue light raced along the storefront windows. Then the first of four diesel locomotives was on the crossing, blocking out our view of the sheriff's speeding vehicle.

"An accident?" Nat said.

"I doubt it. Knowing Mason, he probably just wants the village to see he's still on duty. Elections are coming up in the fall, remember."

Nat chuckled. "You're learning, Kinneson. Slowly but surely, you're coming along. You may still amount to some—"

And that is when all hell broke loose. A fiery orange tongue of flame erupted in the street directly in front of the parsonage, accompanied by a booming reverberation. Even over the clank and rumble of the speeding train I recognized the report as a gunshot. I was vaguely aware of glass shattering below us. This was no ghost and no prank —somebody was firing at the parsonage!

A figure ran off the porch steps into the yard. A sharper report barked out, not so loud, and I heard a man curse. A light came on at Elijah's cottage. Across the hall, Claire cried out in alarm.

Nat and I ran downstairs and onto the porch. Reverend Andrews was standing by the gate in the fence, holding a revolver in his hand. It was pointed straight at Resolvèd Kinneson, standing in the middle of the street with his shotgun.

The study light was still on, and although the shade was pulled partly down, I could see through the bittersweet vines a gaping hole in the window.

"I want her!" Resolvèd shouted. "I want that woman and I intend to have her. I know she's been a-holing up here. You fetch her, mister, or I'll ransack your Christly premises and snake her out myself."

"You'll do no such thing," Reverend Andrews said. "Put down that gun."

In a voice that must have carried halfway out to the gool, my cousin roared, "I paid thirty dollars for her, and I don't intend to stand by and see it go down the drain now that I'm on my feet again. I intend to marry that woman."

"She's hardly a woman, Resolvèd Kinneson, and you know it. She's not yet eighteen years old."

"She's woman enough and whore enough to let half the Frenchmen in Canada put the britches to her, and then come prancing down over the line with that fair show and deny me my lawful rights with her and run off to a so-called preacher that ain't no better than he should be. You'll produce her, by the Jesus, or I'll know the reason why."

"You don't have any rights with her, lawful or otherwise," Reverend Andrews said. "She doesn't belong to you just because you sent her some money. I'll reimburse you, if that's what you're worried about. But I'm not going to let you take her back up to your place. Do you understand that?"

"Yes, I understand that," Resolvèd said. "And I understand why you're keeping her here. And I'll have you understand that one way or another I'll claim what's mine. I aim to marry that woman, goddamn it. We won't be broke asunder by you.

"I aim," Resolvèd shouted, and with no warning fired the second barrel of the shotgun over our heads and through the glass transom above the parsonage door. Then he lifted the gun like a club over his head with both hands and charged the minister.

As Resolvèd rushed toward him, brandishing the shotgun, Reverend Andrews shot twice. Resolvèd crashed into the gate, whirled partway around, and dropped the gun. He held up his right hand. A little geyser of blood was spurting out of it where the tip of his index finger had been. He looked at what was left of the finger in disbelief.

"Resolvèd," the minister said wearily, "go home and put a bandage on that. You've been keeping too much company with your friend Old Duke tonight. He's a bad influence on you."

"You, Preacher," Resolvèd snarled, pressing his hand against his shirt. "You ever hear of a fella name of Ordney Gilson? You hear, Reverend? Ordney Gilson. You remember that name. Ornery Ordney Gilson."

Which was when Mason White showed up in his patrol hearse, blue lights flashing, sirens screaming. "What's going on here?" he demanded in his high voice as he leapt out of his hearse. "What's going on here, I say?"

"No big problem, Sheriff," Reverend Andrews said in his agreeable and now once more mildly amused and ironical tone of voice. "My neighbor here was just telling me that he didn't care all that much for my sermons. That's all."

"Get in the car," Mason snarled at Resolvèd. "I'll deal with you in a minute."

"Who's Ordney Gilson?" Nat said as we headed back into the house while his father filled the sheriff in on the shooting.

I was silent.

"Who is he?" Nat said.

"Oh, nobody," I said. "Just some old farmer who used to live around here."

# 12

"I'm having trouble believing this," my father said for the third or fourth time that morning as we entered Charlie's office.

As usual, I had been brought along as interpreter. There definitely was going to be some trouble.

Still wearing his sweat-stained baseball uniform from the big game the day before, my brother was tilted back in his swivel chair with his spikes propped on his desk, sipping a warm beer.

Although it was still early in the morning, the whole village was buzzing. The Folding Chair Club had already set up a reconnaissance outpost on the courthouse portico, and Charlie had been sequestered with Resolvèd in his jail cell since dawn, when my brother had gotten back from an all-night celebration in Canada with his baseball team.

"I know I shouldn't, James," Dad said, standing with his back to us and staring out Charlie's small window at the distant mountains, "but I'm having trouble understanding what's happening here. A no-good drunken bum fires two blasts of buckshot that can kill a big deer at fifty yards into the home of a law-abiding local citizen. Now your brother's going to represent that no-good bum in court?"

Charlie sighed. "Come on, Jimmy. I've defended Cousin R since the week I opened my practice. How can I stop now?"

"By saying no, James."

"Damn it, Jim, it's my job. I *can't* say no."

My father snorted. "I've said this before, James. A job is something you get paid for doing."

Charlie took a long slug of beer and made a sour face. He set the bottle down on a back issue of *Field & Stream* with a brook trout on its cover far gaudier than any brook trout I had ever seen in Kingdom County, where brook trout were as colorful as any in the world.

"Look, buddy," he told me, though I hadn't opened my mouth once since coming into his office. "Even Cousin R is innocent in the eyes of the law until proven guilty. Lord knows that there's enough circumstantial evidence here to convince a jury to put him away for the next couple of centuries. But that doesn't mean I shouldn't defend him. Somebody has to."

My father turned slightly so that his profile was toward me. He looked more than ever like a somewhat older version of Ted Williams. When he spoke, he seemed to be addressing the statue of Ethan Allen below on the common. "Maybe so, James, but your brother doesn't have to. This is a serious matter. It was well planned. Resolvèd or one of his cronies even went to the trouble of calling Mason White and decoying him off on a wild goose chase just before the shooting. And he used the Montreal highball for cover, just the way the bank robbers did. He ought to be locked up for the next twenty years."

For once Charlie had no rejoinder. In the ensuing silence it occurred to me that none of this would be happening if, right here in this office less than four months ago, my brother hadn't written that stupid letter for Resolvèd. I wondered if he might be thinking the same thing; maybe that was why he felt responsible for defending our cousin now. But none of what had happened in the last twelve hours made much sense to me.

"Look," Dad said, and though he continued to stare down onto the common, he seemed to be talking more or less directly to Charlie for the first time that morning. "This business goes way beyond Resolvèd's ordinary run-of-the-mill outlawry. We aren't talking about a few poached trout any longer. We aren't talking about a rooster fight or a deer shot out of season or a scuffle over at the hotel barroom."

"I realize that," Charlie said.

"I'm glad you do. Because this isn't a question of our family and whatever tribal obligations we both may have or think we have to an outcast shirttail cousin. Whether you defend him or someone else defends him or nobody defends him doesn't matter in the least. The outcome's going to be the same. Zack will throw the book at him, just as he should, and get his big conviction. And he and Mason White will parlay that conviction into at least two more years of disgraceful misrule in this county."

"Maybe."

"There isn't any maybe about it. Resolvèd'll be convicted. You won't find a potential juror in the county who won't be outraged over this. Have you stopped to think what's really at stake here? I'll tell you, mister. The entire moral reputation of the Kingdom, that's what. You can't win. You shouldn't win. And if you do go ahead with this, I intend to do everything I can to make sure you don't win."

Charlie winked at me. "The Civil War is refought in Kingdom County, Jimmy. Father against son. Maybe even brother against brother."

"This isn't amusing," my father said. "It's about the least amusing thing I can imagine. Consider what this will do to your own reputation."

Charlie stood up. "Dad," he said quietly, "do you know what the charges against Resolvèd are as of right this minute?"

"I can easily enough guess. At the very least, assault with a deadly weapon."

Charlie shook his head.

My father raised his eyebrows. "Attempted murder? That's why you feel obligated to defend him? Well, good for Zachariah. For once the old fool's done something halfway right."

My brother sighed. "So far, Resolvèd has been charged with drunk and disorderly conduct and disturbing the peace. Just to get him off the streets for a few days, Zack claims, so that he and Mason can continue their investigation of the incident. The arraignment's this afternoon.

"Now I'm going to tell you something else," Charlie continued.

"Before Resolvèd talked to me, he evidently talked to the sheriff and Zack alone. I haven't been able to find out what was discussed yet. But whatever it was he told them must have influenced Zack's decision to let him off with a light charge."

"James," my father said as he walked out of Charlie's office, "this is going to kill your mother."

Resolvèd Kinneson was arraigned at three o'clock that afternoon. This time he was not wearing a suit and tie and shiny dress shoes. He wore the same tattered green work shirt and baggy green wool pants he had been arrested in the night before at the parsonage. Since his court appearance in the incarnation of the Most Peculiar lawyer last May, his hair had grown out quite long again, and he looked more like the woodcut of Pap Finn than ever.

The courtroom was nearly full. Besides the lawyers, Mason White, Farlow Blake, Julia Hefner, and the Folding Chair Club, there were several out-of-town reporters and at least a couple of hundred local spectators and curiosity-seekers.

Just before the arraignment began, Reverend Andrews strolled in and sat down alone in the back of the room across the aisle from my father and me.

"All rise," said Farlow Blake in his most sonorous and solemn voice as Judge Allen entered, sat down, and immediately began reading the watered-down charges against my cousin.

". . . and with unruly and tumultuous carriage did endanger the general populace." The judge paused. "Do you understand what that means, Resolvèd?"

My cousin, who was standing at the defense table with Charlie to hear the charges, scowled. "I guess it means I don't rub elbows with the right ones in this so-called village."

"It means nothing of the sort," Judge Allen said angrily. "It means that you are being charged with posing a very real danger to a member of this community. Before I ask you formally to state your plea, I want to be certain in my own mind that you understand the charges. Regardless of the wording, you should know that I regard this whole affair as a grave offense and a blight on this entire area. The sanctity of one's home is a basic right in this country, Resolvèd Kinneson. It can't be infringed on with impunity. You wouldn't like to worry about your personal safety every time you turned out your lights and went to bed at night."

"I don't follow such procedures."

"What procedures?"

"Turning out my lights. You see, Jedge, I and my brother don't have electric up there."

"Charles Kinneson, inform your client that if he bandies words with the bench one more time, just once more, I'll slap you both with a cool hundred-dollar fine, payable on the spot."

Charlie turned to Resolvèd. "Be quiet!" he hissed.

Judge Allen finished reading the charges. "What do you plead, Resolvèd Kinneson?"

"No contest."

Judge Allen looked at Charlie for a long time. Finally he said, "Very well. Now, Resolvèd, despite the relatively light penalties of a breach of peace charge, this is in fact a serious offense. Understand that I believe these charges are far too mild, the more so in view of the fact that you have been in front of this bench often before. Understand too that regardless of how you have been specifically charged, I view this latest offense as far more serious than all of your prior depredations taken together. This 'breach of the peace' is a blot on your record not just in this court but in the eyes of all of the law-abiding citizens of this community and this state. For the seriousness of this act lies in its unleashing of violence, which always begets violence—witness your own bandaged hand."

The judge looked straight at my cousin and said, "Resolvèd, do you have anything to say before I set bail?"

My cousin glanced over at Mason White and Zack Barrows; though I couldn't be sure, I thought I saw the prosecutor shake his head slightly.

"Not just yet," Resolvèd snarled.

The judge was caught by surprise. After another pause he said, "I must advise you, Resolvèd, if you have *anything* to say on your own behalf that you believe may have a bearing on your ultimate sentence, and on the amount of bail that I impose, this is the time to make your statement."

Abruptly, my cousin stepped into the aisle between the defense and prosecution tables. "I'll say just this much," he growled. "I ain't admitting to one thing. Not one thing do I admit to about no so-called shooting or nothing else. We'll have that understood right off quick to the start. The rest of what I've got to say I shall say in my own good time."

Resolvèd sat back down.

"Very well," Judge Allen said. "Resolvèd Kinneson, I establish your bail at a thousand dollars. You will be sentenced within the next week. In the meantime, Sheriff White will see you back to your quarters in the county jail in the basement of this building."

NEGRO MINISTER CONFRONTS BACKWOODS GUNMAN

COLORED CLERGYMAN FIRED ON, SHOOTS BACK

RACIAL PERSECUTION IN SLEEPY VERMONT VILLAGE?

WOULD-BE MURDERER GETS SLAP ON WRIST: WHEN WILL HE TRY AGAIN?

It was August 6, the morning after Resolvèd's arraignment, and to judge by the out-of-town newspaper reports, all New England was preoccupied with nothing else. I had just returned to the *Monitor* from the post office with the half-dozen New England papers Dad subscribed to, and even the Boston *Globe* had emblazoned its story across the front page of its northern New England edition.

" 'When asked if racial prejudice existed in northern Vermont,' " my father read from the *Globe*, " 'Reverend Walter Andrews stated that he supposed racial prejudice existed everywhere. But he added that he was inclined to think that Thursday night's shootout in this tiny border town had resulted from a misunderstanding. Queried as to the exact nature of this misunderstanding, the Canadian-born Negro minister of the United Church of Kingdom Common quipped: "The chap who shot at my house and me obviously didn't think I would shoot back." ' "

But no sooner had Dad started to read the Burlington *Free Press* account of the shooting and arraignment than Farlow Blake slithered through the door in his spanking white barber's apron with yet another problem. Some of the Presbyterian session members had just convened a meeting to discuss the minister in the Sunday school room of the church, and for some reason neither Dad nor Reverend Andrews had been notified.

■ ■ ■

"Folks, we can't allow this situation to continue to get out of hand," George Quinn was saying. "Did you read this morning's Boston paper? The Kingdom's getting a black eye clear across New England as a result of all this publicity."

"My main question is, why would a minister or any other law-abiding man keep a loaded gun in his house in the first place?" Elijah Kinneson said. "Not to mention continuing to harbor a girl who's no better than a woman of the streets. This is turning into a full-blown scandal."

"The scandalous thing is Resolvèd's trying to kidnap the girl and firing at the Andrews' house, not Walt's firing back to defend himself," my father said sharply.

I nudged Nat, ensconced beside me in the vestibule just off the main Sunday school room, into which we'd slipped moments before. I was immensely proud of my father. There was no way he was going to let these small-minded people railroad Nat's father.

"We limped along for years before we managed to find anybody willing to venture up here and tackle this job the way it should be tackled," Dad said. "Then we got lucky. We not only found somebody, we found a good man. Walt Andrews has done more for this church in three short months than any other minister has done in years. Now you're saying you want to give him the boot because he's got an enemy or two? You're going to let an event involving Resolvèd Kinneson influence how you run church affairs? You can't do this."

"Nobody wants to eject the man from his job, Charles. We just want some answers here. We want to know about that gun and why he had it. We want that little . . . well, frankly, that little tart out of our parsonage. It just doesn't look right."

"It doesn't look right to hold a session meeting without the minister present, George. Our bylaws clearly state that the minister is a member of the session. Is this an official session meeting?"

"I suppose it is," George Quinn said. "We just didn't see how we could have the man himself sit in here with us today. It would be sort of like having the defendant sit in on the jury deliberation, wouldn't it?"

"This isn't a jury," my father said. "And I, for one, don't for a minute think Walt Andrews has done anything at all that he shouldn't have."

"Well, Reverend Andrews is off in Pond in the Sky conducting a funeral this morning," George said feebly. "He couldn't be here."

"This *isn't* a jury, damn it," my father repeated.

As the session considered what my father had said, it was quiet. It was also stuffy, at least in the cubbyhole where Nat and I were crouched among the musty-smelling folds of the stern dark choir robes, straining to hear every word in the meeting room.

"To tell you the truth, editor," Ben Currier said, "even those of us who support the reverend the most, and I count myself among them, didn't want to embarrass him by asking him to come here this morning. Not until we've discussed the whole situation, at least."

"Embarrass whom?"

Nat stiffened in the dark beside me. In that faintly ironical, richly resonant voice I could not mistake for any other, even if I were to hear it again today after more than thirty-five years, Reverend Andrews said, "Am I interrupting something private, gentlemen? Don't let me disturb you. I just dropped by to hang up my funeral vestments. Or should I leave them on?"

Nat and I burrowed far back into the closet, burying ourselves in the primary grade's Christmas angel costumes. The door opened and a shaft of light fell across the robes. There was a cough that might have been a suppressed chuckle, then the rattle of a coat hanger. The door closed, and all was dark again.

"No need to rush off now you're here, Reverend," George said. "We were just wondering if you'd like to tell us your side of the story."

"That's why you didn't ask me to attend, then?" Reverend Andrews said. "So that I could tell you my side of the story? You know, gentlemen, there's an unpleasant expression for the kind of trial-without-recourse that I've apparently interrupted. I won't offend you by saying what that expression is, except that I fancy it may have originated down under in Australia."

I thought I heard my father snort. But the other members of the session were apparently not amused.

"Where would you like me to begin?" the minister said.

"With the girl," Elijah Kinneson said sharply. "Didn't you know the minute the girl navigated over to your house that in a small town like this there was bound to be trouble? Talk?"

"It wasn't the first thought to cross my mind, to tell you the truth. My first thought was that she needed a roof over her head. Lending a helping hand is one of a minister's duties, you know. And, gentlemen, though there's little so rankling to me as a prattling preacher who cites chapter and text from the Bible to win personal arguments, surely you'll agree that that document holds out more than a few precedents for my decision. It doesn't seem to me that I should have to apologize for trying to follow its dictates."

"You shouldn't," my father said.

"So you'd say you did the right thing then?" George said. "By taking the girl in? And you're still doing the right thing by keeping her? Even in view of her background and all? We're just asking, that's all, Reverend. We need some guidance on this matter. We need to know what you think."

"I'd say it was the right thing to do," Reverend Andrews said. "Especially in view of her background. I'm doing everything I can to find an appropriate alternative for her, if that's any help."

Castor Oil Quinn cleared his throat. "I guess we'll just have to take your word on that, then. Now, on another matter. The matter of your gun. With all the publicity that this trouble's been getting, a number of parishioners have approached us this morning. I mean they've approached us trustees, expressing—ah, surprise. Surprise that a minister would have a loaded gun in his house in the first place, and then actually fire it off at someone. Now don't misunderstand me for a minute, Reverend. None of us at all questions your right to protect yourself and your son. But this shooting fracas at the parsonage—we just wondered why you didn't immediately call the sheriff."

"The sheriff had been decoyed out of town, presumably by Resolvèd Kinneson, whose stated intention was to take Claire LaRiviere out of the parsonage—by force, if necessary."

"Well, we're all relieved that nothing happened to the girl. But if I correctly recall, you were asked by a representative of the Ladies Auxiliary as well as by Elijah here to do something about the girl some days ago, and you apparently chose not to."

"For heavens sake, man, are we back to her again? I have been *trying* to do something about the girl. This isn't as simple as it sounds."

"No, it isn't," George said. "Well, this, ah, inquiry, it's mainly our way of finding out what really is going on so that we can properly support and advise you."

"Indeed? Well, don't think I'm not grateful, but I wish I'd been formally invited to your 'inquiry' because there are some things I'd have clarified right from the start, and will now, with your indulgence. To begin with, I've never in all my life kept a loaded gun in any house I've lived in. The revolver, which was unloaded, was in the bottom drawer of my desk. The clip containing the bullets was locked in an upper drawer. Nor did I fire until after I'd been fired at. I did shoot then but not carelessly. I deliberately fired a disabling, rather than a mortal, shot."

"I understand, Walter," George said. "You don't have to convince me. Probably I would have done exactly what you did."

This I doubted. I would have been astonished to learn that old Castor Oil ever had held anything more lethal than a cough syrup prescription in his well-manicured hand in his entire life.

"It's just that some people will be sure to wonder why a minister would keep any gun, loaded or not, in his desk," George continued. "You know how folks are in a small town."

"I'm learning fast," Reverend Andrews said. "Ordinarily, I don't keep a gun in my desk. But frankly, after some earlier episodes, I thought it advisable."

"So you still think you did the right thing, night before last?"

"I'd say so. What do you think?"

There was a pause. Then Reverend Andrews said, "Why don't you take a vote? I'll wait outside."

"The question before us," George said when the minister had left, "is whether to give Reverend Andrews a vote of confidence. I'm inclined to think we should, but this whole situation still distresses me. All I can say is vote your conscience. A yes means we accord him a vote of confidence. A no means we don't. Written ballots are best in this case, I believe."

I could hear chairs scuffling, paper being ripped for ballots. Beside me in the dark Nat was breathing quicker.

"One thing before we vote," my father said. "Regardless of what any of you may think personally about this matter, don't vote no today. If you do, it'll indicate that you think Reverend Andrews is guilty of something, which he isn't, unless it's being a good minister and a good Christian."

By the end of that fall, it would seem to me that I had spent half of 1952 waiting for important decisions I had no control over, in courtrooms and elsewhere. But the wait in the Sunday school closet with both the minister's and my father's credibility at stake was one of the hardest.

"Seven yes's and one no," George Quinn announced, and a moment later I heard the door open.

"Reverend Andrews, it isn't unanimous but seven out of the eight members of the session have accorded you a vote of confidence. I'm glad of it, sir. I'm glad the air has been cleared. I want you to know that we're behind you all the way."

"That's good," Reverend Andrews said, his voice equable and resonant and faintly amused. "Even the one dissenting vote, now that I think of it. As I've mentioned before, if I didn't have at least one enemy, you wouldn't be able to trust me, would you, now? Gentlemen, good morning to you."

# 13

My father prided himself on never locking the *Monitor* during the day, but just before leaving for the session meeting he'd told me to hold down the fort until he got back, and when I dashed in breathlessly a minute or so after he arrived, he wasn't happy.

Fortunately for me, Reverend Andrews was already sitting in the single chair in front of Dad's desk.

Dad handed me a slip of paper from his notepad. It had two dates written on it: August 6, 1900, and August 13, 1900.

"Reverend Andrews wants to borrow these issues of the *Monitor*, James. Go downstairs and get them, and whatever you do, don't mix up the order of the back issues or Elijah'll have your head, and mine too."

"Didn't I see you and Nathan having a little Sunday school class a short while ago?" Reverend Andrews said to me with a wink.

So he *had* seen us hiding in the Sunday school closet, when he opened the door. It was all I could do not to crack up as I rummaged through the stacks of old yellow *Monitors* in the basement.

Upstairs I heard my father say, "Walter, I must admit, I'm surprised that you can still be so interested in local history at a time like this."

The minister laughed. "What should I do, abandon all hope and start knitting a big red *A*?"

"What do you mean?"

"Well, it's evident to me, and has been since Julia Hefner's first visit to the parsonage to try to bully me into sending that girl packing, that half the people in this town think I'm having an illicit affair with her. No one's quite come right out and said so. But that's what they're thinking."

"Well," my father said, "it's understandable that you might feel resentful. In the past month you've put on the biggest and most successful shindig this town has seen in fifty years, which, by the way, George Quinn just told me brought in a little over four thousand dollars. You've had your household turned upside down by a slightly unbalanced teenage girl, been shot at by a local drunk and would-be kidnapper, and raked over the coals by your governing board for having the temerity to defend yourself."

"Resolvèd doesn't bother me much, Charles. If you look at this from his point of view, it's not hard to see why he's so upset. He honestly believes he has a proprietary right to the girl. He may even be in love with her, in his own strange way. After all, Resolvèd's human. He probably thought he'd waked up in heaven when she walked through his door. Now she's left him for reasons he can't possibly understand, and he's lashing out at me as the person he supposes must be responsible.

"What I want to talk to you about, though, is something else that bothers me. Your local sheriff dropped by rather late last night—to do a bit more investigating, he said."

"He ought to have. It's high time."

"Wait and hear what he wanted. It was around eleven o'clock. I was sitting in the study reading Pliny's *History* when he came up onto the porch and knocked. He was dressed in his uniform, and he asked if we could talk. I said of course, and he suggested that we visit on the porch. I was somewhat surprised, as it was quite cool last evening, but as you'll see, he had his reasons.

"At first White sirred me to a fare-thee-well. At the same time he grilled me like a grand inquisitor. He told me he was getting ready to make his final report to Zack Barrows so that Barrows could decide on a sentencing recommendation for Resolvèd. He said he needed some additional background information, including my exact age, education, and service dates. He claimed this was standard information, and asked to see my service discharge papers. I said I wasn't at all sure I had them here, that they were probably still in Montreal at my mother-in-law's. That was true enough, but frankly, I was hoping to brush him off. I jokingly told him to read his hometown newspaper, that all this 'background information' and more besides was in the interview you conducted with me the week I arrived. He persevered, though, and said he needed some sort of official document to help me prove my credibility.

"That's when I got my back up. I told him I didn't need to prove anything at all, and that I'd never heard of the victim of a crime being investigated more zealously than the perpetrator. White said that he was just trying to establish that a crime had been committed in the first place. Then he said that anyone who wanted to create a local race incident for publicity purposes could have arranged a confrontation such as the one at the parsonage. I was dumbfounded. But it got worse. 'Boy,' he said, 'we are just trying to help you. But we have to know one thing. Do you ever, or have you ever, slept in your study?'

"I wasn't sure whom White meant by 'we.' Himself and the prosecutor, maybe. But I understood the 'boy' all too well. That was the final straw. I told him that where I slept was my own business and that I hadn't gotten much sleep at all lately because I'd been too busy standing vigil night and day to protect my home. White said that if by protecting my home I meant getting involved in a shoot-out in a settled area, he'd think I might have exercised better judgment. That's when I told him to clear off the premises straightaway, before I lost my temper.

" 'I just hope you do lose your temper and lay a finger on me, boy,' White said, 'because that's all the excuse I'd need to bring you in for assaulting an elected peacekeeper.' I don't know what made me look out then toward that hearse he drives around in, but when I did I spotted a man, standing in the shadows by it. Of course, I can't be positive, but I believe White intended to goad me into punching him right there on my front porch, so he could hail in his deputy as a witness. At any rate, I didn't bite, though I must say I was sorely tempted. If I hadn't spotted that deputy, I might be languishing in jail this very moment."

Listening closely to the conversation upstairs had slowed considerably my search for the articles from 1900 that Reverend Andrews wanted.

"James!" my father called down the stairs. "Haven't you located those back issues yet?"

I had just found the second article and I ran up into the shop with both.

"I thought you'd found out everything you wanted to find out about Pliny Templeton when you researched his life for the pageant," my father said to Reverend Andrews. "What else do you want to know?"

"Well, there's still the matter of his alleged suicide. Nothing, and I do mean nothing, about the man suggests to me that he was the sort of person to throw up his hands in despair and kill himself. Especially over a mere matter of doctrine. The use of a piano, for heaven's sake. I simply can't believe that a man of his wisdom and resilience would put a bullet in his head because of a little spat over a piano."

"Well, it's odd you should say that, because as you'll see from these articles, my father felt the same way. Dad and I didn't always agree, to say the least, but he was a shrewd newspaperman, and the whole business of Pliny's suicide bothered him until the day he died. I could never quite understand why, to tell you the truth. It's always seemed plain enough to me."

"Pliny was a battler, wasn't he?"

"Sure was a battler. But the business over the piano wasn't just a little spat, Walter. Trouble had been building for a couple of years, and as I've told you, it finally attained the proportions of a schism, with some of Pliny's closest friends, including my own grandfather, on the opposite side of the issue. The lines were drawn. Reformed Presbyterians were actually yanking their kids out of his school, you know. They say he was suffering from melancholia as a result of the dispute."

"I still can't picture Pliny Templeton putting a bullet through his head."

"Well, the way I see it, Pliny was an idealist. In my admittedly limited experience in that area, when an idealist comes up against a hard reality that contradicts the ideals he's believed in all his life, sometimes he can't cope with the discrepancy. No doubt that's what happened in Pliny's case."

"I suppose so," Reverend Andrews said. "But I'd still like to study these newspaper articles describing his death. This won't make Elijah Kinneson very happy, I fancy."

"To hell with Elijah," my father said. "He's probably the guy who cast the one vote against you over at the church this morning. But don't take it personally. Elijah wouldn't like *anybody* who replaced him in the pulpit. I don't think he's ever forgiven you for getting the job. The man's something of a fanatic and always has been, but it isn't him you've got to worry about. It sounds as though your biggest concern is that self-serving ass Mason White and his sidekick the nonprosecuting prosecutor. I can't imagine what they've got up their sleeves, Walt, but I damn well intend to find out."

"Small towns!" Reverend Andrews said. "Their ways are more mysterious than the armed services'!"

He looked at me and winked again. "Good to see you boys taking such an interest in the church, Jim. It isn't really so boring after all, is it?"

"Dad," I said after Reverend Andrews had left with the newspapers, "what's going on around here? I mean with these secret meetings and the sheriff threatening Reverend Andrews and everything?"

"You overheard that, did you?" my father said. He stood up, straightened his tie, and put on his suit jacket. "I'm not sure, but I certainly intend to find out. Come on, James. You and I have business with Kingdom County's chief elected peacekeepers."

Although it was nearly noon when we arrived at the courthouse, Zack Barrows was nowhere to be found. Not that this was so very unusual—Dad had told me that two or three days a week the old boozer didn't bother to show up until after lunch. But Mason White was sitting at Zack's desk in the prosecutor's big sunny first-floor office, drinking coffee and reading the Boston paper.

"Tell me something, Mason," Dad said, cutting off the sheriff's effusive greetings, "why did you want to run for office in the first place?"

Tipping back in Zack's swivel chair and splaying his long fingers out on the edge of the desk, Mason chuckled. "Well now, editor, if you'd been raised out to Lord Hollow, you'd have wanted to get your *A* out—pardon my French, Jimbo—and run for something, too. I don't mean this personally, now, but you and your boys, Brother Charlie and young Jimbo here, *you* never had anything to prove to anybody. You and your boys grew up speaking good English and contributing to the community. Out in the Hollow, it weren't like that. Oh no, it was not! It was root, hog, or starve, with maybe a country cowboy song or two throwed into it to make us proud of being poor. Now, I, for one, was never all that proud of being poor. Not one little bit. Do you know what 'poor eyes' are, Jimbo? Well, I shall tell you. Poor eyes are all washed-out, drained-out, lived-out-looking eyes, like the eyes on a real old sick person getting ready to die. My brothers had poor eyes. My sisters had poor eyes, too. There was no hope in them a-tall. The only one in my family that *didn't* have poor eyes was Uncle C. V. White. You probably don't remember him, Jimbo, he was a little before your time, but Uncle C.V. ran the undertaking parlor here in town for years. He drove a big new Buick automobile and he never ventured out to the Hollow except to fetch in a client, and then only if you was prepared to pay him cash on the barrel head when he made the pickup. Now there was a man I admired. I can't say I liked him—he never had any more human feeling than one of his own clients. But I did greatly admire him. *And* his Buick automobiles. A brand-new shiny one every year. How old would you be, Jimbo?"

Mason asked this question so suddenly that he caught me off guard. "Twelve," I said. "No, thirteen."

He nodded. "Thirteen years old. When I was thirteen years old, I moved into an unheated back chamber off Uncle C.V.'s basement workroom over to the undertaking parlor. That's when I began working for old C.V. after school in exchange for my room and board. Five years I did that. Five years I filled in at funerals when the bereaved family was shorthanded and needed an extra bearer, and rode out with Uncle C.V. to fetch in clients, and helped Cousin Elijah dig graves over to the churchyard. Five years."

Mason looked out the window onto the common, reflecting with evident satisfaction on the sacrifice of those five years. I didn't see what any of this had to do with his running for sheriff. And why in heaven's name was he addressing me? I hadn't asked him any questions.

"Now, truthfully, Jimbo, most folks back in those days didn't think much about Mason White one way or the other, but even without having to think about it, folks knew old Mason was different. They knew he was one of those poor Whites from Lord Hollow. And Mason knew he was different too and never doubted that he was going to be successful eventually. So he lugged corpses and dug graves and stood in at funerals and bided his time.

"Problem was . . ." the sheriff continued, flexing and unflexing his great hands, "I knew I'd have to go away and become successful *out* of this town first if I was ever going to become successful *in* it. So that's what I did. I went in the service and bided my time and saved up every penny I could. I got an honorable discharge and went straight over to the Simmons School of Mortuary Science in Syracuse, New York, and graduated from that school with honors. And then and only then did I come back here to work for C.V., saved up some more, and bided my time. The truth is, I did a whole lot of biding.

"Now, Jimbo, you know what I used to think whenever a client of Uncle C.V.'s came in that I figured had looked down on me because I was different? Well sir, I'd lay them all out just so, and then I'd think to myself, or maybe even say right out loud, 'Mr. Jones or Mrs. Smith you used to look down on me. Now the tables are turned. Here I am a-looking down on you, naked as a jaybird with a slit in your side. And do you know something, you poor old buzzard? There's *still* a difference between us. A great big *H* of a difference. And would you like to know what that difference is? I shall tell you. You're dead, Mr. Jones, and I'm not.' "

I noticed my father's jaw getting tighter and his lips thinner. He had been flinching visibly during parts of Mason's story, but he was very still now.

Mason gave a great sudden high horselaugh. " 'I'm not,' I'd say. 'I'm alive, and what's more, a-going places. You're dead, Mr. Jones, and I'm alive, and overcoming early obstacles and *on the rise*.' "

But my father had heard enough of the sheriff's poor-boy-makes-good story. "Mason, I didn't come here to do a human interest story. I came to find out why, if you want to be reelected, you and Zack haven't charged Resolvèd with anything more serious than disturbing the peace. What the hell's going on here?"

"Well, editor," Mason said, "the trouble is, we really don't know exactly what did happen over at the parsonage the other night. So far, all we know for a fact is that when I got there your minister friend was holding a smoking gun, and poor Cousin R was missing part of his trigger finger."

"Poor Cousin R! Poor Cousin R had just fired two loads of buckshot through the Andrews' front windows."

"Don't misunderstand me, editor," Mason said quickly. "You know I'd love nothing better than to nail R's *A* to the courthouse door. But like Zacker told me the other day, we just can't leap to conclusions on this one. For one thing, there's that girl staying with your colored man. No doubt she has *all kinds* of unsavory connections in her background—beginning with that girlie show I closed down."

Mason got out a cigar and lit it. It made him look like the quintessential small-town sheriff in the movies: self-satisfied, sly, knowing more than he said yet somehow managing to hint at more than he really knew.

"Mason," my father said, "you know that Resolvèd Kinneson fired that shotgun at Walt Andrews and could easily have killed him. You know that he used the train as cover, just the way the bank robbers did. That's probably where he got the idea. You know that Resolvèd or one of his commission sales cronies called you and disguised his voice and decoyed you to the other end of town just before the highball went through. If you and Zack don't get to the bottom of all this immediately, I'm going to call the attorney general in Montpelier and urge him to send up a special investigator, or better yet come up himself with one or two smart state policemen, and look into this whole situation. And that isn't a threat, it's a promise."

Mason leaned forward earnestly. "Believe me, editor, I and Zack want to get to the bottom of this unpleasantness just as bad as you do. If we don't, there's apt to be merry old *H* to pay, come election time. What I'm saying is, it's more complicated than even you think. If Zack were here now, and frankly I'm sorry he's not because his little 'spells' are getting just a bit tiresome and I for one wouldn't be all that disappointed if Brother Charlie did decide to run against him this fall and trimmed his wick—but if Zacker *were* here, he'd agree. The *last* thing in the world that we need is the distinguished A.G. from Most Peculiar or some other outsider coming up here and airing our dirty laundry for us. We've had outsiders enough in the Kingdom this summer to last for the next fifty years. If you ask me, that's where more than half this problem resides. Outsiders. Can I be frank with you, editor?"

"I haven't the faintest idea. Can you?"

"Yes," said Mason, "I believe I can. Keep this under your hat, but I'm not so very far away from resolving this mess as you may think. There's just one hitch left, really."

Mason leaned so far forward I thought he might fall face first onto Zack's desk. "Don't tell anybody, editor, but I am not, I repeat *not*, entirely satisfied with your colored man's account of what happened at the parsonage evening before last."

"Do you mean Reverend Andrews?"

"He's the one."

"Refer to him by his name, then. What do you mean by calling him my colored man? That sounds like some kind of slur."

"No offense meant, editor. The reverend, then. Mr. Andrews. Call him what you will. My point is, why would a *reverend* need a handgun in the first place?"

"The answer to that is painfully clear if you look at the events of the other night!"

"Maybe. But why? Cousin R is an awful rig and everybody knows it. But all he seemed to want was the girl back again. He's never tried to kill anybody before, has he? We know him pretty well. But we don't know the preacher. Who is he, anyway? What was his real reason for coming down here, where there isn't another of his kind for fifty miles around? Who might he be running from? Or hiding from? Who are his enemies? Who are his friends, for that matter? You're a newspaperman, editor, you know better than I do what's going on with the Negro element in the big cities this summer. Unlawful agitations and rioting and such. How do we know that the preacher wasn't sent here to provoke an incident? How do we know the girl wasn't sent here to help him? They're both from Canada, aren't they? Or claim to be."

"Mason, let me get this straight. Are you seriously suggesting that Walt Andrews and Claire LaRiviere are in collusion? That he arranged for her to come here to the Kingdom and take up residence at the parsonage so he could shoot Resolvèd's finger off and stage a racial episode?"

"I'm not suggesting anything, editor, because I don't know. All I'm saying is that this preacher is a mighty mysterious customer and I'd like to find out a few more things about him before I come to any conclusions."

"Is that why you asked him if he sleeps in his study and demanded that he prove his 'credibility'?"

"Oh," Mason said, chuckling. "I see. I see what the story is. He come a-crying to you over that, did he? The truth is, that was *Zack's* idea, which I'm sure he'd tell you himself if he wasn't off having one of his spells this A. of M. No, editor, we just wanted to know a little more about who it is we're supposed to be protecting here. That's all. There are just a few more little details we need to check, and then I think we'll be cleaning up this whole incident. By the end of the week at the latest, editor."

Mason laid down his cigar in a big green ashtray. "Editor," he said, "I want to tell you something, and I hope you won't think I'm out of line, because all I mean it as is friendly advice. It goes back to what I said about outsiders and strangers. Sooner or later, the new reverend will drift along the way most strangers who come here do. But I and you, now, we'll very probably be here for a good long while to come, God willing. So I and you, we ought to make every effort to get along with each other. Don't you think?"

"I think you can go to hell in a handbasket, Mason."

And on that unequivocal note, the interview ended.

"Falling water is good water to fish, James. Run ahead and ask your mother to wrap up a couple of Spam sandwiches in waxed paper and stick them in a paper bag for us. We'll peddle a few ads this afternoon, and then we'll see what the brook trout are doing up at Red Rocks."

We were standing on the iron bridge looking down into the swift clean river, now dropping again after the big rain of a couple of days ago. The water was still higher than usual, but falling fast and clarifying itself by the hour. We could see all the way to the pebbly bottom, even in the deep amber stretch next to the granite abutment.

It was like my unpredictable father to take part of a day off to go fishing in the middle of what was turning into the biggest story of his career. No doubt he wanted to get away from everything briefly and get a fresh perspective. But also he wanted to fish for brook trout with me just for the sake of fishing. That is how my father was. Always, to him, as to Kinnesons stretching all the way back to Charles I, trout fishing was no mere recreation but a serious avocation. Dad rarely went out of the village at any time in the spring or summer without first stashing his fly rod and hip boots in the trunk of the car, as I still do to this day.

We spent the next few hours riding the steep, twisty back roads of the county from one small store and four-corner filling station and rundown sawmill to the next. The countryside was vibrant with early blue asters and goldenrod and black-eyed Susans and the air was fragrant with second cuttings of hay down and drying, and no sooner were we under way than my father launched into one of his epic monologues, which he sustained between stops all afternoon—a marvelous spoken essay delivered in the same harsh tone he used to address everyone from me to George Aiken and ranging over every conceivable subject that interested him, from major league baseball to the intricacies of selling ads.

"You can always get something on your ad accounts without pressing your customers unduly hard, James. If you can't get two dollars, get one. If you can't get one, get fifty cents. Get a quarter if you have to, and I often have, but get something, however little, and accept it gladly, because that way your accounts will stay open and your paper will stay afloat."

Yet time and again my father kept circling back to his inconclusive interview with Mason White earlier that day, to my brother's cavalier attitude toward his job, and to his own frustration over a story he couldn't seem to get a handle on.

"Let's go fishing," he said finally.

We left the De Soto on a hilltop a quarter of a mile above Whiskeyjack Kittredge's place and cut down across a brushy pasture to the Upper Kingdom. Here the Kingdom was more brook than river, though easily twice as big as our little burn in the gore. It was about thirty feet across in most spots, and its bed was jumbled with big pink granite boulders breaking up the current into ideal feeding spots for the colorful wild squaretails my father so prized.

We worked our way slowly upstream through the woods, fishing with a cast of three wet flies, like our Scottish ancestors. My father fished one pool, I fished the next, and he fished the one after that, leapfrogging our way up into the gorge under a metallic blue sky and bright afternoon sun that should have been far too harsh for trout to feed in but for some reason, maybe because the water was falling, wasn't.

At thirteen, though I tended to cast too far to manage my flies properly, I considered myself to be a first-rate fisherman. I knew just how to hook a fish by watching for the gold-and-bronze flash as it struck, then hesitating a split second before lifting the tip of my rod and simultaneously drawing back the line with my left hand so that the fish all but hooked itself. Once the trout was on I hardly ever horsed it in too fast anymore, or gave it too much slack. Yet when we fished together, my father consistently caught more brook trout and larger brook trout than I did. How come? I wanted to know.

"You fish a lot of water I don't bother with," he told me. "And you change flies too often."

It was true that I did change patterns frequently, partly because I loved to open up my leather-covered fly book, with its soft gray wool dividers, and admire the bright flies with wonderful names inside. My father, on the other hand, stuck with a Gold-ribbed Hare's Ear, a Royal Coachman, and for a lead fly, after the first of August, a red and yellow grasshopper, claiming that the trout would hit these if they would hit anything and that while other fishermen were fiddling with their flies he was catching fish. But there was more than that to my father's expertise on a trout stream. Unlike Charlie and me, he never seemed to hurry, yet he always knew when he had fished a pool thoroughly enough to attract a fish if one was there. For Charles Kinneson, Sr., read a trout stream the way Cousin Elijah proofread the *Monitor*. Never to this day have I known a man who knew so much about brook trout and where they lived as my father. He showed me how to dip my hand into the water from time to time in order to discover cool pockets indicating hidden spring holes where trout liked to lie in hot weather; how to fish an otherwise impenetrable alleyway of alders by floating my flies down the leafy corridor on a chip of wood, then flicking them off just above a suspected lair; how to open a fish with a single quick slit of my jackknife and examine its stomach to see what it had been eating; how to keep trout fresh by lining my creel with damp moss and wild mint leaves. Yet Dad refused to fish in the wind, because he said fishing should be fun, not work!

Around six o'clock, up at the Red Rocks, where the Kingdom was no more than a shallow stream running over a long chute of dark maroon granite exposed by the glacier, we cleaned our fish. Dad looked as immaculate as when we'd started out, though as usual I had stepped in over each boot and fallen down in the alders more times than I could count. We scrubbed our hands thoroughly in the coarse white sand and gravel, cut up the bank through tall fir woods and down through the summery mixed hard- and softwoods, thick with hobble-bush and moose maple, my father walking faster at fifty-five than I could comfortably keep up with at thirteen, and out into the Kittredges' disused browning hayfields toward the car. There we unpacked the supper Mom had put up and ate it sitting at the base of a great granite boulder, dropped on the hilltop ten thousand years ago by the ice sheet—a marvelous vantage spot overlooking most of Kingdom County and a hundred miles of the Green Mountains, all the way from deep into Canada to Camel's Hump in central Vermont.

Instead of Spam sandwiches, supper turned out to be roast pork sandwiches on homemade bread, two slabs of Mom's no-egg wonder chocolate cake, and two long-keeping apples she'd saved through the previous winter and spring. It was as pretty a spot as any in the county, as pretty as any I have ever seen anywhere, and for a time we ate in silence, enjoying our food and the sweeping vista, enjoying just being together after our great afternoon of fishing.

I suspected that my father was still thinking about the trouble in the Common, though. I could almost *feel* him brooding over it as the sun gently lowered itself behind the Canadian peaks far to the north and the sky turned a fiery summer orange all the way up and down the long jagged chain of mountains.

"James," Dad announced suddenly when we'd gotten to the apples, "a newspaperman runs up against situations like this off and on throughout his career. No matter how many ways you come at this kind of story, it resembles nothing so much as a seamless globe with all the information you need sealed inside where you can't get at it. The longer and harder you work without turning up a lead, the more important the story becomes to you. Finally your entire career as a newspaperman seems to depend on finding some sort of seam in that globe."

"What," I said, "does a newspaperman do?"

"It's very simple. He looks for the story behind the story."

I didn't understand. "How can he do that until he finds a seam?"

"I'll tell you how. A newspaperman has to remember what his job is and what it isn't. A newspaperman's job is not to solve crimes. His job is to write exactly what's happening. Or, as in this sort of case, exactly what isn't happening."

Dad looked off at the mountains. "Did I ever tell you why I left Kingdom County when I was eighteen?"

I said no. I knew that Dad had worked for several years in Boston before he met my mother. But I didn't know why he'd gone there.

"Well," he said, "it's time I did. When I was a boy, there wasn't a moment when I wasn't positive that I knew more than my father did about everything under the sun. Whatever Dad said, I disagreed with him. One morning at breakfast when I was eighteen and just a month or so away from leaving for Dartmouth College, we got into a terrible argument. It was over the use of the so-called Harvard comma, of all things—the last comma in a parallel series of items in a sentence. For instance: 'The deer leaped the fence and ran through two fields, a patch of woods, and a river.' The Harvard comma in that sentence comes after 'woods,' and the debate was over whether it was grammatically necessary or not. Dad said it was; I said it wasn't. And my father was so sure he was right that he had the temerity to smile down into his oatmeal!

"Well, James, that smile was too much for my pride. I marched upstairs and packed a valise, put the clips I'd saved from stories I'd begun printing in the *Monitor* inside a big envelope and packed that too, and came back down and left without a word.

"I took the first train south out of the Common and didn't set foot in Kingdom County again for six years. But the truth of the matter is that the Harvard comma wasn't the real reason I left."

"What was? That you didn't want to go to Dartmouth?"

"No, I'd been looking forward to going to college. The real reason I left home was the girl who lived right here on the Kittredge place."

My father pointed far out across the twilit countryside at the white dome of Russia, gleaming brightly in the afterglow high up in the gore above our farmhouse. "When I was about seventeen, I used to hike up there on Sunday afternoons with old Charles I's brass pirate's telescope. At a prearranged time, a girl I knew who lived on this farm would come up here and stand on this boulder and wave. I'd look over at her through that spyglass, and that was our date. The Christmas of my senior year at the Academy I secretly bought her a pair of Montgomery Ward binoculars so that she could look back at me."

I laughed. "Why didn't you just come over and see her?"

"Two reasons, James: my mother and my father. You see, the girl was from a French family. Her parents had come down from Canada knowing no English at all, and without a penny in their pockets, and my folks didn't want me to keep company with her."

This revelation jolted me. It was like Mom and Dad telling Charlie he couldn't date Athena Allen because her mother had been Armand St. Onge's sister. "Why didn't you see her anyway? Sneak over or something? Were you afraid to?"

"I have to admit I was somewhat afraid of my mother," my father said with a chuckle. "It's a curious thing, James. Abiah Kinneson was a little bit of a black-eyed silent creature with a Scottish accent thick enough to cut with a Highland broadsword. She didn't come to this country until she was sixteen years old. Then she came alone, on an immigrant ship, not knowing a soul. She went to work in my grandfather Charlie's family as a sort of live-in cook and housekeeper after my grandmother Kinneson got sick. When my grandmother died and that old rip Mad Charlie married the gypsy girl, Replacement Mari, my mother didn't have anyplace to go. I think my father felt sorry for her, and that's why he married her. That was a bad mistake, along the lines of feeling sorry for a fully clawed wildcat.

"But the point I was going to make is that for all the intimidation she inspired in me and others, my mother herself was afraid of anything she didn't understand. She was certainly afraid of the gypsies who used to come through these parts. After my cousins came along, she was scared of them too, and of their mother Replacement Mari. She was terrified of the river, afraid I'd drown in it. And when she found out that I was interested in a French Canadian girl—and a very nice one, I might add, although she couldn't hold a candle to your mother—Mom was scared of her, too, or of the strangeness she represented."

"Why didn't you just elope, run off together or something?"

Dad shrugged. "That kind of thing simply wasn't done in those days, James. Not much, at any rate. I was just eighteen. I couldn't have supported a wife, much less a family. Anyway, the upshot of the whole episode is that I used the Harvard comma as my excuse and went to Boston, and I'm glad I did, as things turned out, because that's how I got those jobs on the *Post* and the *Globe* and, more important still, met your mother."

"So why did you ever come home, Dad? After working for those big Boston papers? Why did you come back to Kingdom County?"

"I wanted to work for myself. Dad was ready to retire from the

*Monitor* and it was an ideal situation. Besides, there was a notable absence of brook trout fishing in Boston. And finally, as I've told you before, stories in Kingdom County are as good as stories anywhere if you know enough to recognize them—and how to find the stories behind the stories.

"Now, James, a serious crime has been committed, and only a token arrest has been made. No real investigation has taken place, except into the background of the victim of that crime. Incredible as it sounds, Mason White and Zack Barrows are treating Reverend Andrews as the prime suspect in this entire affair. Why?"

I shrugged. "Why?"

"Think about the story I told you."

I thought, and suddenly the entire point of it came clear to me.

"That Mason White and Zack Barrows are prejudiced!" I nearly shouted. "Just the way my grandmother was prejudiced against that French girl. That's the story behind the story!"

"Right you are," Dad said, "and you can bet we'll be looking into it."

On the way back to the car he said, "By the way, James, I wouldn't mention any of this to your mother, especially that part about the French Canadian girl. The last thing in the world I'd want her to think, is that I married her on the rebound from somebody else."

Dad needn't have worried about me spilling the beans. As we clumped up onto the porch with our fishing gear an hour later, Mom met us at the door with a disclosure of her own that eclipsed everything else that had happened that day.

"Reverend Andrews just called with some disturbing news," she told us. "Right after he spoke with you at the *Monitor* this morning he decided to take Nat back to Montreal to stay with his grandmother until things calm down around here. When he got back, about an hour ago, Claire was gone too. He called to say she still hasn't come back, Charles. He left word for you to get in touch with him right away. At first he thought she'd run away to California, but now he's afraid that something may have happened to her because her belongings are still at the parsonage."

# 14

That evening Mom tried to reassure me that no doubt Claire had just decided to return home and was already back in Quebec. I, for my part, was certain that she would never return to Quebec now that her father was dead. California and Hollywood had always been her destination, and I believed in her and in her determination to get there at all costs.

Lying awake in my loft long into that night, I imagined Claire thumbing her way west in her dress of many colors, across the glossy dog-eared map of the United States in my eighth-grade geography book, over the four small emerald triangles of the Green Mountains; past the sparkling blue curtain of Niagara, where surely Claire would stop and view the falls, as I would have; through the flat cornfields of Iowa and Nebraska toward the half-dozen soaring white-capped pyramids of the Rockies, whose lower slopes were speckled with rushing silver trout rivers and spouting geysers; past the shaggy herd of four bison to the two orange trees and one long tan beach of the Pacific, where finally, with her engaging French accent and eyes that changed color with the weather and her uncanny gift for mimicry, she might win for herself a role in a movie like *Under the Big Top*, and my friends and I would see her at a Saturday matinee in the Academy auditorium. . . .

It was the most improbable of romantic fantasies, which I no doubt conjured up as a stay against harsher likelihoods. Yet never since the moment I had first laid eyes on Claire LaRiviere at the tent show had I seen her as anything other than she wished me to: determined, courageous, sure of her gift and confident in her future, young and pretty and exotic and only temporarily unlucky. As my mother had said, she must have left the Kingdom to get on with her life.

Yet Claire had promised that she would never leave without saying goodbye to me, and she hadn't even left a note for Reverend Andrews or Nathan. Remembering our agreement to meet at the granite quarry where she liked to wash her hair and bathe, I made up my mind before going to sleep to hike up there first thing in the morning just in case she was still waiting for me, though that now seemed like the longest of long shots.

Just before dawn the next morning, while Dad was shaving, I slipped out of my window onto the porch roof and shinnied down a post to the misty dim dooryard. It had turned cooler overnight and the wet, cottony river fog hung over the gool like fog on an October morning; but as I climbed up the trace into the gore, past my cousins' place and on into the tall hardwoods, a pale orange blush spread over the horizon away off in the east behind the dark bulk of the Presidential Range of New Hampshire's White Mountains.

At the juncture where the main branch of the trace forked up to Russia, I veered off onto the path Claire had worn beside the fast little burn that rose in the quarry. Before I'd taken ten steps a sharp rattle cut through the still dawn woods like a machine gun. Although I'd heard it a hundred times before—it was only a blue kingfisher, screaming his startled cry of alarm as he zipped up the brook ahead of me —I nearly jumped out of my skin.

I couldn't have said why I was so spooked. Maybe it was the mist or some residual fear of encountering Resolvèd (though I knew he was in jail) or the inexplicable mysteriousness of Claire's abrupt disappearance. Ordinarily I was perfectly at home in these woods, even after dark.

Fortunately it was just a short distance, no more than a quarter of a mile, up the burn from the fork in the trace to the miniature waterfalls spilling over the smooth granite lip of the quarry, where Claire had come to bathe alone and wash her hair. There were no footprints on the sand beside the pool at the base of the falls, not even a set of heron tracks, so I scrambled up onto the ledge under the yellow birch tree where I'd found Claire that morning back in June when I'd mistaken her slip in the tree for a ghost. In the pale early light, the flooded quarry looked as though no one had been near the place all summer.

"Claire?" I called softly. Then, louder, "Claire! Claire!"

Then repeatedly, insistently, "Claire, Claire, Claire, Claire, Claire!"

My voice echoed off the granite cliffs jutting up over the back side of the quarry, and the mocking, inhuman tone of the reverberating echo unnerved me so much I did not call her name again.

Obviously, my friend had either forgotten her promise to meet me here, or had left town in too great a hurry to keep it; the watery quarry, with its opaque jade surface, was as deserted as the village cemetery which it had supplied with monuments for a century.

There is no place anywhere more forlorn than a disused quarry—how Claire could come here to bathe I had no idea—and all I wanted now was to get away from the place. But just before leaving, I picked up a loose fragment of granite and shied it across the pit at the cliffs. It struck with the sharp flinty crack of rock on rock, and ricocheted back into the green water with a good, satisfying splash, followed instantly by a terrifying string of long loud coughing croaks and the specter of two huge black ravens rising up from the wooded ledges on the back side of the quarry.

If I'd been able to, no doubt I'd have turned tail and sprinted down that mountainside faster than ever I pounded home from third on a ninth-inning squeeze play. But I was so scared all I could do was stare at those two hideous creatures now climbing the dawn updrafts along the face of the cliff.

I laughed all the way down the ridge, at my timidity and silliness and earlier fear for Claire, who was undoubtedly already well along on her odyssey west, telling some puzzled potato chip salesman or log-truck driver her odd history and the story of her sojourn in Kingdom

County; yet even with these calming reassurances I was very relieved to see the familiar sight of my cousin Welcome out in his pasture junkyard in the sunrise, hoisting a 1938 or '39 Chevy onto his automobile abacus with his huffing steam crane.

And when I jogged into our dooryard, something entirely new and wonderful, as Charlie liked to say, made me forget all about my spooky morning excursion and the ravens and Welcome and even Claire LaRiviere and her whereabouts.

Standing on a homemade spruce-pole ladder propped against the road side of our barn and refurbishing the faded picture of the leaping brook trout was the deaf and mute Dog Cart Man, with his dogs sitting perfectly still in a tight semicircle nearby, watching every move he made.

The painter worked at an incredible rate of speed. Before my eyes the trout took shape and size and color, its fantastic pinks and oranges as bright as the sunrise, its fin edgings white as milk. It was a splendid creation, arching high over the sparkling blue meadow pool, with more vitality than any gaudy outdoor magazine illustrations I'd ever seen.

Just as she'd promised me earlier that summer, Mom said I could accompany the Dog Cart Man on his rounds that day if I'd like to. "But don't pester him when he's painting, Jimmy. And for heaven's sake, if any of the town boys start to pick on him, make them stop right away."

Mom packed us a lunch big enough for an overnight outing for the whole family, which the Dog Cart Man wedged into his big wagon between the spruce-pole ladder, a dozen or so cans of paint, a metal footlocker, and a White Owl cigar box. Then we set out together toward the red iron bridge.

It was yet another fine summer day, and as we jogged along beside the dogs (I soon learned that the Dog Cart Man never walked anywhere), I studied him out of the corner of my eye. He was tall, thin, and spare, with long stringy arms, and he wore a brown cotton smock, baggy gray gabardine pants and shapeless brown shoes laced with baling twine.

Instead of a cap he wore a faded beret that might once have been blue or green, and from beret to shoes he was spattered with paint of every color so that at a little distance he resembled a trotting painter's palette.

His most remarkable features were his hands, which were long and thin and artistic-looking, and his eyes, which were brown and watchful and at the same time slightly bemused, as though even when he was looking at you he was thinking of his next painting or the painting he had just completed.

Just on the other side of the bridge, the Dog Cart Man swung silently east out the county road and the dogs turned silently with him. We passed Charlie's trailer and the logged-off hillside across from it and continued out to Ben Currier's place, where we turned abruptly into the barnyard. Leaving his dogs hitched to the cart, the painter opened his steel locker and took out a marvelous meerschaum pipe with a massive and beautiful bowl swirled with blue and yellow and pink like an old-fashioned agate shooting marble. He stuffed the pipe with ropy tobacco from a little sack that stank like Resolvèd Kinneson's unlimed privy, and puffed away for a few minutes, studying the faded painting on the side of Ben's barn from several different angles, his pupils getting larger and larger and larger. When I mentioned the pipe later to my father, he laughed and said that the Dog Cart Man didn't smoke real tobacco at all, but hemp leaves, or marijuana, which he both planted and picked in his travels, like a Bohemian Johnny Appleseed.

The painting was a simple scene of Ben's Jersey cows lining up at the pasture bars across the road from the barn, with the barn itself in the background and the house next to the barn. The Dog Cart Man put up his pipe and gazed at Ben's homestead—as dilapidated a set of buildings, nearly, as our own. In the meantime Ben came out of the barn, where he'd evidently just finished milking. Together the old farmer and the half-dozen dogs and I watched as the Dog Cart Man silently set up his homemade ladder and arranged his paint cans and brushes on the ground beneath it. Then he began to paint like a wildman, slapping on each color at such an alarming clip that he hardly seemed to be paying attention to what he was doing. Ben's wife joined us, and we all watched spellbound. On the side of the Curriers' barn, the pasture across the road reemerged, a lovely lush June-green, then one by one the handsome Jersey cows, then the barn itself and the house, no longer faded but as spanking red and white as the cowbarn and traditional farmhouse on my mother's *Vermont Life* kitchen calendar at home.

"My land!" Mrs. Currier said. "That's how the place must have looked back when your grandfather had it, Benjamin."

Ben gave a short laugh. "I much misdoubt it. But it's pretty, all right. Too bad it won't last. Three Kingdom winters will weather that picture to the same state of ruination as the building she's painted on and its owner."

Ben seemed to take considerable satisfaction in contemplating the inevitable weathering of the painting and his own personal ruination as he walked over to the Dog Cart Man's wagon and slipped a five-dollar bill into the White Owl cigar box. The artist looked at neither the cigar box nor his completed painting. He packed up his paints, snapped his fingers to his dogs, and we trotted back toward the village, leaving the Curriers to admire the bright new panoramic picture of the way their farm might once have looked.

The Dog Cart Man stopped again at my brother's trailer, hunched against the dark spruce woods along the river like an overgrown green leafhopper. The Dog Cart Man flicked a finger at the weedy dooryard and the dogs turned in. He went carefully from window to window, looking in at my brother's tiny cramped kitchen and living area, papered with sexy pinups. He looked at me, and for the first time since I'd met him he grinned, a fleeting little brown-toothed mischievous grin gone almost immediately, and before I knew it he was painting again, this time a portrait of a willowy young woman with blond hair, in red high-heeled shoes and an impossibly bright red dress clinging to her shapely thighs. It was Marilyn Monroe, reaching out as though to open the door of Charlie's trailer, and smiling coyly back over her shoulder!

This painting took no more than ten minutes from start to finish, and we were on our way again. For the rest of the day we continued at a nearly frenetic pace from building to building, stopping only once, around noon, when the Dog Cart Man bought two Hershey chocolate bars apiece for himself, me, and each of his dogs.

Late in the afternoon, on the side of Armand St. Onge's hotel, the Dog Cart Man refurbished the black bear climbing a beech tree to shake down beechnuts; then the yoke of Red Durham oxen with gleaming golden balls on the tips of their horns over the big sliding door of the commission sales barn, where Bumper Stevens, to my surprise, gave me a crumpled twenty-dollar bill to put in the White Owl cigar box; and finally the faded black letters that said KINGDOM COUNTY MONITOR on the inside of my father's shop window.

By suppertime he was ready to knock off for the day. We trotted back out to the gool, and although Mom didn't ask him inside to eat with us—she knew he'd never join us—she carried his meal out to him and he ate squatting with his back against the barn under the fresh painting of the brook trout, with his dogs sitting in their comical half-circle waiting for him to finish so they could eat.

Afterward he smoked his pipe for a while; I then took a sheet of newsprint out of the footlocker and folded it into a rectangle and then into a sort of lopsided triangle. From the locker he removed a long pair of gleaming barber's shears. He studied the folded sheet of paper, turning it several times in his hands. Suddenly, so fast I could hardly follow the flashing scissors, he made several cuts and unfolded an uncannily exact replica of a buck deer with a perfect ten-point rack, which he gravely handed to me. He repeated this process several times, cutting out a bear standing on one hind foot, a sitting partridge, a dog resembling his lead dog, a Model T Ford, a modern-looking fire engine, and a steam locomotive with a smoke stack just like the ones that until two years ago had pulled the mile-long Boston and Montreal freights through the Common.

At dusk, the Dog Cart Man and his dogs retreated into the hayloft for the night. All in all, it had been one of the best days I could remember, and just before I went up to bed myself, Mom said I could go with my new friend again in the morning.

We spent most of the next day in the Academy auditorium, where the Dog Cart Man refurbished the mural of the entire village on the stage backdrop—the church, the Academy, the Common with its gorgeous wine-glass elms, the brick shopping block, the hotel and commission sales barn, and the cemetery, with Jay Peak and the Green Mountains in the background.

Around three in the afternoon, we returned to the gool by way of the covered bridge, stopping briefly to touch up the signs over each end that said CROSS AT A WALK. Then we struck off up into the gore, and turned onto the old trace leading to the granite quarry.

Somewhat guiltily, I thought of Claire for the first time since the previous morning; but instead of following the burn all the way up to the falls where I'd called her name in the mist until the echo scared me, we cut off the trace and out around the deep pit. In the bright afternoon sunlight, it no longer looked eerie to me—just empty and forlorn. On the back side of the quarry, the Dog Cart Man unhitched his dogs, handed me four buckets of paint, and hoisted the homemade ladder to his shoulder. In single file we pushed our way through a tangle of blackberry canes, to the faded pictograph he'd painted long ago on the granite face of the cliff above the quarry of the gypsy stonecutters who had once come regularly to Kingdom County. Over the years it had faded almost beyond recognition, and at this time of year it was obscured by the leafy summer foliage of second-growth hardwoods.

As we approached the cliff, something let out a cough. Up from the pit flapped one of the ravens I'd seen two days ago. But if the Dog Cart Man noticed it, he paid no attention.

He propped his ladder against a slanted defile, and climbed up to a shelf just below the faded picture of the gypsies and motioned for me to hand him the paint cans. He pulled the ladder up behind him, got out his pipe, and began to smoke and study the painting.

It was actually more discernible from a distance. Up close, I could just make out the faint tracery of the gypsy figures. The Dog Cart Man smoked a bowlful of the evil-smelling hemp, staring at the painting and the woods and the sky, and all at once he was painting fast.

As the dogs and I watched from the foot of the cliff, the old gypsy stonecutters took shape again, four men in vivid blue pantaloons with wide crimson sashes and billowing green and yellow shirts, hauling a block of granite out of a pit of opaque green water below. It was wonderful to watch the painter at work, and he worked so fast that the painted figures taking form above me seemed themselves to be working and sweating in the great heat.

I was so absorbed by the wonderful tableau that I jumped when the lead dog, a spaniel-hound cross with floppy ears and long legs, tugged at my pants cuff.

"What do you want?" I said.

The dog released my cuff and ran into the blackberry patch nearby, then returned and tugged at my pants again.

This time I followed it.

I bulled my way through the briers, trampling on the tough thorny canes. The dog was thrashing somewhere out of sight ahead. I was pretty sure it scented a partridge and braced myself for the sudden roaring whir of wings; I expected it to flush thundering out from under my feet at any moment.

Abruptly, I came out of the blackberry cane patch by a pin cherry tree growing on the very brink of the quarry. The spaniel-hound ran to the very edge and wagged its tail and looked back at me. I snapped my fingers. "Come back here, boy."

The dog looked at me inquiringly.

I crept closer and peered over the edge. Fifteen or so feet below me was a ledge, and below the ledge the surface of the flooded quarry. As I started to turn away, something on the ledge gave an odd sort of jerking heave. I grasped the slender trunk of the pin cherry and leaned far out over the edge and peered down again.

An enormous raven was standing on something long and bright, sprawled on the ledge below. Except for the torn bright garment I would not have recognized it because it had no face where its face should have been; the ravens had seen to that. I yelled. I reeled back, tripped over the dog, and fell crashing into the blackberry bushes. I was on my feet, screaming for help and plunging back through the bushes, heedless of the raking thorns on my arms and hands and face, shrieking Claire's name at the Dog Cart Man on the shelf above me, who, oblivious to my screaming and to all the sounds of the world worked rapidly on under the hot afternoon sun beating down on him and his painting and the dogs, on me and the quarry and the shattered body of Claire LaRiviere on the ledge in the quarry.

Fleeting, jumbled, indistinct nightmare images remain: woods flying by me, the silvery falls spilling over the lip of the quarry, riffles and pools I would never fish again; Welcome Kinneson looking up and waving at me from his steam crane; a jarring spill on the gravel at the junction of the gool and the gore that cut the heels of my hands to bloody shreds. Somehow I was on the porch at home, where my mother sat in her sun hat snapping green beans, and then I was in my mother's arms and pieces of beans were raining down on us both and I was crying and shouting something about Claire, an accident, ravens.

Finally my mother managed to understand what had happened. Her hand shot to her mouth as though to keep herself from crying out. Then we were inside the house and she was on the phone to my father, and then she was hugging me again.

"That poor, poor waif," Mom said over and over again. "Oh, Jimmy. That poor little girl. . . ."

Within minutes, Sheriff White and Doc Harrison and Zack Barrows and Deputy Pine Benson and Reverend Andrews and my father were standing on the porch and I was trying to tell them how I had found the body.

"On the back side, the *woods* side, you say, Jimbo?" Sheriff White kept asking me. "You say it was on the *back* side of that old hole up there? You'd best come along and show us where."

Mason reached for my arm, but Reverend Andrews told him that there was no need for me to go back up there now, they'd locate the body all right.

Mason whirled around and pointed at the minister. "Reverend, I'm going to tell you something. I don't know how they work things where you come from, but up here the preachers stick to preaching and leave the elected officials to take care of enforcing the law. In case you didn't know it, you're in enough hot water as it is."

"Just what do you mean by that?"

"For God's sake, gentlemen, let's not start quarreling between ourselves," my father said. "There's a dead girl up on that mountain."

The last thing I heard as they went down off the porch was Doc Harrison saying in his dry sardonic voice, "Leave your siren off this time, will you, Mason? She isn't going to get any deader than she already is, you know."

How I got up to my bedchamber I have no idea. I cried my eyes out there and pounded my pillow furiously, overwhelmed by grief and my first encounter with a great indifferent universal injustice, which, if I had suspected its existence at all, had never before touched my life. My mother sat beside me, trying to comfort me, trying to explain that with all her problems, poor Claire was better off out of a life that had never shown her a day's kindness since the death of her father. But to me at thirteen, any life seemed better than no life, and I was inconsolable.

Besides being infatuated with Claire from the moment I'd set eyes on her, standing scared half out of her wits on the tailgate of a truck in a tent show, I had genuinely liked her. The contrast between the affectionate, engaging and good-natured girl I had known and the faceless, crumpled heap of bones on the ledge in the quarry was terrible. I cried for a long, long time, before falling into an exhausted broken sleep in which I dreamed of Claire's body, floating down through the green water of the quarry, her long hair trailing above her, while Resolvèd stood sneering on the brink above, under the pin cherry tree, with his smoking shotgun crooked in his arm, and the woods behind him ringing from the shot.

It was pitch dark and the phone was ringing. It rang for a long time before my father answered it, so I knew it must be very late.

"Mister Baby Johnson!" he said.

I got out of bed and tiptoed to the head of the stairs.

Dad listened another moment, then said he'd be right over.

"Charles? Who is it?" My mother had come into the kitchen too now.

"You'd better sit down, Ruth," Dad said. "That was Perry Harrison with some very bad news. The LaRiviere girl didn't just wander up into the woods and stumble into that quarry the way we thought. According to Harrison, she was shot and thrown in."

Often and often my father had said and written in the *Monitor* that there was little or no law in the Kingdom. Yet so far as I knew, nothing like Claire's murder had ever happened here before. With the possible exception of the Ordney Gilson lynching, to find anything as brutal in the annals of local lawlessness you would have to go back at least as far as the shooting of the slave catcher, Satan Smithfield, in the pulpits of the church by my great-grandfather Mad Charlie Kinneson, nearly one hundred years ago. And even that shooting, as horrible as it was, had been regarded by my ancestor and most of his New England contemporaries more as an act of war than a crime. Dad said there had never even been an official inquiry.

Now, almost literally in our own backyard, a young girl had been murdered in cold blood, apparently with a botched attempt to conceal her body, since presumably whoever threw her into the quarry had expected her body to sink and Claire LaRiviere never to be seen again.

Somewhere, quite possibly in Kingdom County and perhaps in the village itself, a murderer was at large. There were no more fishing trips alone for me that summer, or with anyone else for that matter. I was forbidden to stray out of sight or earshot or our dooryard, forbidden even to go to the meadow pool or up the burn. Nor was

I at all inclined to. Besides being more frightened than I had ever been in my life, I actually felt partly responsible for Claire's death because I'd waited until the morning after she turned up missing to search for her at the quarry.

On the afternoon of the day after Sheriff White drained the quarry, I confided to Mom how terrible I felt and why.

"Tell you what, Jimmy," she said, "let's go see if the red raspberries are out in that cut-over woods across from your brother's. On the way we can talk all this over."

I didn't feel like going anywhere, except possibly to California on the next freight, but before I knew it Mom had gotten her sun hat and a stack of quart berry baskets, and we were climbing up the hillside where, just as she had hoped, the raspberries had sprung up like magic. The warm, sugary fragrance of ripe raspberries suffused the slashed woods for acres around, but although I had always loved berrying with my mother, I couldn't stop thinking of Claire, wondering whether she'd picked berries at her Laurentian grandmother's, wishing she were here with us on this sunny hillside picking berries today.

"You know, Jimmy," Mom said, "when your grandfather the poor captain died in the typhoid epidemic, and then my poor mother, I remember feeling just the way you do now. I kept thinking that if only your dad and I hadn't gotten married and left Boston, somehow the captain and my mother wouldn't have caught that dreadful illness. And I felt terribly guilty, as though I was completely to blame for their dying. Even at the time, I knew it was silly of me to think that way, and goodness knows I loved your father so much I never for a second regretted marrying him. But still I felt very, very guilty. I cried for days over it. And that made your father feel bad, which made me feel worse. But I couldn't help it."

This was exactly the way I felt about Claire's death, with the added problem that I couldn't stop thinking that if I had gone up to the quarry sooner, maybe somehow I really *could* have prevented it. I was so teary-eyed all over again that I couldn't say a word.

Mom patted my arm. "I stopped feeling that way after a while, and you will too. What happened to Claire undoubtedly happened before we ever knew she was missing. There wasn't a thing you could have done to prevent it, then or earlier, any more than I could have prevented the Boston typhoid epidemic."

As usual, Mom had hit the nail right on the head. Still and all, I didn't see how she or anyone else could truly know how bad I felt, and despite her assurances I was very certain, with all the certainty of my thirteen years, that I would never feel any different.

In the meantime, the biggest manhunt in the history of northern Vermont was under way. With the help of two bloodhounds and their trainer, a hatchet-faced hunting guide from across the state line in New Hampshire, Sheriff White combed the spruce thickets and blackberry brakes around the quarry. But no clues turned up.

Before the bloodhounds went home, their trainer and the sheriff beat through several acres of swamp along the Boston and Montreal tracks, in the outside hope of finding a bloodstained tramp or hobo; and Zack had ordered the Dog Cart Man to remain in the county, where he could be questioned if need be, as soon as anyone could think up a way to question him. But I doubt that Zack or anyone else ever believed for a minute that the deaf and mute artist had anything to do with Claire's death.

On the morning after the bloodhounds left, Zack decided to drain the quarry in search of evidence. Around ten o'clock I heard the siren of the volunteer fire department's twenty-year-old American LaFrance hook-and-ladder, and a minute later it appeared on the gool, with the equally antiquated town pumper truck chugging along in its dust. Sheriff White manned the wheel of the hook-and-ladder, with Zack in the seat beside him. A dozen or so volunteer firemen were riding the sideboards of the truck, and several carloads of veteran local fire-engine chasers, including Plug Johnson and the entire Folding Chair Club, brought up the rear. Seeing those old ghouls made me sick, but when Dad showed up a few minutes later and asked if I wanted to walk up with him to the quarry I went along, knowing that if I didn't I'd probably never be able to go near the place again.

"Good morning to you, editor!" Mason said, when we arrived, as though we were all on a picnic together. "Morning to you, Jimbo."

The sheriff lowered his voice confidentially. "Between I and you, boys, I don't believe we're going to find anything in this old hole much more incriminating than a few of Cousin R's Old Duke empties. Zacker, though, he's got his mind made up that she's got to be flushed out."

In fact, I think that Zack and Mason both felt that a major public spectacle as appealing as draining the quarry would increase their political stock in the county; and by eleven o'clock there was already a big crowd at the quarry, mostly made up of town folks, though a fair number of farmers were there, as well.

Around noon the first major discovery was made. The sinking water had revealed first the rusted tin roof, then the broken windows and hood and trunk of a 1929 Packard, balanced precariously on a rock shelf a few feet below us.

"I believe that would be one of the vehicles Henry Coville lost smuggling Canadian booze down over the line years back during Temperance time," Zack Barrows said. "Go down and have a look-see, will you, Mace?"

Somewhat reluctantly, Mason climbed down on the fire department's extension ladder and promptly discovered a dozen cases of Seagram's whiskey in the Packard's trunk. Many of the bottles were broken but some were still intact, and soon an argument broke out between Zack, who wanted to confiscate the contraband as "evidence," and Cousin Welcome Kinneson, who claimed that since the quarry was on his and Resolvèd's property, everything in it belonged to them. The dispute was resolved only when Plug Johnson suggested sampling the Seagram's on the spot "to see if it had gone bad or not." To everyone's relief, both Welcome and Zack pronounced it excellent; the evidence was passed around liberally, and from then on, the work seemed to go much better.

Almost despite myself, I was interested in the accumulating heap of relics from the various levels of the quarry. Besides the bootlegger's Packard, the sheriff and his crew salvaged a flintlock rifle; several flawed or broken granite gravestones, including three or four spooky ones with the beginning letters of names carved on them; any number of Old Duke bottles and several antique bottles, including a flat glass flask inscribed with the name KINNESON from our ancestors' potato whiskey distilleries; and a rusty set of bed springs.

Bumper Stevens poked the springs with his cow cane. "Look at these, boys. Some enterprising young blade from days of yore lugged his own girling equipment up here along with the girls!"

"A girl's been murdered, for God's sake," my father said angrily. "You're all making a circus out of this. Come on, James. Let's get the hell out of here."

"What did they find up there?" my mother asked us when we got back to the house.

"A set of bed springs and a few empty wine bottles," my father said. "Nothing more."

But just as we sat down for supper an hour later the hook-and-ladder's siren shrieked out again and the old truck came careening down the gore road past my cousins', swerved onto the gool, and screeched to a stop in front of our dooryard.

"Editor!" Mason called as we hurried out onto the porch. "We just stopped to say if you see that dog cart fella before we do, you can send him along on his way now."

"You mean he's no longer a suspect?"

"I mean, as of this evening, he's free to go. Period. Let's get this rig over to the village, Mace. We've got a great deal of work to do in a short time."

This, at least, was good news. But the following evening, the evening before Claire's funeral, my father came home from work furious. Not only had Zack Barrows excluded Charlie from a secret hearing to be held the next day in front of Judge Allen to determine whether there was enough evidence to bring charges in the murder case—a hearing at which Charlie's own client, Resolvèd, had been subpoenaed to testify—but Reverend Andrews had just minutes ago told Dad that he hadn't been able to prevail upon the church cemetery committee to allocate a space for Claire except in the so-called pauper's corner—under the cedar trees where Satan Smithfield and other outcasts were buried.

The funeral was held at two o'clock the following afternoon—the same day the inquest convened at the courthouse. Neither Dad nor Charlie had been able to find out exactly what (if any) "evidence," besides the Seagram's bottles, Zack and Mason might have discovered in the quarry, and at two o'clock a dozen cars were still parked along the common across the street from the courthouse.

I had dreaded Claire's funeral terribly, in part because I'd been tapped as a pallbearer. Worse yet, there was a large crowd of curiosity-seekers, most of whom had probably never even said hello to Claire on the street when she was alive. With Julia Hefner tied up at the courthouse in her capacity as clerk and stenographer, my mother had been recruited to play the organ; Dad and Athena and Charlie and I slid into the Kinneson pew just as Reverend Andrews started the service.

He began by speaking about Claire's unusual childhood in Quebec, her ambition to become a movie star, and her marvelous talent as a mime. To this day I do not know precisely what Reverend Andrews' metaphysical convictions were. But I recall his saying in Claire's funeral sermon that no human being ever dies without leaving a spiritual gift behind—a legacy not measurable in money or property, but infinitely more meaningful. Claire's gift, he said, was her courageous faith in a providential future, to which she herself had now passed. And her presence in the village left us with an example of how providence gives each one of us many opportunities to exercise our Christian and human obligation of charity—however far short we are all bound to fall of that obligation.

When Reverend Andrews finished his last prayer consigning Claire's soul to an immortal eternity, which to this day I do not know for certain he himself literally believed in, and my mother began the funeral processional on the organ, Dad and Charlie and George Quinn and I remained seated until everyone else had left. Just as we picked up the coffin (so light that it hardly seemed to contain a body), Elijah began tolling the funeral knell on the Revere church bell my great-great-great-grandfather, Charles I, had brought over the mountains to Kingdom County by oxcart one hundred and fifty years ago.

"Easy does it, gentlemen," George whispered as we headed out the door and down the church steps. "Watch your footing now."

The old fuddy-duddy acted as though he'd been drinking too much of his own castor oil, but of necessity I did watch my footing and so didn't see the two men coming toward us from the courthouse until they were halfway across the baseball diamond.

It was Sheriff White and his deputy, Pine Benson.

For a moment, as the bell continued to toll, I thought they were going to intercept us and prevent us from sliding the coffin into Mason's hearse. But as we eased the box along the silent rollers and into the hearse—"Watch your fingers, gentlemen, let's not have any pinched fingers today!"—Pine and Mason passed us without so much as a glance in our direction.

They strode through the crowd to the top of the church steps, where Reverend Andrews was standing in his funeral robes. Mason said something to him that I couldn't make out over the reverberations of the bell.

"What the—" my father started to say.

Reverend Andrews was jerking his hands away from Sheriff White. To my astonishment Mason pulled out his gun.

The coffin safely in the hearse, my father sprinted toward the church, but Mason and Pine were already on their way down the steps with the handcuffed minister between them, and the shocked crowd of people were in an uproar on the same lawn where nearly a hundred years ago their ancestors had watched, shocked and outraged, as my great-grandfather Mad Charlie Kinneson had ridden out of the church with the corpse of Satan Smithfield slung over his saddle and thundered furiously across the same green and into the same courthouse toward which Mason and Pine were now hustling the protesting minister.

Then the three men were through the courthouse door, with Charlie right behind them, and Reverend Andrews was not seen again until the inquest adjourned at six o'clock that night, this time with his hands cuffed behind his back and Charlie at his side, to be led downstairs to jail.

"What in hell is going on here, Farlow?" my father demanded when the bailiff appeared a minute later.

"Good news and bad, editor. Which do you want first?"

I thought that my father was going to muckle onto Farlow Blake on the spot. "Just tell me what's happening here, damn it. I don't care how you tell it, just tell it."

Farlow nodded sagely. "Then I'll give you the bad news first, and save the good for last. The bad news, I'm sorry to report, is that the inquest has just handed down their decision to indict our friend the reverend for first-degree murder!"

My father looked at the bailiff as if he didn't understand him.

Farlow leaned toward him. "I don't know if I should tell you this yet, editor, but strictly off the record, it was the preacher's revolver that Zack and Mason dredged up out of the granite quarry yesterday. Doc H identified it as the probable murder weapon in front of Judge A this afternoon.

"And that's not all the good physician said," Farlow continued. "He also testified that the LaRiviere girl was at least a month pregnant when she was found."

"Mister Baby Johnson!" my father said. "What in the name of Ethan Allen and the First Continental Congress is the good news?"

Farlow Blake leaned closer to my father. "Don't breathe a word of this to anyone," he said. "But the good news at this point would appear to be that the reverend's asked Charlie to defend him, and Brother Charlie's agreed."

# 15

"very bit of the evidence is circumstantial, James."

"That's true, Jimmy. But circumstantial evidence is just as admissible in court as any other legitimate evidence."

In the background, over the windowsill radio in Charlie's office, Mel Allen was waxing rhapsodic over the routine trouncing being administered to our Red Sox by the Yankees, who were coasting toward yet another easy pennant.

It was evening, several days after the traumatic arrest of Reverend Andrews on the church steps. The minister was being held in the Memphremagog city jail, ten miles to the north, both in order to spare him the humiliation of being incarcerated in the village where he had lived and preached and because Judge Allen wasn't entirely sure that it was safe for him to remain in Kingdom Common. And once again, Dad and Charlie were trying to make sense of the whole mess.

"So the girl was pregnant, James. What does that prove? Nothing. I can think of any one of a dozen different explanations for that, beginning with Resolvèd himself or somebody connected with that traveling strip show, or somebody back in Quebec. Maybe that's why she left Quebec, for God's sake. That stepfather might have raped her."

"I've got a question," I said. "Can I ask a question?"

"Of course you can ask a question," my father said, though once he and Charlie got going hot and heavy, getting a word in edgewise was no simple matter.

"Does Nat know about his father? Being arrested and all?"

Charlie nodded. "Nat knows the gist of it, buddy. He knows Claire's dead, which he took pretty hard, and that his father's in jail, which he's taking even harder. He doesn't know all the details. They let Reverend Andrews call him from jail. He told Nat as little as he could, and ordered him to stay put at his grandmother's."

"How Zack Barrows, as incompetent as he is, can believe that Walt Andrews killed that girl, is beyond me," Charlie said.

"Look, James," my father said. "I'm not saying Zack Barrows is terribly prejudiced himself—but Mason White's an outright bigot. With White at Barrows' elbow night and day to spur him on, Barrows will believe anything and do anything to win his big case and get reelected. Of the two, White's by far the more dangerous. The more I see of that pair, the more convinced I am that appearances notwithstanding, Barrows is at least as much White's flunky as vice versa."

Charlie sighed. "Look, Jimmy, I don't for one minute think that Walt Andrews murdered that girl, and I very much doubt he slept with her and got her pregnant, all the rumors notwithstanding. I asked him both questions point-blank—I *had* to before we could decide on an innocent plea—and he denied doing either, and I believe him. But I'm pretty sure that the only way we're going to get a *jury* to believe him is to find out who actually did kill her and then framed him into the bargain."

"And?"

"And I'm still at square one on that."

"Then let's go back to square one, James. Let's make another list of all the possible suspects."

Charlie sighed again, but reached for a fresh yellow legal pad and tore off a sheet. At the top he wrote Resolvèd's name.

"Resolvèd Kinneson," he said. "Resolvèd had a motive. He was furious with the LaRiviere kid for running away from him and with Walt Andrews for harboring her, not to mention shooting off part of his trigger finger. But the girl wasn't killed with Resolvèd's shotgun and Resolvèd was in jail at the time of the murder. Unless he escaped or was temporarily released, which seems most unlikely, and then sneaked into the parsonage and got Walt Andrews' revolver, he couldn't possibly have committed the murder. Besides, I still don't think that Resolvèd would do such a thing."

"Of course he'd do it, James," Dad said. "But I must say I don't think he did, either. So that leaves us with whom?"

"Frenchy LaMott?" I ventured. "Frenchy's used to carrying a revolver. He told me he'd like to get Claire alone."

My brother shook his head. "It wasn't done with Frenchy's little .22, buddy. This is light years beyond Frenchy LaMott. Way out of his league. If Reverend Andrews was framed, and we have to assume that that's the case, whoever did it made it look as though Andrews shot the girl, threw her into the pit intending for her body to sink and never be found, and then chucked the gun in after her."

"Then why wouldn't he notice that there wasn't any splash?" Dad said.

"He would have, of course. That's a point I intend to emphasize. But I'll need more than that to prove Walt Andrews was framed.

"Bumper Stevens?" Charlie said, writing down the auctioneer's name. "I've always suspected that he and that warped pygmy Titman White know a hell of a lot more about ornery Ordney Gilson's untimely end than they ever admitted. But again, what's the motive? Stevens has hated Andrews ever since that cockfight episode. But enough to kill the girl in order to frame him? I can't believe that."

"Well, Stevens ought to remain a suspect, in our minds at least, James," my father said.

"I suppose so," Charlie said. "But not a very strong one. Here's one for you: Cousin Elijah. He certainly disliked Reverend Andrews. And he had access to the parsonage, to boot."

My father snorted. "Elijah never broke so much as a jaywalking law in his life. He'd have dearly loved to see Walt Andrews struck dead in the street by lightning and the girl, too, but you don't commit murder and then frame somebody for replacing you in the pulpit. There's no plausible motive."

"I guess not," Charlie said. "Much as I'd like to think so. Then how about Mason White? He hated Walt Andrews with a passion."

My father shook his head. "White's a weasel. He's the worst sort of small-town opportunist. I can't believe he'd murder an innocent little girl just to frame an enemy, though."

"That's just the trouble with a case like this one. It's hard enough to believe that *anyone* would do such a thing for *any* reason. But somebody did, so we can't really rule out anyone at this point, however farfetched they might seem."

"I suppose your brother's right about that, James. But if Mason had a hand in this, which I still can't believe, he'd do a more convincing job of framing the minister. Who could possibly believe for a minute that an intelligent man like Andrews, and an ex-soldier to boot, would throw the murder weapon in the quarry right by the body, where it was bound to be found?"

"A jury, that's who," Charlie said. "Unfortunately, unless we can come up with a more convincing candidate, I'm afraid that a jury might very well believe that he panicked and that's just what happened."

"So why did you take the case?"

"Why not? Besides the fact that this is already the biggest challenge of my career, I don't think for a minute that the guy's guilty, and one way or another I intend to prove it. You can bet on it. As I told Athena the other day, it's about time I defended somebody who's actually innocent. I'll tell you one thing though. There's no way in all this world that our minister friend is going to get a fair trial in Kingdom County. Bright and early tomorrow morning I'm going to beard old Uncle Forrest in his chambers and demand a change of venue. After what's happened this summer, the only way this trial's going to be held here in 'God's Kingdom' will be over my dead body."

"Good luck to you," my father said. "But if I know Forrest Allen, and after fifty-some years I think I do, he's going—what's that? Oh, brother! Mister Baby Johnson!"

" . . . going, going, gone!" the euphoric Voice of the New York Yankees hollered over the static. "The kid from Oklahoma has just hit his *third* home run of the game, making it New York twelve, Boston—"

Snap! Dad reached out his long arm and off went the radio. Mickey Mantle's third home run of the game, as far as my frustrated father was concerned, was the final straw.

"Who is this man Mantle, anyway?" Dad said as he and I headed out to the gool a few minutes later. "Ted's gone, Joe's gone—the game's being taken over by parvenus and upstarts, James."

But at that point, I don't think it would have mattered much to any of us if the Sox had staged a comeback and gone on to win their first World Championship since 1918.

The next morning I went over to the post office to pick up the mail for my father and discovered a letter for me, postmarked in Montreal. It said:

> What in the bloody hell is going on down there? Claire *murdered*? And *my father* thrown in jail? I can't believe it. Nothing makes sense. But I do know one thing, I'd like to see Kingdom County, Vermont, disappear from the face of the bloody earth.
>
> Dad called from his cozy little cell and told me of his pleasant accommodations, then he made it perfectly clear that I was not under *any* circumstances to set foot in Vermont without his express permission, which, by the way, he was not offering. Now I wish I'd never come back to Montreal.
>
> Listen, Kinneson, I know I wasn't always the friend you hoped I'd be but we both know I'm just not a small-town person and never will be. You're a good chap, and I hope you still think well enough of me to do me a favor. I need to know—I *have* to know—just what's happened down there. Are your fascist sheriff and prosecutor actually accusing *him* of being connected with Claire's murder? And *how* was she murdered? Dad said something about being shot at the quarry and "other complications," but he wouldn't go into it. You *have* to write to me in care of the address on this envelope and fill me in. Or better yet call at the number I've enclosed. If you don't, I'm bloody well going to come back, orders or no orders, and find out for myself.
>
> Please write or call immediately.
> N. Andrews
>
> P.S. Don't breath a word about this letter to anyone. Act on your own for once.

I must have thought about Nat's letter fifty times that morning. I wanted in the worst way to show it to someone—if not Dad, then to

Charlie or Mom. But Nat had asked me not to and challenged me to act on my own, besides. So late that afternoon, while Mom was out in the garden picking sweet corn for supper, I called him from the farmhouse, and told him the entire truth, how I'd found Claire's body in the quarry, how the gun was discovered, the autopsy results, and how Nat's father had been arrested on the church steps after the funeral.

Two or three times during my recitation I nearly broke down, and finally, when I got to the part about his father's arrest, I *did* break down. To make matters worse, Nat began swearing and yelling into the phone. He was furious, angry with *me*, mainly, for not letting him know all this as soon as it happened, calling me a bloody fine friend and yelling that he was coming down on the very next train to straighten things out.

Then he was crying, too, which, thank heavens, is when Mom came in with her apron full of sweet corn and gently took the phone away from me and talked to Nat for a long time, while I went out on the porch and sat on the stoop and just cried my eyes out like a little kid. Looking back on that dreadful day in that dreadful summer so many years ago, I truly believe that Ruth Kinneson was the only person in Kingdom County who could have persuaded Nat to remain in Montreal. Somehow she made him understand that coming back would only make matters harder for his dad.

"I don't think it was a mistake to call your friend, Jimmy," she said afterward, sitting down on the stoop and putting her arm around me. "Nat had to know the truth sooner or later, and you were just being a good friend. No harm's been done. I promised Nat that if there's anything he can do to help, we'll be in touch with him right away. In the meantime, you're doing just fine. We're all doing just fine. What's more, I'm sure your brother will get Reverend Andrews out of all this trouble."

"Do you really believe that, Mom? I mean *really*?"

"Yes, I do, Jimmy. I really do believe that. You'll see. I know you can't help worrying. But one way or another, Charlie will get to the bottom of this, with your dad's help, and everything'll turn out right in the end."

"But what if Reverend Andrews really did—"

"I'm sure he didn't, sweetheart. Charlie's going to prove he didn't. Okay?"

"Okay," I said. But how Mom could be so certain of Reverend Andrews' innocence and Charlie's ability to prove it was beyond me.

During the weeks before Reverend Andrews' murder trial, the Kingdom was overrun with reporters. The Kingdom County Affair, as the whole tragedy had come to be called in the papers, was headline news throughout New England. The editorial pages of every paper from Burlington to Boston blazed with questions, innuendos, and denunciations of racial prejudice in northern Vermont. Letters poured into the *Monitor*, too. Dad said the paper had never received so many on any single issue. From their content, it was obvious that local battle lines had been drawn, though nearly everyone seemed determined to refute the allegations of racism in the out-of-town newspapers.

George Quinn submitted a long-winded treatise to the *Monitor* pointing out to "downcountry muckrakers and other rabble-rousers" that not only had Vermont been the first state in the union to outlaw slavery, it had sent the highest ratio of soldiers per capita to the Civil War of any northern state. And numerous other Kingdom County natives wrote to remind readers that Pliny Templeton had been a Negro and that neither his students nor neighbors, nor anyone else, for that matter, had seemed to give his race any thought one way or the other.

Yet one had to wonder. There were other letters, ugly ones, mostly unsigned, which my father did not print but filed away along with clippings from the out-of-town papers. Some of these anonymous diatribes were postmarked Burlington or Rutland or Montpelier; but some had been mailed in the Common and Memphremagog. One averred that Kingdom County had gotten along very nicely for a century and a half without "the colored element that was stirring things up and causing trouble in the big cities," and there was no call to change matters now. Another reiterated Mason White's earlier speculation to my father that Reverend Andrews had come to the area as part of a nationwide Communist-Negro conspiracy. Many people seemed to assume that the murder charges against the minister had already been proven, and as the days went by, fewer and fewer visitors went up to the Memphremagog jail to give him even the slightest support.

As angry as I still become when I look through that yellowing file of anonymous hate mail, I am sure that my father was even angrier when he received them. Of all the Kingdom County natives affected by the Affair, I think Dad was the most distressed.

I should stress here just how deeply my father believed himself to be free of romantic illusions about country living. How could he harbor illusions, this newspaperman's newspaperman who routinely flailed the town for its anti-intellectualism and provincialism and shortsightedness?

And yet, in the end, I believe that my father was the most incorrigible idealist I have ever known. For at the heart of every single one of his excoriations was the unswerving belief that for all its flaws, Kingdom County was a basically good place to live and work. Flog the Kingdom the old man did, relentlessly and tirelessly, much as our stern Scottish ancestors had flogged their own offspring, and for approximately the same reason: He believed most of its failings were correctable.

Dad's great dilemma in the late summer of 1952, however, was that until now he had never believed that such deep-seated and widespread racism was among the village's evils. True, from the start he had recognized the existence of a certain latent prejudice in the Kingdom. But he was genuinely shocked to discover that, at least in the instance of a sizable number of anonymous letter writers and perhaps some members of the congregation as well, he had underestimated its prevalence. So he found himself in the almost impossible position of attacking the bigots yet at the same time trying to defend the village as a whole against the blanket charges of outside reporters and editors who labeled it a northern pocket of rampant racism—a "little piece of Mississippi in northern New England," as one editorial in the Boston *Globe* put it.

It was at this time that Dad, following his own advice to me about the "sealed globe"—that a newspaperman's job is not to solve crimes but to report what is or is not happening—wrote his famous "Conspiracy of Silence" open letter in the *Monitor*. It appeared in the August fourteenth issue and was immediately reprinted in dailies throughout New England and far beyond.

"A Conspiracy of Silence," an Open Letter by Charles Kinneson, Sr.:

> For many years, the United Church of Kingdom Common has experienced difficulty recruiting and retaining qualified full-time ministers. Our church is far from unique in this respect. Small congregations in

outlying rural areas of northern New England have always faced the same problem. This past spring, however, a remarkable clergyman came to our town to live and preach. Almost as soon as he arrived he started to make himself a part not just of the church but of the town as well. When the high school baseball coach fell ill, he stepped in and took over. When he perceived that there were factions in his congregation, he rallied everyone to a wonderful common cause, organizing the first annual Old Home Day Celebration in honor of the church's sesquicentennial anniversary. Yet so far from imposing his ideas and convictions upon us, he listened to our concerns and needs, our plans and desires, even to our history, which became the theme of Old Home Day. His sermons were concise and literate, his counsel witty and humane. Within a month of his installation the size of the congregation, the Sunday school enrollment and the choir had more than doubled. He visited sick people and elderly people, and not just those belonging to his congregation but from the entire community.

Who, precisely, was this remarkable clergyman? His name was Walter Andrews. He was a former Olympic athlete, an outstanding scholar at his college and theological seminary, and a brave and decorated chaplain in the Canadian armed services. He was also a widower, who had known tragedy and sorrow in his life but transcended it through a wholehearted commitment to his spiritual beliefs and work and his son—for whom, naturally, he wanted a normal and happy life. It was in part so that his son could enjoy such a life that he had chosen to come here to our beautiful Kingdom, which (as we all assure one another constantly) is "a fine place to raise kids and have a family."

Now this will no doubt come as a very great surprise to some members of the United Church Congregation and local Rotary Club, but Kingdom County, for all its virtues, is still not quite a perfect place. We have our shortcomings, as well as our strengths, from the sewerage we hourly pump into the Lower Kingdom River to the novels we sanctimoniously deem "unfit" and ban from the hallowed rooms of the Ira Allen Memorial Library. Chief among these shortcomings is an innate suspicion of strangers, outsiders, and, if the truth be known, almost anyone who is much different from ourselves. So it is all the more remarkable that Walter Andrews was so quickly able to win our trust and acceptance and admiration. For not only was he a stranger, from another country—he was the first Negro to live in Kingdom County in more than fifty years.

Yet soon after Reverend Andrews' arrival he and his son were subjected to racial slurs and outrageous behavior on the part of some local bigots whom most of us failed to take very seriously, saying to Walter Andrews and to each other, "Ah, yes. It exists everywhere, even here to a degree.

But it isn't a big problem. These unfortunate instances are only the exceptions that prove the rule that there is next to no serious prejudice in this fine place to live, this bastion of traditional New England ideals so remote from the teeming cities and the steamy South. Not here in God's Kingdom where (nearly a century ago) more than half of the men between 18 and 40 years of age enlisted to preserve the Union and put an end to an institution founded on the very bigotry and contempt for human rights we claimed to abhor. After all, wasn't the founder and first headmaster of our very own Academy himself a Negro? (Of course, our prejudice, or lack of it, had not been tested in over fifty years, since not a single member of the Negro race had lived in Kingdom County in that time.) Besides, Walter Andrews and his son seemed able to handle the isolated instances of prejudice very well themselves. So in general our reaction, when, for instance, our Negro minister and his son were obliged to defend themselves from town drunks and bullies, was silence. Better to let them handle these difficulties themselves, we thought.

Then Reverend Andrews did something that many of us neither totally understood nor totally approved of. He opened his home (and *our parsonage*—we were quick to point this out—his home was *our parsonage*) to a homeless French Canadian girl who came to town with one of the infamous tent shows at Kingdom Fair. She was not a member of the show; she had been picked up on the road into Kingdom County, had been offered a ride by people who said they were performers. The young girl was also a performer—a mime like her famous, deceased father. Pretty and confused, she was told that she could repay the kindness of the ride by "performing" with them at the Kingdom County Fair. Little did she know what they were up to, but when she found out—the night of the performance—she fought to get away and ran. Many of the people from whom she was forced to run were our own townsmen. Yet in opening "our" parsonage to this waif, Walter Andrews outraged and offended many of us almost unforgivably, and from that very day began to lose standing in the eyes of the community for taking in a confused and needy minor — for doing his Christian duty!

A few of us complained directly to him, and a considerable number murmured one to another. But most of us expressed our disapproval by simply remaining *silent* in a sort of unspoken agreement to wait and let events run their course. Certainly no one else stepped forward to help the girl, the outcast, the stranger. Oh, we didn't form a mob and try to stone her or ride her out of town on a rail. Those aren't our tactics here in God's Kingdom these days. We just said to each other, maybe a little baffled, "But what has she to do with us? A girl from the tent show? What has she to do with us and *our* minister and *our* parsonage?"

Then soon afterwards, when one of our local ruffians fired upon our parsonage, breaking our windows and leaving buckshot in our furniture, and Reverend Andrews fired back, actually taking up arms to protect his home, more of us broke our silence, going to him and saying, "What are *you* doing with a gun? How is it that you, a minister, have broken the peace and silence of our streets by firing a gun?"

True, some few of Reverend Andrews's close friends and supporters thought that perhaps he *might* have had a right to defend himself and his son. But even then most of us maintained our silence—even after the local outlaw who fired on the parsonage was charged merely with disturbing the peace (and, temporarily, the silence) of our town; even after the local sheriff went to our parsonage, as directed by our local prosecutor, and questioned the minister about *his* past, and why *he* had a gun and had the temerity to use it (never mind in defense of his life and our property) addressing the Negro minister twice as "boy"!

And though some few of us considered "boy" an improper form of address for our minister, the vast majority of us still maintained our silence, though with considerable curiosity to see what would happen next, because by now it was clear that this affair was fast turning into high social drama of a sort not usually connected with the Kingdom or Vermont or New England.

We did not have to wait long. Three days later the unfortunate homeless girl turned up shot to death at a local quarry. The gun with which Reverend Andrews had had the temerity to defend himself was found nearby, and the minister was arrested on his church steps, during her funeral and charged with murder.

And now it must be acknowledged that at last many of us did break our silence, though only briefly, to repudiate the charges in the out-of-town newspapers that a Negro minister in Kingdom County had been systematically persecuted, fired upon, harassed by the law and finally framed for a murder no one really thought he committed or could commit.

Then we lapsed back into that constitutional taciturnity for which we Vermonters are renowned (for the most part erroneously, since we are laconic only with strangers), and no one except for a reporter or two and the minister's lawyer went to the sheriff and said, "Can't you see that this man has been framed? That it's inconceivable that he would murder the girl with his own gun and then throw it into the water beside her body?"

And although most of us know there are at least five other possible suspects in the case, none of whom our sheriff (who does not deny calling Negroes "boy") has chosen to question, we have thus far remained silent on this point too.

And where, you may well wonder, are those who undoubtedly could come forward with information about this case?

They are silent.

And why hasn't the sheriff questioned local people who had access to our parsonage? No doubt he has his own good reasons, for he too has remained silent.

And what of those leading members of the congregation who literally applauded the arrival of Walter Andrews and might now at least visit and comfort him in his travail? From them we hear, mostly, silence. And I am here to tell you that this conspiracy of silence is, in kind, if not degree, every last bit as heinous as the conspiracy of silence that caused us to stand by for years and do nothing while Nazi Germany was murdering millions of its own citizens in cold blood, not to mention the conspiracy of silence that has allowed an opportunistic and mendacious politician from our own Midwest to destroy the careers and lives of thousands upon thousands of good and loyal American citizens, who are supposedly entitled to freedom of thought and expression.

We may counter these charges by saying, "Yes, but now there will be a trial. Now justice will prevail."

But how can justice prevail if those of us with information continue to remain silent?

We may say, "But only a very few have actually persecuted this man." To which I say that persecution takes many forms. Our fault here is that the majority of us have been more or less indifferent to him, except, of course, as Reverend Andrews's plight embarrasses our town or provides diversion to us. Why? Because like the poor girl he tried to help, Reverend Andrews is an outsider, and still, essentially, a stranger himself, despite all he has done for us.

Don't mistake me. I don't mean to give the impression that we here in the Kingdom are hopelessly intolerant of all strangers. Yet there is some accuracy in what I read in the southern newspapers, that it is too easy for us to be tolerant of the oppressed and of minority races elsewhere. For as a result of geography and chance, we have had astonishingly few outsiders in the Kingdom over the past century and a half, with the exception of French Canadians, many of whom have their own sad tale to tell about what it means to be strangers here; for as most French Canadians can tell you, we are, at the least, innately suspicious of almost anyone who is different from ourselves. This suspicion prevents us from extending to strangers in need the very assistance we pride ourselves most on extending to one another. And without this code of mutual assistance no community could survive.

And yet, the Kingdom *is* still a good, if eminently improvable, place

> to live and work and raise kids. The fact that it can still be improved may be its greatest strength. It is by no means too late for those of us who have information about Claire LaRiviere's murder to come forward, or for our sheriff and prosecutor to begin a vigorous and honest investigation, or for the people Reverend Walter Andrews led, comforted, and supported to provide him with some of the same comfort and support, so that years hence we will never have to say that a stranger came to our village, and we failed him, and by doing so failed ourselves and what it truly means to live in "God's Kingdom."

Charlie told me that Dad's letter was bound to provoke a barrage of self-justifying and angry rejoinders. But for the most part it didn't. For a week or so Reverend Andrews had a few more visitors at the Mephremagog jail, and the sheriff did make an attempt, however cursory, to interview Ida LaMott and Elijah Kinneson and a few others who had access to the parsonage. The hate mail tapered off. But this is all that happened, and, in the end, Dad said that if anyone needed additional proof of a conspiracy of silence, the almost total silence with which his open letter was greeted provided it.

To say that the Affair changed our lives radically seems the feeblest of understatements. Our entire late summer routine had now been usurped by a single ugly event growing uglier by the day. Yet ironically, out of the turmoil came one good thing. As a direct result of Charlie's decision to defend the minister, the estrangement between him and my father that had been deepening all spring and summer as a result of Charlie's refusal to run for the county prosecutor's job was mended. And this was a small miracle for our family, because, though I never doubted for a minute that the differences between my brother and my father were very real, neither did I ever doubt that Dad loved Charlie with a nearly Old Testament (or at least old Scottish) harshness no less profound for its sternness.

But the defense of Reverend Andrews would not be easy, and more, much more, was at stake than in any of my flamboyant brother's other cases, especially after Judge Allen ruled against a change of venue. "We've made this mess ourselves," the judge privately told my father, "and by God, we'll clean it up ourselves. For once in my life, I'm going to see to it that justice is done here in Kingdom County, however painful it may be for everybody involved. If I'd done this last January, Ordney Gilson's murderers might well be behind bars this minute."

What, in the meantime, of Reverend Andrews? Dad and Charlie continued to visit him at the Memphremagog jail nearly daily. And though they usually didn't go together, their reports were discouragingly alike. Without giving way to despair (which any good Presbyterian would make every last effort to resist), the minister was becoming more low-spirited with each passing day.

"I'm worried about him," Dad told us at one of the family war councils we'd begun to hold in our farmhouse kitchen almost nightly. "I don't believe he thinks he's got a chance. He's even quit talking to downcountry reporters—not that I blame him, but these days they're about the only visitors he has."

"I advised him not to," Charlie said. "It's never a good idea for a defendant to talk to reporters in a situation like this. But I couldn't agree more about his low spirits. For a born two-fisted fighter, which I for one still think he is, the guy seems too quiet. I can't figure out why he isn't angrier; God knows he has a right to be. One small piece of good news, though, is that he knew the girl was pregnant. She told him so, and he actually called a home for unwed mothers over in Burlington about it. The doctor he wanted to talk to wasn't in, but we've got a record of the call."

"What does that prove?" I said.

"Not a whole hell of a lot, to tell you the truth. It just makes Zack's contention that the minister murdered her to keep her pregnancy from coming to light seem a little shakier. Why would he kill her after calling the home in Burlington? Or call Burlington if he intended to kill her?"

"He wouldn't," Mom said. "And he didn't. And you, Charlie Kinneson, Esquire, are going to prove beyond any doubt that he didn't. I'm positive of it. What upsets me most right now is thinking of poor Reverend Andrews sitting alone up there in that jail cell all day with only you and your dad and a few curiosity-seekers for visitors. Why, even most of his own congregation's stopped visiting him now that the novelty's worn off. Worst of all, he's got no family nearby to help him."

"Nat's not all that far away," I said. "He's family."

"Nat's the last one he wants around, Jimmy," Charlie said. "Above anything, he doesn't want Nat involved and I don't blame him."

"He's been rereading Pliny Templeton's *Ecclesiastical History* to keep from going crazy," Dad said. "Though how he can concentrate on it I have no idea—Mister Baby Johnson! That's another thing. He asked me to stop in at the parsonage this morning before I came up and bring along his notes on Templeton and those two newspaper clippings on Templeton's death. I went through his desk from top to bottom, but Mason White had evidently beaten me to it. The papers weren't there, and neither was much of anything else. White's apparently confiscated everything in the desk for 'evidence.' "

Charlie frowned. "I don't think White's got those Templeton notes or the clippings. I've seen a list of all the evidence the prosecution's going to use. There's no mention of the Templeton papers. Check the desk again."

"They aren't there, I tell you. I don't need to check again. White took them, whether he intended to use them or not."

"What else does Reverend Andrews do all day in jail?" I said quickly, to avert an argument. "I mean besides reading old Pliny's *History*? It must be terribly boring for him."

"It is," Mom said. "It's high time you and I went to see him, Jimmy. We'll drive up in the morning."

I knew that my father was not happy about my mother's driving our rattletrap De Soto up to Memphremagog, even though it was just ten miles away and she was a very capable driver, and he was even less happy about our venturing into the jail in that rough little Canadian-border paper mill town. But with one exception, which had it not reflected the deeper problems of the adults of the Kingdom would actually have been amusing, the trip went as well as anyone could expect such a trip to go under the circumstances.

Reverend Andrews' cell was in the police station on the main street of town, overlooking Lake Memphremagog. The chief just waved us on down the corridor. As we had hoped, Reverend Andrews seemed very glad to see us, though we had to stand outside his cell and talk through the bars. I was relieved to see that he was wearing his suit pants and dress shoes and a clean white shirt with the sleeves rolled up; I'd been worried that he might have on a striped uniform. Mom had brought him a carton of Luckies, and he thanked her and assured us with a grin that his "help" at the jail were all very attentive, and the view from his high barred window was capital.

He winked at me. "How's next year's starting shortstop?"

Remembering how Reverend Andrews had found my baseball position for me, I had to blink back tears. How, I wondered, could he possibly concern himself with *my* trivial hopes and dreams at such a time? Yet I believe that it was in a large degree just this kind of unselfishness that made him an effective minister. And there was no trace of irony in his voice when he asked Mom how my father and Charlie were holding up through this whole mess. There was that touch of greatness about the man, that capacity to transcend his own circumstances, however grim, that I suppose he had cultivated as a chaplain in World War II and Korea. Yet I could tell by looking at his eyes, which were grave and unamused and worried, that he was undergoing a terrible ordeal.

"Have you been in touch with Nat, Jim?" he asked after we had settled down.

This caught me completely off guard. I stammered something about a letter and a phone call, until Mom rescued me and told Reverend Andrews that Nat and I had talked on the phone, and she'd talked to Nat, and her impression was that things were fine in Montreal. "I want you to know something, though, Reverend," she said. "If the time ever comes when, for whatever reason, you need Nat here in Kingdom County, he'll stay with us and be part of our family for as long as he wants to."

"That's very, very kind of you, Ruth. But please understand that it's imperative that Nat not be mixed up in all this. I'd never forgive myself if I let that happen. I've come to think that it was a bad enough mistake to bring him here in the first— Oh, no! Will you look at those blooming little urchins! They've been at that for the past three days."

Reverend Andrews was laughing. He pointed at the window, where I caught just the briefest flash of a kid's face, popping into and fast out of sight. Then I saw it again! Only this was a different kid, a redhead. What in blazes was going on?

Still chuckling, Reverend Andrews explained. And as he did, his eyes briefly assumed that wonderful amused expression, his voice that mellifluous delight in an irony, any irony, that I'd sensed the first time I saw and heard him, back in the Ridge Runner Diner. "What we've got here is a prime example of old-fashioned North American small-town entrepreneurship, folks, in the tradition of Tom Sawyer. It seems that the local police chief's son is a bright young chap of about twelve years of age, who's been operating a sort of sociological peephole show out behind the jail. What he's doing is selling glimpses of me, for a dime a shot, to younger kids who've apparently never seen a Negro. At least not in jail! He boosts them up outside my window and holds them there until they're satisfied—though most are too scared to take full advantage of the opportunity— Where are you off to, Jim?"

I was already halfway down the corridor.

"I'm going to kick their damn asses into the lake!" I shouted.

"Hold up, chum!" Reverend Andrews called. "That's not the ticket. Let 'em have their fun. It's a diversion to me, and at this point any diversion is welcome."

I don't think it really was a diversion, though, and apparently Mom didn't think so, either, because on our way out she marched into the chief's office and told him he should be ashamed to let such a disgraceful circus go on outside his jail and if he didn't put a stop to what his boy was doing, she would.

The chief was a big, tired-looking man of about fifty. "Judas Priest, missus, how do you expect me to do that?" he said. "Put a twenty-four-hour guard outside that window? How would *you* stop it?"

"Just let me get my hands on that son of yours for five minutes," my mother said, "and I'll show you."

"Oh, Judas," the chief said, and stood up and started heavily for the door.

The last thing we saw as we drove out of the police station parking lot was the chief, lumbering down the sidewalk behind a gaggle of kids, but I could tell his heart wasn't in it the way mine would have been.

I have mentioned that in many ways it was my mother who helped us all pull through that terrible summer intact. Besides that visit to the jail, which I believe was critically important, if not for the minister then for us, and perhaps for me in particular, she did everything in her power to preserve as many of our ordinary routines as possible during those weeks before Reverend Andrews's murder trial. Two such instances in particular come to my mind.

The early fifties saw the tail end of what to me was a wonderfully fascinating type of entertainment in rural northern New England. Here and there in outlying corners of Maine, New Hampshire, and Vermont, the very last remnants of the myriad itinerant one- or two-night performers who once toured the entire country still occasionally turned up. I am not thinking of vaudeville performers or chautauqua lecturers so much as, say, the little one-elephant circuses, the family carnivals with half a dozen or so rides and games, the four- or five-man barnstorming baseball teams, and best of all, an individual called "Mr. Mentality," who came to town every three or four years when I was a boy and who was a mind reader.

Although my father printed up twenty or so big four-color posters advertising Mr. Mentality's amazing one-man performance to be held on the Saturday night after Mom and I visited the minister in jail, such excursions into the realm of the extrasensory not only brought out the skeptic in him but, I believe, disconcerted him—as anything that was not entirely accessible to strict journalistic scrutiny and reducible to logic and Newtonian physics tended to disconcert him. Mom said that once, years ago, he had sat through a single performance of Mr. Mentality's show with the objective of demystifying the mind reader's act in an open letter in the *Monitor*. When he could not entirely, for at the very least the traveling clairvoyant was a sort of specialized genius, Dad lost all interest in him and wrote him off as a shrewd purveyor of parlor games for pay.

My mother, on the other hand, was endlessly intrigued by all aspects of Mr. Mentality's performances, and regarded him as the last of a breed and someone I should see while there was still time.

You might suppose that with the terrific uproar over the murder during the past couple of weeks, interest in a magic show many Commoners had already seen three or four times would run rather low. Not so at all. The "hall," as everyone in town called the Academy auditorium, was jam-packed by 7:30 that Saturday evening when George Quinn stepped out onto the stage and introduced the astonishing Mr. Mentality: a stooped, solemn-looking man of an indeterminate age in a rusty black cape, with a pointy dark beard, who for the next hour and a half kept us delighted and baffled by various astonishing mnemonic and intuitive feats. He could accurately multiply in his head any two numbers you gave him, up to four digits apiece; instantly name the day of the week in which you were born; and recite verbatim any page of that week's *Saturday Evening Post*. He could tell you numbers you were thinking of in your head, the dates of the coins in your pocket, the names of books you'd checked out of the library, the topic of a conversation you'd had in Farlow Blake's barbershop two days before. (My father had said that for most of these feats Mr. Mentality undoubtedly employed a stalking-horse who acted as advance man and spy as well as in-house confederate—quite possibly a native of Kingdom County—though who this might be even Dad had no idea.)

I kept thinking how much Claire, with her flair for the dramatic, would have loved his performance, his low-keyed panache even on the infrequent occasions when he guessed wrong (shrugging as though to say, "So what? Now you *know* I'm no humbug. A humbug wouldn't ever be wrong, would he?"). Suddenly I realized that this was the first time I'd been able to think about Claire without despair, and I was both relieved and surprised, yet slightly sorry, that as Mom had promised, time had already healed some of my grief. But at the end of the evening, during the question-and-answer period, when that ignorant old smart-aleck Plug Johnson stood up and asked Mr. Mentality who "rubbed out the Canuck gal staying at the preacher's," a question so tasteless and outrageous it shocked the entire room into total silence, the mind reader just shrugged, held out his hands palms up, and said that was up to us to determine, not him—after which he walked off the stage without a backward glance and was never seen or heard of in Kingdom County again. This bad ending put such a damper on the evening that I almost wished Mom and I hadn't come at all, and I think she felt the same way.

Ruth Kinneson was nothing if not resilient, though. And the very next day, when Dad remarked that he'd told Judge Allen we wouldn't be spending our usual end-of-the-summer week's vacation at his fishing camp on Lake Memphremagog, Mom made him call the judge on the spot to reserve the camp for that last week of August before he offered it to someone else. She said that with me going off to high school in the fall, and only four years away from college, there was no telling how many more chances we'd have to be together as a family, and Kingdom County Affair or no, we were going to have our week on the big lake. It was a good and wise decision, and a good week, though of course there was no way to escape from the Affair there, any more than there had been at Mr. Mentality's show—just some easing of the day-to-day tension and a welcome break from our routine at the farmhouse on the gool.

Every morning at dawn, when the huge lake was at its calmest, I'd start the judge's old motorboat and ferry Dad the five miles south from the island to the town dock at Memphremagog. After a brief visit to the jail to see if Reverend Andrews needed anything, he'd drive down to the Common to work and I'd troll a big red-and-white spoon slowly back to the camp, sometimes picking up a smallmouth bass or a land-locked salmon or two, which Mom would cook for our breakfast. I spent the rest of the morning exploring and fishing the nearby bays and coves, and afternoons I swam off the dock, and read on the screened-in camp porch overlooking the lake and high mountains to the west. Evenings Mom and I played parlor games while my father read or returned to town to visit Reverend Andrews at the jail.

On our last night at camp, Mom had a big steak cookout, and Charlie, who'd been busy all week in the Common preparing for the trial, came up to eat with us. I hadn't seen him since our vacation had started, and he looked tired and frustrated when I met him and Dad at the dock. As soon as we got out to the island, my mother went right to work to perk him up.

"How's Vermont's best-looking defense lawyer tonight?" she said, and gave him a big hug.

"Tired, Ruthie," Charlie said. "I still haven't come up with a single lead on another suspect. I'd make a hell of a prosecutor at this rate, wouldn't I?"

"Don't call your mother Ruthie," my father said.

"*You* look good, Ruthie," my brother said. "How old did you say you're going to be on your next birthday? Thirty-nine?"

"Me and Jack Benny," Mom said, but I could tell she was pleased because she unconsciously brushed back her lovely long hair with her hand and laughed the way she always did when Charlie teased her.

Usually on the last night of our vacation week at the Allens' camp, my mother asked Athena and the judge for supper. But Athena was off taking courses at the state university in Burlington, and as my father had tried to explain to me the night before, with the trial coming up and Charlie representing Reverend Andrews, having my brother and the judge both for a meal would be a conflict of interest. At thirteen, I didn't know the difference between a conflict of interest and the Korean conflict, but Charlie himself had told me that lately when he ran into the judge he would barely grunt at him.

"Sure as hell old Uncle Forrest'll go out of his way to give me a hard time at that trial just to show everybody how impartial he is," Charlie said as we sat down to eat.

"Just don't *you* go out of your way to give *him* a hard time, mister," Dad said. "You want to play this one straight the whole way."

Then Mom declared a moratorium on the topic until supper was over, which was fine with me. After dessert Charlie and Mom walked arm-in-arm around the island while Dad and I played catch in front of the camp, and then we sat out on the screened porch in the split-cane chairs that had been there as long as I could remember and watched the lights of Memphremagog came on far down across the water. Dad smoked a cigar, and its rich fragrance blended with the familiar camp scents of spruce needles and woodsmoke and the camphor-soaked ball of cotton on the screen door to keep the flies away. I thought Dad or Charlie might recite one of William Henry Drummond's marvelous French Canadian dialect poems, "The Voyageur" or maybe "The Habitant," as they liked to do when we got together at the judge's camp. They did not, though, and Mom didn't tease Dad by suggesting that we all play a parlor game, either. I knew they were all thinking about the Affair.

"All right," Charlie said in a flat, unhappy, determined tone of voice. "All right. Suppose he *did* sleep with the girl? I'm not saying I think that's what happened. But what if it did? Here's a healthy guy, vigorous and in his prime, with no wife and no girlfriend and no social life with the opposite sex at all. And here's an attractive and lonely and, for all we know to the contrary, rather promiscuous young woman under his roof. So what if he succumbed to the temptation and did sleep with her? That sure as hell doesn't mean he killed her."

"Temptation is one thing," Dad said. "Anybody might be tempted. He might even have been tempted when Julia offered him her precious favors back a couple of months ago—she was a handsome enough woman at one time. But the fact is he *didn't* succumb to whatever temptations he may have felt. Besides, he had a much more normal social life than you might think. I wasn't going to mention this, but he once told me he had a close woman friend in Montreal, a teacher at McGill University."

"Well, he can't have seen her very often since coming here."

"What is it you're saying? There's some sort of new evidence that he got the girl pregnant?"

"No, not really. I don't know. I don't want to get into it just yet. I just want to be prepared to show in court that even if he *did* succumb to the temptation, he didn't necessarily kill her."

"Didn't necessarily kill her! I can't and won't believe that there's a shred of truth to these trumped-up charges."

"Neither can I, sweetheart," Mom told Charlie.

Charlie stood up. "Who wants to go for a dip? We aren't going to have many more warm nights, or days either, for swimming."

"Fall's coming and that's a fact," Dad said. "The swamp maples along the river between here and the Common are already starting to turn red."

"I think fall's my very favorite season," Mom said in a musing voice.

Charlie laughed. "You say that about every season. 'Spring's my favorite, summer's my favorite, fall's my *very* favorite season!' "

"Well, suppose I do? They can *all* be my favorite. Right now, fall's my favorite."

"This fall won't be, Ruthie," Charlie said, heading inside to change into his swimsuit. "I'll guarantee it. Win or lose, we're in for the nastiest trial in the history of Kingdom County and maybe the whole state. This'll make the Gilson debacle look like a traffic court case. And that, Editor Kinneson, is—"

"—the beginning and the end of it," my father grunted without even bothering to rebuke my brother for calling Mom by her first name.

As Charlie had predicted, it increasingly looked as though in order to prove that Reverend Andrews didn't commit the murder, my brother would have to prove who did—a job that at best would be difficult, given the slender list of suspects and Judge Allen's refusal to grant his request for a change of venue, though I must admit that I was secretly pleased by that decision, since it meant that I might be able to see the trial myself.

One morning in early September I started high school. To my puzzlement, many of my classmates seemed actually to have shrunk over the summer. But I soon realized that contrary to all my expectations I had actually grown, shot up three inches during the past three months.

For the first few days of school Reverend Andrews' upcoming murder trial, now formally scheduled to begin on the Friday of Harvest Festival weekend, was all the kids could seem to talk about. In the hall before classes, again at lunch, yet again at soccer practice, they pumped me for all I was worth both because I was Charlie's brother and because I had been Nathan Andrews' closest friend. But beyond the generally known facts that Nat was going to school back in Montreal and living with his grandmother, and Reverend Andrews was still in jail in Memphremagog, I knew little more than the rest of the kids.

Once or twice I went so far as to start a letter to Nat. But what under the sun could I say—"Your dad's doing fine in jail, wish you were here"? I rationalized my failure to write by falling back upon that oldest and lamest of excuses, telling myself that, what with classes and homework and soccer and daily chores both at the shop and on the gool, I simply didn't have time.

# 16

Kingdom County's Harvest Festival traditionally fell on the first weekend in October. It began on Friday, a local school holiday, and was held principally on the village common. There in a final informal celebration of the short northern growing season, farmers and gardeners from the Canadian border all the way south to St. Johnsbury brought every kind of produce that could be raised locally to sell out of the backs of pickups or from makeshift stands and benches set up under the tall yellowing elms.

In the fall of 1952, for the first time in more than twenty years, my mother would not be taking vegetables to the common on Harvest Friday, though when I got out of school on Thursday afternoon for the long holiday weekend I found two Harvest Figures waiting for me in the dooryard—the pumpkin-headed straw men emblematic of autumn in the Kingdom, and which to this day you will see sprawled in barnyard wheelbarrows, propped nonchalantly against mailboxes, and lounging incongruously on porch roofs, leering out at passers-by with macabre or comical grimaces.

On Saturday morning the Harvest Figures would be judged by a panel of local dignitaries, who would then present awards in several categories that afternoon.

My mother was the only person in our family with artistic ability, and in the fall of 1952 her figures were especially wonderful: a roly-poly old farmer in overalls and a battered straw hat, sitting in a chair and watching his wife toiling over my grandfather James' wooden cider press. In the farmer's crooked arm was a half-full glass gallon of hard cider, and carved on his pumpkin face was an obviously tipsy smile, while Mrs. Pumpkin-head looked on with pursed lips. On a cardboard placard around the straw woman's neck my mother had carefully stenciled the words NEW ENGLAND GOTHIC.

At the time, I wondered how Mom could fool with Harvest Figures on the eve of the biggest murder trial in the history of the county. Now I realize that she wanted to make our fall as normal as possible, but such sweet and familiar acts just served to underscore the bizarre twist our otherwise happy lives had taken.

Harvest Friday dawned crisp and clear, with a coverlet of October mist over the river, and the hardwood ridges around the village as beautifully red and gold as I could ever remember. As my folks and I started out to the village the sun rose above Lord Hollow, blood-red and magnified to ten times its normal size, and for the first time that fall I remembered that tomorrow was opening day of partridge season. Ordinarily, Dad and Charlie and I would be planning to slip up into the brilliantly colored hills with our shotguns. But not tomorrow. Tomorrow, no doubt, we would still be at the trial, and neither Dad nor I mentioned a word about bird hunting, or even paused to assess the river for fall fly fishing as we crossed the red iron bridge. We passed the empty parsonage without a word and turned silently south past the Academy, toward the courthouse, where a small crowd had already gathered on the sidewalk.

"Hit 'em hard, Editor K," Plug Johnson called out. "Give 'em hell!"

But Mom and Dad and I went immediately to the small side door on the ground level, which Charlie opened just wide enough for us to squeeze through, then shut quickly behind us.

"What's the news?" my father said immediately.

"As Farlow would say, bad and good," Charlie told us as we started upstairs to the courtroom. He was wearing the gray Brooks Brothers suit that he had lent to Resolvèd for our cousin's poaching trial last spring. His wing-tip shoes were polished, his white shirt was starched stiff, and he wore a conservative dark necktie, and although his sharp black eyes looked very tired, he also looked more determined than I had ever seen him.

We stopped on the landing at the head of the stairs. "There's still no doubt in my mind that there's only one way I'm ever going to convince a jury that Walt Andrews didn't murder that girl, and that is to find out who did. That's the bad news."

"So what's the good news?" Dad said.

Charlie ruffled the back of my head and shook his own. "The good news, I'm afraid, is that Vermont has outlawed the death penalty."

Except for Athena Allen, who was sitting directly behind the defense table, the courtroom was still empty when we walked in. Sure enough, Farlow Blake had left three sheets of paper with KINNESON printed on them taped to the backs of three chairs beside Athena.

Soon after we were seated the tall steam radiators under the windows clanked on. Julia Hefner bustled in with her stenographer's notebook. Farlow Blake appeared with a great glass pitcher of ice water and began filling the glasses at the defense and prosecutor's tables and on the judge's bench. Mason White, dressed in a brand-new flashy seersucker suit, appeared with Zachariah Barrows and an ordinary-looking middle-aged man in a plain gray suit and matching gray tie, whom I didn't recognize. As they sat down together at the prosecutor's table, I noticed that Charlie was staring hard at the stranger and grinning. It was not a pleasant grin, but reminded me of the way my brother had grinned at the French Canadian ringer who had tried to bean him in the big grudge game back on Old Home Day.

Instead of his shiny old bottle-green jacket, Zack too was wearing a new suit, a pin-striped affair, with what must have been the last red zinnia from his flower garden in the lapel. And although his nose was as crimson as the bright fall flower, when he nodded over at Charlie and said good morning he sounded sober and alert. His white hair was cut neatly and carefully parted in the middle. Projecting from his left ear was a large flesh-colored button.

"Mister Baby Johnson, James!" my father said in a low voice. "The old codger's gotten himself a hearing aid!"

"Well, Zachariah," Charlie said, "are you ready to do battle this morning in the best interests of the county and the law of the land?"

"My boy," Zack said, "I've forgotten more about the law of the land than you'll ever know."

"What good does it do you, then?" Charlie shot back.

Zack laughed, and the stranger looked over and smiled a little tight-lipped smile. But I didn't understand how the lawyers could joke this way before a murder trial. Within an hour they would be at one another's throats, and somehow their banter seemed callous, when a man's fate was hanging in the balance.

At eight o'clock on the dot, Farlow threw open the courtroom doors. Spectators began filing in, filling first the downstairs chairs, then trooping upstairs to the gallery where, a little more than three months ago, Nat and I had hidden to watch the arraignment of the Paris Revue entourage. Still, there were not enough seats to hold the huge crowd, and people lined up two and three deep along the walls. They were quiet, even the out-of-town reporters, and acted more like spectators coming into a courtroom just before a jury was to return a crucial verdict. There was no jostling for position. Like me, most of the people did not quite seem to believe that any of this could be happening in Kingdom County.

No one was turned away. The courtroom had been built for a maximum of three hundred people, but now held half again that number. Yet except for a few coughs and the shuffling of a few feet, it was as still as when my father and mother and I had first entered it.

At eight-fifteen Farlow ushered in thirty-six potential jurors, who sat in a reserved section near the front of the room across the aisle from us.

Reverend Andrews was already halfway to the defense table when I saw him. He was dressed in the same dark suit and dark tie he had preached in, taller by inches than the two deputies he walked between, looking dignified and even aloof, although his wrists were handcuffed. He paused at the end of the defense table and remained standing while Pine Benson unlocked the cuffs. Totally ignoring Pine fiddling nervously with the cuffs, he looked from right to left and then unhurriedly up to the gallery, taking in the entire room in one long appraising glance—a man so entirely accustomed to being at ease with large groups of people that for a moment I actually thought he was going to say something to them. He looked at the jurors. He looked back at our side of the room and noticed me, and as soon as his hands were free he gave me his small two-fingered salute.

Suddenly the buzzer over the judge's chambers went off.

"All rise," Farlow Blake said loudly, and Judge Forrest Allen strode in from his chambers, looking neither right nor left.

"Be seated, please," Farlow said after the judge had sat down. "Those that have a place to sit down at, that is. The rest may remain standing."

And on that nearly comic note began the ultimate adjudication of the Kingdom County Affair. All I could think of, however, was the last thing my brother had said to us on the landing outside the courtroom door: that the only good news that morning was that Vermont had no death penalty.

Judge Allen began the empaneling by asking if any of the jurors were in any way personally acquainted with Reverend Andrews; several put up their hands and were automatically excused. By the time the judge had finished his general questions, including one asking whether anyone had any doubt about his or her ability to render an impartial decision in a case involving a Negro defendant (no hands went up in response to this query), only nineteen of the original thirty-six prospective jurors remained.

Now it was Zack's turn to weed out the field. He used only two of his six peremptory challenges. After a whispered consultation with the middle-aged stranger beside him, he disqualified a retired history professor from the state university and a yard foreman at the American Heritage Mill with a reputation as a labor union advocate. Now the pool had been reduced to less than half of its original size.

The first person Charlie questioned was a young attendant at the Memphremagog Socony station, a man named Rip Coleman. "Have you ever been in the service, Mr. Coleman?" Charlie asked.

Rip Coleman said yes, he'd gotten back from a tour of duty as a marine in Korea just three months ago. After a brief pause, my brother inquired if there had been any Negroes in his company.

"More than enough," Rip Coleman said.

A murmur ran through the room as Charlie immediately challenged for cause and Judge Allen upheld his challenge. But when my brother asked another veteran, an older man who'd served in World War II, if he'd formed any opinions about Negroes or other minority races in the service, the stranger at the prosecutor's table leaned over and whispered something to Zack, who quickly got to his feet to object.

"That question is redundant, your honor. You've already made that inquiry, and no one felt that the defendant's color would be in any way a problem."

"Including Rip Coleman, who's just been disqualified from sitting on this jury for making a blatantly prejudiced remark!" Charlie said angrily.

"All he said was—militarily speaking, I presume—that—" Zack started to say.

"All he said was that there were more than enough Negroes in his company!" Charlie said loudly. "That's pure bigotry, Zack, and you know it."

The judge brought down his gavel hard. "Gentlemen, race is *not* to be an issue in this case."

"I wholeheartedly agree that it shouldn't be, your honor," Charlie said. "But the reality of the matter is that in some cases it is. To refresh your memory, I'd like to ask Mrs. Hefner to read Rip Coleman's—"

"My memory does not need refreshing, thank you, Mr. Kinneson. Matters of race, creed, and color are not, never have been, and never will be an issue in any courtroom I preside over. I will settle this issue once and for all, now and forever. Once more, is there *anyone* left on this panel of prospective jurors who has any doubts at all about his or her ability to arrive at a fair and impartial verdict based on the evidence of this case and the evidence alone? If so, I'll excuse you without further question."

The judge waited. Finally, a man from Pond in the Sky, a logger of Portuguese descent, stood up and left the room. It was, I suppose, a courageous thing to do, although at the time I did not know his reason. Later that week my father interviewed him, and to everyone's considerable surprise, the logger said that his grandfather had always claimed to be part black, and he thought that he might be prejudiced on *behalf* of Reverend Andrews!

"Your honor," Charlie said, after he'd gone, "I would still like to question some individual jurors on this delicate matter. This case is too important—"

"Come forward, sir!" the judge barked. "Mr. Barrows, you may approach the bench also."

For the next two or three minutes, Charlie and Zack and Judge Allen conferred in low, heated voices. I looked inquiringly at my father, who wrote on his pad, "Judge A trying to keep nasty business from becoming even nastier. Issue here is murder."

Meanwhile, Charlie made one final impassioned whispered plea. But the judge just shook his head, his silvery hair looking as icy as February hoarfrost on Jay Peak, and motioned impatiently for the attorneys to return to their tables. Although I didn't completely understand what was happening, it seemed to me that, while trying to be totally fair himself, the judge had tied my brother's hands—or one of them, anyway—behind his back. Maybe race wasn't an issue in the murder itself; but what about potential jurors, who despite what they themselves might think, could be prejudiced? Did the judge just expect that they would all admit biases that they might not even recognize? Or did he expect them to suspend these biases during the trial? It seemed to me that Forrest Allen was being downright wrongheaded.

One thing was clear, though. However discouraged he might be with Reverend Andrews' case, Charlie was going to do everything within his power to make sure that the man received a fair trial.

The final jury of twelve members and two alternates was composed of three farmers, three housewives, an independent lumberman, two mill workers, a Northern Vermont Telephone Company installer, a young woman teacher from Pond in the Sky, a sales clerk from the IGA in Memphremagog, a retired Boston and Montreal Railroad engineer, and a traveling licensed practical nurse who gave physical exams at the Academy once a year and had a reputation as a no-nonsense individual who could summon in Painless Doc Harrison and have him yank out your appendix if you so much as batted an eyelash at her. Of the jurors, I knew only the traveling nurse and the telephone installer, a man in his thirties named Yves St. Pierre, who was an expert deer hunter and frequently had his picture in the *Monitor* with a big buck.

The trial began at exactly ten o'clock with the opening statement of the prosecution. Ordinarily, Zack would have spent a good half minute fussing with his papers. This morning, he appeared neither hungover nor confused as he stepped forward to address the jury. In the same orotund style with which he had declaimed the Gettysburg Address each Fourth of July for the past forty years from the base of the statue of Ethan Allen, he boomed out, "Your honor, officers of the court, my young brother-at-the-bar, ladies and gentlemen of the jury. It is a signal privilege to speak before you on this glorious morning in the 'season of mists and yellow fruitfulness,' as the immortal Bard put it."

"Objection, your honor."

Charlie stood up. "If the prosecution is going to drag in literary allusions by the heels, he ought at least to check his sources. It's 'mellow fruitfulness,' not 'yellow.' And the immortal Bard never said any such thing. John Keats wrote that line, and if you don't believe me you may check with our resident literary expert who's sitting just behind me."

Charlie motioned to Athena, who indicated with a nod that he was right. My father got out his handkerchief and blew his nose. The out-of-town reporters wrote furiously. Zack Barrows merely looked puzzled.

"Let the prosecutor proceed, Mr. Kinneson," Judge Allen said.

But as Charlie had undoubtedly hoped, Zack had lost his train of thought. Now his customary fumbling ensued. For a moment he actually seemed to forget that he was holding his opening speech in his hands. But at last he recovered himself and blustered ahead.

"At any rate," he said, "the task of sitting on a jury is neither an easy nor an envious one—"

"Objection, your honor. The word is envia—"

"SILENCE! Charles Kinneson, you will allow the prosecutor, who has as unenviable a job today as yours, to complete his statement in peace or I will interpret your fractious interruptions as contempt of this court and slap you with a cool hundred-dollar fine payable on the spot. Do you take my meaning?"

"Yes, your honor," Charlie said.

In the meantime, my father had written in his notebook: "Look at jury."

Two or three of the jurors, including Yves St. Pierre, were smiling. The rest looked bewildered, but as Zack started in again, most of the jury members continued to glance over at my brother as though trying to anticipate what he would come up with next. If Charlie had meant by his interruptions to distract their attention from Zack, he'd succeeded.

But today Zachariah Barrows was not to be sidetracked for long. And if there was ever any doubt in anyone's mind about the boozing old prosecutor's native cunning, that doubt was removed by his opening speech—if in fact it was *his* speech.

"As I see it, ladies and gentlemen," he read, "the case before you is a clear one, though by no means an easy one to sit on. An especially brutal murder has been committed in our county. The victim, a simple and innocent young woman, was killed senselessly and savagely, in a town where no murder of any kind has taken place in recent history."

What about Ordney Gilson's untimely demise? I thought. Wasn't he murdered? Or did he just hang *himself* in the elm tree on the common?

"A good town," Zack continued. "A town where people come and go safely, leave their keys in their vehicles while they shop, and don't for the most part bother to lock their doors at night. A place where hunting and fishing are the main sports and high school soccer is the most violent activity.

"Kingdom County," Zack continued, "has the reputation as a place where things are done in old-fashioned ways. Neighbors still take pains to be neighbors. Friendships last a lifetime. And"—gesturing at the big Seth Thomas wall clock—"even the time is an hour behind the rest of the country.

"Nonetheless, this wonderful and special place is not immune from all of the horrors of our era. We have a railroad here. We have a U.S. highway. Tramps drift through. Travelers of all kinds between Montreal and Boston pass through: outsiders, most of whom, though they may live at a faster pace than we do, are basically no different from you and me. But unfortunately, there are exceptions. For with a total lack of involvement from any native of Kingdom County, a heinous crime has been committed here, a crime in which both the victim and the accused perpetrator came from far away, leaving those of us who have always lived here, and will continue to live here, with the unpleasant but necessary work of picking up the pieces and determining what happened and how and why, and meting out justice. That, ladies and gentlemen, is what we the prosecution are here to help you do.

"Toward that end, we will prove not only beyond any reasonable doubt, but beyond the slightest doubt at all, that the defendant, Walter Andrews, knew the victim well before the murder took place. Further, we will prove that Walter Andrews murdered Claire LaRiviere, shooting her brutally and repeatedly with his own gun. We will produce photographs of the mutilated victim, along with highly qualified medical testimony.

"Now, folks, I must warn you in advance that some of the photographs you're going to be asked to look at here today are extraordinarily gruesome. Nonetheless, you must examine them closely and thoroughly, however repulsive you may find them, in order to form an accurate opinion of the nature of the crime and discharge your own sworn duty.

"We will produce the murder weapon. We will show that it came from the defendant's house and that it belonged to the defendant.

"We will show, moreover, that there are discrepancies in many public statements that have been made by the defendant, who has a history of compulsive and sudden violence in this community—where, in less than six months, he has broken a man's jaw in an encounter having all the earmarks of a back-alley brawl and been involved in a shoot-out in the village streets with the same gun he used to murder Claire LaRiviere.

"What was this volatile and violent-minded man's motive for murdering an innocent girl? you may well wonder. We will answer that question by producing a witness whose testimony will establish as clear and compelling a motive as any I have ever encountered. I will warn you in advance that the defense will undoubtedly argue that his client was somehow mysteriously framed for the murder. But we will show that no one had the slightest motive to frame him and, moreover, that he was the *only* person in Kingdom County with a motive to murder Claire LaRiviere. Finally, we will produce an unimpeachable final witness who will offer testimony that will dispel all remaining doubt of the defendant's guilt.

"I appreciate your patience, ladies and gentlemen. I'll ask for just a moment's more of it. A short while ago, Judge Allen made it clear that one issue is totally irrelevant in this trial. That is the issue of race. That the defendant happens to be a Negro has absolutely no bearing on the matter at hand and, as the judge has stressed, must have no bearing on your ultimate determination. The issue here is whether Walter Andrews did or did not murder Claire LaRiviere. Nothing else. You cannot and must not allow yourselves to be swayed by sympathy for him any more than you could allow yourselves to be swayed by bias against him. The fact that he happens to belong to a minority people is absolutely immaterial, period. Thank you very much."

But instead of sitting down, Zack held up his index finger to indicate that he wasn't quite finished. "At this point, your honor, I'd like to introduce my colleague and associate who'll be assisting me with the prosecution of this case—Mr. Sigurd Moulton."

Zack made a gracious motion toward the stranger at the prosecutor's table, who made the very slightest bow. "Mr. Moulton is a former county prosecutor with extensive experience in first-degree murder cases and currently a partner of the law firm of Moulton, Greaves, and Greaves, of Montpelier."

I grabbed my father's arm in alarm but no doubt he had known from the moment the stranger walked into the courtroom. Sigurd Moulton was the hotshot "Most Peculiar" prosecutor my cousin Resolvèd had impersonated this past spring at his own trial—the man rumored to be the best lawyer in the state, who had lost only one case in his career, and that to Charlie, in the Ordney Gilson murder trial!

My brother was on his feet like a shot. "Objection!" he roared. "Attorney Barrows was elected by the voters of Kingdom County to prosecute his own cases. That he believes himself fully competent to do so is indicated by the fact that he's running for the same office again this fall. Hiring outside help to do what he's paid for is a highly questionable way to spend taxpayers' money."

Sigurd Moulton stood up. "Your honor," he said in a voice as dry as the pages of the oldest books in the courthouse law library, "I'm gratified to inform my esteemed colleague Mr. Kinneson that Attorney Barrows is paying my retainer out of private funds. The taxpayers' trust is quite secure."

"Is this true, Mr. Barrows?" the judge said loudly.

"Yes. I've hired Mr. Moulton from private funds."

"Your honor," Charlie said, "I'd like to ask Mr. Barrows right here and now why he didn't apply to the Vermont attorney general's office for assistance if he didn't feel competent to prosecute this case himself."

"Mr. Barrows?"

"Well," Zack sputtered. "I—I did. But the Most Peculiar bureaucracy, in its infinite wisdom, didn't see fit to provide that assistance."

"Judge Allen," Charlie said angrily, "my client and I, and the taxpayers of this county, including the members of the jury, have every right to know what's going on here. Why does Kingdom County need to be represented or assisted by a downcountry law firm? What are these mysterious 'private funds' the prosecutor claims he's using to pay Mr. Moulton's fee? Where did they come from? I want to know who's financing the prosecution of this case—the people of Kingdom County, or somebody else? If it's somebody else, I want to know who."

For the first time since we'd come in, my father was writing fast. Sigurd Moulton, in the meantime, took a fat tan-colored book out of his briefcase, stood up and said, "With permission, your honor, I'd like to read from the Vermont statute pertaining to the prosecution of cases in county courts."

Looking as though he'd just lost a state-record brook trout, Judge Allen rapped his forefinger on the bench. "There'll be a short recess while I meet in chambers with counsel for the defense and prosecution."

"All rise, please," Farlow Blake said.

When we sat down again, my father turned to me. "Your brother," he said in the general buzzing, "was always a pretty fair first-pitch hitter."

I was amazed. It was the first time I had heard my father compliment Charlie for anything in a long, long time! Reverend Andrews swung around in his seat at the defense table. "I'd say he knocked the first pitch of the game clean over the centerfield fence."

Dad shook his head. "More like a sharp single up the middle. I very much doubt that there's any law on the Vermont books to prevent Zack Barrows from hiring anybody he wants to as long as he doesn't use county funds to do it."

My father was right. When the lawyers came out of the judge's chamber ten minutes later, I could tell from my brother's expression that Sigurd Moulton, whatever his exact role might be, was going to be with us for the duration of the trial.

Judge Allen tapped on the bench. "Let the record show that nothing in any Vermont statute prevents a county prosecutor from seeking qualified outside legal assistance at his own expense. I find myself obliged to overrule the defense's objection and will only remind the jury that their decision must be based on the merits of the case and the preponderance of the evidence rather than upon the reputation or expertise of the respective lawyers."

Sigurd Moulton rose again. With the slightest smile he said in that paper-dry voice, "Thank you for the prompt ruling, your honor. I will add only that while it may be unusual for prosecutors in this area to engage in specialized legal assistance, it certainly is far from uncommon elsewhere, particularly in first-degree murder trials."

Judge Allen leaned forward. "Mr. Moulton, you are not in a position to add *anything* to my ruling, which is sufficient unto itself. I will also warn you that I won't have any impromptu speechifying in this courtroom. Kindly confine any remarks you feel moved to make to the case at hand, sir."

From my angle, it appeared as though Moulton's miniscule smile widened momentarily. "I stand corrected, your honor. Except to reiterate that race must not be an issue in this case, a point with which my youthful colleague Mr. Kinneson would, I'm sure, be the first to agree, I have nothing more to add at this time."

"Defense may make its opening statement," Judge Allen said tersely.

Charlie stood up. "Except to request that Mr. Moulton refrain from telling the jury what his youthful colleague would or wouldn't be the first to agree with, I'll defer my opening statement until later on."

Charlie sat back down. Deferring his opening statement was his prerogative, of course. But I'd assumed that my brother would outline his argument ahead of time. I'd been looking forward to hearing him speak and I was disappointed.

Zack's first witness was Mason White. At first Mason seemed nervous and "sirred" Zack Barrows to a fare-thee-well; but within a couple of minutes he was perfectly at home again, telling how Claire LaRiviere had come to Kingdom County in late June with the Paris Revue show at the Kingdom Fair and how she had slipped through his fingers during his celebrated raid; landed at Resolvèd Kinneson's; run off to Reverend Andrews', where she had stayed for more than a month; then turned up missing two days after the sesquicentennial celebration and been found dead in the old granite quarry by the Dog Cart Man and a minor.

"Who is this so-called Dog Cart Man, sheriff?" Zack asked.

"Well, he's a more or less harmless old duffer that floats around the countryside painting pictures on the sides of barns and sheds and such. He lugs his gear in a cart pulled by half a dozen or so old mutts. That's why they call him the Dog Cart Man."

"Did you consider this Dog Cart Man a suspect at any time during your investigation?"

"Not really. It never came out that he'd hurt anyone in his comings and goings. Like I say, he's the one that discovered the body. Or his dogs did, rather, and the minor. It was after five o'clock in the P. of M. of August eighth when the office phone rang, but I quite often work late and—"

"Sheriff," Zack interrupted, "did you make a positive identification of the victim at the quarry site where her body was found?"

"What was left of her, I did. After the blackbirds and such got done. It was that French prostitute that come with the fair, all right."

"Objection, your honor. There isn't the slightest evidence that Claire LaRiviere was ever a prostitute, and to characterize her as such is misleading and irresponsible."

"Sustained. The jury will disregard Sheriff White's previous statement, and it will be stricken from the record."

"All right, Sheriff. Now tell me. Do you recognize this gun?"

Zack took a revolver out of a big manila envelope on his table and handed it to Mason.

The sheriff nodded. "Yes, sir, I certainly do recognize it. This would be the gun that was found when we drained the quarry a couple days after the victim was discovered out there. It's a .38 revolver, of the kind carried by Royal Canadian Air Force officers!"

A murmur ran through the room, but Zack cut it off. "Can you tell us who it belongs to?"

"Yes, I can, sir. According to the serial number, it belongs to one Walter Andrews. It was issued to him by the Royal Canadian Air Force in 1943, and apparently he just kept it when he retired from the service—not that a lot of them don't, you understand. Fact is, though, he should have declared it to the customs when he entered this country over in New York State last April. But for some reason he didn't."

"Objection, your honor!" Charlie said angrily. "Unless Reverend Andrews was specifically asked at the border, he was under no obligation to declare his gun."

"Sustained," the judge said.

In the meantime, Sigurd Moulton wrote something on a yellow legal tablet and handed it to Zack. "So you aren't denying that the gun belongs to Walter Andrews, Charlie?" Zack said.

Charlie was on his feet and shouting, his great booming voice filling the courtroom. "Your honor, I'd like to request some guidance from the bench. How should I answer that question, orally to our nonprosecuting prosecutor, or in writing to Sigurd Moulton? Since the moment this trial began the elected prosecutor of Kingdom County has been taking his instructions from that sawed-off little city slicker, and I just—"

"*Mr. Kinneson, sit down.* One more such outburst and I'll slap you with a cool hundred-dollar fine so fast your head'll spin."

"I'm sorry, your honor," Charlie said, looking at the jury to make sure every word of his protest had registered. "It's just that this two-on-one situation seems a tad unfair, to say the least. To get back to the question, what I'm denying is that my client used that gun on Claire LaRiviere and then threw it in the quarry."

"We'll get to that soon enough," Zack said sarcastically. "Your honor, I'd like to enter this gun as Exhibit A and then pass it around among the jury members."

"Mr. Kinneson?"

"No objection, your honor."

After Julia Hefner tagged the revolver, Zack handed it to the juror nearest the judge. The jury gingerly passed it from hand to hand. Most held it no more than a very few seconds.

After setting the gun in plain view on the evidence table near Julia, Zack had Mason describe how he discovered it by draining the quarry. "Thank you, Sheriff," Zack said when Mason finished. "That's all for the time being. Your witness, Charles."

My brother stood up and said, "Sheriff, who actually found the revolver in the quarry?"

"I did," Mason said. "It was in the very lowest level, down in the mud. Like I said, it took us all day to get that old hole pumped out."

"Were there witnesses there at the time to see you actually find it?"

"Yes, sir, Charlie. Both my deputy Pine Benson and Prosecutor Barrows were on hand, among others."

"Were they down in the quarry with you when you found the revolver?"

"Pine was. Zack, he couldn't be expected at his age to be scrambling around down there."

"Did you check it for fingerprints?"

"Yes, I did. Well, actually, I had the state police up to Memphremagog do it. But after being underwater for two, three days, there weren't any."

"What did you do next? I mean in your investigation?"

"Well, I dropped by the reverend's and asked him if he knew where his gun was."

"You suspected that it might be Reverend Andrews' revolver?"

"Yes, sir. I'd already had occasion once before to question him about that revolver and I was pretty sure it belonged to him."

"So you dropped by and asked him if he knew where his gun was?"

"That's correct. He looked for it, or at least pretended to, and of course he couldn't produce it. So then I came back to the office and made a few phone calls up to Canada and ascertained that the side arm belonged to him—or at least to the Royal Canadian Air Force, and had been issued to him. Like I said, legally it still belongs to the Air Force."

"Then what did you do?"

"Then I met with Zack, and we went straight to Judge A with the evidence, and the next day we convened that formal inquest."

"Now Sheriff, you've testified that you already had occasion to talk to Reverend Andrews about the gun. So your trip to his house to inquire whether the gun was in his possession wasn't your first trip there?"

"No, sir, Brother Charlie."

"Could you please explain why you went to see him about the gun the first time?"

"Well, there'd been a little mix-up over to the parsonage involving the LaRiviere girl and a . . . well, I guess you could call him a fun-loving local scamp, Resolvèd Kinneson. Resolvèd got hot, as you know, and went up to the parsonage with his shotgun, and instead of waiting for the law to arrive, the preacher began to shoot first and ask questions later."

"Sheriff, isn't it true that by the time you did arrive at the parsonage on that night this 'fun-loving local scamp' had fired two shotgun blasts into the parsonage?"

"I couldn't attest to that, Charlie. If any such goings-on did take place, it was before I got there. When I arrived, Andrews there had his gun out and had shot off one of Resolvèd Kinneson's fingers."

"We have signed affidavits from three persons telling a very different tale, Sheriff. At any rate, you went to the minister's house on the following night and questioned him about his gun?"

"I most certainly did."

"Did you, on two separate occasions during that conversation, address Reverend Andrews as 'boy'?"

Mason paused. "I can't precisely recall how I addressed him. He wasn't cooperating. He was pushing me."

"Did you, Sheriff White, call Reverend Andrews 'boy' and invite him to take a swing at you?"

"He was getting up on his high horse, Charlie. Wouldn't give me the information I'd asked for."

"His service discharge papers, for instance?"

"Among other documents."

"Sheriff, is it customary for you to investigate the victim of a crime more vigorously than the perpetrator?"

"Charlie, to this day I don't really have any evidence that any crime was ever committed."

"I have no more questions for this witness at this time, your honor."

"Redirect, Mr. Barrows?" the judge said.

"No, your honor. Not at this time."

"You may call your next witness, Mr. Barrows."

"I call Dr. Perry Harrison," Zack said. "Because of his expertise and experience in forensic medicine, your honor, Mr. Moulton will question Dr. Harrison."

The judge nodded, and Painless Perry Harrison moseyed up to the stand, took the oath, and identified a box of slides entered as Exhibit B as those that he had taken of Claire's corpse. Sigurd Moulton set up a screen and projector in the railed-off space below the judge's bench while Farlow Blake, at the judge's instructions, lowered the window shades. It was not very dark in the courtroom, but that was fine with me; this was a show I'd been dreading.

As Moulton slipped in the first slide, the projector jammed. "I never was mechanically inclined," he quipped. "I'll warn you ahead of time, I have an infallible gift for breaking every machine I lay my hands on."

I suppose he wanted to alleviate the tension, since everyone in the room, with the possible exception of the old ghouls of the Folding Chair Club, must have been nervous about what we were going to view. Farlow Blake came gliding to the rescue, all but apologetic as he flipped a lever and fixed the projector. Moulton focused in on an enlarged image of Claire's body lying on the quarry ledge.

If it was not quite as bad as I'd imagined, the only reason was that nothing could be. The mutilated body looked frail and doll-like. Her torn, bloodstained dress of many colors was hiked up around her waist and she was slumped on her side on the ledge, exactly as I had discovered her. All that was missing was a raven! Thankfully, her face was largely obscured by her hair.

"Dr. Harrison, can you identify this body?"

Moulton spoke in clipped, almost bored accents, as though he'd asked similar questions hundreds of times before. The jury members, who'd seemed somewhat confused by Zack's ramblings earlier, looked attentively from him to Doc Harrison.

"Yes, sir," the doctor drawled. "The young woman's name is—was—Claire LaRivière."

"Did you take this slide of her?"

"I had that inestimable privilege."

"Did you perform an autopsy on this body?"

"On what was left of it."

"What do you mean when you say 'what was left of it'? What *who* left of it?"

"The crows. They arrived first and did their own autopsy. They picked her face clean down to the bone."

Moulton cut off the gasps from the audience after the briefest pause. "Were you able to ascertain the cause of the young woman's death?"

"Multiple gunshot wounds."

"By multiple, Doctor, could you please be specific?"

"The girl was shot six times. Including twice in the chest and once in the head."

"Could you tell us, Doctor, which of the wounds were responsible for her death?"

"Look at slides number four, five, and six," Dr. Harrison said. "Any one of them could have been fatal."

With the occupational irony for which he was famous, Painless Perry added, "Once she was dead, I don't suppose she could be killed again."

A couple of the jurors smiled sickly. Two or three of them looked as though they might actually be ill.

In the successive slides, the body was lying on an examining table, partially covered by two white sheets. As Moulton clicked them through the projector one after another, Doc Harrison quickly described the nature of each wound. "Gunshot wound to the lower left abdomen, gunshot wound to the right lung, gunshot wound passing through the left temple into the cranium and penetrating the cerebrum . . ."

Once Judge Allen asked for a layman's equivalent of a medical term; this was the only interruption.

"Dr. Harrison," Moulton said, "were you able to form an opinion of the nature of the murder weapon?"

"Yes."

"Would you share your opinion with us, please?"

"It isn't an opinion, it's a fact. The murder weapon was a .38 caliber revolver. Three .38 bullets were found in the girl's body."

Without fanfare, Moulton entered the bullets as evidence. Then he said, "Doctor, you mentioned six shots. So far we've viewed five different wounds. You've testified that any one of three of these could have been fatal. I would now like to show you another slide."

Moulton clicked his final slide onto the screen. "Can you please identify this wound, doctor?"

"That slide depicts a wound to the victim's vagina, slanting upward into the uterus. It was fired at point-blank range and caused massive internal damage to the genitals and uterus. But not massive enough."

"Not massive enough, Doctor?" Moulton asked in the stunned silence of the courtroom. "What exactly do you mean by that?"

"Not massive enough," Doc Harrison said, "to conceal the fact that the girl was at least one month pregnant."

When the uproar in the room subsided, the prosecutor said, "Could we have light again, please?"

Everyone in the room was grateful to Farlow Blake for pulling up the shades. I blinked, still not quite able to believe what I had seen and heard.

"Just two or three more questions, Doctor. How long have you been the chief county medical examiner?"

"Thirty-four glorious years."

"In your personal opinion, judging by your nearly three and a half decades of experience, how brutal was this murder?"

Doc Harrison yawned. "The most brutal I've ever seen."

"And finally, would the nature of these wounds lead you to conclude that the murderer was a trained killer?"

"A trained killer?"

"Yes, trained in mortal combat with small weapons. Such as a serviceman is."

"Objection, your honor," Charlie said. "He's leading the witness."

"Sustained."

Moulton fixed his mild gaze on the jury for a moment, as though inviting them to consider the implications of his stricken question.

"Thank you, Doctor. Your witness, Mr. Kinneson."

Charlie stood up. "Just one quick question at this time, Dr. Harrison. You referred to the crime as the most brutal you've ever seen. Would you call it the work of a deranged person?"

Moulton was on his feet. "Objection, your honor! Dr. Harrison is a general practitioner, and a very capable one, but no psychiatrist."

"I'm not asking for a clinical assessment. I'm merely interested in Dr. Harrison's personal opinion, based on his three and a half decades of experience and his common sense. I hope we aren't going to rule common sense out of the courtroom, too."

"You may answer the question, Doctor."

"Well, as Mr. Moulton pointed out, I'm not a psychiatrist. But yes, I'd be very tempted to call this murder the work of a deranged individual, or at least of someone who temporarily turned into one. In my admittedly limited experience, rational people, even cold-blooded murderers, don't shoot their female victims in the vagina after killing them."

"Thank you, Doctor. I don't have any more questions at this time, but I'd like to request that you remain within hailing distance, since I may well want to recall you a bit later."

Moulton stood up. "Your honor, Dr. Harrison is an extremely busy man with a full schedule. If my young colleague for the defense has any additional questions, he should ask them now."

Judge Allen asked Dr. Harrison if he had appointments that afternoon, and the doctor looked thoughtful.

"Yes," he said, "but I'll postpone them. I'm willing to stay."

Which, I supposed, was a small victory for Charlie.

The judge looked up at the clock. "It's almost noon," he said. "We'll break for lunch and reconvene at one-thirty sharp."

"All rise," said Farlow as the judge left. As soon as the judge departed, Charlie and Reverend Andrews sat down again and began to hold a whispered, intense conversation. Charlie seemed to be reassuring him about something; but Reverend Andrews just smiled that ironical smile and shook his head.

Across the aisle Moulton gathered his papers together like a bookkeeper putting his desk in order before going home for the night. As far as he and Zack Barrows were concerned, the case already seemed to be won.

# 17

I was restless from having to sit still all morning, but Mom made me eat a sandwich with her and Dad over at the *Monitor*. Then I wandered around on the common for a while. I ran into Justin LaBounty and Al Quinn by the baseball backstop and we made a quick tour of the Harvest Figures around the green, casting a critical eye over the straw shopkeepers in front of the brick shopping block; the lone red-coated straw sentry, dozing with his back against an elm, with a placard around his neck that said SLEEPING ON DUTY, while nearby the statue of Ethan Allen prepared to take Fort Ticonderoga unmolested; and, our favorite, the straw ball player standing at home plate in pinstripes and knickers and a little round pinstriped cap, with a red devil's tail and horns and a placard announcing, ANOTHER PENNANT FOR THE DAMN YANKEES. Yet like the resplendent hills above the village, the farmers' displays and Harvest Figures seemed only to accentuate by contrast the grimness of the business inside the courthouse.

"What do you think, Jim?" Justin said. "Does it look as though the jury's going to find the reverend guilty?"

"Charlie says you never know how a jury's going to vote until they vote, Justin."

"Weren't those slides sickening?" Al said. "I don't think Reverend Andrews could do anything like that in a million years."

"Me neither," Justin said loyally. "But if he didn't, who in hang did?"

"That's the question—right, Jim?" Al said.

"That's the question, all right," I said. "That's still the big question Charlie's got to find the answer to."

"Well, I'm glad I don't," Justin said. "I wouldn't know where to start."

"Me neither," Al said. "There's your folks, Jim. Your old man's waving to you. Must be the trial's about to start."

"You didn't try to call us over at the *Monitor*, did you, Jimmy?" Mom asked me, when I caught up with her and Dad on the courthouse steps.

"Call you? You mean on the phone?"

"Yes. Twice after you left the phone rang, and both times when your father picked it up the line went dead."

I shook my head. "I was on the common the whole time. Why would I want to call you?"

"Well, somebody did," Dad said. "Probably some prankster with a warped sense of humor. If I find out who, by God, I'll muckle—"

"—onto them and throw 'em into the biggest snowbank south of Labrador," I said.

Dad never cracked a smile. With each passing hour, it seemed he was becoming less optimistic that, as resourceful and determined as Charlie was, he would be able to prove the minister's innocence.

For once in his career, it seemed that Zack Barrows had all the evidence, and all the help, even he would need to get a conviction.

When the trial resumed, Zack called Julia Hefner as his next witness. Prof Chadburn's secretary from the Academy, a woman named Vida Potts, temporarily took over Julia's post at the stenographer's table.

Zack began by asking Julia if she could recall where she was on the morning of July twenty-eighth, a few days before Old Home Day. Julia said yes, that was the morning she went to the parsonage on a mission.

"What was this mission, Mrs. Hefner?"

"Well, some of the ladies of the church had talked to me and asked me to persuade Reverend Andrews to find more appropriate living arrangements for that LaRiviere girl. Frankly, they didn't think it looked right. Knowing her background and all."

"Was that the only purpose of your visit?"

Julia replied by saying that she had also reiterated her plea to Reverend Andrews to look for a housekeeper, partly because if he wouldn't get rid of the girl, at least it would look better if he had another woman in the house.

"How did the minister reply to your request that he find alternative living arrangements for the LaRiviere girl?"

"Well, he got uppity. He said, very sarcastic, you know, 'Would you take her, Julia?' I had the impression, Mr. Barrows, that he had . . . well, private reasons for wanting to keep the girl at his place."

"Do you recall anything else that was out of line about the minister's behavior during your visit?"

"Objection, your honor. Nothing that Mrs. Hefner has told us so far indicates that Reverend Andrews was in any way 'out of line' during her visit."

"Strike the question," Zack said. "Mrs. Hefner, did you notice anything else that struck you about the minister's behavior during your visit?"

"Yes, to tell you the truth, I did. I was sitting on the couch, and he was sitting at his desk chair, which was swung around facing me, and all the while we were visiting, I had the feeling that I was being looked at, if you know what I mean. He was looking at me and smiling in a way that made me uncomfortable—just the way he did once before when I asked him and his son to eat dinner with my son and myself. So as soon as I saw I wasn't going to get anywhere with him about the girl, I high-tailed it out of there as fast as I could!"

I was astonished by this outright lie.

Charlie, however, who knew the whole story was smiling broadly.

"Thank you very much, Mrs. Hefner. That's all," Zack said. "Your witness, Charles."

Still smiling, Charlie got up and walked over to the witness table.

"Julia, you've testified that Reverend Andrews sarcastically asked you if you'd take in Claire LaRiviere."

Julia tossed her head. "Yes, that's so."

"He wasn't serious, then?"

"Oh, he may have been serious and sarcastic at the same time. I think he knew very well that I wasn't about to take in a stray who had come to town with that filthy fair show. I had the strongest impression that he was determined to keep her right there at the parsonage, no matter what."

"Why did you decline to have her stay with you, if you were so concerned about Reverend Andrews' reputation?"

"Well, Charlie Kinneson! I've got a teenage son I wouldn't have exposed to the likes of her for anything in this world. Unlike certain others I could name."

"Julia, you testified that during your conversation in the parsonage study the minister smiled at you in a certain way that made you uncomfortable, and that he'd done this once before. Exactly what way is that?"

Julia turned red as a beet. "Well, you know. Bedroom eyes and all. He kept looking at my legs."

"Now, Julia," Charlie said with a very broad smile this time. "Who could blame any man for admiring an attractive young woman like you?"

Here the courtroom broke up. Even Julia laughed, more from embarrassment, I think, than for any other reason.

But Charlie cut the laughter off himself by saying loudly, "So he was looking at you in a certain way?"

"Yes. Absolutely. In fact, he kept smiling."

"The way I am now?"

Again the courtroom broke out in laughter, and Judge Allen did nothing to stop it. I think that he may have felt that Julia deserved exactly what she was getting.

"So he looked at you and smiled. Was that when you invited him to dinner and said your son would be gone that evening and you two would have a 'quiet little chat and a few brandies together'?"

"Objection, your honor! He's leading the witness."

"On the contrary, your honor. In my opinion the witness was leading Reverend Andrews—straight down the primrose path!"

Now the whole courtroom sounded like the Saturday matinee in the Academy auditorium during a Three Stooges movie. But once again Charlie restored order himself by saying, "Mrs. Hefner, did you, during your first visit to the parsonage, invite the minister to dinner and tell him that your son would be out that night?"

"I can't recall where Bobby was going to be that evening, but I'm not ashamed of inviting the local pastor to dinner. It's customary, you know. Besides, I was desperate to get out of there. When you think you might be molested on the spot, you'll say any old thing."

"Did Reverend Andrews say he'd be glad to come to dinner, if his son was invited, too, and did you say no, you had some private matters to discuss with him?"

"Objection, your honor, the defense attorney is entirely out of line himself to pursue these idiotic speculations."

By now Julia had begun to snuffle into a little embroidered handkerchief.

"Sustained," the judge said.

"Just one more question, Mrs. Hefner. Are you familiar with the old phrase, 'Hell hath no fury like a woman spurned'?"

"OBJECTION! This is disgraceful!" Zack roared.

"Well, Zack," Charlie said, "for once, you and I agree. Strike the question."

"You may call your next witness, Mr. Barrows."

Zack stood up. "Thank you, your honor. I have just two more witnesses. I'd like to thank the jury for its patience and attentiveness so far, and ask only that each juror please pay particular attention to the testimony of these last two individuals, who will amply clarify the one remaining question in this case: Walter Andrews' motive in brutally murdering and maiming Claire LaRiviere. Sheriff White, will you please bring Resolvèd Kinneson forward to the witness stand?"

To say that I was astonished, to say that the entire local population of the courtroom was astonished, does not begin to describe our collective amazement as my outlaw cousin made his way down the far right-hand aisle beside the sheriff. He was wearing neither a suit nor his ratty old poaching clothes, but a clean pair of green work pants and a new green work shirt and new hunting boots. He was clean-shaven and his hair was slicked down, as though he'd just wet and combed it a few moments ago.

Zack began by having Resolvèd establish how he had written away for a housekeeper with Charlie's assistance and how Claire had shown up out of the blue one morning late last June, stayed a week, and then left.

"By the time she split the coop, I was laid up with a broken leg," Resolvèd continued in a voice that was already half a snarl. "But as soon as I was up and around, I decided to get her back again. So on the night of August the fourth, I went out a-hunting for the woman in question, who I'd bought and paid for through the mail and then run off on me. I knowed where she was. I knowed she'd gone to ground at that parsonage, and I intended to snake her out. So around eleven, eleven-thirty I slipped up onto the property through the empty lot next door and past that old sugar maple tree without no top and so along beside them red bitterberry vines a-clinging to the porch. It wasn't any light on inside the house, but I can see good in the dark, always have, and I says to myself, says I, I'll just go 'round by the windows and take a look-see inside and see if she's to home. Well, sir, I slid up onto the porch real quiet-like and then I could hear two voices coming from inside the front room. I crept up closer until I could look in the window where the voices was. It was open some and I could hear everything very distinct, only now it weren't so much voices as this moaning-like, a-moaning and a-groaning, just like a heifer cow coming into heat for the first time. And by God, I stuck my head in the window and switched on the lamp that set on the preacher's desk, and there on that di-van, ladies and gentlemen all"—Resolvèd was on his feet, and Judge Allen had already begun to rap on the bench, but it was too late; unless he'd had a gun, there was no way in the world that the judge could have stopped my cousin, now pointing directly at Reverend Andrews—"there on the di-van, I see that big buck nigger setting over there beside Charlie Kinneson *a-putting the britches to my housekeeper*."

The courtroom was in an uproar. Charlie was roaring objections, Judge Allen was banging for order, Farlow Blake was shouting at Resolvèd to sit down and trying to yank him forcibly back into his seat. Once again, Judge Allen had to call a recess, this time to talk to Resolvèd and Zack Barrows. I would have liked to be a little bird on Forrest Allen's shoulder during that session; but all I know for certain is that ten minutes later, when they reemerged, Resolvèd looked considerably subdued.

"Mr. Kinneson," Zack said when Resolvèd resumed the witness stand, "would you please tell us in polite and appropriate language what you saw in the United Church parsonage study on the evening of August fourth when you put your head inside and turned on the light?"

With a snaggle-toothed smirk, Resolvèd said, "Yes, sir. I seen the preacher, Andrews, and the LaRiviere woman engaged in sexual innercourse."

"Your honor, is that answer acceptable?" Zack said.

"It's close enough," Judge Allen said dryly.

"What did you do then, Mr. Kinneson?" Zack said.

"Well," Resolvèd said, "I weren't very god— I weren't at all well pleased with the situation, let us say. But I kept my manners and only said good and loud, in a pretty sarcastic way, 'Excuse me!' "

"Did either of the two people on the divan speak?"

"Yes! He did, preacher fella there. He hollered, 'Shut off that bloody light.' La-de-da Englishman's accent and all."

"Resolvèd, I'm going to ask you just one more question," Zack said. "Please be assured that you do not have to say anything further to me or to the defense attorney, Charlie Kinneson, that would in any way prejudice the outcome of any further legal dealings in which you yourself may already be involved. I'd just like to ask you if you're absolutely sure of what you saw on the divan that night?"

"I be."

"Thank you very much, sir."

Charlie wasted no time with preliminaries. "Resolvèd, you say you looked in the window and saw the preacher and the LaRiviere girl engaged in sexual intercourse. Remembering Judge Allen's instructions to keep your language acceptable, what precisely were the people in the parsonage study doing?"

"Going right at it two-forty."

The judge's gavel was poised; but except for a few suppressed laughs, the courtroom was silent.

"There are a thousand and one ways to 'go right at it,' even on the relatively cramped quarters of a couch," Charlie said. "Please describe exactly what you saw."

Oddly, Resolvèd turned nearly as red as Julia Hefner had. I had never seen my cousin in any way flustered, and in other circumstances I would have been amused.

"Well, now. The first thing I see when I reached in and snapped on the light was the back of the girl's head. Blondish-color hair. Back of her neck. Back of her smock."

"By 'smock' do you mean a dress?"

"Smock, shift, gown, or dress, call it what you will. It was that rainbow-color one she wore down from Canady. It was all bunched up around her waist, and her legs and behind was nekkid as the day she was borned."

"Was she lying down or sitting up?"

"You really want to get into all this smut here, Cousin? Well, the fact is, not to offend the judge's nor nobody else's ears but just to tell the strict truth, she was setting up and a-straddling him, if you must know. He was sort of slumped into one corner of the di-van, and his bare feet and bare legs was sticking out under her."

"Could you see the man's face?"

"Not all that plain. No, I couldn't see his face plainly. But I knowed who it was, all right."

"How did you know who it was if you couldn't see his face?"

"I knowed because, as I said, I could see his feet and legs and they was a nig—a colored fella's."

"You've testified that immediately after you turned on the desk lamp, the man in the room said, 'Shut off that bloody light.' What did you do then?"

"I decline to answer."

"Did you go home and get your shotgun and come back and fire at the parsonage and order the LaRiviere girl outside?"

Resolvèd looked at the prosecutor's table. Zack looked at Moulton, who shook his head. Zack, in turn, shook his head at Resolvèd.

"I decline to answer that question, Charlie Kinneson, on grounds that it might in—get me into more hot water!"

"Your honor," Charlie said, "I don't see how the defense can be expected to present its case if Resolvèd Kinneson refuses to tell us the rest of the story. We have a right to know what happened next."

"I'm sorry, Charles," the judge said. "But Mr. Kinneson has a right not to incriminate himself. If he doesn't wish to answer that question, that's his constitutional right."

"It's his constitutional right not to say yes or no when I ask him if he fired on the parsonage and ordered—"

"Mr. Kinneson, one more word and I will slap you with a cool one-hundred-dollar fine on the spot," the judge said. "You have my ruling."

"Resolvèd, did you tell the sheriff these allegations about the minister and the LaRiviere girl early on the morning of August fifth, after the shooting episode at the parsonage that we can't discuss?"

Resolvèd looked at the prosecutor's table. Again, first Moulton, then Zack shook their heads.

"Your honor, I'm going to request that Mr. Resolvèd Kinneson answer or decline to answer these questions himself, without signals and assistance from the prosecutors."

The judge sighed. "And I'm going to request, Mr. Charles Kinneson, that you rephrase your question without any reference to a shooting. Then I'll consider ruling whether he has to answer it."

"Resolvèd, on the morning after this alleged incident at the parsonage, did you tell the sheriff what you'd seen?"

"I decline to answer on the grounds that it might 'crim'nate me."

"Your honor, telling the jury whether or not he informed the sheriff of what he allegedly saw at the parsonage when he looked in the window cannot, by any stretch of my imagination, incriminate this witness. I request that you instruct him to answer the question."

The judge thought briefly. Then he said, "I'm sorry, Mr. Kinneson. Resolvèd Kinneson does not at this time have to answer that question."

"Resolvèd, I noticed that the sheriff escorted you down the aisle to the witness stand. Why is that?"

"I decline to answer."

"Resolvèd, are you currently residing in the Kingdom County Jail?"

"What if I am?"

"One more question, Resolvèd. How many times have you been in this courtroom?"

"I don't know the answer to that, Charlie K. A dozen? Two dozen?"

"Which?" Charlie said. "One dozen? Two dozen? Three dozen times? Fifty times?"

"You ought to have some idea, Cousin," Resolvèd said. "Over the past few months, you've rupresented me here every time."

"You may call your last witness, Mr. Barrows."

Zack nodded to Mason White, who disappeared through the double swinging doors at the rear of the room. He was gone for perhaps fifteen seconds.

Accompanied by the sheriff, Zack's final witness entered the courtroom and walked stiffly down the center aisle. He wore green work clothes and work shoes with holes and dull little scallops of printer's lead cooked into them. His cropped gray hair looked like a sprinkling of lead filings. As he passed us I caught a whiff of that sulfurous redolence he carried everywhere, and his great ring of keys clanked sternly at his side.

"Your honor," Zack said, "as its final witness, the county calls Elijah Kinneson. Once again, because of his expertise in first-degree murder cases, Mr. Moulton will conduct the questioning of Mr. Kinneson."

After Farlow had sworn Elijah in, Sigurd Moulton said, "Mr. Kinneson, would you please state your full name, your profession, and your place of business."

"Elijah Kinneson. Printer and linotype operator for the *Kingdom County Monitor*."

"I believe that printing demands close attention to details, Mr. Kinneson?"

"I don't make many mistakes."

"So I've been told. Now, Mr. Kinneson, will you please tell the court where you were and what you were doing on the evening of August fifth of this past summer?"

"That was Production Night at the shop. From about eight o'clock on I was putting out my newspaper."

"Were you alone in the building?"

"Yes and no. The other fella skipped out around midnight. After that I was alone and could get something done."

"Who is the other fella?"

Elijah thrust out a sallow talon in the direction of my father. "Fella out there in the congregation. My cousin, Charles Kinneson. So-called editor over at the *Monitor*."

"I see. Editor Kinneson left around midnight and then you were alone. Do you recall what time you finished your work that night?"

"Not to the exact minute I don't. It was in the vicinity of one-thirty A.M. I would say that give or take a few minutes either way I put my paper to bed at just about half-past one o'clock in the morning. I locked up, which I might not otherwise have done except that so-called Old

Home Day had been held the day before and you can't tell what riffraff such an affair as that might draw. Then I started on home."

"Did you drive home?"

"Drive home? No, I did not. I don't own a motorcar. Never have, never will. Unlike some I could point out, I'd rather pay my bills than make car payments."

"Elijah Kinneson," Judge Allen said sharply, "you will answer the questions put to you and only those questions. You will kindly restrain yourself from favoring the court with your opinions on borrowing and lending, automobiles, and all other topics not directly related to the questions you are asked. Do you understand me, sir?"

Elijah gave the judge the barest curt nod.

"Answer yes or no," Judge Allen said angrily. "The court stenographer has no way of recording a surly gesture."

"Yes," Elijah muttered.

"Where do you live, Mr. Kinneson?" Moulton said.

"On the edge of the churchyard, heading out the county road toward Lord Hollow. Last house on the right going away from town."

"By the churchyard, do you mean the precincts of the church?"

"I do not. The church would be clear across town at the south end of the common. I mean the graveyard. Cemetery. Final resting place. Call it whatever you want, everybody in town winds up there. Except the papists, that is. They're planted up on Anderson Hill."

"Do you customarily pass by this cemetery on your way home from work?"

"I customarily pass through a corner of it. It's a shortcut. From the shop I cut cross the common, and down between the courthouse and the Academy, and so on through the edge of the churchyard to my house."

"On the evening of August fifth—actually it would have been the early morning of August sixth, by then—did you see anything unusual as you approached your house?"

"If I hadn't, I wouldn't be here today, now, would I?"

"What did you see?"

"Well, I didn't actually *see* much of anything. It was black as pitch. But I heard something."

"Tell the court what you heard, please."

"Two voices."

"Could you tell where these voices were coming from?"

"Yes, from the parsonage porch, just across the street."

"Were you startled?"

"Startled! Startled by what?"

"By the voices. You said it was a dark night. I thought you might have mistaken them for ghosts."

Elijah snorted. "Ghosts don't jangle," he said. "At first I thought it was fishermen navigating around on the lawn and picking up nightwalkers, which they frequently do over in the churchyard, and trample all over my plots into the bargain. But this wasn't nightwalker pickers. These voices were coming from the parsonage porch. It was a fella and a woman. Jangling."

"Jangling?"

"Yes. Back and forth."

"Could you please explain the term 'jangling,' Mr. Kinneson?"

"Jangling," Elijah said impatiently. "Like these."

He half rose and gave his key ring a great clangorous jerk.

"Arguing," he said.

"I see. Did you hear any of the words of the argument?"

"Yes. I stepped out toward the street a short ways, so I could hear clearly, just to be sure it wasn't housebreakers, you know, or one of the preacher's enemies, of which he'd made a goodly number. As I say, it was a fella's voice and a girl. Once I got out in the street, I could tell that the girl talked like a Frenchman. Anyway, the fella said, 'Well, what's done is done. If you are, I shall see to it that it's taken care of straightaway. I have a good friend in Burlington, who runs a home where you'll be taken care of.

"The girl with the Frenchman's voice said, 'Oh, I know I am, me.' Then the fella said, 'Have you told anyone else yet?'

"Well, that's all I heard because then they started back into the house, and I wasn't really comfortable standing there eavesdropping, you understand."

"Did you recognize either voice?"

"I recognized one, all right. The man's."

"Is the man whose voice you recognized here in the courtroom this afternoon?"

"He be."

"Will you identify him, please?"

Elijah nodded grimly.

"Andrews," he said. "So-called preacher, at the table behind you."

"The prosecution rests, your honor."

And on that note, Judge Allen ended the proceedings for the day.

"It's still sealed, James," my father said. "I am here to tell you that it is still sealed as tight as a drum."

"What's sealed?" Charlie said.

"Dad says this case is like a globe," I explained. "With all the information shut up inside and no way to get at it."

Charlie was sitting in Elijah's vacant linotype chair, wearing my cousin's green eyeshade and eating a ham sandwich left over from lunch. "Maybe we should get an ax and whale the hell out of this globe," he said.

"Maybe," Dad said, accepting a sandwich from Mom.

"On the other hand," Charlie said, "maybe we wouldn't like what we found when we did."

"I'll tell you one thing you aren't going to find," my father said. "You're not going to find that Walter Andrews had the least thing to do with that girl's murder."

"Are you going to put him on the stand, Charlie?" Athena said, taking a bite of homemade potato salad.

Charlie frowned. "To tell you the truth, I haven't made up my mind yet."

"Isn't it getting rather late in the game to decide?"

"I know what I'm going to ask him if I do put him on the stand. The trouble is, his testimony may hurt his case more than it helps. Elijah's a splenetic little factotum, as I've said a hundred times before, but there's no doubt in my mind that he heard what he said he heard. Andrews himself has admitted that he and the girl had that conversation."

"What about Resolvèd's testimony?" my father said. "Do you believe that?"

Under other circumstances, I would have been delighted that Dad and Charlie were actually holding a direct conversation with each other. Now I hardly noticed.

"What Resolvèd claims he saw is hard to swallow. Him, I intend to get back on the stand first thing tomorrow morning. But whether he's telling the truth about what he saw when he looked in the parsonage window is anybody's guess. There's one encouraging thing, which is that Walt Andrews flatly denied to me that he was in the study with that girl on the night before Old Home Day. In fact I think we can place him at the common until about that time, maybe even a tad later. That's one of about a hundred things I've got to look into between now and tomorrow morning at eight o'clock."

"One thing I'm going to look into," my father said, "is who is paying Sigurd Moulton's retainer. Private funds indeed! I can't believe that Zack Barrows wants to win this case badly enough to shell out thousands of dollars of his own money to pay somebody else to prosecute it for him."

"Well, whoever's paying Moulton is getting his money's worth," Charlie said. "There isn't any more feeling to him than a rattlesnake, but he knows exactly what he's doing, including when to shut up, which Zack has never learned. Also he wants to clip my ears in the worst way after that Gilson trial last winter."

"He isn't half the lawyer you are," my mother said. "And what's more, if Reverend Andrews denied he was in the study with Claire, he wasn't there."

"I agree with you, Ruth," my father said. "But I'm beginning to suspect that he's holding *something* back, whatever it is."

" 'The wise old owl sat in an oak; the more he knew, the less he spoke,' " my mother said, and laughed ruefully. "Remember that one? I used to say it over and over for you boys when you were tiny."

Charlie looked affectionately at Mom out from under Elijah's green visor. "I hadn't thought about those nursery rhymes for years and years. How about the Grimm stories you used to read me at bedtime? I thought that was great stuff, hot off the press.

"You know," my brother continued, "growing up around a newspaper office, I somehow got the idea when I was a little shaver that a lot of the stories you and Dad read to us and told to us were printed right over here."

"I did, too," I said. "And when people used to call Dad 'the press,' like when old Hefty Hefner would shoot him a dirty look and say,

'Shhh! The press will have this all over town'—well, I thought they meant that bloody old *Whitlock* press of Dad's. For years I wondered how it could get out the door and all over town."

My father nodded, seeing the logic behind my childhood assumption without really appreciating the humor; but my mother laughed out loud. When she laughed, I saw the wrinkles around her eyes deepen, and then to my great surprise I noticed for the first time that her blond hair had a few streaks of gray in it. I felt a pang of guilt. Somehow, I had been so caught up in the events of the summer and fall and in my own changing life that I had neglected to see this change in her. Although I couldn't remember a time when Dad had not had gray at his temples, it came as a shock to see that Mom, too, was getting older.

Charlie looked at Mom and Athena. Then he looked at me. "Jim, that story you told about the printing press. What was it you called it?"

"The Whitlock?"

"Yeah, the Whitlock. But you used a word to describe it. You called it 'that *bloody* old Whitlock.' Where'd you pick up that expression?"

I shrugged. "I don't know. Some book, probably."

"What book?"

Charlie had slid out of Elijah's seat and was looking at me intently.

"I don't know what book. *Kidnapped*, maybe. Plus I've heard Nat and his dad use it. They say it all the time. That and 'blooming.' I got used to hearing it, 'bloody' this, 'blooming' that. That's what Resolvèd said in court today, right? That when he looked in the window he heard the minister tell Claire, 'Shut off that bloody light'?"

Now my father and Charlie and Athena and Mom were *all* staring at me.

"What'd I say? What is it?"

"I'll tell you what it is, mister," my father said. "I never once heard Walt Andrews use the expression 'bloody.' 'Blooming,' yes. 'Bloody,' no."

"That globe you and your father were talking about?" Charlie said to me. "It's looking more and more like a box."

"A box?"

"Yeah," Charlie said grimly. "Pandora's."

Still I did not understand.

"Jimmy," Charlie said quietly, "have you got Nathan's phone number in Montreal?"

"At home," I said, suddenly remembering that I had intended to call Nat after the first day of the trial.

My brother was already on his way to the door. "In the eloquent words of a certain ex-client of mine, Jim, let's shag ass. I need that phone number and we need Nathan Andrews in Kingdom County—pronto!"

As I hurriedly struggled into my hunting jacket, the phone began to ring. The last thing I heard when I went out the door behind Charlie was my father's voice saying "Hello. Hello? Damn, Ruth! It's that crank caller again. If I could find out who's doing that and were ten years younger . . ."

The next few hours rushed by in a flurry of phone calls, a trip to the train station to check schedules and timetables, and hurried consultations at the *Monitor*.

As soon as Charlie and I got to the farmhouse, I called Nat and told him that the first day of his dad's trial had gone as well as could be expected. But when he impatiently demanded a specific account of the proceedings, as of course I knew he would, I put Charlie on.

"Hi, buddy," my brother said in his loud, harsh voice, as though he was talking to somebody at the far end of the farmhouse. "Listen up. The trial's going fine so far, okay? But the time has *definitely*—*definitely*, understand?—come when I need you here. I'll tell you right now that you're very probably going to have to testify in order to help clear your dad. What? No, I don't want you to call him. He'd just order you to stay put. Don't even think of calling. Just get on the train and come, okay? You still willing to do that? Good. No, we'll call you back with the details in half an hour or so."

We made a flying trip back to the village in Charlie's woody, stopped at the railroad station for a train schedule, and were back at the *Monitor* no more than twenty minutes after we'd rushed out the door to call Nat.

"Mister Baby Johnson! Did you speak with his grandmother? She isn't going to let him come back down here and get caught up in this mess," Dad said when we told him the news. "If that happens, you'll have to get a subpoena from Forrest Allen. Hell, you'll have to get *extradition* papers to get him out of Canada."

"Maybe not," Mom said. "Why don't *I* call Nat's grandmother? I wouldn't be a bit surprised if she is completely understanding."

I can't recall everything Mom said in her conversation with Nat's grandmother, but in her serene way, while my father paced back and forth across the room like Vermont's legendary last mountain lion, she explained that Reverend Andrews was now in deeply serious trouble and we had reason to believe that Nat's testimony might be able to help him.

Mom listened to the voice of Nat's grandmother in Montreal. After perhaps half a minute she gave Charlie a sudden smile.

"He's coming!" she mouthed silently, and after thanking the grandmother she handed the phone back to Charlie to give Nat the departure time of the Early Bird Special from Montreal.

"Ruthie, you did it," Charlie said when he hung up. And he picked Mom right up off the floor and hugged her and swung her around like a square dance partner.

"For heaven's sake, put her down before she has a stroke," my father said. "And quit calling her Ruthie!"

For all Dad's concern for my "finely tuned" mother, he seemed impressed by her persuasiveness.

As for me, I was still in the dark concerning the reason for these phone calls and the urgent need for Nat to return and appear in court. All I knew for certain as I trudged upstairs to my loft chamber an hour later, dog-tired, more tired than I could ever remember being, was that I was very relieved that my friend was coming back to the Kingdom, however temporarily, and for whatever purpose.

# 18

It was going to be another fine day, with the splendid fall foliage at its peak, glowing with an intense internal light of its own, though today the morning haze, rather than muting the colors, caused them to burn with a fierce vehemence I found disconcerting. Mom and I were to meet the Early Bird at the train station, while Charlie and Dad met with the minister at the courthouse to break the news of Nat's imminent arrival. This was a good arrangement. Of all us Kinnesons, Mom was the one Nat trusted the most, and since Dad was the minister's best friend in all Kingdom County, he could talk him into cooperating with Charlie's plan for Nat to testify if anyone could. That was essential now since just before Mom and I had left the shop the night before, Charlie had said that he'd decided to put both Reverend Andrews and Nat on the stand today.

The pink Scotch granite blocks of the courthouse and Academy sparkled softly in the hazy sunshine, suffusing the Common with a rosy light as Mom and I headed down the sidewalk toward the train station. The clock on the courthouse tower said 7:02. The Early Bird hooted at the trestle north of town, followed immediately by the rumble and the single bright headlamp—almost brighter by day, it seemed, than by night—of the blue and yellow and silver engine pulling eight passenger cars, a mail coach and a caboose. My mother surreptitiously took out her compact, frowned, then hastily shoved it back into her pocketbook.

The platform vibrated under my shoes with the train's approach, and the engine screeched and hissed into the station. Inside the cars, passengers were reading or tilted back asleep or looking incuriously out the windows. For perhaps thirty seconds nothing happened. The big diesel locomotive throbbed powerfully, the platform vibrated sympathetically, the passengers continued to read or sleep or look with bored expressions out the windows. A horrible thought crossed my mind. What if Nat hadn't come, after all?

Then the door of the third car opened and my friend stepped out onto the platform.

He was thinner than I remembered him. And he looked older, too, maybe because he was wearing a necktie and his blue school jacket with the school crest. He was carrying a leather overnight bag with wide straps and tarnished gold-colored buckles, and as he walked toward us across the platform he looked as tired as I felt.

I was tongue-tied and didn't know what to say or do. But my mother went right up to Nat and gave him a big hug and a kiss, just as though she were welcoming Charlie or me back from a long absence. "Welcome back, Nathan," she said. "We're all so glad you came."

Nat smiled wearily. "How about my father, Mrs. Kinneson? Does he know I'm here?"

"He will in a few minutes if he doesn't already," Mom said. "He'll be delighted, too."

"I hope so," Nat said, and turned to me. "So how are you, Kinneson? I see congratulations are in order."

"Congratulations?"

"You've grown three inches since I saw you. Your big brother better watch out. If this keeps up, you're going to break all his athletic records at the school, eh?"

Nat gave me a friendly punch on the shoulder, and I laughed and jabbed him back, relieved that the tension had been broken. At the same time I was filled with admiration for a friend who, like his father, could extract a gracious sentiment out of all the fatigue and anger and uncertainty he must have felt. Then and always, there was a genuine dignity about both the Andrewses, father and son, a determination not to be abashed by anything, however unpleasant or unfair, that our town could deal out to them. I could not have named the quality at the time. But certainly it was human dignity, founded on decent human conduct.

The Early Bird was pulling out of the station. It gave a long, alluring hoot as it rumbled through the lumberyard of the American Heritage Mill, but for once I didn't wish myself aboard it. And although I knew that the hard part of the day had not yet begun, I was very happy to be with my friend Nat Andrews again.

Charlie and Dad were meeting with Reverend Andrews in the sheriff's office on the first floor of the courthouse, and Sheriff White was sitting in a straight-back chair, on guard just outside the closed office door. When he saw Mom and Nat and me, he broke into a big horse-toothed smile. "Well, if it isn't young Andrews!" he said, jumping to his feet and thrusting out his hand as though he and Nat had been good friends over the years. "Good to see you, son! Dad Andrews is expecting you."

Even then I suppose Sheriff White was currying our goodwill just in case something went haywire with the prosecution of Reverend Andrews. Nat never so much as glanced at the sheriff, now making some sort of weird herky-jerky gestures to me. He was pointing first to one ankle, then to the other, bent over and flapping his long arms around his lower legs, tying himself all up in knots and silently mouthing something. For a moment I thought the man had gone completely off his rocker. Then Nat was through the door like a shot, with Mom and me right behind him.

Reverend Andrews was sitting next to a low radiator in front of the window overlooking the common. Dad was standing at the opposite side of the room and Charlie was sitting in the sheriff's swivel desk chair with his feet propped on the corner of the desk. Nat had stopped short just inside the door. He was staring at his father, who for the first time since the trial had started, and probably since he was arrested on the steps of his church, was smiling a genuinely happy smile.

"Nathan," he said, half rising. "Nathan!"

In an odd, awkward motion, Reverend Andrews stood up. As he did so, he accidentally knocked over his chair. Incongruously, it occurred to me that this was the very first uncoordinated movement I had ever seen him make. And although he was not an openly emotional man and had always maintained a sort of affectionate aloofness, even in his bearing toward his own son, he now said Nathan's name again, and with unmistakable love and feeling in his expressive voice. He took half a step toward Nat. Again he appeared uncharacteristically awkward, as though fighting back great emotion. Then he was grinning that same amused, friendly, yet slightly detached and ironical grin I knew so well. "I'd come over and give you a hug, son," he said. "But I'm afraid I can't."

"Jesus!" Nat said suddenly. "Jesus Christ, Dad! The bastards have got you chained like a bloody slave!"

Then he was across the room and sobbing in his father's arms, and Reverend Andrews was standing awkwardly, holding Nat and patting his shaking shoulders.

"Let's get the hell out of here and give them a minute alone together," my father said, and he and Charlie started for the door.

For a moment, though, all I could do was stare with horror at the heavy iron ring around Reverend Andrews' leg and the short chain manacling him tight to the radiator as he tried to comfort his son.

"Sir, would you please state your full name and profession?"

"Reverend Walter Andrews. I'm a Presbyterian minister."

"Let's begin right at the beginning, Reverend Andrews. Where and when were you born?"

"Toronto, Canada, on January twenty-third, 1912."

"Would you please summarize your education?"

"I attended grammar school and secondary school at St. Gilbert-on-the-Lake. St. Gilbert is a private Presbyterian Academy about twenty miles from Toronto. I took undergraduate studies in history and literature at the University of Toronto and received my divinity degree from the Presbyterian seminary affiliated with that university."

Step by step, my brother led the minister through his career as an

RCAF chaplain, his service in France during World War II, his medals for bravery, his most recent tour of duty with the United Nations forces in Korea.

"You seem to have had a highly successful military career, Reverend Andrews. What rank did you hold when you resigned?"

"Major."

"Why did you resign from the Air Force?"

"Well, sir, I was weary of it. I wanted a more stable situation for myself, in part so that my son could rejoin me. He'd been living with his grandmother, in Montreal, since my wife died, fourteen years ago."

"How would you describe your initial reception here in Kingdom County, Reverend Andrews?"

"I would characterize it as generally very friendly and helpful."

"You say 'generally very friendly.' Did anyone in Kingdom County demonstrate any signs of prejudice toward you?"

"Objection, your honor," Sigurd Moulton said. "Prejudice is not the issue here today. That's been clearly established."

"Sustained. I personally instructed you, Mr. Kinneson, not to introduce that subject. You may, however, rephrase your question."

"Did anyone, for any reason, behave in a hostile way toward you during your first weeks in Kingdom County?"

"There were one or two unfriendly incidents involving my son."

"Could you please describe these incidents?"

"On one occasion a man addressed him with a racial slur. On another, he was taunted in the same vein by a local boy about his age."

"How old is your son, Reverend Andrews?"

"He's just seventeen."

"And how did he react to these two situations?"

"Well, he'd encountered similar difficulties before. He's learned to shrug them off. At the same time, Nathan isn't a fighter. That's partly why I came here, in the hope of finding a place where he'd be able to have a more or less normal boyhood, a place where he and I both could be happy. He handled the taunting as well as any youngster could, given the circumstances."

Charlie nodded. "We'll come back to Nathan later on. Now I'd like to skip ahead a bit. Could you please tell the jury how you first met Claire LaRiviere?"

"Well, sir, I was familiar with her story from my parishioners, particularly your father, Editor Kinneson. I knew that she'd come here as a species of mail-order bride—"

"Hearsay," Zack honked. "Witness is not answering question as put."

"Please just answer your attorney's question, Reverend Andrews," Judge Allen said. "Under what circumstances did you first meet the young woman?"

Sitting erect in his chair, betraying not the slightest impatience, looking as self-assured as though he were in his own pulpit winding up a particularly persuasive sermon, the minister nodded. "I was working in my study, doing some historical research around eleven or eleven-thirty on the night of June twenty-eighth. She appeared at the door and said she was in trouble and needed a place to stay."

"What did you do?"

"What nearly anybody would have done, I suppose. I asked her in, heard her out, and said I'd try to assist her."

"Did she say what sort of trouble she was in?"

"She told me that Resolvèd Kinneson, with whom she'd been staying, wanted to marry her. She said she didn't want to marry him. She said he'd threatened her with his gun, and she was afraid he might shoot her."

Sigurd Moulton stood up. "Objection, your honor. We have no way of ascertaining whether any of this hearsay from the deceased murder victim is accurate. None of that testimony is admissible here."

"I simply asked Reverend Andrews to describe how he met Claire LaRiviere," Charlie said. "If the prosecution can prove that any of this information is inaccurate, they're welcome to go ahead. But surely Reverend Andrews has a right to explain how he came to take her in in the first place."

"Then I'm going to request, Mr. Kinneson, that you confine your questions, and Reverend Andrews confine his answers, primarily to what he did and said at the time, rather than what Claire LaRiviere said."

"Reverend Andrews, how long did Claire LaRiviere stay at the parsonage?"

"Approximately five weeks."

"How did you feel about her staying there?"

"I did everything under the sun I could think of to try to find an alternative for her. She absolutely refused to go back to Quebec, and with the exception of your family, to which she was unwilling to return because of your cousin Resolvèd's proximity, no one was willing to accommodate her. The fact that she was an outsider seemed to work very much against her. One or two individuals went so far as to suggest that I have the sheriff transport her to the county line and simply leave her there with orders not to come back. Someone else advised me to report her to the immigration authorities. Frankly, I was at my wits' end to know what to do with her."

"How would you describe her behavior during those five weeks that she stayed at the parsonage?"

The minister shrugged. "Peculiar. Sometimes erratic. To begin with, she seemed to have a compulsion to tell and retell how she'd come to Vermont in the first place. Also, she was obsessed with becoming a movie actress. She was determined to find a situation for herself in Hollywood.

"At the time, I was extremely busy with preparations for the church sesquicentennial celebration. I was concerned for the LaRiviere girl, and she tried to be helpful around the house, but frankly, her presence was never really anything but disruptive. To compound matters, I'd received threats against her safety and mine from Resolvèd Kinneson."

"We'll get to those threats in a moment, Reverend Andrews. In the meantime could you please tell us what you were doing on the evening of August fifth and in the very early morning hours of August sixth this past summer?"

"Yes. I was working in my study."

"Were you alone?"

"I was alone for most of the evening, with the exception of a short visit from Sheriff White. But sometime after midnight, I'm not sure exactly when—it could have been one o'clock or even one-thirty or two—I stepped back onto the porch to smoke a last cigarette. Claire LaRiviere came out and asked to talk with me."

"What did Claire LaRiviere tell you on the parsonage porch on the very early morning of August sixth, Reverend Andrews?"

"Well, sir, she told me that she believed she was pregnant."

A murmur ran through the courtroom.

"Did you tell her you had a friend who could help her?"

"That's part of what I told her. I went on to explain that my friend worked at a home for young unwed mothers in Burlington—it's the Mary Margaret Simmons Home for Unwed Mothers, sponsored by the

Catholic Diocese of Vermont, and well known throughout northern New England. I explained that I would ring up my friend and refer her to the place in the next couple of days."

"Did she seem willing to go to the home for unwed mothers?"

"She didn't seem unwilling. She was distracted, to some degree, as she often was. But she didn't indicate that she was reluctant to go to the home."

"Did she give you any idea of who the baby's father might be?"

"No, and I didn't ask. I assumed that the pregnancy probably dated from before she left Quebec for Vermont. I believed, and still do believe, that it might have been a factor in her departure."

"I see. Did you make the call the following day?"

"Yes."

"Did you talk to your friend?"

"No, he was on vacation for that week and the next. I talked to a receptionist at the home and explained that I would call back in a week."

"Your honor," Charlie said, "I have here Reverend Andrews' August bill from the Kingdom Common Independent Telephone Company, recording a long-distance call on August sixth of this year to the Mary Margaret Simmons Home for Unwed Mothers. I'd like to submit it, along with the page of the Burlington telephone directory listing the number of the Mary Margaret Simmons Home, as Exhibits E and F."

"No objection," said Sigurd Moulton.

"Reverend Andrews, you heard Resolvèd Kinneson testify that around eleven o'clock or eleven-thirty on the evening of August fourth, he came onto your porch and looked into your study, where he claims to have seen you and the LaRiviere girl together on the couch. Is that possible?"

"It is not."

"Why not?"

For the first time since he had taken the stand, Reverend Andrews hesitated for a moment before replying. Then he said quietly, "Because I remained on the common to clean up after the celebration until nearly midnight. I was the last person to leave."

The courtroom was still. What could this mean? That Resolvèd had fabricated his whole story?

"Could you please tell us what happened after you got home from the common on the night of August fourth?"

In his dispassionate military manner, the minister told the jury how, shortly after he had arrived home, two shotgun blasts had been fired into the parsonage and he had confronted Resolvèd in the street. When he finished, the only sound in the room was the persistent scratching of Sigurd Moulton's fountain pen as he continued to write on his inexhaustible supply of yellow legal paper.

"How did you spend the afternoon of August sixth, Reverend Andrews?"

"Around noon I decided to drive my son to his grandmother's place in Montreal. I didn't think the village was safe for him any longer."

"Was Claire home when you returned from your trip?"

"No. That noon was the last time I saw her alive."

"When did you report her missing?"

"That evening, the evening of the sixth. When she hadn't shown up by dark, I called your parents' house and left word that Claire was missing and for your father to call as soon as he got home. About ten I called the sheriff's office and the state police and filed a missing person's report."

"What time did you arrive home from Montreal?"

"Around nine."

"You've clarified a number of very important things for us, Reverend. I have only one further question for you at this time. You said earlier in your testimony that you assumed that Kingdom County would be a good place for you and your son to live, a place where you could both be happy. Have you been?"

The minister hesitated. Then he nodded and said, "Until recently, I thought we were."

"Thank you very much, Reverend Andrews. I have no further questions for you at this time."

Sigurd Moulton glanced briefly at his thick pad of notes. Then he fixed his shrewd gaze on the minister.

"Mr. Andrews, did you visit Kingdom Common for a personal interview before you were hired as minister of the United Church?"

"No, sir. The interview was held over the phone."

"Isn't that an unusual procedure? To hire a minister without a personal interview?"

"You'd have to ask the church trustees that question, sir. But the job here had been vacant for nearly a year. The three trustees I spoke with on the phone all indicated that they were most eager to find a qualified minister, and as I've testified, I was eager to relocate in a small town."

"That's all well and good, Mr. Andrews. But during the interview, did you at any point tell the trustees that you were a Negro?"

"Objection, your honor. As the prosecution has pointed out more than once, you've already ruled that race is not an issue here."

"Strike the question," Sigurd Moulton said, and looked carefully at the jury.

The Montpelier attorney glanced back down at his notes. "Mr. Andrews, you testified that until recently you were happy in Kingdom County. But earlier you alluded to 'one or two unfriendly incidents' involving your son."

"They were straightened out."

"Indeed? Did you straighten out one of those problems by striking a prominent local businessman with your fist and breaking his jaw?"

Charlie was up like a shot. "Your honor, my client is not on trial for defending his son against town drunks and bullies. The prosecution is trying to prejudice the jury against Reverend Andrews through highly misleading innuendo."

"Strike the question," Moulton said again, now that the damage had been done. "Mr. Andrews, you testified that on the night of August fourth or the early morning of August fifth you fired your revolver at Resolvèd Kinneson, though you failed to mention that you shot off part of his right index finger. You seem to be very handy with this revolver. Do you practice with it frequently?"

"Not since taking up residence at the Memphremagog jail."

Some titters broke out; but I saw Charlie give Reverend Andrews a warning look, as if to say this was no laughing matter.

"Did you carry your revolver with you in the line of your chaplain's duties in the service?"

Now Charlie was roaring mad. "Your honor, the prosecution is insinuating that my client is somehow predisposed to violence because he's a decorated war hero with the courage to protect his home from an armed assailant. Moreover, my client is an ordained Presbyterian minister and I'm going to insist that the prosecution accord him the professional courtesy of addressing him by his title, the Reverend Mister Andrews."

"Now see here, both of you," Judge Allen said. "I'll have no more public squabbling and no more public insisting and no more public innuendoes in my courtroom. You, Mr. Moulton, will confine your questions to the case at hand and address the defendant by his title. And you, Charles Kinneson, will indulge yourself in no further tantrums. Is that understood?"

Both attorneys indicated that it was.

"Then you may proceed, Mr. Moulton."

"Mr.—Reverend Andrews, is it fair to say that even before Claire LaRiviere appeared in Kingdom County, you felt that you and your son had been subjected to certain injustices here?"

"In isolated instances."

"Were you frustrated by those isolated instances?"

"Yes."

"Were you angered by them?"

"Yes."

"So ministers do sometimes experience anger? Just the way doctors experience pain and some few lawyers are actually rumored to harbor human feelings?"

Reverend Andrews smiled. "Of course."

"All right. Then let's move along to the evening of August fourth. Resolvèd Kinneson has testified that he discovered you and Claire LaRiviere engaged in sexual intercourse on the divan of your study—"

"Objection, your honor. That accusation was never even remotely substantiated."

"Your honor," Moulton said, "Mr. Barrows and I are laying a foundation, as we pointed out in our written brief, for establishing the motive for the murder of Claire LaRiviere. I will go no further into the matter than is necessary to lay that foundation. If you'll permit me to proceed, I will establish that motive quickly and clearly."

"Proceed," Judge Allen said after a brief pause.

Moulton stepped out from behind the prosecutor's table and walked toward the minister. "Reverend Andrews, did you engage in sex with Claire LaRiviere?"

"I did not."

"A citizen of this county testified that he saw you in your parsonage with her on the night of August fourth. Were you there with her?"

"I was not."

"Reverend Andrews, I'm going to ask you to think very, very carefully before answering this question. Are you saying that Mr. Resolvèd Kinneson is lying?"

"I'm saying he's wrong."

Once again Moulton looked carefully at the jury. "Reverend Andrews, isn't it true that, fearing Claire LaRiviere's accusation that you had gotten her pregnant, and its consequent effect on your job and your standing in this community, you met her by prearrangement in the granite quarry in the Kingdom Gore on the late afternoon or early evening of August sixth just after you returned from taking your son to Montreal, and shot her there, brutally and repeatedly, with the same gun you had fired two evenings ago at Resolvèd Kinneson? Your .38 service revolver, which was subsequently found in the quarry near the site of the girl's corpse? And only then returned to the parsonage and notified the police that she was missing?"

"That is false."

"Who did kill her then? Do you know of any other likely candidate who could have smuggled the gun out of your house and committed the murder?"

"No."

"Do you have any witnesses who can testify that you returned to the village from Montreal at nine and not, say, seven or eight?"

"No, *sir*."

"These questions seem to upset you."

"Everything about you and your questions upsets my stomach, Mr. Moulton."

"That's understandable," Sigurd Moulton said, turning his dry smile toward the jury. "That's very understandable. Your redirect, Mr. Kinneson."

"No redirect at this time, your honor."

Charlie waited until Reverend Andrews had stepped down. Then my brother said quietly, "I'd like to call Nathan Andrews to the witness stand."

# 19

"Your honor, I must protest that a minor, and moreover a member of the defendant's family, can hardly be a credible witness. The testimony of Walter Andrews' son should not be admissible to this trial."

"There's no Vermont law to prevent a minor from giving relevant testimony, Mr. Moulton," Judge Allen replied. "Nathan, you just speak up loudly and clearly so that all us old folks can understand, and tell the strict truth, and you'll be all right."

"Nat," Charlie said, approaching the witness stand, "why don't you begin by telling us your full name and your age?"

"Nathan Andrews. I just turned seventeen."

"When did you first learn that your father intended to take a job here in Kingdom County, Nat?"

"Last spring. It would have been March, I suppose."

"Where were you living at the time?"

"With my grandmother in Montreal."

"Were you going to school at the time?"

"I was attending a private high school, St. Stephen's."

"How would you describe yourself as a student, Nat?"

Nat shrugged. "I've always gotten my A's."

"Did you like living with your grandmother and attending school in Canada?"

"Very much."

"What was your reaction when your father told you that you and he were going to be moving to Vermont?"

"Well, I was happy to be with Dad. But I didn't really want to leave Canada. I was pretty well established there. Baseball practice had just started, and I had some close friends, you know."

"I understand, Nat. Now let's talk about your first days and weeks in the Kingdom. Did you like it here?"

Nat paused. "School was all right, except that I was ahead of my class, especially in math. The other kids at school were friendly enough, most of them. They wanted me to play ball, and so forth. I don't know. It wasn't so bad here, but I missed my friends up home and Gram. She and I sort of looked after one another, you know. And I missed the city."

"You mentioned that you'd played baseball in Canada. Did you join the Academy baseball team?"

Nat shook his head.

"Please answer yes or no, Nathan," Judge Allen said.

"No, I didn't play baseball here in Vermont."

"Did anyone else besides your classmates urge you to play?"

"My father did. He was helping out with the Academy team, after Coach Whitcomb got sick. Dad wanted me to play. He'd been a standout player in secondary school and at university, himself."

"Nat, putting aside all modesty for a moment, how good a baseball player are you?"

"Well, I pitched for my Canadian school's 'A' team in my freshman and sophomore years."

"Why didn't you play ball for the Academy? You obviously love the game, you're an outstanding player, your dad coached, your school friends begged you to play."

Nat looked down at his hands. "I don't know," he said quietly.

"There were times, are times, when I don't feel like playing or doing much of anything else. This was one of those times, I guess. About the time I moved here and baseball began."

"Was there anyone you could talk to about those times?"

"Well, Jim Kinneson was my best friend here. He and I talked quite a bit. I talked to Dad some, but he's pretty much of the philosophy that you grit your teeth and bear things, you know."

Nat paused again, looked at his hands, started to say something, then stopped.

"Go ahead, Nat. What else were you going to tell us?"

"There was another person I liked talking to."

"Who was that?"

"Claire LaRiviere."

"How did things go for you after Claire came?"

"Better."

"How much better?"

"A lot, at first. She was an outsider too, and she'd lost a parent herself. Her father. They were very close; he was some sort of street performer. He was teaching her how to perform, too."

"How much time did you spend with Claire, Nat?"

"Well, I guess you could say I spent a whole lot of bloody time with her."

"I'm sorry. Would you please repeat what you just said?"

"I said we spent a great deal of time together."

"What, exactly, did you just say, Nat?"

Nat shrugged. "I said a lot of time. We spent a lot of time together."

"Julia," Charlie said, turning to the stenographer, "would you please read Nathan Andrews' first answer to my question, 'How much time did you spend with Claire?' "

Julia flipped back a page. " 'How much time did you spend with Claire, Nat?' 'Well, I guess you could say I spent a whole lot of bloody time with her.' "

"Thank you, Julia. Now Nat, I'm going to ask you some questions about what happened on Old Home Day. These questions aren't in any way meant to embarrass you or put you on the spot. Just answer them as truthfully and as completely as you can. Do you recall where you were that evening?"

"Yes. I was home. At the parsonage."

"Were you alone?"

"No."

"Who was with you?"

"Well, that was the night that old Pliny Templeton's ghost, his skeleton, was supposed to walk. Jim Kinneson and I had planned to sit up and wait and see if it came to the parsonage. Anyway, Jim had come in about nine and gone upstairs to my room and fallen asleep."

"Were you and Jim Kinneson alone in the house at the time?"

"No. Claire was there, too."

"Around eleven o'clock, Nat, precisely where were you in the parsonage?"

The courtroom was deadly still.

"We—I mean Claire and I—were in my father's study. Jim was still asleep upstairs in my room."

"What were you and Claire doing in the study?"

Nat paused and looked at his hands. Then he said softly, "We were necking on the couch. It wasn't her idea as much as mine. I mean, she never forced herself on me or anything like that, no matter what people might think about her coming to town with that show. It wasn't like that at all. We were friends. Anyway, we left the window open so we could hear when the shindig on the common ended."

A murmur passed through the room, and Judge Allen's gavel rose; but immediately it was quiet again.

"What happened next, Nat?"

"I thought I heard a noise on the porch. But then I didn't hear anything else, until all of a sudden the desk light went on. I thought, oh, no, my father had somehow come into the room. Then I saw this man's head in the window."

"Did you recognize the man?"

"Yes. It was Resolvèd Kinneson. He said, 'Excuse me!' in this very sarcastic voice."

"Did either you or Claire say anything?"

"I said, 'Shut that bloody light off.' "

"And?"

"And he did."

"What did you do next?"

"Well, I was going to tell my father, but I couldn't figure out what to say to him, without . . . you know, admitting what we were doing on the couch. So I just went up and woke up Jim, and pretty soon after that Resolvèd showed up with his shotgun."

"Nat, you said you were necking on the couch. What do you mean by that?"

Looking at his hands, Nat said, "We were . . . making love. Going, you know, all the way."

"Was this the first time you and Claire had 'gone all the way'?"

Very softly, Nat said no.

"When was the first time?"

Nat sighed. "The second night she stayed with us."

"During the five weeks that Claire stayed with you, how many times would you guess that you and she made love?"

"A great many. As often as we could arrange."

"Nat, did Claire ever tell you that she was pregnant?"

Nat looked at his hands. "Yes, she did. She told me on the night after Old Home Day. At first I didn't know what to tell her. I asked if she was sure, and she said yes. I asked if—if she thought I was the father. She said yes. She said I was the only *possible* father. I suppose in a way that made me feel good—I mean, that she hadn't been with anyone else—but I didn't know what she should do, until it occurred to me that she ought to tell my father. That's what I told her to do."

"Thank you, Nat. That's all for the time being."

To my surprise, Zack Barrows rather than Moulton stood up to cross-examine Nathan. He walked threateningly toward the witness stand and stopped not more than a foot away from my friend.

"Young Andrews," he said, "I'll remind you that you are sworn to tell the truth. Do you know the term for lying in a court of law?"

Nat just looked at him.

"That term, young man, is perjury. Perjury is not a nice term. The punishment for perjury is not nice. The punishment for perjury is severe. Now, young Andrews, do you know your Vermont geography? I assume you do, since you seem so quick to tell us about your high marks in school. Very well. Do you know where Vergennes is? Vergennes is some miles south of Burlington. Vergennes has two distinctions. It is the smallest incorporated city in the United States of America. And it is the home of Vermont's reform school for boys who are ungovernable and commit perjury in a court of law. This school is not noted for being a nice place, either. Over the years I have sent many boys—"

"Objection!" Charlie said.

"Sustained! That's quite enough, Zachariah, and I do mean enough. If you want to question the witness, go ahead. But I won't have you terrorizing him."

"I just want him to be certain in his own mind what will happen if he commits perjury, your honor. I want him to know about that reform school, that's all. Now Nathan Andrews, you've testified that you felt you didn't fit in here, that you felt like an outsider, that you couldn't cope with adjusting to a normal boyhood in this village. You couldn't cope with playing baseball like any other boy. Is that what you're telling me?"

"At times."

"Well, Nathan Andrews, you've had some rough sledding, all right. Going to a good school, being asked to play a game you yourself have told us you excel at, 'necking' every night with a pretty little girl who didn't know any better. Let's go to the night she disappeared, the night of August sixth. Did you neck with her that night?"

"No, I didn't. How could I? She was gone and so was I. I was in Montreal."

"Just before you left you didn't slip up to the quarry with her? And maybe take along your father's gun—"

"Your honor, this is sheer idiotic speculation. Nat Andrews isn't on trial here. The prosecutor seems to be badly confused. He's grasping at straws to try to prove that somebody named Andrews was involved in this murder."

"Sustained," Judge Allen was saying. "Mr. Barrows, I am telling you right now to stop this impertinent line of leading questions. Nathan Andrews is certainly not on trial here today. You're undercutting your own case, sir."

"I'm sorry, your honor, but let's not forget that an innocent girl was murdered. In between all these melodramatics, a young girl was brutally killed."

Zack turned back to Nat. "Let's go to another episode. Did you or did you not, Nathan Andrews, knock the LaMott boy off the Boston and Montreal train trestle back in June, and nearly drown him?"

"Your honor, once again I must object that the prosecutor is deliberately leading the witness, or trying to, with inaccurate and totally unsubstantiated innuendo."

"Sustained. You will rephrase that question, Mr. Barrows."

"Nathan Andrews, did you knock the LaMott boy off the trestle?"

"He fell off the trestle, and I jumped in after him and pulled him out."

"Did you hit him before he fell?"

"He tried to hit me. I ducked and reached out and swatted him. He fell and I went in after him."

"Nathan Andrews, you have testified that you advised Claire LaRiviere to talk to your father and tell him that she was pregnant."

"Yes."

"After you proffered this wise counsel, did it occur to you that when the baby was born, your father would certainly know that you, and no one but you, had to be the father?"

"I suppose so."

"I know so. And on that illuminating revelation, I shall turn this versatile young witness back over for your redirect, Charles."

"Nat, I want to ask you just one more question," Charlie began. "Did you at any time before or after Claire's death tell your father that you were very probably her baby's father?"

"No. Never."

"Thank you, Nathan. If Mr. Barrows has no further questions, I'd like to recall Reverend Andrews to the stand, your honor."

The judge glanced up at the clock. It was nearly noon. "We'll break for lunch," he said. "Court will reconvene at one-thirty. In the meantime, I'd like to see both sets of counsel in my chambers."

At the *Monitor*, Dad pulled down the blinds, put the CLOSED sign on the window, and locked the door in order not to be bothered. But no sooner had Mom started to unpack our lunch than the phone began to ring.

My father snatched the receiver off the hook. "Hello? Hello?"

He put his hand over the mouthpiece. "It's that damn crank caller," he said. Then he spoke again into the receiver. "Listen, whoever you are, I am here to tell you that—What? What's that?"

My father listened for perhaps fifteen seconds, then said, "All right; we'll be here," and hung up.

"Well, that's one mystery solved," Dad said. "We know who the crank caller is."

"Who?"

"Ida LaMott. Apparently she's been working up the courage to identify herself. She said she and Frenchy are on their way over here with something very important to tell us.

"Did she say what it was about?" Mom said.

"Only that it had to do with the trial. James, run across the street to the courthouse. As soon as your brother comes out of the judge's chambers, tell him to get over here as fast as he can. This may not amount to a hill of beans, but whatever it is Ida wants to tell us, he ought to hear it."

"I'd like at this time to recall the Reverend Walter Andrews," Charlie said an hour later when court reconvened.

Although he maintained his erect bearing, the minister looked dreadfully tired as he took the stand.

"Reverend Andrews, you've testified that on the evening of June twenty-eighth, the evening Claire LaRiviere appeared at the parsonage you were doing some historical research. What was the exact nature of this research?"

"I was interested in the background of Pliny Templeton—the founder and first headmaster of the Kingdom Common Academy."

"How did you first hear of Pliny Templeton?"

"From your father, Charles Kinneson. Not long after I came to town this past spring, he told me how Pliny ran away from slavery, with the help of your great-grandfather, and established the Academy here in northern Vermont. The tale captured my imagination."

"Was there any particular reason for this, apart from the fact that Pliny was a Negro?"

"Well, my own great-grandfather had come north from Mississippi via the Underground Railway. His son, my grandfather, was the first Negro Presbyterian session member in Canada, and at divinity school I wrote my thesis on the Presbyterian church's efforts to help fugitive American Negroes become established in Canada."

"Was there anything else that especially intrigued you about Pliny Templeton's story?"

"Well, there's the legend that Pliny was the first Negro college graduate in America. Actually, although Pliny did graduate from Middlebury College he had several Negro predecessors at other American colleges, including both Harvard and Yale. What really intrigued me about the man was the end of his life."

"What particularly intrigued you about the end of Pliny Templeton's life, Reverend Andrews?"

"To begin with, the fact that he allegedly committed suicide over a doctrinal dispute between the church and his school. I was curious about it and decided to look into the entire situation."

"Your honor, this has nothing to do with the murder of Claire LaRiviere!" Sigurd Moulton cried out.

"Judge Allen, if you'll let me proceed free from the interruptions of the various prosecutors, I'll demonstrate the relevance of this line of questioning in good time."

"Go ahead, Mr. Kinneson. Get to your point as quickly as possible."

"Thank you. Reverend Andrews, I'll come back to the matter of your research into the life of Pliny Templeton in a moment. Before I do, though, I'd like to ask you who, besides you and your son, had ready and free access to the parsonage this past summer."

"Anyone who wanted or needed to come there was welcome, Mr. Kinneson."

"I understand that. What I'd like to know is who came and went on an informal basis? Without knocking, let's say. Or at odd hours."

"Well, sir, as far as I can remember he always knocked, but your father quite often dropped in of an evening. Many nights he'd stop off on his way home from covering a meeting or working late at the newspaper office, and we'd visit until all hours. Your younger brother, Jim, used to call for my son. And in late July I hired a local woman, Mrs. Ida LaMott, to come in to clean three times a week. She came and went without knocking. So, for that matter, did Claire La-Riviere."

"What there anyone else who had access to your house? Anyone from the church? A session member, for example?"

"The sexton, Elijah Kinneson, held keys to both the church and the parsonage. So far as I know he never came to the house except when I called him, though, say to fix the furnace or plumbing or some other practical matter."

"But the sexton did at your request assist you with those matters? The furnace and plumbing?"

"Yes, upon request."

"How many times did you request the sexton's assistance over the course of the spring and summer?"

"I'm not sure. Four or five, perhaps."

"Was he prompt in responding?"

"So far as I can remember."

"How would you characterize his attitude toward you at those times?"

"Irrelevant, your honor," Moulton said. "The church sexton's attitude is hardly at issue here today."

"The sexton has already given critical testimony in this trial, your honor. Surely the jury has a right to be aware of any information that might have a bearing on that testimony."

"Proceed with care, Mr. Kinneson."

"Reverend Andrews, how would you characterize Elijah Kinneson's attitude toward you when he came to the parsonage?"

"I don't recall that I was ever at home when he came. The work would simply be done a day or two after I'd spoken to him about it."

"Can you think of a specific instance?"

"Yes. After the shooting episode at the parsonage, I asked him to replace both the front and back door locks with modern locks. Two days after the shooting, when I returned from a morning meeting with the session and just before I drove Nat back to Montreal the locks had been installed and the keys were on my desk and labeled."

"So Elijah Kinneson had complete access to your house at any time?"

"Objection! It's been established that the sexton had access to the parsonage only in connection with his job and upon the minister's request."

"Strike the question," Charlie said casually. "How would you characterize Elijah Kinneson's attitude toward you in general, Reverend Andrews?"

"He rarely spoke to me directly. I had the impression he avoided me when possible."

"Do you have any idea why?"

"Immaterial, your honor," Moulton said. "We're speaking of the vaguest impressions here."

"Sustained," Judge Allen said.

"Let me inquire more precisely," Charlie said. "Reverend Andrews, did you ever have any difficulty, any arguments with Elijah Kinneson?"

"We disagreed on occasion," the minister said. "I recall asking him one Saturday morning to change the text on the bulletin board outside the church. I thought the message he'd put up was inappropriate, and we exchanged some sharp words over it. He walked away in a huff, so I changed it myself. After that, he refused to have anything more to do with the bulletin board.

"On the other hand, I never had any cause to complain about the sexton's regular work; he kept the church in apple-pie order. Doctrinally, we never pretended to agree. Mr. Elijah Kinneson is a Reformed Presbyterian, one of the very last in the congregation. I was brought up as a United Presbyterian."

"Was Elijah Kinneson aware of your interest in Pliny Templeton's life?"

"Yes, he was. That was a curious thing. More than once he gave me to understand that he didn't at all approve of the research I was conducting on Templeton. When I began looking into the circumstances of Pliny's alleged suicide, he went out of his way to tell me that wasn't any of my business. He objected when your father lent me Pliny's book, *The Ecclesiastical History of Kingdom County*. Elijah said that Pliny was a born troublemaker who was at the root of a turn-of-the-century feud between local Reformed and United Presbyterians. I presumed that Elijah thought Pliny richly deserved to languish in obscurity because of the changes he sought to effect in the church and Academy."

Sigurd Moulton, who once again seemed to have resumed the duties of chief prosecutor, was on his feet. "Your honor, these speculations and presumptions on the part of a defendant in a first-degree murder trial have no place in this courtroom. They're totally unrelated to the case at hand."

"The jury will disregard Reverend Andrews' presumptions. You may proceed with this line of inquiry, Mr. Kinneson, if and only if Reverend Andrews confines his replies to what he knows for a fact, with no presumptions."

"Thank you, your honor. Reverend Andrews, where do you keep your research papers on Pliny Templeton?"

"Until recently, I kept them in the lower left-hand drawer of my desk in the parsonage study."

"Why did you say 'until recently'?"

"A few weeks ago I asked your father if he'd bring my research notes up to Memphremagog for me. He checked in my desk and found they were missing. So were two newspapers from the summer of 1900, the summer Pliny died, which I'd borrowed from the back files at your father's office."

"What, specifically, did those two newspapers contain?"

"One contained an article on Pliny's suicide. The other contained a notice concerning a sudden illness of Charles Kinneson—your great-grandfather and Pliny's close friend and benefactor."

"Did you keep your desk locked, Reverend Andrews?"

"Yes, always."

"Do you have any clues as to who might have taken your research notes and the two newspapers?"

"Not without presuming again."

"Thank you very much, Reverend Andrews. Your testimony has been very illuminating. That's all for the time being."

Sigurd Moulton stood up. "Reverend Andrews, I'm not going to conduct a class up here on local history. We're all sure that your interest in Pliny Templeton is a very fascinating little hobby to take up your spare time when you're not out getting into fistfights or shooting matches with local citizens, but—

"Objection, your honor. That's exactly the sort of misleading, gratuitous insult that you've warned the prosecutor against."

"Sustained. Mr. Moulton, if you insult anyone in this courtroom just once more, I'll slap you with a cool one-hundred-dollar fine on the spot."

"I was simply going to say, your honor, that I intend to back up and ask the defendant some much more relevant questions. Now, Reverend Andrews, I want to explore in more depth your relationship with your son. I'd like to ask you whether you were aware that he was going to testify here today."

"Not until my attorney told me so this morning. I wasn't even aware that Nat was back in Vermont until Charlie Kinneson informed me this morning that he'd called and asked him to return from Montreal last night."

"Why did you spirit your son off to Montreal in the first place?"

"As I've said, this simply wasn't a safe place for him after the shooting at the parsonage. He'd been happy at his grandmother's before moving to Vermont, and both he and I thought that it was best for him to return there, at least temporarily."

"Did your son ever tell you or hint to you that he had slept with the LaRiviere girl?"

"No, he did not."

"Did the LaRiviere girl tell you or in any way intimate to you that it was your son who had slept with her?"

"No, she did not. And I'm not at all ready to concede that he was the only one who did."

"Do you know that from firsthand experience?"

"Objection, your honor. Once again, the prosecutor is using innuendo to try to trap and discredit my client."

"I don't mind answering that question, your honor," Reverend Andrews said. "No, Mr. Moulton, I do not know that from firsthand experience. My sole interest in the girl was in trying to help her find a suitable situation, and frankly, a situation as far away from Kingdom Common as possible. As I've testified, I knew better than any of my congregation that the parsonage was no good place for her to be."

"Well, then," Moulton said, "the obvious question, Reverend Andrews. Did you *suspect* that there might be something between your son and Claire LaRiviere?"

"I suspected that if there wasn't something between them already, there soon might be. Human nature would only lead one to that conclusion."

"Did your knowledge of human nature also lead you to suspect, when Claire LaRiviere told you that she was pregnant, that your son might be the father of the baby?"

"She'd been with us for only five weeks. I must own that the thought crossed my mind, but I more or less dismissed it because I thought five weeks would be too soon for that to happen, or for her to be sure about it if it had happened."

"Then why on earth, if you suspected that your son and Claire LaRiviere might have been sleeping together, didn't you say something about it earlier in this trial?"

"Several reasons. One, no one's on trial here for sleeping with the girl, and I was under no legal obligation to mention any suspicions that I may have harbored on that head. Two, I saw no reason why Nathan should have to answer questions on this matter. Even if I suspected that there might have been something between him and the girl, I didn't see how his testimony could be relevant to my case. Finally, I didn't want him to have to go through just this type of ordeal."

"You seem very protective of your son."

"Is that a question?"

"You've testified that it was partly on your son's behalf that you decided to come here to Kingdom County. Isn't that correct?"

"Yes."

"Didn't you also want to protect your son, as well as yourself and your own professional and personal reputation, from the criticism that inevitably would have resulted from the unsavory disclosure that he was involved in a sordid sexual affair with a girl who had worked as a stripper in one of the notorious tent shows at Kingdom Fair?"

"As I've already indicated, I had no proof at all that my son was engaged in such a liaison with the LaRiviere girl."

"But you've admitted that you suspected that he might have been. Weren't you concerned about your reputation and his then?"

"If my reputation had been my principal concern, I wouldn't have allowed the girl to stay with us in the first place."

"Let's get back to Elijah Kinneson. Are you seriously suggesting that a man with an impeccable reputation, not only as a sexton and a citizen of this village, but as a pillar of the church, broke into your house and stole a bunch of haphazard notes on a man who died fifty years ago?"

"I'm not suggesting that. But someone took them. I have no way of knowing who."

"Exactly. If in fact they were stolen at all. Reverend, since coming to Kingdom County you've punched a local man in the jaw, fired shots at a local citizen in the street in front of your house, maiming that citizen for life, and spirited your boy back off to Canada after the girl who was staying at your house informed you she was pregnant—all in the interest of protecting that boy. Just how far would you go in protecting your son?"

"I suppose I'd go as far as necessary."

"What do you mean by 'necessary'?"

"I mean that short of violating the law or my personal conscience, I would do what I had to do to keep him out of harm's way."

"I'm going to ask you a question, then, in the interest of, shall we say, broadening the field of suspects. Would you, Reverend Andrews, protect your son from murder charges by remaining silent, even to the point of throwing suspicion onto yourself?"

"OBJECTION, YOUR HONOR! Nat Andrews is not on trial here. That's the most ridiculous—"

"Sustained! Don't let me warn you on this issue again, Mr. Moulton."

"Ridiculous?" Moulton said. "Quite possibly. Quite probably. Almost definitely, in fact. So my last question, at least for the time being, is this: Would you, Reverend Andrews, murder someone *yourself* to protect your son from being named as the seducer of a homeless girl staying in your house? Would you do that, sir? Did you do that? Did you murder Claire LaRiviere in order to prevent what you yourself suspected from becoming public knowledge—that your son had gotten her pregnant?"

I thought that Reverend Andrews might leap right out of the witness box and coldcock Sigurd Moulton on the spot, the way he had Bumper Stevens the past spring. But he betrayed no emotion at all as he said, "No, I did not. Or for any other reason."

"We'll let this group of twelve Kingdom County natives determine that," Moulton said, with a nod at the jury. "I have no further questions."

Charlie next recalled Cousin Elijah. Now as Elijah took the stand he looked as triumphant as his Biblical namesake.

"Mr. Elijah Kinneson," Charlie said, "would you mind telling the jury again why you passed through the United Church cemetery on the early morning of August sixth?"

"I don't chew my cabbage twice."

"Mr. Barrows and Mr. Moulton," Judge Allen said, "your witness is now standing on the thinnest of ice. A mere skim of ice, in fact. Unless otherwise instructed from the bench, he will respond to the defense attorney's questions promptly and courteously."

"Just answer the question, please, Elijah," Zack said from the prosecutor's table.

"I passed through the cemetery because it's a shortcut home from work," Elijah said in a surly tone. "Besides that, as I indicated earlier, I quite often detour out around through the graveyard in order to check on this or that in my capacity as sexton."

"I'm interested in your sexton work, Elijah. What, exactly, does it entail?"

"Irrelevant," Moulton said.

"The witness has just testified that he was checking up on things in the cemetery in connection with his job as sexton on the night he overheard Claire LaRiviere tell my client she was pregnant."

"Answer the question, Elijah," Judge Allen said.

"What does being a sexton entail? Well, mowing the cemetery grass. Planting the dead. Keeping the church clean, the church walk clear in the wintertime. Maintaining the parsonage."

"Are you paid for these duties?"

"Yes and no. I compute my time at a fair hourly rate and donate it to the church as my tithe. Fact is, it comes to way more than your standard tithe. This way I tithe for a number who won't, or at any rate don't."

"You said you maintained the parsonage. Do you have access to it at all times?"

"I don't go there unless I'm summoned."

"When you changed the front and back door locks at the parsonage on the morning of August sixth, did you keep a duplicate set of keys for yourself?"

"Objection, your honor. Counsel for the defense is adopting a prosecutorial stance with the witness."

"Your honor, the prosecution has just finished adopting exactly the same stance with Nathan Andrews. It's as though if they can't prove their case against my client, which they can't because my client is totally innocent of these absurd charges, they're going to go out after my client's son. Well, they're the ones who wanted to 'broaden the field of suspects.' That's all I'm doing."

"Your objection is overruled, Mr. Moulton. Elijah Kinneson may answer the question. Put your question again, Attorney Kinneson."

"Elijah, when you changed the locks at the parsonage, on the morning of August sixth, did you keep a set of new keys for yourself?"

"I may have. What of it? That's only standard procedure."

"Do you have the new keys with you now, and if so, could I please see them?"

"Objection. The only way I'll agree to that, your honor, is if those keys are going to be entered as evidence."

"They are," Charlie said. "Toward the end of broadening the field of suspects, Mr. Moulton."

"That murder didn't take place in the parsonage, it was committed in or near the stone quarry."

"The revolver presumed to be the murder weapon came from the parsonage, your honor. The prosecutor is using this fact as prima facie evidence that my client himself must have used the revolver to commit the murder. I'm only broadening the—"

"We know, Mr. Kinneson," Judge Allen said. "We know. Do you intend to enter the keys in question as evidence immediately?"

"Yes."

"Proceed."

Elijah unclipped his great key ring and scowled at it as though the dozens of keys had offended him personally and unforgivably. From the ring he selected two new keys and handed them to Charlie, who had them duly entered as evidence.

"Do you have any other keys belonging to the parsonage, Mr. Kinneson?"

"Not that I know of."

"Could I please see the ring?"

Elijah, who had clipped the keys back on his belt loop, gave a long exasperated sigh. He unfastened them again and handed them to Charlie.

"What's this one go to?" Charlie said, fingering a very small key like the key to a cedar chest or padlock.

Elijah hesitated. "I couldn't say for a certainty."

"Might it go to the desk in the parsonage office?"

"I can't tell you. I'm not in the habit of going into other folks' private desk drawers."

"Just one more question, then. Did you, Elijah Kinneson, go back to the parsonage on the afternoon of August sixth, after Reverend Andrews had left with Nathan for Montreal?"

"Objection! Elijah Kinneson's whereabouts on that afternoon are totally irrelevant."

"You're basing a large part of your case on his whereabouts the night before," Charlie roared. "If you can ask him where he was on the night of August fifth, I can damn well ask him where he was on the afternoon of August sixth."

"Answer the question, Mr. Kinneson," Judge Allen said.

"I'll tell you where I was," Elijah said angrily. "I was at the newspaper office from one that afternoon until well on into that evening, whilst my cousin and his boy were off fishing. Anyone who says otherwise is a bold-faced liar."

"Fine," Charlie said. "Then unless the prosecution wishes to redirect questions to Mr. Elijah Kinneson, I'd like to call Claude 'Frenchy' LaMott to the witness stand."

"Your honor, I must protest again that in a case of this gravity a mere boy's notions cannot be taken seriously."

"Mr. Moulton, kindly be seated. We will entertain no 'notions,' I'll assure you, and I, not you, will continue to determine who may and may not testify before this court. Administer the oath, Mr. Blake."

As Frenchy LaMott came forward, his black hair slicked back with tonic, wearing an ancient herringbone suit coat over a flannel shirt open at the collar, he looked a good thirty years old.

Charlie had obviously coached Frenchy about the swearing in, because he gave his actual name, Claude, when he took the oath.

"Just relax, Frenchy," Charlie said. "You've been waiting for what, an hour already? You probably know more about how a courtroom's run than some over-the-hill persecuting attorneys and their flatlander hirelings."

*Bang!* Judge Allen's hand hit the top of the bench as hard as a gavel.

"Charles Kinneson, I am fining you a cool hundred dollars, payable on the spot. You will disburse this amount, in full, to Mr. Blake before we proceed one step further."

"I'm sorry, your honor. I can't."

"What do you mean, you can't?"

"I don't have one hundred dollars."

"Then write him a check."

"I don't have a checking account."

"Well, how much cash do you have?"

Charlie took out his wallet and looked inside. "Eight dollars and change," he said.

Beside my mother, Athena had her hand over her mouth and was trying not to break up with laughter.

"Then you will step over to Mr. Farlow Blake and pony up that eight dollars and change and write him an IOU for the balance. Payable within thirty days," the judge added.

Not one person in that crowded room dared laugh, though I'm sure that, like Athena, everyone wanted to, as Charlie followed the judge's orders.

This transaction completed, my somewhat subdued brother said,

"Frenchy, I'm going to make all this as short as possible. Could you please tell us what you were doing on the afternoon of August sixth when your mother got home from her housekeeper's job at Reverend Andrews'?"

"Grinding up pig brain for headcheese."

"Did you make headcheese all afternoon?"

"No. 'Bout middle of afternoon or so I go overstreet."

"By 'overstreet' you mean to the village?"

"That what I mean," Frenchy said.

"For what purpose?"

Frenchy LaMott looked defiantly out from under his great glistening mop of hair and said nothing.

"Why did you go to the village, Frenchy?"

"I just told you this noon, Kinneson. You written it all down on you yellow paper. Why I got to say it again now in front of all these people? Read you yellow paper to them."

"The jury needs to hear this directly from you, Frenchy," Charlie said patiently. "Otherwise it won't mean anything in court."

"Old jury be a lot more apt believe you than me," Frenchy muttered.

"Tell us why you went to town on the afternoon of August sixth, Frenchy."

"Went to see that girl."

"What girl?"

"Canuck girl. LaRiviere."

Frenchy glared at my brother. "I knowed she was alone because the old woman said so. Said the preacher had took his kid back to Canady and weren't expected home till nighttime. So I went to see her. That give you a thrill, does it, Kinneson?"

Charlie grinned. "Was this the first time you had ever gone to see Claire LaRiviere?"

Frenchy turned his head aside as if to spit out a jet of tobacco juice, just caught himself, and instead blew air out through his compressed lips. "Hang no! I see her over at that Old Home fair for a while. Had a talk with her."

"What did you and she talk about?"

"You know what. I already told you."

"Tell the jury, please."

"Well, we got to talking in French. I asked if she had a boyfriend. She said sort of. I said I had fifteen dollars that Bumper Stevens owed me that I'd give a certain girl to be my girlfriend. She knowed what I meant, all right. She said she was saving up to get to Hollywood and go into the movies and needed money, but she wasn't going to take no fifteen dollars to be nobody's girlfriend. So I said what if I showed her that fifteen. And she tell me it still don't make no difference, she already got a boyfriend. I ask her who, but she won't say."

"Did you have the fifteen dollars with you on the afternoon of August sixth, Frenchy?"

"Matter of fact, I did."

"Where did you get it?"

"I took it outen Bumper Stevens' cash box at commission sales barn that afternoon. He owed me wages for two, three weeks. Kept telling me he'd pay up, then forgetting or something."

"What did you do after you took the money from Bumper's cash box?"

"I cut through back lot behind old undertaker's place and come out in preacher's backyard and went up and knocked on the back door."

"Did anyone answer the door?"

"Naw. I get in, though. I get in with the old woman's new key that the preacher give her."

"Did you know it was wrong to go into the house uninvited, Frenchy?"

"I didn't think 'bout it. I wanted to call that girl's bluff. See if she still turn me down after I show her that fifteen."

"Had you ever been inside the parsonage before?"

"Once. Spent a night in there once when it was empty to see old skellington 'post to come snooping 'round every summer, only it never show up. Scared to with me there. Anyway, I look all 'round, call that girl's name. No answer. I go upstairs, look in all the rooms. No girl, no nobody. So I figure she overstreet at store. Then phone ring downstairs. In room off the porch where I watch for old ghost."

"The minister's study?"

"Right. Where desk is. Ring one, two, I don't know, maybe dozen times. 'Course no one there to answer. Kind of spooky."

"I imagine it was. What did you do then?"

"Well, I know preacher don't be back all afternoon, so what the hang, I go snooping 'round a little. Didn't take nothing, neither, mister man! 'Cept for wages Christly old Bumper 'post to pay me, I never took nothing off nobody. Even old Barrows tell you that!"

Judge Allen smiled. "We believe you, Frenchy. No one has accused you of theft."

"They hadn't better," Frenchy told the judge.

"Where did you snoop, Frenchy?"

"Well, I look 'round in girl's room, look at things on dresser, you know, lipstick and that. Then I go in room 'cross hall and see all those smelly old funny books. I couldn't believe it. They must have been thousands. I sit down on bed and read a few—well, look at pictures anyway, 'cause I don't read that good. Then I hear the back door open and close and footsteps in kitchen. Jesus! I nearly crap my britches! Then I think, must be that crazy Canuck girl. I set tight as pa'tridge in a spruce tree, thinking she come upstairs and I show her that fifteen dollars. Then I hear rummaging 'round down below in preacher's office, drawers opening, closing."

"Objection, your honor. This entire performance smacks of an eleventh-hour desperation strategy on the part of the defense to drag in a red herring. If there's any truth to this testimony at all, why didn't young LaMott come forward with his information sooner? Why didn't he report what he knew to Mr. Barrows' office?"

"You'll have an opportunity to ask that question in due course, Mr. Moulton. Defense may proceed."

"What did you do when you heard the desk drawers opening, Frenchy?"

"I sneak over and look down stovepipe hole in floor and see somebody there. Round top of head, short gray hair like pig bristle, green shirt and trouser. Fella take some papers out of bottom drawer, read them over quick, and stuff inside shirt. Then go through more drawers, and take something out of top one and put that inside shirt. Then go out of room. Next thing I know, I hear footsteps coming upstairs."

"What did you do when you heard the footsteps coming?"

"I roll under bed! Door to room open, footsteps come in. Then leave, go across hall into girl's room. One, maybe two minutes pass, then come out and go back downstairs and out through back door. I never been so scare in my life, mister man, and that the truth."

"What did you do next, Frenchy?"

"Stay right there under bed till I sure he gone. Then come out, look out window onto street, make sure coast clear."

"Did you see anyone on the street?"

"Didn't seen nobody at all, 'cept old E-li Kin'son, out on him porch 'cross street."

"What was Elijah Kinneson doing on his porch?"

"Couldn't tell for sure. At first, it look like he cutting on crazy old wood chain he always carving."

"Could you describe this wood chain for us?"

"Describe?"

"Could you tell us what it is? What it looks like?"

When Charlie asked Frenchy to describe Elijah's Endless Maze, I could see the thing as clearly in my mind as if it were right there in the courtroom in front of me. Describing it was something else, though.

"Don't look like nothing else I ever see. Big old block of wood he keep up on sawhorse on porch. Made out of trunk of old white pine tree. Maybe three, four feet long. This big 'round."

With his long arms, Frenchy described a circle about three feet in diameter.

"Anyway, old E-li always cutting away at pine log wit' big knife like butcher knife, cutting and carving old log into wood chain wit'out no beginning or no end. Make you old head spin like fair ride to look all them coils, too, Charlie K!"

"So when you looked out the upstairs window of the parsonage Elijah Kinneson was on his porch carving on his endless chain?"

"No. Only look that way. Old E-li, he not sitting on bench, way he do when he carve. He standing up, bending over chain and reaching down inside 'mongst all them coils make you dizzy to see."

"Your honor, I can't see the relevance of this," Sigurd Moulton said. "Assuming that any of this fellow's tale is true to start out with, Elijah Kinneson was minding his own business at his own home. He had nothing to do with whatever young LaMott here did—or, more likely, didn't—see at the parsonage that afternoon."

"Is that an objection, Mr. Moulton?" Judge Allen asked wearily.

"Yes."

"We'll demonstrate the relevance, your honor. Among other things, Elijah Kinneson has already testified he spent that entire afternoon at work in the newspaper office. I'd like to resolve that discrepancy, at the least."

"Your objection is overruled, Mr. Moulton. Proceed with your witness, Mr. Kinneson."

"Thank you, your honor. Frenchy, you were saying that Elijah

Kinneson was reaching into the coils in his endless wooden chain. Did you see him take anything out?"

"No. Look more like he stuff something in, maybe. But can't be sure. He only there short while. Then he come down off porch and walk away up street."

"Which way did Elijah go? Back toward the village? Or out toward the county road and the red iron bridge?"

"Toward red bridge."

"What was he wearing at the time, Frenchy? Do you remember?"

"Green shirt and trouser, just like always."

"Like the man you saw in the parsonage going through the minister's desk?"

"He's leading the witness again, your honor. Besides, half the men at your local furniture mill no doubt wear the same green work clothes. That doesn't prove anything."

"Nobody said it necessarily did," Charlie said. "But I withdraw the question. Now let's get back to the parsonage, Frenchy. You said that after the man in the parsonage left, you stayed under the bed until you were sure he was gone. You said you were never so scared in your life. Why were you so scared?"

"You be scare too, Charlie K, you see what fella take out of top desk drawer after he steal papers."

"What did he take out of the top desk drawer?"

"Preacher's gun!"

"OBJECTION, YOUR HONOR! How could this boy know that? How could he tell what it was he saw, looking down through a dim grate into a dim room that way?"

"I see what I see," Frenchy said angrily. "Was gun. Look just like same gun right over on that table!"

"Your objection is overruled, Mr. Moulton," Judge Allen said.

"Did you ever see the face of the man who took the gun and came upstairs while you hid under the bed?" Charlie said.

"No. Didn't need to, neither. I know pretty well who it be when I look down and see his round old head, like somebody spill salt and pepper all over old cannonball. Then I know for sure when I look out from under bed and see them green trousers and shoes of his, all shiny little bits of lead cooked all over them, and here and there holes in them, most bad as my boots. I see them shoes before, me."

"Whose shoes were they, Frenchy?"

"Your honor, this is the most outrageous, trumped-up—"

*"Mr. Moulton, sit down and close your mouth."*

"Whose shoes were they, Frenchy?"

"They was full of holes as Christly old cheese," Frenchy said excitedly. "I never see pair of shoes like that in all God's Kingdom, 'cept on feets of old E-li Kinneson!"

# 20

"Claude LaMott, where did you spend the bulk of the year 1950?" Sigurd Moulton said.

Frenchy shrugged. "Can't remember."

"You can't remember where you spent nearly a whole year?"

"Can't remember which year I there. I know what you driving at, you. No doubt that when I down the line to Vergennes, right?"

"Yes, that's right. And where at Vergennes did you stay?"

"*Vergennes.* Reform school. They make you get up early, milk cow, go school, do chores again."

"Why were you sent to the reform school, Claude?"

" 'Cause Judge A here and old man Barrows ship me there. Wouldn't go to old Academy, me. That all. No thieving. No looking in window at night at old ladies get undress like crazy Titman White. No nothing 'cept not go school."

"How did you like reform school? Would you like to go again?"

"Wouldn't mind a bit."

"Surely you're jesting?"

"Not doing nothing but telling truth. You work for Hook LaMott and see if you don't want go there, too. Down Vergennes, they pretty damn decent to you, long's you keep you nose clean. Nobody crack you with meathook upside head. Nobody kick you with steel-toe boot."

"So you were sent to the state reformatory for your idyllic year because you refused to attend school locally. When you got back here, did you return to school?"

"Year ago this deer season, yes. Till I turn sixteen this past spring. Then I get out once and for all."

Moulton glanced at his tablet. "You claim to have gone to the parsonage with your mother's key on the afternoon of August sixth for the purpose of soliciting the LaRiviere girl to sleep with you for fifteen dollars. Is that correct?"

"Didn't say nothing about sleeping. You heard what I told Charlie K. Ask her if she want to be my *girlfriend*."

"And you claim she was gone when you arrived?"

"That right."

"This all sounds like very suspicious behavior, Claude LaMott. How do we know that you didn't take the gun out of the desk yourself? Maybe rape her at gunpoint, order her out of the house, and take her up to the quarry and kill her?"

Charlie was on his feet to object; but Frenchy was even quicker. Pointing at Reverend Andrews, he said, "Then what you got that fella there on trial for? You all mixed up, mister."

"Exactly!" Charlie shouted. "Judge Allen, the prosecutors don't seem to know who *is* on trial here today. First they brought charges against Reverend Andrews. Then they tried to implicate Nathan Andrews. Now they're implying that Frenchy LaMott, who hardly even knew the girl, raped and killed her. I respectfully request that you direct Mr. Moulton and his assistant to make up their minds once and for all who the real defendant is here today."

"Withdraw the question, please," Moulton said. "Your honor, at this point I'm going to request a mistrial on the basis of this witness's total incompetence to testify. He's a juvenile delinquent, a low-life illiterate without even an eighth-grade education, and nobody in town will say a good word about him."

"Oh, yes, someone will, Mr. Moulton!"

Two chairs down the row from me, Athena Allen was on her feet.

"Please, Athena, be seated!" the judge cried out.

"Don't you 'please Athena' me. I've got something to say and I intend to say it. Sigurd Moulton, I've listened to your pompous bullying for two days. But now you've gone too far. I'll say a good word for Frenchy LaMott and no one's going to stop me. I've known him since he was five years old. I taught him in the eighth grade for three years. And I never knew him *once* during all that time to tell a lie. *Not once.* There, now I've had my say. Go ahead and have me arrested, Father, if you must. I'll go peaceably."

"Even your most recalcitrant former students would rise up in protest if I did so ungallant a thing, Athena," the judge said. "I will accept your promise not to interrupt these proceedings again. The jury will of course disregard the most recent out—the most recent interjection. Go ahead, Mr. Moulton."

If Sigurd Moulton was nonplussed by Athena's "interjection," he didn't show it. "All right, young LaMott. If you're such an honest and upright young gentleman, why didn't you step forward sooner to tell your story?"

Frenchy snorted. "Who believe me if I do? Frenchy LaMott? Town clown, town bastard, no school, can't read, can't even tell time. Why anybody believe me? Plus I scared."

"What were you scared of? A big rugged fellow like you?"

"Two thing. Scared old Barrows and Mason White try to pin what happened to girl on me. Or that same one that kill girl kill me. Kill one already. Why not two?"

"So what changed your mind? Did someone offer you money to change your mind?"

"I don't know what change my mind. Couple of thing. Mainly my old lady. She talk to me for good long while, and the more I think about it, the more I think I going speak out. Finally today she tell me I don't say something, she going to."

"I'm not in the habit of putting any stock in the fabrications of juvenile delinquents, and I doubt the jury is. I have no further questions for the moment, but we'll visit again, Claude LaMott, I'll assure you. Your honor, I'd like to request that this trial be suspended until Monday in order to give the prosecution adequate time to look deeper into this witness's testimony. These latest theatrics caught the county totally off guard, as I'm sure they were meant to. I need time to prepare for a more extensive cross-examination."

"Your honor," Charlie said, "I have just one more witness to call, and then if Mr. Moulton still insists on a postponement I won't object. In the meantime, I'm going to object to the prosecution's use of the term 'theatrics' to describe my witness's testimony."

"Your objection is well taken, Mr. Kinneson. I don't much care for the word myself. And I have no intention of postponing this trial at this point. For the time being, however, I'm getting hungry, and I imagine the jury is. It's five-thirty. We'll recess for supper and reconvene at seven o'clock sharp."

"I'd like to recall Elijah Kinneson, your honor."

I had never before seen the courtroom occupied at night. The suspended globe lights shone brilliantly on the bird's-eye maple attorneys' tables, on the judge's bench and the polished railing around the jury box; glints of lights played off Forrest Allen's high domed forehead and off Frenchy LaMott's shiny black mop of hair and the bright ring of keys jingling at Elijah's belt as he walked forward. Outside the tall windows, the village lights twinkled in the autumn gloaming; for a few moments the room seemed like a different room in another courthouse in an unfamiliar town.

Partly my disorientation was the result of the nap I'd taken at the *Monitor* during the supper hour. While I slept and Charlie worked feverishly in his office preparing his summary speech my father continued to call anyone and everyone he could think of to try to find out the source of the "private funds" Zack Barrows had used to hire Moulton. But so far as I knew, he had drawn a complete blank.

"Elijah," my brother was saying, "could you please tell the jury what your feelings are concerning the Reverend Walter Andrews?"

"Objection," Moulton said wearily. "Our witness is not on trial."

"Your honor," Charlie said, "I'm more than willing to leave the investigation and legal prosecution of the likeliest suspect in this case to the proper authorities. I simply want to broaden the field of suspects, as Mr. Moulton himself has chosen to do today, however facetiously he did that and for whatever purpose. I intend to establish that someone did in fact have a motive to frame Reverend Andrews. Moreover, I intend to establish that this motive dates back almost to the time of Reverend Andrews' arrival in Kingdom County."

"That's a fine point you're making, Charles Kinneson," Judge Allen said. "But I'm going to permit you to continue your line of questioning, so long as you don't ask this or any other witness to incriminate himself. That rules out inquiring about 'feelings.' "

"Then, I'll be more specific. Isn't it true, Elijah, that you resented the minister from the day he arrived and supplanted you as preacher in the United Church?"

"Nay! I was merely filling in as lay preacher. I was willing to serve in the pulpit in that capacity, and just as willing to step down when a qualified permanent clergyman could be found."

"You must have had quite a bit of extra time on your hands after you 'stepped down,' Elijah. No more sermons to prepare. No other ministering duties. How did you fill it? Do you have any hobbies?"

"Hobbies!" Elijah stared at my brother as though he was crazy. "What do you mean, 'hobbies'?"

"I'm sure you understand what a hobby is, Elijah. You know. Golf, hunting, fishing. Do you have any hobbies at all?"

"None!" Elijah said angrily, as though Charlie had asked him to confess to a shameful secret vice. "Absolutely none. We were placed here in God's Kingdom to work, Charles Kinneson, not play and have 'hobbies.' "

"Well, that's an interesting point of view," Charlie said, and he casually walked around in front of the defense table and dragged out from beneath it an object as large as a big steamer trunk, covered with a brown rug. With a prestidigitator's flourish, my brother whipped off the rug. There before us, looking every bit as outlandish as some arcane reliquary from King Tut's tomb, sat Elijah's gigantic endless wooden chain.

"Do you recognize this object, Elijah?"

"Aye," he said furiously. "It's the Endless Maze of the Kingdom, which I've been carving for these past forty years and more, and before me my grandfather. You have no right to display it here in a vulgar public spectacle, Charles Kinneson!"

"Well, since I obtained a warrant from Judge Allen during the supperhour to go to your house with the sheriff and pick it up and bring it here, I believe I do have that right, Elijah."

Over strenuous objections from Sigurd Moulton and Zack Barrows, Charlie promptly entered the wooden chain as evidence.

"Now, tell us, Elijah. What does this wonderful maze of yours signify?"

"Signify? Why, it signifies all the subtlety in the world, Cousin. The Endless Maze of the Kingdom signifies the confusion we Reformed Presbyterians must guard against at all times. It signifies Old Chaos and Evil."

"Old Chaos and Evil?"

"Aye," Elijah said grimly. "For lo! behold its twists and canny turns and snaky byways. They represent the numberless paths of evil to be avoided only by the one true path of Reformed Presbyterianism."

My brother did a curious thing. Reaching far into the coiling, alive-looking spirals of the convoluted wooden rings, he withdrew two rolled-up yellowing documents and a fat sheaf of plain white papers with typescript on them.

As carefully as if he were handling an ancient scroll, Charlie unrolled one of the yellowing documents and handed it to our cousin. "Do you recognize this, Elijah?"

"You have said so."

"What is it, then?"

"An issue of the *Kingdom County Monitor*, dated August sixth, 1900."

Charlie then asked Elijah to identify the second scroll.

"This is an issue of the *Kingdom County Monitor*, dated August thirteenth, 1900," my cousin said.

They were the issues I'd found in the basement of the shop and brought upstairs for Reverend Andrews on the morning of the church session meeting—the same issues that had turned up missing from the minister's desk and that Frenchy claimed he saw Elijah purloin and stuff into his maze!

"And finally, Elijah, would you please identify these sheets of typescript?"

"They appear to be the notes that the preacher spoke of earlier. The notes he took on Black Pliny's life and times."

"Your honor, I'd like to enter these three documents as evidence," Charlie said, and immediately received permission.

"Elijah, did you remove these documents from the parsonage desk and place them inside your Endless Maze of the Kingdom?" Charlie said.

Silence.

"Mr. Elijah Kinneson, did you understand the question?" the judge said.

Silence.

"Our witness has every right not to answer incriminating questions," Moulton said. "He is not on trial here today."

"Then your witness should decline to answer those questions on the grounds that they might incriminate him," Charlie said. "I'll repeat the question. Did you, Elijah Kinneson, as Frenchy LaMott testified, place these documents inside your Maze of the Kingdom?"

"I decline to answer."

"Your honor, I'd like to read excerpts from these two newspaper articles," Charlie said. "I believe they'll shed some light on the conflict between Elijah Kinneson and Walter Andrews."

"Objection, your honor! Any such imagined conflict is as irrelevant to these proceedings as the contents of a newspaper article fifty years old."

"Not if it resulted in the motivation to frame my client for murder, it isn't!"

Judge Allen frowned. After a moment he said "I see no reason why you shouldn't be permitted to read those documents, Mr. Kinneson. Go ahead."

My brother proceeded to read first the August sixth, 1900, article by our grandfather James Kinneson, describing the suicide of Pliny Templeton in his own study after his falling out with the church and Academy Trustees; then Charlie read the August thirteenth, 1900, article describing Mad Charlie's sudden "brain fever" and removal to the infirmary of the state asylum at Waterbury.

When he finished, my brother placed the two old issues of the *Monitor* on the evidence table.

"Elijah, would you please tell us how you're related to the Charles Kinneson who discovered Pliny's body and who was shortly afterwards stricken with 'brain fever'?"

"He was my father."

"Did he ever recover from this affliction?"

"Nay!" Elijah said angrily. "He spent the last two years of his life chained to his bed in a madhouse with certified howling madmen. How could he possibly recover under such conditions?"

"Was he mad himself?"

"He was not. He was brain-fevered from the shock of Black Pliny's betrayal, the betrayal of a man he had single-handedly raised up from slavery and educated and placed in a position of trust, only to see that man turn on him, his benefactor, and foment a schism in the church, and seduce half the members of the congregation over to the heresy of United Presbyterianism. It is as disgraceful a chapter in our history as any imaginable. It required no further so-called research."

"Did you, Elijah, in order to put a stop to the Reverend Walter Andrews' research on the church schism and Pliny's suicide and your father's brain affliction, enter the parsonage on the afternoon of August sixth and go through the minister's desk in search of papers relating to your father and Pliny Templeton?"

"Inquire of the Black Man."

"By the 'black man' do you mean Walter Andrews?"

"I mean the Black Man who has navigated over these hardwoods and softwoods both by day and by night since they were first settled, and for many a long century before that, since his fiery expulsion from the Realm of Glory."

"Do you mean the devil?"

"Some call him by that name. Call him what you will. I mean mankind's one great implacable enemy. Inquire of him, Charles Kinneson!"

"Elijah, did you enter the United Church parsonage on the late afternoon of August sixth and go through the minister's desk and remove the articles I've just read, along with the minister's notes, and secret them in your Endless Maze?"

Moulton was on his feet. "Your honor, what proof does the defense have to support this wild conjecture—apart from the highly unreliable testimony of a juvenile delinquent? Anyone could have planted those documents in the maze."

"Yes," Charlie roared. "And anyone could have come into the parsonage and stolen the minister's gun and gone out the county road to the red iron bridge and up into the gore to the quarry and shot Claire LaRiviere. Right, Elijah?"

In the shocked silence that ensued, Charlie took three quick strides toward the witness stand. "Did you, Elijah Kinneson, on the late afternoon of August sixth, steal the minister's revolver from his desk, follow Claire LaRiviere to the quarry, and murder her there? Did you mutilate her body and throw it onto the ledge on the back side of the quarry, where you expected it to be discovered or planned to discover it yourself? Did you then throw the murder weapon into the water where it was bound to be found?"

On the witness stand, Elijah Kinneson was silent.

*"Did you murder Claire LaRiviere with the minister's service revolver on the afternoon of August sixth at the granite quarry in Kingdom Gore?"*

"Our witness is not on trial here!" Moulton said, raising his voice for the first time.

"Well, he damn well should be, and I'll see to it that eventually he is!" Charlie shouted. "Elijah Kinneson, I'd like to ask you to remove one of your shoes and place it on the witness stand."

"I object, your honor!"

"Sustained. That's going too far, Charles."

"No more questions, your honor."

But when Elijah walked down from the stand past the jury, though he walked very fast, every pair of eyes was fixed on his work shoes, which were covered with shiny little scallops of lead and pocked like Swiss cheese from the hot lead that had spattered on them from his linotype.

It did not seem like enough for a defense to be built on. A pair of pockmarked shoes. A delinquent's testimony and a zealot's raving. An old family skeleton, literally and figuratively, the baffling story of Pliny Templeton and my mad great-grandfather, who spent his last years in the lunatic asylum raving at a dead man over the use of a piano in his school—a story which, for some unknown reason, Elijah Kinneson did not want told. Yet that my old cousin would go so far as to murder an innocent girl for the purpose of framing an innocent man was nearly impossible for me to imagine. The facts remained that Claire LaRiviere had been killed with Walter Andrews' revolver, and at the time she had been pregnant, very probably with Nat's child.

What Charlie could make out of it all in his summary, and what the jury would make out of it, I had no idea.

Sigurd Moulton made the closing statement for the prosecution, and it was brief and bitter. He began by citing a number of serious breaches of standard courtroom procedure. He characterized the day's events as bush league, and stated that regardless of Elijah Kinneson's final testimony, and his silence, which he was guaranteed the right to maintain by the Constitution, there were still far more unanswered questions about Reverend Andrews than about Elijah, beginning with where the minister was at the exact time of the murder—on his way home from Montreal or already in Kingdom County.

Sigurd Moulton pointed out that the defense's chief witness was a juvenile delinquent who made Huckleberry Finn look like a model boy. Despite Elijah's theological differences with Reverend Andrews, Moulton said, the sexton had no reason to kill the girl or frame the minister over a piece of long-forgotten history and there was not a shred of real evidence that he had done so. Moulton emphasized that both the minister and Nat had plausible reasons for wanting Claire out of the way, but the minister had more reasons, whether the jury believed Nat's story that he was with the girl on the parsonage couch or not, and Nat had almost certainly been in Montreal at the time of the murder.

Moulton admitted that the case was more complicated than even he had realized at first. But he asked the jury to make the clearest distinction in their minds between complications introduced by my brother to cloud the issue, and the legitimate complications of any murder case. By far the likeliest chain of events, he said, involved Nat sleeping with Claire early on in their acquaintanceship and getting her pregnant; Claire informing Reverend Andrews that she was pregnant on the very early morning of August 6; and Reverend Andrews deducing that Nat was the child's father and killing Claire on the early evening of that day, after returning from Montreal, to protect his son's reputation and his own.

"Rely on the facts," Moulton advised the jury. "Don't be misled by extraneous complications. Fact number one: the murder weapon was the minister's gun, which he had already used against a local citizen just two nights before the murder. Fact number two: Nathan Andrews has admitted that he repeatedly slept with the girl, who was found to be pregnant. Fact number three: the chief witness for the defense is a village outcast with a reform school record. Fact number four: the minister was overheard by a prominent local citizen and churchman making arrangements to help the girl take care of her pregnancy, and so was clearly aware of her condition. Fact number five: the minister has a history of protecting his son, which is good and admirable and natural, too, until it results in violence and murder. Fact number six: by his own admission, the defendant arrived home from Montreal on August 6 at nine o'clock and didn't notify the police of Claire LaRiviere's absence until ten—leaving a full unaccounted hour during which he had plenty of time to take her to or meet her at the quarry and kill her.

"Reaching the proper conclusion this evening, ladies and gentlemen, now requires only common sense. Common sense, as the defense attorney himself has pointed out, is a quality we Vermonters—and we are all Vermonters, whether we live in Kingdom County or Montpelier or Brattleboro or White River Junction—have valued and prized for generations. Exercise that common sense for which we are so justly famous and you can come to only one conclusion, despite the defense's extremely clever attempts to cloud the fundamental issues by dragging in irrelevant information and incompetent witnesses. Mere cleverness must not win the laurels tonight. The victory tonight, if victory there can be in the most gruesome murder case I have ever seen in this state, must result from common sense and a dedication on your part to preserve the law of this land, and particularly that most supreme law that forbids the taking of a human life. I don't envy you your task. But Mr. Barrows and I urge you to do your duty, however unpleasant you find it. We have every confidence that you will discharge it responsibly and correctly."

Charlie's summary speech was entirely different from what I had expected. I had expected a thunderous oration. There was none. My brother made relatively little reference to the ubiquitous lined yellow legal pads, which he, like Zack Barrows and Sigurd Moulton, had filled with notes during the past two days. He spoke instead extemporaneously in a down-to-earth, natural way, as though visiting with two or three of the jury members on the street in front of the brick shopping block or in the post office.

Charlie began by saying that several months ago a minister, a stranger from another country, had come to Kingdom County with his son to live and to work. He said that to the credit of this stranger and of our community, he had been well-received. He pointed out that

Reverend Andrews had made considerable efforts on behalf of the church and the congregation. He mentioned Reverend Andrews' taking over the Academy baseball team, and reminded the jury how genuinely interested the Canadian minister had been in our community, its people and history, and how eager he had been to make himself and his son a part of it from the start. By incorporating himself into the community rather than imposing himself and his ideas on it, Charlie said, Reverend Andrews had quickly established himself as a leading citizen.

Speaking quietly but with feeling, Charlie conceded that Reverend Andrews had also earned a few enemies, to whom, for the worst possible reasons, he and all Negroes would always remain strangers. My brother cited the episode with Bumper Stevens at the cockfight back in late May and the shooting at the parsonage and the subsequent investigation of Reverend Andrews rather than Resolvèd Kinneson. Finally, he cited the murder charges, which he said were based on the flimsiest circumstantial evidence.

"In his summary speech," Charlie said, "the hired prosecutor asked you to rely on facts. That's a spectacularly ironical request on his part because over the course of this trial he's presented so few of them. Nonetheless, I'm going to echo his sentiments here, because the only way you folks on the jury can come to a fair decision is by sticking close to the facts that we do have available.

"The first fact I'd like to remind you of is that in this country, everyone, stranger and native alike, is equal before the law. And in this country, everyone is presumed innocent until proven guilty beyond a reasonable doubt. What constitutes a reasonable doubt? I'm sure Judge Allen will explain that to you in his final instructions far better than I could. I want to remind you only that you must base your decision concerning Walter Andrews' innocence or guilt on facts, not suppositions. And the facts all lead to the same conclusion—that this case is rife with reasonable doubts about the identity of the killer, who by the prosecutor's own arguments today could conceivably be any one of several persons.

"To make my summary as simple as possible, I'm going to focus primarily on the facts as they transpired on just three days this past summer, August fourth, fifth, and sixth. I want to ask you to review, first with me now and then later in the privacy of your deliberations, not whatever guesses and surmises and conjectures we may share about those days, and the weeks and months that preceded them, but what we know for a fact to have taken place during that seventy-two-hour interval.

"August fourth dawned raining. That was a huge disappointment for nearly the entire Kingdom. But under Reverend Andrews' sterling leadership, the sesquicentennial celebration went forward with great success despite the rain.

"As you know, however, there was an ugly incident afterwards at the parsonage, in which Resolvèd Kinneson saw Claire LaRiviere and Nathan Andrews together on the study couch, mistook Nat for his father, went home and got his shotgun, and fired two blasts of lethal buckshot through the minister's window.

"The prosecution has tried to make something, I'm not quite sure what, out of the fact that Reverend Andrews fired back in self-defense. But he fired only to protect his home, which I believe every man and woman in this room would have done.

"That brings us to August fifth, when, after a lengthy private conversation with Resolvèd Kinneson, Zack Barrows elected to charge him not with assault with a deadly weapon—but with *disturbing the peace*.

"August fifth. What else do we know for a fact about August fifth? Well, we know from the testimony of both Reverend Andrews and Elijah Kinneson that in the very late hours of August fifth, or more probably the very early hours of August sixth, Claire LaRiviere went to Reverend Andrews and informed him that she was pregnant. We have no evidence, no facts, to suggest that either then or later did she or Nat Andrews indicate to him that she believed herself to be pregnant with Nat's child. Indeed, given the hand-to-mouth existence Claire LaRiviere had led in Canada and both while traveling to Kingdom County and during her first days here at Resolvèd Kinneson's, combined with the fact that she had been staying at the parsonage for only about five weeks, it can be very logically argued that Reverend Andrews had no reason to suspect that Nat, of all the possible candidates, was the baby's father. And I submit to you that without that suspicion, Reverend Andrews would have had no conceivable motive for doing what he is accused of doing here today.

"Fine. We know for a fact, from both Reverend Andrews' testimony and from Elijah Kinneson's, that during that conversation on the parsonage porch in the very early morning hours of August sixth the minister recommended to Claire that she go to the Mary Margaret Simmons Home for Unwed Mothers in Burlington, which he might or might not logically have done if he had known Nat was the father of the baby, but never, certainly, if he intended to murder her. We know furthermore that he even went to the trouble of calling the Simmons Home.

"Let's move along to the daylight hours of August sixth. Elijah Kinneson was a busy man that day. He had to change the locks on the parsonage and get back to the newspaper office where he worked by noon. Sticking just to the facts, we know that Elijah Kinneson has testified that he never left that newspaper office from noon until well into the evening. Yet Frenchy LaMott has testified that on the afternoon of August sixth he went to the parsonage and saw a man with short gray hair and green work clothes and shoes with holes in their tops go through the minister's desk and remove some papers and a revolver.

"Whether Frenchy LaMott actually saw this you must judge for yourselves. But I suggest that in making this judgment, you ask yourselves what conceivable motivation Frenchy could have for coming forward, at his own risk, and lying about what he saw. Keep in mind Frenchy LaMott's and his mother's reputation in this community for truthfulness when you make this judgment.

"What further facts can we be sure of? Well, that at ten o'clock on the evening of August sixth, after returning from Montreal, Reverend Andrews called the police to report that Claire LaRiviere was missing, which I, for one, can't imagine his doing if he were in any way implicated in her disappearance; and that late in the afternoon of August eighth, a minor and the so-called Dog Cart Man discovered Claire LaRiviere's dreadfully mutilated body in the granite quarry in the Kingdom gore, lying on a ledge just above the water approximately fifteen feet below the edge of the quarry, as though someone had thrown her down there after dark—supposedly assuming the body would sink out of sight in the water. Now I ask you, ladies and gentlemen, in the name of the common sense invoked by the Montpelier prosecutor, is it remotely believable to you that, not hearing the splash of that body striking the water, a murderer who wished to conceal the body would just go away and leave it exposed to plain sight there? Or, for that matter, toss the murder weapon after it into the water, where it would be bound to be found? Hardly!

"Now let's return to Elijah Kinneson. It is a fact that his name, more than any other except that of the Reverend Walter Andrews, persistently comes up in connection with this entire affair. We know that Elijah Kinneson was a most determined adversary of Reverend Andrews. We know that Elijah Kinneson, for whatever private reasons he may have had, above all else did not want the minister investigating the death of Pliny Templeton or the sad conclusion of the life of his father, 'Mad Charlie' Kinneson, in the state lunatic asylum. And we know that Elijah Kinneson, and this is a *fact, refused to answer yes or no when I asked him here in this courtroom whether he murdered Claire LaRiviere and framed Reverend Andrews!"*

"That's more than enough, Charles," Judge Allen said angrily. "I warned you about incriminating anyone else in any of your remarks. The jury will disregard Mr. Kinneson's last statement regarding Elijah Kinneson's refusal to answer that question!"

Charlie cleared his throat. His voice was raspy from talking all day. He looked carefully at each jury member—the same people he had seen on the street most of his life.

"When I asked Elijah Kinneson why he resented Reverend Walter Andrews, he had no real answer for me. The reason, of course, is that there is no answer to that question. That particular kind of hatred has no rhyme or reason. The most unfortunate and dangerous thing about any kind of human intolerance is that you'll find it wherever there are humans, because, ladies and gentlemen, it's potentially as much a part of the human heart, including yours and mine, as its opposite, tolerance, and we all have to guard against it every single day of our lives, whether we live in deepest Africa or up here in what we're pleased to call God's Kingdom.

"Of course we know that this isn't a perfect place. But as a close relative of mine likes to say, it's an eminently improvable place, and the fact that it can be improved and that we're in a position to do that may yet be its greatest strength and ours. Now I'm nearly finished."

Charlie turned back to the defense table. He took a long drink of water, emptying the entire glass. With his profile to the courtroom, he pointed a long arm at the jury, looking for all the world now like a preacher himself. I could feel my father go tense beside me, no doubt waiting for the torrent to come, for Charlie to roar like an evangelist about the girl whose blood had drenched our town and the innocent man who had been crucified for her death. I know Charlie was tempted to do just that because he told us so afterwards. But when he spoke again he didn't say anything about murder or martyrdom or racism. Instead, he dropped his arm, shook his head sadly, and as much to himself as anyone else said:

"Folks, you're left with a hard decision. Who do you believe? A pillar of the church or a young man who by his own admission is an outcast—an outcast with a reputation for always telling the truth? I remind you of the courage it required for Frenchy LaMott to come forward. I remind you of all the facts that we've reviewed together. I remind you too that by finding Reverend Andrews innocent, you're in no way pre-judging any other individual, only affirming that you have been unable, beyond a reasonable doubt, to find him guilty because in fact, as Sigurd Moulton himself said, we have drastically broadened the field of candidates during these past two days. That is what all this now comes down to, ladies and gentlemen. Reasonable doubt. If in your minds there is a reasonable doubt that Reverend Andrews murdered Claire LaRiviere, my client must go free.

"An innocent verdict won't atone to this good man for what we've done to him. It won't expiate us or our town from the guilt we all have to share, the guilt of knowing we stood by and allowed this to happen, if nothing else. But it will be a small redressing of some of the injustice that's taken place. I'm not as religious as many people. No doubt I'm not the best one to say this. But I hope the Lord can forgive us for what we have done here in this town this summer, because I don't see how on earth any mere human being could be expected to."

As my brother sat down, my father wrote something in the ensuing silence. I looked at his notebook, and my eyes filled with tears to see scrawled there the single word:

"AMEN."

"So what, precisely, constitutes a reasonable doubt?" Judge Allen was saying. "The best way I can put it, ladies and gentlemen, is that if your collective common sense tells you that for whatever reason or reasons you can't be sure who killed Claire LaRiviere, then you must find the defendant not guilty. Now understand that if you come to that conclusion, you aren't in any way incriminating anyone else. If you can't be sure the defendant is guilty, that doesn't mean that you're pointing your finger at another person and saying you think he or she did it.

"If, on the other hand, after considering all of the evidence, including admitted circumstantial evidence, common sense tells you that the defendant very probably committed this crime, then you must find him guilty. And as I've said, the fact that he's a Negro or the fact that he is a good father or the fact that he's a good minister mustn't enter into your decision at all. In other words, you can't be swayed by sympathy, any more than you can be swayed by prejudice. That's what the blindfold on the figure of justice means.

"Now, it's getting late, and you people must be getting tired. I'll tell you what I'm going to do. I want you to begin your deliberations now, while everything you've heard over the past two days is still fresh in your mind. If you don't come to a clear decision tonight, you can sleep on it. As soon as you do go into deliberation, I'm going to send Mr. Blake to the hotel and have him bring you back some hot food and coffee, and I'm going to have him reserve rooms there for you. When and if you get tired, just let him know, and I'll recess court until tomorrow morning. Above all, I want you to take all the time you need because this is an extremely important decision, not just for this defendant, but for the town as well. Like it or not, the eyes of the county are on us tonight; but once you begin deliberating I want you to forget that, too, to forget the reporters and the tape recorders and the newsreel cameras outside the courtroom and, as both Attorney Kinneson and Attorney Moulton said, just pay attention to the facts of this case.

"I'm going to say one more thing; then I'll pipe down and you folks can take over. I want to say that despite everything that's happened here in this county this summer, I have faith in two things. First, I have faith in our legal system, however unwieldy it may seem at times. And just as important, I have faith in you twelve folks and in your ability to sort out everything that you've heard over the past two days and to bring back the right and just verdict. That's why I never for a single minute considered transferring this trial out of Kingdom County. Discuss the case until you come to a decision or get tired; then let me know. Take your time. A year from now, nobody's going to remember whether you reached your decision tonight or tomorrow or the next day. All they'll remember is that decision itself. Good luck, ladies and gentlemen—good luck!"

"They're going to need it, editor," Plug Johnson said a minute later as we jostled our way out of the courtroom. "That luck the judge wished them. I wouldn't want to be in their shoes tonight, no sir. Jim here, though, he's probably come to a decision already. What is it,

Jim, heh? Guilty or innocent? Use your common sense now, boy, like the old judge said. Don't be swayed by sympathy or nothing else."

"They won't come back with a verdict tonight. I'm positive of it," Farlow Blake half-whispered to us as he headed down the stairs on his way to the hotel for provisions. "Don't breathe a word of this to anyone, boys, but on his way into the jury room I heard Yves St. Pierre say they should have brought their nightcaps."

Instead of going over to the shop, Mom and Dad and Athena and I went upstairs to Charlie's office. (There were only two chairs in Charlie's office, so Mom and Athena sat down, I perched on the edge of Charlie's desk, and Dad stood by the window looking out over the dark common below.) And there we were, waiting again, right in the same room where all of this had first begun last spring, on my thirteenth birthday, when I had come back from Burlington to find Charlie just finishing Resolvèd's letter to *Young Love, True Love*.

Charlie appeared a few minutes later with Nat, looking tired and tense. He squeezed Nat's shoulder. "Thanks, buddy. Thanks for coming back and for testifying. It had to help."

"So what will they decide?" Nat said.

My brother shook his head. "I'd like to say they'll be back in ten minutes with an innocent verdict, Nat. But you never, never know. It's almost impossible to predict. One thing I'm pretty sure of, though. The longer they take to make their decision, the better our chances are. That means that at least somebody in that deliberation room, probably more than one somebody, is seeing something our way.

"Where's Elijah, by the way?" Charlie asked.

"The last I saw of him, he was still downstairs in the courtroom," Athena said. "I'm surprised that somebody isn't keeping a closer eye on him."

"Why should you be surprised? He hasn't been charged with anything yet."

"It's going to snow pretty soon," Athena said, winking at me. "There'll be some big snowbanks, right, Jim?"

"Right!" I said; but my heart wasn't in it.

"I loved it when you got up and delivered your unsolicited testimonial for old Frenchy," Charlie said.

"My father didn't," Athena said. "You can bet that the minute this trial is over, he'll be on his way up to the big lake for a week or two."

"Duck hunting's coming, and that's a fact," Charlie said. "I'd like to go with him. But I doubt he'll invite me. He was pretty mad over that hundred-dollar mistake I made."

"I'm going over to the shop," Dad said. "James, keep an eye peeled for Farlow Blake. If it looks as though the jury's going to come back in with the verdict tonight, which I very much doubt, come right over to get me."

Nat and I went back downstairs and peered into the courtroom only to find Elijah carving away on his chain, intent as old Dr. Manette at his cobbler's bench in *A Tale of Two Cities*. It made my flesh creep to watch him. Even then I did not believe that the old sexton was capable of murder; but if ever pure evil seemed compressed into a single form or being, it seemed compressed into Elijah Kinneson and that dizzying chain, as he carved on and on under the courtroom lights, oblivious to everything around him, with the thin curly shavings flaking off and accumulating around his pitted shoes.

We wandered back out to the second-floor landing, where Farlow Blake had buttonholed me last spring to tell me about the Most Peculiar lawyer. Nat went downstairs to the jail to wait with his father, and I drifted aimlessly here and there, from the second-floor landing to the first floor of the courthouse, back up to Charlie's office, down onto the street. The straw Harvest Figures around the common looked spooky in the dim streetlamps, and wherever people were gathered I heard bits and snatches of opinions about the outcome of the trial; but the only opinion that counted that night was the opinion of the twelve men and women sequestered in the jury room of the Kingdom County Courthouse.

Farlow popped outside two or three times, looking solemn; but he wouldn't say a word. Charlie came back downstairs to sit with the minister and Nat in the jail cell. In the adjacent cell, an uncharacteristically morose Resolvèd was working on a bottle of Old Duke someone had passed in to him through the bars of the tiny basement window. On the sidewalk in front of the courthouse, Welcome shared glimpses of the full October moon through my great-great-great-grandfather's telescope.

Plug Johnson nudged me with his elbow. "Can you see them green fellas up on Mars with that spy glass, Welcome?"

"Aye, and more besides," Welcome said, "for with this wondrous device, a man may peer deep into the far reaches of creation and view the comings and goings of many a distant civilization. In fact, I was just about to take it up into the church steeple with me, to get a closer look at Old Mother Moon. You come, too, Jimmy.

"You like local history, don't you?" Welcome asked me as we toiled up the steep winding steps of the church steeple. "Do you know that, except for Sundays and funerals and weddings, this bell's been rung just two times in the past hundred and fifty years? Both times in 1918. Once when the Red Stockings won the World Series and then again a month later on Armistice Day.

"Now here's my idea, Jimmy. I shall ring this bell myself, tonight, when the reverend's innocent verdict comes in, as I have no doubt it will. And it's very possible we'll have others on hand to celebrate along with us."

Welcome pointed significantly up at the sky.

Step by step, one hundred and twelve steps in all, my cousin and I labored up into the four diminishing coffins of the United Church's steeple to the little rope-pull belfry overlooking the town and the lighted courthouse. There Welcome spoke to me earnestly for a short time, making me repeat my instructions twice, to make sure I had them right.

I left my cousin humming a tuneless little song and gazing from time to time at Mother Moon through his telescope, and hurried back down to the common. On the courthouse steps, I met Frenchy LaMott.

"Well, Kinneson, what you think? They going to send me back down to Vergennes, or what?"

"Hell, no, Frenchy. Nobody's going to send *you* anywhere."

"They never frigging believe me, though. Old Andrews going to get the chair, Kinneson. Him or his boy. I never should have come out of Christly woodwork."

"Tell me something, Frenchy," I said in a low, confidential voice. "Why *did* you come out of the woodwork? I mean, really? Was it because Nat saved your life, or did your mom make you, or what?"

Frenchy laughed. " 'Member that time I tell you 'bout, when old E-li hire me dig up them coffin over at graveyard? That mother and baby, hair all turn to dust when he open it? Well, he say he pay me two dollar, but old bastard never gave me a frigging cent. 'Member I tell you I do for him some day? Like old Bumper always say, it a goddamn long road that don't have no bend. That why I tes'fy. Fix E-li good, me!"

Frenchy let fly a great jet of tobacco juice. "Every word I say in there true, too. I don't give a frig you believe me or not."

With that, he slunk off toward the common, satisfied that, at last, he had "done for" Elijah Kinneson for welching on the two dollars that day in the cemetery more than a year ago!

On the common, kids raced here and there setting off lady fingers left over from the Old Home Day celebration, but no one seemed to care. Normal order did not quite pertain tonight. I wandered over to the hotel, where Mason and Zack and Sigurd Moulton were eating a late supper. When I went by their table, Zack handed me a small campaign button that said, BARROWS AND WHITE IN '52. The sheriff reached out and slapped me on the back, glad-handing it as though the jury's verdict had already come in in their favor and he'd just been reelected by a landslide.

Disgusted, I drifted outside again.

Just as I started back across the common toward the courthouse, I noticed a commotion on the knoll on the east side of town. A crowd was milling around in the street in front of the empty parsonage and talking excitedly.

As I approached, I spotted something unusual on the porch. At first it looked like a man, standing on the railing and clinging to the thick bittersweet vines, dimly illuminated by the porch light.

"Jesus Christ," I said aloud.

Hanging in the tangled bittersweet vines running from the porch rail to the roof, by a stout noose around its neck, was a body.

No, not a body. A Harvest Figure. But this Harvest Figure was unlike any I had ever seen before. This Harvest Figure was a pumpkin-headed straw effigy of a caricatured black man in a dark suit and a white clerical collar. His face had been crudely outlined in black paint or shoe polish, with grossly distorted lips and a huge nose, and the effigy was grinning hideously.

And that is when someone up the street shouted that the jury had come to a decision, and the crowd around the porch broke and surged toward the courthouse. I ran with them, but as I raced along, I could still see that terrible Harvest Figure before me and the placard pinned to its suit below its white collar.

In huge capital letters it had said, THE WAGES OF SIN.

■ ■ ■

Now there was a great press and bustle inside the courtroom, and Dad had to kick four downcountry reporters out of our seats. But I remembered my cousin Welcome's instructions and slipped back down the aisle to the side of the room by the light switch under Farlow's sign, DO NOT TOUCH WITHOUT PERMISSION UPON PAIN OF A COOL ONE-HUNDRED-DOLLAR FINE.

I could feel my heart going faster as the attorneys came in. Sporting his election button, Zack Barrows was smiling and shaking hands with everyone near him. Reverend Andrews came in between Pine Benson and another deputy and sat down at the defense table. Across the common, high in the belfry tower, I thought I saw a reflected glimmer off Welcome's telescope.

The jury appeared and a sigh like a long retreating wave went through the room.

"All rise," Farlow said as Judge Allen entered the room.

"Mr. foreman, have you reached a verdict?" Judge Allen asked.

Yves St. Pierre stood up. In his hand was a folded piece of paper. "Yes, your honor."

"Will you please hand your verdict to the court bailiff."

Farlow took the piece of paper from Yves St. Pierre and walked to the bench and handed it to Judge Allen, who read it carefully, looked up at the jury, read it again, then said, "Mr. Blake, please carry this verdict to the court clerk, to be read aloud."

I inched my hand toward the light switch.

"Reverend Andrews, will you please stand while the verdict is read," Judge Allen said.

Julia Hefner took the verdict from Farlow and stood up. In her hand, the paper shook slightly. She cleared her throat.

"The jury finds the defendant, Walter"—here her voice gave out momentarily, and she cleared her throat again. "The jury finds the defendant, Walter Andrews, not guilty of the charge of murder in the first degree."

In the joyous shock of that moment, I momentarily forgot what I was supposed to do!

At the defense table Reverend Andrews turned and shook hands with my brother and stood up and turned around to hug his son.

And across the aisle, from his seat behind the prosecutor's table, Elijah Kinneson sprang to his feet, with his long gleaming carving knife held high over his head in both hands.

"The wages of sin is death!" he shrieked.

*Bang!* Down came Judge Allen's gavel. "Sheriff White, secure that man immediately and remove him from the courtroom!"

The judge was too late. Fast as a striking snake, the knife held high above his head in both his hands, my mad cousin leapt across the aisle toward the minister. He moved so quickly that I saw only the blurred motion of his hurtling body and the dull metallic flash of his carving knife. The knife disappeared into the minister's side, appeared again bright red now, and vanished into Elijah's own throat. A jet of blood flew out over the first rows of spectators as Charlie and Mason White wrestled the madman to the floor. Reverend Andrews slumped forward onto the defense table. Dr. Harrison was bending over him, Judge Allen was pounding for order, and then, as though to block out the horrible scene Welcome's instructions came back to me:

*One by land*
*Two by sea*
*Three means Reverend A is free.*

Without thinking what I was doing, I reached for the lights and flicked them off and back on once, twice, three times. Later people would tell me that they had no recollection of this. But not two seconds afterwards a long glad peal rang out over the town from the steeple, followed by another and another and another, peal upon clangorous peal, while below in the courtroom, pandemonium reigned.

It has always seemed to me incongruously appropriate, an irony of the kind that Reverend Andrews himself would enjoy, that it was Mason White, in his patrol car–hearse, who rushed the bleeding minister across the common to Dr. Harrison's office, actually driving straight through the baseball diamond from the first base side toward left field, while Cousin Welcome, still ensconced in the belfry, continued furiously to toll out the happy tidings on the great Revere bell.

"Get that maniac out of the steeple!" I recall my father roaring to Pine Benson—though later Welcome said that when he saw the raging crowd on the common he thought it was a torchlight victory procession or a welcoming party to greet the arriving Martians, and rang the bell all the harder.

The crowd shifted in a quick erratic surge from the courthouse to the common to the brick shopping block, now lighted from the *Monitor* all the way up to Quinn's Drugstore at the north end of the block and packed with horrified spectators, some sobbing, some still and waxen in the eery light, waiting for word of Reverend Andrews from Dr. Harrison's office.

My mother and father and Athena and Judge Allen and I waited in stunned silence in the *Monitor*, and it was Charlie, his suit spattered with blood, who jostled his way down Painless Doc's steps, up which he and my father and Judge Allen and Mason White had rushed the minister on a stretcher half an hour ago, and into the shop with the good news.

"He's going to be all right!" he said. "Thank God, he's going to be all right. The knife went between two ribs and just missed a lung. He's awake and Nat's with him."

Suddenly a great cheer went up from the crowd outside the shop; apparently the news about Reverend Andrews had just reached them. But I was still too stunned by all of the events of the past two days and the past summer to do anything but stare at the rest of my rejoicing family.

"Charlie," I started to say. "Charlie—"

The room began to spin slowly. The shop floor tipped, the great Whitlock printing press and Elijah's massive linotype loomed over me. Then I collapsed onto the deacon's bench by the door, and everything went black.

"James. James!"

Far away yet quite distinctly, I heard Claire LaRiviere calling my name. I was back at the quarry, trying to locate her in the thick summer mist, and she was calling to me from deep in the opaque green water; but when I opened my eyes, Mom and Charlie were anxiously bending over me.

Then I was sitting up and crying, and Mom was hugging me and she and Charlie were both assuring me that the minister was going to be fine, just fine—not knowing, having no way to know, that I was not crying for Reverend Andrews, but for Claire LaRiviere, whose voice, except in dreams, we would never hear again.

▪ ▪ ▪

"Doc says he's got the constitution of a prize fighter," Dad said an hour or so later as he hung up the phone and sat down at the kitchen table.

He and Mom and Charlie and Judge Allen and Athena were working on their second potful of coffee and a fresh batch of sandwiches, and I was perched on the woodbox, finishing my third Coke. Nat had ridden up to the Memphremagog hospital in the ambulance with his dad, and Doc Harrison had just called to say that Reverend Andrews was resting comfortably.

"I doubt he'll be going too many rounds for the next few days, Jimmy," Charlie said, winking at me.

"Don't bet on it, James," Dad said. "If I've ever met a guy who enjoyed a good battle, it's that fella. Just before they loaded him into the ambulance tonight, he told me he might have missed his calling, that sitting through the trial made him regret that he hadn't taken up the law. He said the *action* appealed to him."

"You'd think by now he'd have had enough action to last a lifetime," Judge Allen said dryly.

The judge put his hand on Charlie's shoulder. "But I want you folks to know that whether Walt Andrews missed his calling or not, this young man didn't. That was a first-rate defense, Charles. A first-rate defense."

It was Judge Allen's highest accolade, and we all knew it.

The judge turned to his daughter. "And you, my dear, although this is strictly off the record, your eloquent testimonial for Frenchy LaMott came at exactly the right time."

"What about Cousin Elijah?" I said. "Is he—did he—?"

"Let's put it this way, buddy," Charlie said, "Cousin Elijah's navigating days are over, thank heavens. The guy turned out to be totally insane, didn't he? Like father, like son, I guess. In the end, he was the most prejudiced one of all.

"Uncle Forrest," Charlie said, "let me ask you something now that the trial's over. Didn't you know from the start that there was a good deal of prejudice involved in this case? How could you not see it?"

"I did see it," Judge Allen said. "Some of it anyway. But I honestly didn't think it was relevant to the murder charges."

"So you thought that Reverend Andrews was guilty?"

"It was never my job to determine whether Reverend Andrews was innocent or guilty. That's the jury's job. I just couldn't believe that we couldn't find twelve impartial people here in the Kingdom to get to the bottom of things. As bad as the whole Affair's made the Kingdom look, we would have looked a hell of a lot worse if we'd let somebody else clean up our mess for us. Besides, I had faith in Yves St. Pierre to do a good, fair job as foreman of the jury. I've known Yves since he was Jimmy's age, and I knew he'd keep those folks from getting off the track. As for conjecturing ahead of time about Reverend Andrews' guilt or innocence, I try never to think along those lines during a trial. A judge has to keep his mind open as long as possible. I'm sure you understand that, son. When you get to be a judge, you'll understand it even better."

Judge Allen looked at my father. "The fickleness of a small town, eh? A day or two ago people were crying for the man's blood, most of them. Tonight they're celebrating his acquittal."

He shook his head sadly. "I think I'll be going up to the big lake for a few days, Charles. I shall leave at dawn, as a matter of fact. I want to catch a few more fish before the season's over. Any chance I can persuade you to come along?"

"It's tempting, Forrest. But I've got a paper to get out here. The story isn't over yet, by a long shot. For one thing, I intend to find out just exactly what it was about Pliny Templeton that Elijah wanted to prevent Walt Andrews from unearthing enough to try to kill him right there in the courtroom. I've never seen anything like that stabbing in all my born days. It makes Satan Smithfield's shooting look like a day at the county fair. Then too, I have to ferret out who kicked into that 'private fund' Zack Barrows said paid Sigurd Moulton's retainer."

"You still think Zack had help raising that money?" Charlie said.

"I wouldn't be at all surprised. Moulton's services can't come cheap. And don't forget the silent conspiracy. Elijah killed the girl and framed Reverend Andrews, and Zack and Mason jumped at the chance to prosecute him and win a big case. But I don't think any of it could have happened without a tacit agreement on the part of a very substantial number of local citizens not to come to Walt's defense. Very probably, some of those same citizens helped underwrite Moulton's fee."

Judge Allen nodded in agreement. "Well, Charles, I'll save a few fish in the lake for you."

He stood up, bent over and kissed the top of Athena's head. Then he started for the door, a big, courtly man as solid-looking as the granite courthouse he presided over.

Suddenly he turned back and pointed at Charlie like a man swinging his shotgun up to a flock of incoming ducks. "Speaking of saving . . .

you, young man, had better start saving your pennies. You owe the court ninety dollars and something. Don't forget it."

Then he paused. "Pay for it out of your first prosecutor's check," he said as he went through the door.

"Don't tell me your brother's running," my father said to me, just as I started up the stairs for bed.

Charlie shrugged. "As your father said, Jimmy, there still seem to be a number of unanswered questions about this whole affair. I haven't quite decided whether I'm going to run or not, but I'm sure as hell going to get to the bottom of all this one way or another."

"So am I, mister," Dad said. "I'll tell you something, though. There will probably always be some unanswered questions about this situation. Nonetheless, James, I'm glad about your brother's decision. Your mother's glad, too. His lack of direction over the past year or so has been killing her."

I nodded, but as I climbed the stairs, all I wanted was to be on the Montreal Express, barrelling out of Kingdom County and on my way to a life that *I* could control—where the people I loved didn't die violent deaths and all things were fair.

# 21

Election Day, 1952.

Shortly after midnight, my father had driven over to Dixville, New Hampshire, across the upper Connecticut River from Vermont and Kingdom County, to be on hand for the nation's traditional first presidential returns. In that Republican stronghold, the results were predictable: Eisenhower 22; Stevenson 0. Dad was back by breakfast to announce that in Kingdom Common, anyway, Adlai would get at least one vote.

Locally, the really important races were for county attorney and sheriff. How Zack Barrows had the temerity to run for prosecutor again I have no idea, but he did just that. Even though Charlie had to conduct a write-in campaign, my father predicted that Zack would be lucky to get fifty votes. In the sheriff race, Pine Benson was running against

Mason White, and while Charlie didn't think White could possibly win, Dad said he would wait until the results were in to make his prediction.

A few downcountry reporters had checked into the hotel the night before to cover the race between Charlie and Zack and write the final follow-up stories on the Affair; but for the most part, talk about the tragic events of the summer had died down.

A few days after the stabbing, a close friend of Reverend Andrews, a RCAF general, had personally flown the minister from the county's small airstrip in Memphremagog to Ottawa, where he'd spent another two weeks recuperating in a military hospital, then promptly reenlisted in the Air Force. Nat was back at his grandmother's, going to school once more in Montreal, and I had neither heard from him nor, I am ashamed to say, written since he'd left on the day after the stabbing.

Just before leaving Memphremagog with the general, Reverend Andrews had met with a delegation from the session, who hoped to reinstate him as minister of the United Church. Dad said he'd listened to them from his hospital bed with a polite but slightly amused expression, then courteously, yet with that same undercurrent of irony so characteristic of the man, told them that even if he were inclined to resume his old job on his own behalf (the clear implication, Dad said, was that he wasn't), it was obvious to him now that uprooting Nathan and bringing him to Kingdom County had not been the right thing to do. Plainly, Nat had never been happy in Vermont; and although Dad agreed with him, and had never for a moment thought Reverend Andrews would accept the session's offer, he always said that next to Claire LaRiviere's death, the saddest consequence of the Kingdom County Affair was that Reverend Andrews' desire to locate in a place where he and his son could be happy together had been so cruelly thwarted. Probably it was simply too late in their lives to try such an experiment Reverend Andrews told him, in Vermont or anywhere else. But there is no question in my mind that Dad, with his own iron determination to be a good father, nursed a special anger for those individuals who actively or passively made it impossible for his friend Walter Andrews to raise his son in "God's Kingdom."

As for the rest of the congregation and the residents of Kingdom County as a whole, I believe that most of them were secretly more relieved than disappointed that Reverend Andrews decided not to remain. What, after all, could he ever have been to us but a reminder of that terrible summer in our lives and our failure to help him and stand by him when we should have?

Of course my father wasn't about to let the matter drop; throughout the fall he continued to unseal that metaphorical globe, unearthing unsavory additional bits and pieces of information every week—though to his endless frustration, Dad never was able to determine beyond the level of rumor who besides Zack contributed to the "private fund" to pay Sigurd Moulton's legal fees—who, incidentally, after Elijah's attempt to kill Reverend Andrews, never did appeal the verdict, or return to Kingdom County, either, so far as I know. Dad always said that he strongly suspected the whole idea to import an out-of-town lawyer was not Zack's, but Mason White's; but there was no way to prove that, either, especially since White had spent the past month trying to ingratiate himself with both Dad and Charlie now that he saw the handwriting on the wall for Zack. But with the presidential, state, and local elections to cover, in addition to the constant round of village meetings and school events and regular news items, and the time-consuming job of breaking in Julia Hefner on the linotype, my father had been far too busy to devote more than a fraction of his time to the ugly aftermath of the Affair, anyway.

Over in the village, things had pretty much returned to normal by Election Day. Armand St. Onge hired Ida LaMott to go through the Common Hotel scrubbing every vacant room in preparation for the downcountry deer hunters who would be flocking in at the end of the week. The leaves had all blown off the tall elms on the common, and the town had its customary battened-down fall look. Two candidates for the vacant minister's job had come to preach and be interviewed on two separate Sundays; but the old-guard Presbyterian faction wanted one, and the ex-Congos wanted the other, so, running true to form, their idea of a good workable compromise was to hire neither.

Reverend Andrews' things were still in the parsonage, though he'd written to my father from Ottawa to say he expected to drive down to pick them up some time before the snow flew, and to "clear up one more small matter," though he didn't say what this matter was.

The single most maddening remaining mystery, as far as the Kinneson family was concerned, was Elijah's motivation. Charlie continued to maintain that the old sexton had acted from a pure bigotry that he'd kept secret until the very end; but Dad said there was far more to it than that, and that though Elijah had, with great subtlety and malevolence, used the racial biases of people like Mason White and Zack Barrows and the many members of the congregation and community who would certainly have come to the defense and support of a white man in a similar predicament, he did not believe that bigotry alone could account for Elijah's intense personal hatred of Reverend Andrews.

One turn of events caught me totally by surprise. Elijah had left a will naming my father as his sole heir, and at Welcome's request, Dad had sold the sexton's cottage in the village to him and Resolvèd for "a dollar and a consideration"—the consideration, according to my father, that it would be worth nearly anything to get my outlaw cousins out of our backyard, though how they would adjust to village life, and how the village would adjust to them, remained to be seen.

Election day dawned cold, with a solid gray Canadian sky. Charlie had gone duck hunting with Judge Allen up on the south bay of the big lake—he couldn't campaign once the polls opened, anyway—and my father pulled in from Dixville just as I finished filling the kitchen woodbox.

"I'll tell you something, mister," he said. "It's going to snow before this day is over."

I thought I'd smelled snow coming when I first stepped into the woodshed that morning—that faint, spent-shotgun-shell scent over the familiar old redolence of dry seasoned maple and cherry and yellow birch.

"What have you got going on after school today?" Dad said.

"Same thing I always do. Sweep up over at the *Monitor*, come home and chop wood, do my homework. Sound exciting?"

"This boy has his smart mouth on," my father said. "Well, never mind your chores for one night. Let's you and me sneak up on the ridge behind the house and see if we can scare up a partridge or two, if it isn't snowing too hard by then. This'll be the last chance we'll have to go for birds before deer hunting starts.

"Put a couple of Spam sandwiches and a apple in a paper sack for us, will you, Ruth? We probably won't be back much before dark."

The snow held off, and at three o'clock I met Dad at the *Monitor* and we walked home quickly, past the desolate-looking parsonage, over the red iron bridge above the cold river, along the gool, and into our dooryard—where we were greeted by three clangorous crows from Ethan Allen Kinneson, Resolvèd's huge old fighting cock, now parading back and forth in front of half a dozen of my mother's Banty laying hens under the refurbished picture of the brook trout on the side of our barn.

"Resolvèd brought him down earlier this afternoon," Mom told us. "He said that now that Ethan's stopped fighting, and he and Welcome are moving into the village, this would be a better place for him to live."

"Great," my father said. "I always hoped to open a retirement home for superannuated roosters."

My mother smiled. "That's not all the boys brought down this afternoon, Charles. Look what's in here."

We followed Mom into the other side of the house. She opened the parlor door and switched on the old-fashioned overhead light. Gazing solemnly at us from the wall above my mother's piano was a framed daguerreotype of a fierce-looking, dark-featured young woman in a plain black dress.

"Welcome said he didn't have a proper place to hang his mother in the cottage in the village," Mom said. "He asked if we'd keep Replacement Mari down here."

"Mister Baby Johnson!" said my father. "Enough's enough! Let's go bird hunting, James."

Just as we got ready to leave, Charlie roared into the dooryard in his woody with his limit of ducks: a mallard with a wonderful iridescent green head, a golden-eye, and two male wood ducks as colorful as tropical parrots. Exchanging his camouflaged hat for a red one, he joined us.

"I would think, James," my father said, "that Kingdom County's next prosecuting attorney might want to spend at least some part of Election Day over in the village."

"What would I do over there, Jim? I voted this morning as soon as the polls opened, saw my duty as a good citizen, and did it. Now I've just got to wait for the outcome like everybody else."

During the past month or so, my father and brother had gradually reverted to talking to each other via me again, and to arguing ferociously over all kinds of minor matters—politics, the weather, the King's English. Two nights ago they had haggled into the wee hours over which was the better pastoral poem, Thomas Gray's "Elegy Written in a Country Churchyard" or Oliver Goldsmith's "The Deserted Village"!

The events of the summer just past had brought them closer together for a time; but as I said at the start, Charles Kinneson, Sr., and Charles Kinneson, Jr., were simply too much alike to be easy with each other for very long.

Now as we walked up the lane past Welcome's and Resolvèd's toward the remnants of my great-great-great-grandfather's apple orchard, it felt ready to snow at any time. My cousins were evidently home. Black, pitchy smoke from the final remains of the barn they'd been burning for the last ten years was pouring from the stovepipe sticking horizontally out of the rear wall of the kitchen.

"Some day, James, those crazy sons-of-bitches are going to burn themselves out of house and home," my father said. "Tell your brother what we've got hanging down in the parlor."

When I then told Charlie how we'd inherited Replacement Mari's portrait, he laughed his great booming laugh and said he'd seen the daguerreotype hanging in a cluttered upper chamber at our cousins'.

"Sheepsnose," my father said, changing the subject. He was looking at an ancient gnarled apple tree with a few oddly tapered bluish pearlike apples still clinging to its twisted branches. "Summer St. Lawrence. Alexander. Smokehouse. Over there by the stone wall is the last Scarlet Pippin I know of in these parts. This, James, is a Wolf River; you can make a small pie out of a single apple, they're so big. Next fall, when I've got more time, I intend to write a column or two on old-fashioned apples while there're still a few of them around to write about."

"Here we go again, Jimmy," Charlie said. "More local history."

As we stopped to load our shotguns, my brother said, "What about Replacement Mari, anyway? Mad Charlie's second wife, the gypsy? Was she crazy too?"

"If she wasn't to start out with, she got to be that way in a big hurry after her husband was carried off to the lunatic asylum," Dad said. "Living up here with those three little boys and bringing them up to hate the great majority of humankind the way she did. Of course, none of it ever took with Welcome. He was an anomaly from the start. Your grandmother wouldn't speak to Mari, you know. Mother always claimed to have second sight, and though she never said what she saw when she looked at Replacement Mari Kinneson, I don't think it was a pretty sight."

"The summer of 1952, maybe," Charlie said.

"I doubt that, James," my father said. "I still lay only about half of all that's happened this summer to Elijah and Resolvèd's door."

Walking three abreast about thirty feet apart, we skirted the quarry and crossed a brushy pasture overrun with dead goldenrod, purple asters, faded pink steeplebush. Forty-four minutes later we came out at Russia, on the height of land where, in the spring and early summer, we had driven in my father's De Soto to hear the Red Sox games. Charlie had three of his limit of four partridges and I'd shot one, in a beech grove halfway up the slope. My father had watched us shoot without comment.

Now he looked out across the bleak gray countryside, at the far hill where the French Canadian girl had sat on the big boulder and, as a young man, Dad had looked over at her on Sunday afternoons through Charles I's pirate spyglass while she looked back at him with the Montgomery Ward binoculars he'd bought her.

"Everywhere I go this fall, James, I get the sense of a pervasive relief that the trouble's over at last and now we can go about our business as usual. Well, dammit we can't go about business as usual. We won't ever go about business as usual again until we know the truth, and not just what happened, but why. Take it out and look at it so it won't happen again. Why *didn't* more folks come to the defense of Walter Andrews? He was a good and decent man, never anything else. Was it fear that motivated them? The kind of fear that caused my mother and father to forbid me to keep company with that French girl? If it was fear, fear of what, exactly? Of Negroes? Of outsiders, strangers? Of change? I won't stop until I'm satisfied that I understand this entire Affair."

"Nobody's without some responsibility for what happened," Charlie said. "A hundred times a day I think if I hadn't written that idiotic letter for Resolvèd, the whole mess would never have happened."

"Don't be so sure," Dad said. "It was here all the time, I think, waiting to happen. It's everyplace."

I had wandered over to the edge of the clearing and was looking off down at the gool. "What's that down there?" I said.

"Down where, buddy?" Charlie said.

"There. Welcome's silo. It looks like smoke."

Charlie and Dad walked over and peered down where I was pointing. There was no question about it. An ominous twist of coal-black smoke was rising up from the tilted silo beside my cousins' place.

"Jesum Crow!" I shouted. "Cousin W's silo is on fire!"

Under ordinary circumstances, it was a half-hour walk up the road through the gore to Russia and a fifteen-minute walk back down. But I'm sure that I made it to Welcome's that November afternoon in under ten minutes. As I pounded into his cluttered dooryard, flames were shooting out of the top of the silo. Welcome was standing near the watering trough, rubbing his hands like a man warming himself at a campfire. Resolvèd was leaning against the shell of the old Model A nearby, sipping on a bottle of Old Duke.

"Hello, Jimmy," Welcome said. "How's high school going?"

"Jesus!" I shouted. "Jesus, Welcome! Your silo's on fire!"

"We know that," he said. "Quite a little blaze, isn't she? I imagine," he continued, looking up at the leaden sky and tipping me a cunning wink, "that she's visible to those on high."

"On high?"

"Saucering over the firmament."

"Aren't you afraid your house'll catch on fire?"

"No, goddamn it!" Resolvèd said angrily. "We're afraid she won't!"

I was flabbergasted; but far greater surprises were yet to come. For just as my brother and father came into the dooryard, the entire wooden framework of the silo collapsed. Inside, enveloped in flames, stood the tallest automobile totem of Welcome's illustrious career. It was a good thirty cars in height, nearly as tall as the silo itself had been. On the tip-top, spouting flames from its crushed roof, was the white armored Brink's vehicle used as the getaway vehicle in last summer's bank robbery!

" 'Now Sam McGee was from Tennessee,' " Welcome began to recite. "Do you know that one, Jimmy?"

"Mister," said my father. He shook his head. "Mister Baby Johnson!"

"Stand away, boys," Welcome said cheerily.

"TIM-BER!" roared Resolvèd.

No sooner was the warning out of his mouth than the fiery column of cars toppled over, the Brink's car first, crashing through the roof of my cousins' house and burying itself in the cellar where Resolvèd had held his cockfights and Welcome had kept his homemade wine, where Mad Charlie had hidden runaway slaves and his father James had stored arms and powder for the Fenian invasions of Canada.

"What the frig you crazy outlaws doing now?" said a familiar voice behind us.

Spinning around, I found myself staring at Frenchy LaMott.

"Pay attention, Frenchy," Welcome said sternly. "You're witnessing the end of an era."

"End of something, all right," Frenchy agreed.

To me he said, "Say, Kin'son, who you think I see out front of Christly minister's house short while ago? Your color friend from Montreal and his father, that who, packing stuff in trailer. You want to see 'em before they go, best shag you ass right down. Look like they in pretty big hurry to get going, by Christ!"

" 'I traveled mainly by night, guiding myself by the stars and by some instinct that told me where north and sanctuary lay. I kept mainly to the thick woods, leaving just enough of a trail to lure the murderer Satan Smithfield to his just fate at the hands of the man who would turn out to be my great friend and mentor, Charles Kinneson. . . .' "

Reverend Andrews paused; but his resonant voice still seemed to hang on the frigid air of the parsonage study, like his breath, which I could see with each word. The house seemed even colder than the outdoors. Nat and I stood by the window where, in midsummer, Resolvèd had looked in and seen my friend and Claire on the couch where Charlie sat now. My father stood near the desk. Except for the couch, a chair, the desk and Pliny's great *Ecclesiastical History* open on it, the room was bare.

"So," Reverend Andrews said to us, "even then as a young man, he was never anything but a survivor. Pliny, I mean. Then and always. I felt it the first time I heard his story. And I simply couldn't comprehend why a man so positive in everything he did, so affirmative about life, a man who had educated himself in the classics, escaped out of slavery, built a wonderful school and written a wonderful book, and served with distinction in your state legislature—how such a man could possibly succumb to despair over a piano and a small-town dispute between two local religious factions and take his life with his own hands. It ran counter to everything I knew about him."

"But it was exactly that schism you referred to that caused Pliny's suicide," my father said. "Because the schism caused the falling-out between best friends. As for my grandfather, with the help of his gypsy wife, he was already more than half-crazy. Hell, he'd been half-crazy most of his life. Pliny's suicide just drove him the rest of the way over the brink."

"No," Reverend Andrews said.

"No? Pliny's suicide didn't push him over the brink?"

"No."

"Then what did?"

"Pliny's murder."

"Pliny's *murder*?"

"Pliny never committed suicide," Reverend Andrews said quietly. "He was murdered."

My father thumped his hand down on the parsonage desk. "Mister Baby Johnson!"

Reverend Andrews shook his head. "I've always felt that Pliny Templeton did not and never would and never could commit suicide. The man was committed to *life*, Charles. Every word in this book affirms that premise. It's true that he introduced the use of a piano in the Academy. It's true that your grandfather and the session objected to that piano and to the singing and to his proposal to introduce dancing lessons as well. It's true that the session met and that the United Presbyterians, led by Pliny, voted to withdraw from the church. But it is *not* true that Pliny Templeton borrowed your grandfather's horse pistol and committed suicide with it."

"How do you know?" My father's voice was strained, but excited.

"Because of this." From his inside jacket pocket Reverend Andrews took out a folded piece of paper. "I know because of this document, which Elijah Kinneson did not find when he went through my desk on the afternoon of August sixth last summer for the simple reason that it wasn't there."

"What is that?" Dad said.

"The court committal of your grandfather to the Waterbury State Lunatic Asylum."

My father shook his head. "I've looked for that document over in the courthouse a dozen times, Walt. That can't be authentic. The court-ordered committal was washed away in the Flood of '27, along with ninety-nine percent of the other pre-1927 county legal documents."

"I didn't find this in the courthouse," Reverend Andrews said. "This is an exact copy of the lost committal papers, which I found in the records room of the Vermont State Hospital, formerly the state lunatic asylum, earlier this afternoon. Read it, Charles. And read the statement, in your grandfather's handwriting, that's attached."

By now Charlie was standing up, and so were Nat and I. But my father moved a little ways apart from us and, characteristically, he read the papers without expression. He handed them back to Reverend Andrews. Then he nodded.

"I should have guessed," he said. "It was under my nose the whole time. I should have figured it out."

"Figured *what* out?" Charlie said. "What the hell is going on here?"

"I shall tell you what. This document is nothing more or less than the last window into that sealed globe I've been talking about. It explains everything. Why Elijah killed the girl to frame Reverend Andrews, why he was so adamant that Reverend Andrews not look further into Mad Charlie's committal. Everything! Because these committal papers include the signed confession of my grandfather, Mad Charlie Kinneson, written at Waterbury State Lunatic Asylum a week before his death in the fall of 1903."

"Confession for *what*?"

"For the murder of Pliny Templeton," my father said, and he took the papers back again and read:

" 'I, Charles Kinneson, to clear my conscience, do hereby swear upon my immortal soul that on August fourth, in the Year of Our Lord 1900, I entered the study of my beloved friend Pliny Templeton and shot him twice in the back of the head with my pistol whilst he sat writing at his desk, murdering him in cold blood. And with my own hand I hereby clear him from the charge of committing suicide or any other crime against himself or God or mankind.' "

"But *why*?" Charlie said. "This is incredible; I don't believe it. So Mad Charlie and Pliny Templeton quarreled? So what? People quarrel all the time. You mean to tell me that my great-grandfather shot his best friend dead in this room fifty years ago because of a disagreement over a *piano*?"

"It was fifty-two years ago," my father said. "And it wasn't over a piano. What was really at stake was the survival of a religion. And not just a religion, either, but a way of life as encompassing as Quakerism or Islam or what have you. Because that's exactly what Reformed Presbyterianism was. A way of life. Music was the least of the devil's work as far as your ancestors were concerned. They couldn't vote, they couldn't take an oath to hold office, they couldn't formally enlist in any army—which is why your great-great-great-grandfather had to resort to piracy to fight the British during the Revolution and why James I fought along the Canadian border with the Fenians and Mad Charlie fought with John Brown at Harper's Ferry but never enlisted in the Union Army, despite his hatred of slavery. When Pliny and his faction voted to secede from the church and affiliate themselves with United Presbyterianism, your great-grandfather's entire *way of life* was threatened. Reformed Presbyterianism was the main reason his grandfather had come here in the first place, remember. And I'll tell you something else, mister. What Reformed Presbyterianism, for all its strictures, *really* represented to Charles I and James I and most of all to Mad Charlie, was personal independence—independence from the British, from the Americans, from the rest of Vermont, including the legislature. And that independence is a legacy you and I and every Kinneson have inherited and pride ourselves on practicing to this day. So *of course* Mad Charlie, who knew all this and was crazy besides, couldn't just stand by and watch everything he believed in, and everything his father and his father's father believed in, just disintegrate."

"*So he shot his best friend?*" Charlie said. "He murdered his friend in cold blood? Just the way he gunned down Satan Smithfield in the pulpit of the church? And with the same horse pistol, no less?"

"Yes," Reverend Andrews said. "He felt he had to kill Pliny for all the reasons your father's just enumerated. But afterwards, the rational part of his mind couldn't accept what he'd done. He was faced with the consequences of an impossible choice. It wasn't really like the Smithfield episode at all."

"My God!" Charlie said. "And Elijah knew this? Elijah knew that Mad Charlie shot Pliny Templeton?"

"I'm sure he did," Reverend Andrews said. "That accounts for his determination that I cease my inquiries into the matter; he was afraid I'd discover the truth and change his father's reputation to that of murderer."

"It accounts for everything," Dad said. "But when did *you* first suspect all of this?"

Reverend Andrews smiled. "Have you ever taken a good close look at the skull of Pliny's skeleton?"

My father shrugged. "Not in years. Why?"

"Because there are *two* holes in the back of it. At first glance, it looks like one large hole, but if you look closely—I checked with Dr. Harrison, and he agreed with me—it's obvious that he was shot twice. Now, in a weak moment a man who's disturbed enough might shoot himself in the back of the head once, even an affirmative, positive man like Pliny Templeton. But not twice. Elijah must have figured that out too. Also it's very possible that your grandfather, Mad Charlie, told the truth to Replacement Mari before he died, and she told Elijah. At any rate, I'm positive that Elijah knew about the murder, and not only did he know, he was willing to go to any lengths to keep me or anyone else from finding out about it. He thought I might figure out what happened from the account your father wrote in the newspaper, Charles, which is why he wanted those articles back. But Elijah overlooked one thing. He overlooked your grandfather's records at the state hospital."

"And these records never came to light before?" Charlie said. "That's hard to believe."

"Why should they have? Somebody just stuck this in his file with the court committal and left it there."

"How did you get access to the hospital documents?"

Reverend Andrews grinned. "Ask and ye shall receive. I just asked the hospital superintendent. He didn't see any reason why I shouldn't see them. After all, Mad Charlie died fifty years ago."

"And now?" Dad said. "What do you intend to do with the information?"

"I've already done it," Reverend Andrews said. "I've passed it on to you. What do *you* intend to do with it?"

"Print it. All of it. In the *Monitor*."

"Tell the truth and shame the devil, eh?" Reverend Andrews said, chuckling. "Well, you always said, Charles, that up here in God's Kingdom the past is still as much a part of the present as ever. All this tends to bear that statement out, I fancy."

The minister looked at Nat. "How are you coming on your room, old man? Have you got it about hoed out?"

"I'm ready," Nat said.

"What about your funny books, Nat?" I asked. "There must still be four or five big boxes of them up there."

"You hang onto them for me, Kinneson. There's some good reading up there and you could use even such a small corrupting influence in your life."

We stood awkwardly together on the porch, while Reverend Andrews made one final check of the house. It was snowing now.

The minister came back outside and locked the door and handed the keys to my father. Turning away from the wind, he lit a cigarette, as he had done on that night I'd first met him in the April sugar snow. He shook hands with me and with my father and Charlie.

"Charles the Younger," he said, "I thank you. I thank you and your father for your help and for your friendship. I wouldn't be here now if it weren't for you folks. I'd be languishing in state's prison, no doubt."

"Hell, I can't imagine you languishing for long anywhere, Reverend," Charlie said. But just the same, I could tell that my brother was moved.

"And again, Charles," Reverend Andrews said to my father, "thank you once again. I'll never forget how you stood by me."

"I shouldn't think you'd soon forget anything about this place, Walter. I'm sorry for what happened here. But I want you to know one thing. For all its shortcomings, the Kingdom's a better place for the time you and your son spent here."

Reverend Andrews did not reply. He put his arm around Nat, and they walked out to the car together.

"Now, you wait," my father said. "You wait just a minute."

He took something bulky out from under his overcoat. He handed it through the passenger window to Nat, and I saw then that it was Pliny's *History*.

"I can't—" Reverend Andrews started to say.

"Oh yes you can," my father said. "This belongs to you, my friend."

Reverend Andrews looked at my father. He leaned across the seat and grinned, and flicked Dad that marvelous two-fingered salute. "Oh, one thing, Charles. If you see Julia Hefner, tell her I made it a point to leave the parsonage as clean as I found it."

Then the car was moving. It eased out of the driveway and past the vacant lot. The red brake lights of the canvas-covered trailer flicked on as it approached the hotel, and it was out of sight in the snowstorm.

"He'll land on his feet," my brother said. "As I said once before, there goes one tough hombre. As a matter of fact—"

But whatever else my brother might have been going to say was drowned out by a siren blast. Flashing blue lights appeared in the snow, a long dark vehicle pulled into the dooryard, a long figure unfolded itself from the driver's side, and Mason White's high voice piped out, "What the *H* is going on here? Oh, is that you, editor? Charlie? Just checking up, boys."

"You don't mean you're still sheriff?" Charlie said.

"Still sheriff?" Mason said. "Why, haven't you heard the news, Charlie K? I and you, we both won our respective races hands-down."

He reached out his long arm and grabbed my brother's hand and began to pump it.

"It looks, Brother Charlie, like I and you are going to be working hand-in-glove to bring law and order to the Kingdom for the next two years at least. Congratulations!"

Even today Kingdom County is isolated enough from the rest of Vermont so that an out-of-state license plate in the village is something of an event. So with my mind still on the story I was banging out for Production Night deadline, I watched with curiosity as the car with white and blue tags cruised slowly into town between the United Church and the south end of the green, swung north, and slowed almost to a full stop in front of the courthouse.

Whoever it was seemed to be looking for something, probably directions. But on this cold gray afternoon in late October there was no one on the street to ask. The car eased over the disused Boston and Montreal tracks, passed between the Common Hotel and the statue of Ethan Allen taking Fort Ticonderoga on the far north end of the green, turned south along the three-story brick shopping block. Directly across from the *Monitor*, it nosed diagonally in against the west side of the green. And there, for perhaps thirty seconds, the driver sat stock-still with his back to me, staring over at the courthouse.

Then his door opened and a ghost got out and came straight across the street toward my office.

Even thirty-six years ago, when I had last seen him, I had not really believed in ghosts, and I certainly did not believe in them now. But for just a split second, I didn't see how the man coming toward me with that same ironical and amused expression I remembered so well could be anything else.

Then he was close enough for me to recognize. He was discernibly taller than his father, and rangier, though I was so astonished by his presence after all these years that not until he actually came into the office did I notice that he was carrying a good-sized box under one arm.

"So, Kinneson. You've followed in your father's footsteps, eh?"

"Editor, reporter, ad manager, janitor," I said. "Not to mention school board member, Little League coach, church trustee—I'm running out of fingers."

We shook hands across my desk and he set the box down beside my typewriter and sat down. "Married? Kids?"

"Two boys."

"Charles and James. Right?"

"Half right. Charles and Lucien. After their grandfathers."

He nodded, and turned to look out the window with the words KINGDOM COUNTY MONITOR written across it in faded black letters. "I don't know just what I expected. Boutiques, maybe. Gift shops selling maple syrup. This hasn't changed at all."

I smiled. "It's changed. A lot's changed."

"Like what?"

"Well, I print the paper on offset now. I have for ten years. And the elm trees. Remember the big elms out there on the green? They're all gone, along with half the farms and nearly all the old-timers."

He shrugged. "I don't suppose I'd notice their absence. You never did manage to get me interested in your woods and fish and local characters, did you, Kinneson? Lord knows you tried. But I was your inveterate city kid if there ever was one. And I have to confess, I like them all a hell of a lot better in your books, anyway. I was lost up here in these hills. Totally lost."

I smiled at his reference to my story collections, pleased that he'd read them, amused by his way of letting me know.

"You were interested in the ghost," I said.

"The ghost?"

"Sure. The footsteps on the parsonage porch. Remember? I was thirteen that summer, you were what, sixteen? We had that crazy plan to wait up and—"

He held up his hand. "I remember. I remember."

He told me that he'd been divorced for several years and had a daughter in college in Toronto. He said he was in sales, something having to do with educational computers. He was on a trip to the Maritimes and on the spur of the moment he'd gotten off the Trans-

Canada Highway, thirty miles to the north, to have a quick look at the Common. Yet even then I did not believe that he'd come back entirely on impulse. There was more than mere passing curiosity to this visit, though I had no idea what until he asked me to open the package he'd set on my desk.

Whatever it was, was inside one of those big cardboard express mailers, the kind that fold out into a box. For its size, it was weighty. As I lifted it out and pulled away the tissue paper it was wrapped in, I caught a whiff of the unmistakable scent of very old leather and paper, and then, by God, there it was in my hands, still in good condition after nearly a century, all eleven hundred and fifty-five pages of it, with the title and author's name standing out bright and sharp in tall gilt letters on the leather cover:

THE ECCLESIASTICAL, NATURAL,
SOCIAL, AND POLITICAL
HISTORY OF
KINGDOM COUNTY
1781–1900
by
PLINY TEMPLETON, A.B., M.A.

"It's yours, Kinneson. I don't know how many times I've started to mail it to you, including just yesterday, but then I thought, what the hell, maybe I'll just deliver the thing. Anyway, it belongs to you now. Do with it as you please. I'm delighted to have it off my hands."

I looked at the book and up at him and back at the book again. I wanted to thank him; but all I could do was gaze at Pliny Templeton's book, as memory after memory swept over me from a time now gone as irrevocably as the magnificent New England elms on the green across the street.

"So, how about your hotshot big brother, Kinneson? Did he wind up marrying the good-looking schoolteacher? The judge's daughter with the unusual name and the temper?"

"He did. And never lost a case as county prosecutor. But the funny thing is, Zack Barrows went back into private practice, and they continued to face each other in court off and on for three or four years. Later, Charlie ran for attorney general, and he won that election, too."

"It changed all of us," I said. "But yes, Charlie especially. Dad used to say before the Affair that my brother was going to hell in a handbasket. But Mom was fond of saying that there's no great loss without some small gain. Charlie's transformation must have been the small gain. He's a federal judge in Burlington, believe it or not."

"Of course," Nat said. "Why wouldn't I believe it? Moving on, what became of your racist sheriff?"

"Mason White? About the time Charlie ran for attorney general, Mason ran for the state legislature and lost, went back to being a full-time undertaker, then ran again and won. He retired from politics ten years ago, something of a laughingstock and a fairly wealthy man."

Nat shrugged. "What about your dad?"

"Dad retired in the late sixties, after making sure that everyone knew where he stood on Vietnam. I've never known for sure how much he had to do with it, but it was right after a long private meeting he and George Aiken had together that Aiken announced on the Senate floor that we ought to just declare a victory there and get out. Dad thought we were dead wrong in Vietnam from the start. That didn't make him many friends in these parts; but as he used to tell me, he wasn't in the newspaper business to make friends."

I hesitated. Then I said, "You know, every year before he retired, he wrote an editorial on the Affair. That's how determined he was that we should never forget what happened here or let such a thing happen again."

"He was a good man," Nat said quietly.

It was the first completely unironical statement he'd made since he arrived, and I appreciated it.

"So was your father."

"Yes," Nat said thoughtfully. "He died there, you know."

"Died where?"

"In Vietnam. He rejoined the service right after we went back to Canada, and died there in '66."

I hadn't known, and I started to express my condolences; but Nat held up his hand and waved it impatiently, exactly as he'd done years ago to cut off a conversation he didn't want to pursue. "He fell near the thick of the action, just as he'd have wanted it, no doubt, though I never did learn whether he was toting his Bible or his service revolver at the time—probably both. Unfortunately, we were somewhat estranged at the time. Like a good number of Canadians, I was inclined toward your father's side of the issue.

"But I didn't come back to hash over old times, Kinneson. Just to deliver the book. It's getting late, eh? I've got an hour's drive back to my motel and you've got a paper to get out."

I stared at Pliny's great book on my desk, and as I did, a wonderful idea came to me.

"Nat, to hell with the paper. You and I have a piece of unfinished business."

"What do you mean, unfinished business?"

I stood up and put on my hunting jacket. "What I want to do'll only take an hour—two at most. That's a short time, compared to thirty-six years."

"It's ten degrees colder here than up in Montreal, Kinneson. This is insane. Probably the ground's frozen already."

Despite my wool hunting jacket I was cold, too, as we crossed the common and the B and M tracks and sneaked through the dark lumberyard of the American Heritage Mill. Then we were there.

As I'd hoped it would be, the far south window of the Academy locker room was unlocked. The place smelled strongly of liniment and sweat and the victories and defeats of fifty years and more. I led the way out through the gym, into the foyer and the redolence of chalk dust and old books, floor wax and uneasy anticipations. I set down the cardboard box I was carrying and took out my flashlight and ran it briefly across the trophy showcase.

"You shatter any of your big brother's records?" Nat said.

"Not a one. I turned into a good soccer player and, thanks to your dad, a pretty fair country shortstop. You were the one who would have broken Charlie's records."

"We'll never know," Nat said. "Up these stairs, right?"

"Up these stairs."

The door of the science classroom was unlocked, and there was just enough light filtering up from the street lamp below for us to make our way through the lab tables to the closet, which was also unlocked. The place reeked of formaldehyde. For a moment, I felt as though I was ten or eleven again and Charlie was showing me the thing for the first time.

In fact I hadn't seen it for years, and I wasn't entirely sure that it was still here. But it was, dangling from its slim pole in the light of the pocket flashlight like a forgotten prop left over from a Halloween party or some long-ago school play.

"I'd forgotten how small it was," I said. "I've always thought of him as a big man."

Nat grunted. "You were small when you saw him for the first time, so he seemed big."

I eased the yellowing old bones out of the closet and laid them on a lab table. They glowed softly in the faint light cast up from the street below. The skeleton was as short as a child's, nearly.

We began disassembling it, stacking the individual bones without particular order inside the cardboard box. We set the skull in last. "There you go, Yorick," Nat said.

"Look at the poor old guy," I said. "He was missing half his teeth."

"Let's not wax sentimental, Kinneson. No doubt he's laughing at us with the few he has left."

We left the building through the locker room exit, stepping out into a bitter wind gusting hard between the dark looming stacks of lumber in the mill yard, and I remembered what Nat's father had said on the night I first met him outside the parsonage: "Your blooming weather is worse than Korea's!"

The door to the cemetery toolshed was padlocked, but the hasp was so old and rusty that I easily wrenched it and the lock away from the punky jamb. Inside, we found a shovel leaning in a corner.

In front of Pliny's tall monument the ground was hard with frost for an inch or so, then nearly as hard with the ubiquitous blue clay of Kingdom County. We took turns with the shovel until we were down about four feet. That was enough. As we filled the hole in, it began to snow lightly; by the time we were finished, the flakes were coming fast.

"Kinneson, we may be a pair of bloody damn fools, but I'm glad we did that," Nathan said suddenly.

Then we were laughing—two middle-aged men in a snowy cemetery in an end-of-the-line little northern hill town, which was dying fast now like a thousand other hill towns, laughing the way we had laughed on those half-dozen or so other occasions in a long-ago summer when we had done something we thought was sneaky and gotten away with it.

Ten minutes later we shook hands in front of the *Monitor*, and then he was gone as suddenly as he had appeared, and I was alone on the street in the snow.

As I walked out to the gool from the village, away from the protection of the houses, the wind drove the hard pellets of snow against my face, and I huddled into my jacket as I had on the night of my thirteenth birthday when I'd met Reverend Andrews for the first time. On my right, invisible in the falling snow, was the cemetery where so many of my own ancestors lay buried, and now Pliny Templeton with them.

No ghosts accompanied me home that night, but as I stood on the red iron bridge, listening to the muffled river running below me in the snow, I thought of my great-great-great-grandfather, Charles I, who had come to the Kingdom because he loved to angle for trout.

I thought of my great-great-great-great Abenaki grandfather, Sabattis, coming up the same river in the fall of 1781 and discovering Charles I building a cabin where no man had ever built before, and I thought of Charles' Indian bride, Memphremagog, and their son James I, who with the wild Irish Fenians had launched his abortive attacks down the river against Canada.

I thought of James' son, Mad Charlie Kinneson, who had ferried runaway slaves to Canada by canoe and fought with John Brown at Harper's Ferry and finally shot and killed his best friend Pliny Templeton; and I thought of Claire LaRiviere, the daughter of Etienne, coming boldly out from the village across the river to our farmhouse kitchen on a rainy summer night in my youth.

I thought of the Dog Cart Man trotting over the bridge on a summer day and turning down the county road toward Ben Currier's. I thought how Resolvèd loved to sit under the bridge with his friend Old Duke on a hot summer afternoon, and I thought of Frenchy LaMott approaching Nat and me on the trestle half a mile downstream and Nat diving in one long perfect arc into the water and pulling Frenchy out.

All these things occurred to me as I stood on the bridge in the falling snow.

I thought too of my father's statement in the *Monitor* and Charlie's paraphrase of it in his great speech at Reverend Andrews' trial, that our Kingdom was a good but eminently improvable place, where the past was still part of the present, and for the first time in my life I believed that I fully understood what they had meant.

"We should have taken him brook trout fishing, James," I heard my father say, his voice harsh and gravelly, as it had been that election night in 1952 after Reverend Andrews and Nat had left town and Mason White had gone back to the village to celebrate his election victory.

"Who, Reverend Andrews?" Charlie said. "Hell, he didn't care anything about fishing, Jimmy, for brook trout or anything else."

"Just the same, James, we should have taken him," Dad said.

They were still arguing as I headed out along the gool toward home, and the last distinct words I heard were "James" and "Jimmy."

*Book Mark*

The text of this book was set in
Weiss and the display in Orpheus
by Crane Typesetting Service, Inc.,
Barnstable, Massachusetts.

It was printed on 50 lb. Glatfelter
by Berryville Graphics,
Berryville, Virginia.

DESIGNED BY MARYSARAH QUINN